'PUNCH FOR PUNCH,' HE SAID. 'MAN TO MAN. NO
WEAPONS. NO DODGING OR DEFENDING. LAST
MAN TO GET BACK UP LOSES. THAT'S WHAT I
CALL AN HONEST BOUT.'

He knew as well as I did that those were impossible
terms; it was my skill at dodging, defending, and blocking blows that made up for my lack of height and bulk.
'Fine,' I said. 'You strike first.' I dropped my candy-
striped nunchuck and put my hands behind me.

As I expected, he swung for my chin. As the punch
came in I leaned foward slightly and dropped my jaw.
He punched me in the teeth. For anyone but myself it
would have been a fatal gambit, but my teeth are a
sturdy legacy from dear Old Dad. They were all false,
tooth-shaped white ceramic over a crystalline metal
core, anchored solidly to one of the thin ceramic plates
that armored my skull. He screamed and drew away his
hand, dripping blood.

RoC

**Exploring New Realms
in Science Fiction/Fantasy Adventure**

BATMAN™ IS BACK IN ACTION!

Batman™: To Stalk a Specter
by Simon Hawke

Gotham City Blackmailed!

Drug Lord Caught by U.S. Commandos! Desiderio Garcia to Stand Trial in the U.S.! The headlines — and the authorities — are jubilant, but not for long. For Garcia has a deadly would-be rescuer: the superassassin known as Specter. And Specter's reign of havoc and horror has already begun. The people of Gotham City are held hostage and destined to die by the thousands unless Garcia is freed. The people's only hope lies with Batman's bold and dangerous plan. In a war with only one winner and one survivor, he's going to make himself the archkiller's target, matching his enemy weapon for weapon, deception for deception — and with good for evil!

BATMAN™ CREATED BY BOB KANE

Bruce Sterling

The Artificial Kid

A ROC BOOK

ROC

Published by the Penguin Group
Penguin Books Ltd, 27 Wrights Lane, London W8 5TZ, England
Penguin Books USA Inc., 375 Hudson Street, New York, New York 10014, USA
Penguin Books Australia Ltd, Ringwood, Victoria, Australia
Penguin Books Canada Ltd, 10 Alcorn Avenue, Toronto, Ontario, Canada M4V 3B2
Penguin Books (NZ) Ltd, 182–190 Wairau Road, Auckland 10, New Zealand

Penguin Books Ltd, Registered Offices: Harmondsworth, Middlesex, England

First published in the USA by Harper and Row 1980
Published in Penguin Books 1985
Reprinted in ROC 1992
10 9 8 7 6 5 4 3 2 1

 Roc is a trademark of Penguin Books Ltd

Printed in England by Clays Ltd, St Ives plc

1

Reverie shines, the planet's edge lined in luminous atmospheric haze, her broad, shallow seas sparkling, her big coral-atoll continents brown and green and white through rifts in scattered clouds. The sky over Telset, my island city, is clear as glass as the camera zooms in; I was careful to check with the weather satellites before I did the taping. The effect is serene and hypnotic; and the camera accelerates downward and the gridwork of my city expands with nearness, to a single block, a single street, a single person, me, and my own image swells to fill the screen. The soundtrack says:

"Ladies and gentlemen, the Artificial Kid. This tape is made possible by Mr. Richer Money Manies and the Artificial Kid. Copyright C.R.Y. 499 by the Artificial Kid for Cognitive Dissonant Enterprises, Reverie."

Most of my audience are floaters, who circle our coraled planet in city-sized orbital oneills. I draw them down to the planet's surface, I involve them personally during those first thirty seconds of tape. Orbital Reverids think of Reverie as lovely, but remote, and surface dwellers like myself as rather quaint and sweet. I break down that distancing effect. I stare right into the descending camera, my slightly slanting eyes blacklined in kohl and as cold and mean as an adder's. I challenge the viewer. I believe in direct challenges; they're at the heart of combat artistry.

People used to ask me how I became a combat artist and why I'm called the Artificial Kid. People stopped asking such prying questions after I ruthlessly beat them up. Every formal interview I've given has ended with me "losing my temper" and soundly clubbing the journalist. Now, the days have passed when I found it necessary to establish a reputation for fury and volatile violence. Now, I intend to tell all.

Why, then, do people call me the Artificial Kid? My answer is that all combat artists must have a gimmick, and mine has always been my childishness and wild artificiality. "Kid," on Reverie, means a young person, but the word also has a certain raffish air of irreverent disrespect.

I'll explain further with an analysis of my tape image, an image I know well, an image, in fact, that obsesses me. Many times, I have risen at sunset and worked straight through the eighteen-hour Reverid night, editing and polishing my own tapes for Mr. Manies and the market. The image on the tape is that of a very young man. He is resiliently, but not heavily, muscled; his skin is suntanned dark brown under a thin, shiny film of green skin oil. He is short, about five feet four. He wears a thick armored leather surcoat over his torso, held up with two wide shoulder straps; a stiff, heavy collar shields the back of his neck. He wears a pair of gleaming metallic scale trousers with elastic waist and cuffs, and shiny black combat slippers. His head seems slightly oversized for the childish body; his face is unlined and beardless, with wide cheekbones, a pointed, narrow chin, and eyes with an epicanthic fold, heavily outlined in black. His hair is unusual; each strand of hair is separately laminated in plastic, forming a jackstraw array of stiff, black, pointed quills. Floating about him in the air are six small, silent camera modules, each with two lenses and sound recording equipment, each carefully programmed. These floating cameras are with him always.

In his right hand he casually grips his nunchuck. This weapon consists of two slightly tapering eighteen-inch clubs of blood-repellent padded black plastic, linked at their thin ends by eight inches of crystalline metal chain. He grips one club about half-way up its length and lets the other dangle. The solid metal core beneath the plastic assures a satisfying kinetic impact, while the slight malleability of the plastic provides stunning bruises rather than the actual mangling and spattering that a solid metal 'chuck would cause. Above all the Artificial Kid believes in theater. Theater is having opponents fall at your feet, stunned, numb, and nerveless. Theater is not gouging out great bloody chunks of flesh.

The Artificial Kid moves with resilient grace. He is aware at every moment of the exact position of every inch of his body, and his nunchuck moves like a living thing, absolutely obedient to his will because of his ninety-eight long years of practice. "Ninety-eight years, Kid?" I can hear my audience ask. "Isn't that seventy years longer than you've been alive?" So it is. And *that's* why I'm the Artificial Kid.

I happen to have the first moments of my "birth" on tape. They were taped by Professor Crossbow, my tutor and mentor for the first twenty years of my life, a person to whom I owe a profound debt. It was clever of it (Professor Crossbow is a neuter, so I will refer to it as "it," the pronoun it always preferred) to put the close-up on my face. In the first few minutes of the tape it is obvious that, despite the fact that he says nothing, we are looking at Rominuald Tanglin, my previous personality. He is two hundred and seventy-one standard years old and looks every day of it. The lines of madness are in his face; his eyes shift rapidly from side to side like hot black ball bearings; there is tension in the pale thinness of his grizzled lips. He is about to commit mental suicide. His hair is shoulder length and frivolously curled in the old style; there are half-a-dozen shaven spots where the metal contacts will touch his head, and they lend the proceedings a peculiarly makeshift air.

The machine that will kill him descends from above him, extruding six gleaming contacts. Tanglin still says nothing, but his throat moves visibly. The contacts touch; there is a discharge; Tanglin dies instantly and his eyes close. His face sags in total relaxation. The narrow jaw drops and a thread of drool forms at the corner of the lower lip; Crossbow's hand appears to touch it away with a sponge. The body, momentarily empty of any personality, sags in the chair, but transparent plastic braces, barely visible, keep the head upright. Tears form in the opened eye ducts and slide down across the broad cheeks. The memory eraser has done its work. Tanglin's mind is gone, his personality is scorched away. The machine rises from the head. Quickly, Crossbow touches away the tears and removes the head brace. Within seconds, consciousness returns, I am born, and I lift my head.

"Hello," Crossbow says gently. Wondering, I lift my hand and touch the cool dampness on my cheeks. "Hello," I say as I rub my eyes with two fingers.

CROSSBOW: Do you know who you are?

SELF: Yes. I'm R.T. [pause] R.T. Arti. [I move my mouth, tasting the words]

CROSSBOW: And do you know who I am?

SELF: Yes. You're my friend, Professor Crossbow. And we're in your house, on Reverie.

CROSSBOW: [with infinite gentleness] Very good! [I smile radiantly] Let's try to walk a little now, Arti, shall we? That's right. [I get up from the chair. Though I am newborn, my body has not forgotten its reflexes. I begin to pace around the room with the unnatural assurance and grace that comes from hundreds of years of experience. The camera follows us. The memory device looks ugly, bulky, and angular in Crossbow's room, amid its warm, tasteful driftwood panelling, its dangling mobiles and air chimes, its glass terraria and aquaria, its tape display screen.] There. How do you feel now, Arti?

SELF: I feel just fine, Professor.

CROSSBOW: Wonderful! Now drink this [it hands me a ceramic cup full of a thick dark liquid practically crystallizing with testosterone inhibitors] and then I'll take you for a swim out on the reef. After that we'll have a nice lunch, and then we'll start your lessons. You're not sleepy, are you?

SELF: [putting aside drained cup] No! [eagerly] Let's go swimming!

The tape ends when we go out the door. Crossbow was not especially enthusiastic about taping, except of course in its scientific work, where a rigorous recording of every step of scientific procedure is demanded by the Academy.

Not so Rominuald Tanglin. Tanglin, or "Old Dad" as my friends and I have come to refer to him, was a fanatical believer in the potency of tape. He was an image builder, at one time one of the planet Niwlind's most powerful politicians (and that on a world known for the maddening intricacy of its intrigue). I can't help but feel that I've inherited some of his remarkable abilities in this field.

It must have hurt Tanglin to erase the hundreds of years of taped memories in the personal computer I inherited from him, but he knew that the vast bulk of memory there would have crushed a young, developing personality. Even so, he left me the record of his last two years, severely edited, as his echoing, gesticulating legacy. This computer, a highly advanced Niwlindid model, was specially designed for Tanglin; he understood it far better than I ever will. He cunningly hid his last tapes in there somewhere, part of a virus program that resurrected them and played them at apparently random times. The tapes were addressed to me personally, usually by a full-faced, insanely earnest Old Dad. He always addressed me as "Kid" or "Son," so that not even my closest friends knew our true relationship.

How often have I been playing breathless tapes of my own combative exploits, only to have Old Dad pop up, raving? Dozens of times at least; in fact, his projected hologram was constantly haunting my house. He would lecture me on politics, or on the perfidy of his wife Crestillomeem, or on the lurking presence of the alien creatures he called "leeches." These "leeches" were his particular obsession during his last months. He claimed to have learned his nunchuck techniques to protect himself from "Them." "They" were degenerate survivors of the Elder Culture, he insisted; gray-skinned and rubber-boned, with brittle, hollow skulls lined inside with coarse black fiber. Of course, his insane assertions had no shred of backing evidence. Once I'd grown up, I no longer believed him.

There were hundreds of tapes. He must have done at least one a day during the two years of decontamination in the orbiting emigration oneill. During his last week, in Professor Crossbow's house off the Tethys Reef, sixty miles from Telset, he edited them. Some tapes, especially the ones where he gives the details of his paranoid theory regarding the Elder Culture, radiate an intense conviction that demonstrates how he managed to rise to the exalted position of First Secretary of the Niwlindid government.

Why did I become a combat artist? Well, what else was there? I was young, though I still had the habitual grace of age. My body still remembered its combat training. And combat art is a young person's pursuit; it takes the vitality of youth, its carelessness, its reckless self-assertion. This modern age is a hard one for the young. Our remote ancestors, and some contemporary humans dumb enough to live on low-technology planets, died early, sometimes before a single century of life. They didn't live on and on, smothering their sons and daughters with the weight of their centuries of power and experience. It's hard to find room to breathe when you're young; it's hard for someone two hundred years old to acknowledge the adulthood of someone eighteen. One answer on Reverie has been the Decriminalized Zone, an area freed of legal and social restraint.

When the Decriminalized Zone was first opened, twenty years ago, corporate citizens were shocked and titillated by the spontaneous anarchic violence that broke out among the small gangs of roving, idle, bored, and defiant delinquents. Their vicious activities aroused interest and sympathy among others suffering from a similar frustration. Bootleg tapes of people being savagely beaten up found a larger and larger audience, and not only among the young. Viewer money began to pour into the industry. Combat art forms sprang up, the original undisciplined hoodlums were quickly disposed of, and combat art became a profession.

In the Professor's house northeast of Telset on the shore of the continent Aeo, I was a devoted follower. The Professor disapproved at first, but it wisely left me to my own devices as I grew older. In fact, I saw less and less of the old neuter as it spent longer and longer hours exploring the reef and documenting its incredibly intricate Reverid ecology.

One day I simply left the Professor a note and took my sailboat to the city. In two weeks I was established and I came back for my computer. My note was gone, but so was the Professor. My departure had freed it of its last responsibility. I imagined that my old tutor had gone completely marine and simply moved under the surface of the Gulf of Memory.

I soon found that I loved Telset. She is an island, twelve miles long, five wide, set like a jewel in the shallow gleaming waters of the southern Gulf of Memory. She is shaped like the footprint of a pointed slipper. The northern tip is Prospect Point; the original city, Old Telset, is in the middle of the eastern shore. Orbiters can see the Gulf as a whole: an ocean-sized lagoon, almost completely encircled by the vast coral-crusted arms of the continent-sized atoll we call Aeo.

Five hundred years ago, the pioneer Reverids cooked Telset to a state of red-hot viscosity with powerful orbital lasers, killing all native life. When she cooled, they stocked her sterile soil with their own flora and fauna, mostly Niwlindid stock. The alien species did well, but as the centuries passed they began to succumb to highly evolved native species that were washed ashore or carried by birds. Now the island is a riotous scramble of species from a dozen planets, each seeking a niche in a chaotic, cosmopolitan ecosystem.

The boundaries of the city of Telset are vague; her modern villas, of limestone, travertine, marble, metal, and wood, are scattered throughout the island. They are hidden in the woods and half-buried in the reefs; they loom from the shoregrass, they nestle in dells and creeks and hollows. Telset is wired, which does away with the need for compactness. The primary recreation of her citizens is tape: drone tape, art tape, life tape, memory tape. That's the way we are.

I've explored all of Telset on foot or by drone. I know the dense-packed, thickwalled, deserted buildings of Old Telset like the back of my hand; most of Old Telset is now the Decriminalized Zone, my stage and arena. I know the channels of the Telset Reef well, too; I've sailed them all in my little skiff, the *Sea Whip*, and explored them while swimming or with aquatic drones. I've seen sea beavers, mudcumbers, skates, and rays; I've seen kittiwakes, skeiners, skimmers, and cormorants. I've seen great mud-belching holothurians, as big as houses, hauling their rubbery bulk to shore, and I've touched them with my hands. I've seen great crusted cylinders of Tower Coral, two stories high; I've climbed them and dived from the top. I've seen Telset, touched her, heard her, tasted her, and smelled the sharp brine of her ocean air. And best of all, I've known her people.

Those among my audience who have closely followed my career (and I've known some to have whole libraries of my tapes) know that I started my career as a junior gang member of the Cognitive Dissonants, a group led for the last eight years by that resplendent couple, Chill Factor and his Ice Lady. Chill and Icy were responsible for my development as an artist and tape craftsman. The fact that I have sometimes challenged and beaten up members of their gang (Six Fingers, Hammer, Million Masks, Happy Daze, Flying Bill Flatbeak, Chains, Brains, Sumo, Hobble, and Twinkles) should not blind anyone to the sincere affection I feel for all these extraordinary fighters and artists.

They bought me my first cameras. They gave me innumerable tips on the correct dramatic presentation. They bought me my first smuff, helped me find my first home. They taught me gang etiquette, and the rituals of combat art and the artists' Code. The Code rules our lives. If not for the Code, we would all have killed each other years ago.

Of course, that was eight standard years past. Since then I've climbed to the top of the bloody flagpole.

Combat artists, even in this day of technomedicine, spend a lot of time healing up. You can't fight all the time, there are limits: medical bills and smuff. Limits enough so that even the top ranks are only moderately well off by the standards of Reverid richesse. But money isn't everything; in fact, to my youthful mind, fame and a fearsome reputation meant much more. And I had enough money to live comfortably and securely in the Decriminalized Zone, thanks to computerized alarm systems, royalty payments, a steady supply of smuff, and my housekeeper, Quade Altman.

Why did I have a human housekeeper when I could have had all her not-very-onerous tasks done by machine? Not for sexual gratification, obviously; I've stayed on libido suppressants ever since Professor Crossbow first gave them to me. My hairless face and high-pitched voice attest to that. Nor was it an attempt to conform to the typical practices of status-conscious, dominance-conscious Reverids. No, I kept her because she begged me to.

I still have the tape of our first meeting. I just couldn't resist her plea when she knelt amid the rubble of her three-dimensional mosiacs to look me eye to eye. (I'm five feet four, while Quade approaches eight feet.) Two members of the Perfect Stranglers had broken into her Zone studio to hide from the Cognitive Dissonants during a gang clash. Being uncouth louts, they amused themselves by smashing her works of art—excellent three-dimensional mosaics, if you like that form of expression, which I do. Unfortunately for them, Quade's falsetto screams and the brittle crunching of the mosaics' multilucent panels alerted me and I broke in to gloriously beat them both to pulps. It was wonderful; the cameras caught everything, and Quade took her cue beautifully in an impromptu performance that had me gasping with admiration. She fell to her knees, threw her incredibly long, skinny arms around my neck, and begged, literally begged me to protect her and take her to safety. I hesitated; in those days I was obsessed with projecting an image of utter inhuman ruthlessness. Finally, reflecting that I could always edit the tapes for publication, I agreed, and she actually swooned with relief. I later learned that she swoons a lot anyway, due to various blood circulation problems caused by Reverid gravity, but it was a great performance and she's done some of her best mosaic work in my house.

She'd been with me two years. I was healing up from a fractured shin, watching a drone tape, doing a little nicotine. Quade came into my tape room, carrying a light nighttime brunch. "The stars are beautiful tonight," she said vaguely. Her face was flushed; her eyes were glazed, and the peculiar yellowness that sometimes filmed her eye-whites was gone. I didn't know what was wrong with Quade but I naturally assumed it had something to do with sex; she had no lover. I had been trying for two years to get her onto libido suppressants, but with sporadic success. "Rub your back?" she piped. "Shift your pillows? Help you rub on your skin goo? Bring you your weights?"

"Quade, you're spoiling me," I said. "But get me an apron. I don't like eating hot food without clothes." I lifted the cover of the tray: steam curled upward. It was diced roast ray with stir-fried marshgrass; none of your corporate-issue oneill-imported proteins for me. I like an idiosyncratic taste, even when it's far short of synthesized perfection. Some fanatics might blame me for eating wild game; but since we humans have already taken this island, why not enjoy it to the full? To do otherwise is to insult Reverie; we should partake of her bounty, with the appreciation she deserves.

Quade left the room with three incredibly long strides. I was about to dig in when I heard the ping-ping-ping of a personal communiqué. I cut into my personal channel to see the genial, froglike face of Mr. Richer Money Manies, my friend and patron.

"Hello, Money Manies," I said. "Nice to see you."

"So, Kid," said Manies, licking his everted lips. "Trying to tempt me with your atrophied, hairless link, are you? You've missed your true calling, dear fellow. You should have been in pornotapes."

"Sorry," I said, pulling a pillow over my loins. "I didn't intend to pander to your depraved tastes." Quade returned with an apron; I threw it over my body. "Quade, doll, stay and rub my feet," I told her, more to get to Manies than for any other reason. As she knelt at the end of the couch to adoringly rub my feet, I picked up a mouthful of crisp marshgrass on my chopsticks and offered it to her. She ate it gratefully. I checked my camera with one eye to make sure all this was registering on Manies. "Lovely sunset today, wasn't it, Money Manies? I was up in time to see it."

"Yes, lovely, lovely," agreed Manies distractedly, his blue eyes goggling a little. "I would have put in a trace more scarlet, myself. Listen, my dear. I intend to have another of my breakfasts in twelve hours. Shall we make it three hours before dawn? I really need a combat artist to round out the group, and you know you're my prize of prizes, Kid."

"I bet you tell that to all the fighters you can't seduce," I said. "Of course I'll be there. It would be futile to offer this shattered leg as an excuse." I lifted the leg in question, showing the transparent cast and the electrodes that were helping to regrow the bone. "It'll hold my weight already; I'll walk over."

Manies sniffed. "How mundane! Is this the Artificial Kid, my star of stars? Let me send over a quartet of my most luscious pornostars to transport you in a scented, canopied litter. Why risk meeting some brainless belligerent not fit to kiss the hem of your nunchuck? No, allow me to deal with transportation." He waved his pudgy fingers, dismissing the topic. "How have you been occupying your convalescence, dear Kid? Viewing?"

"Exactly."

"What channel?"

"Nothing special; a drone taping from the wilderness. Done by some floater; the computer work's excellent. Channel 85. One thing interests me; she's using a manipulative drone. She doesn't just passively observe—she picks things up and looks at them. She's an innovator." We cut off our visual and put on Channel 85 with our audio as voiceover. "Oh, I recognize this woman's work," Manies said. "That's Cewaynie Wetlock. She's very new—no older than you are."

I'd never heard of her. We proceeded to a minute criticism. We spent two hours on it. Manies got me to promise to do a tape for him for his critical broadcast (a broadcast that was eventually to reach the eyes and ears of Cewaynie Wetlock herself). Time means nothing to a three-hundred-year-old Reverid, but it was decent of the ugly old antique to make the effort to amuse me.

2

The third hour before dawn found me at the northern tip of the island, at Many Mansions, the sprawling, limestone, colonnaded dwelling place of my friend and patron, Mr. Manies. I marveled at my friend's stamina, his continued gusto for life amid such demanding surroundings. As usual, his beautiful seaside villa was stuffed with servants, clients, house guests, flatterers and sycophants, rising pornostars, and ambitious tape craftsmen, not to mention the usual unclassifiable oddities: Manies' surgically altered pets, the mutant and hybrid products of his huge, flourishing terraria and aquaria, grotesque wandering holograms, and at least one actual resident alien. Amid all this even his far-famed breakfasts must have been a relief to him. Certainly he seemed relaxed and completely at ease as he performed his hostly duties.

He had invited five of us—about the usual number. And, as usual, we were a markedly heterogeneous group. Alruddin Spinney, the poet, and "Ruffian Jack" Nimrod, the explorer, were already known to me; they were two of Manies' closest friends. But I had never before seen Professor Angeluce of the Academy or Saint Anne Twiceborn, a Niwlindid political refugee. Both had only recently made planetfall, after the long and painful decontamination process in an orbiting oneill.

Spinney was a small, scrawny man, with a prominent adam's apple and a thick shock of kinky red hair. With an air of quiet melancholy, he pulled a fist-sized gobbet of raw meat from his pocket and offered it to his pet mantis, a green, arm-long, chitinous monster that followed him everywhere. It accepted the gift with a gentleness and restraint that matched Spinney's own and began to nibble it, breathing audibly through spiracles as big around as my little finger.

"The Morning Star's beautifully bright tonight, isn't it?" said Ruffian Jack, looking off the airy balcony across the slow surf of the reef. "Did I ever tell you about the time I went there?"

"Come now, Ruffian," laughed Money Manies. Conversation was his element. "We mined the Morning Star four hundred years ago. We're all intelligent people here. Surely you won't try to hoodwink us with some grotesque and impossible brag about your longevity?"

"Who said anything about four hundred years?" demanded Jack. "I was there not fifty years back. My floater days, you know. The final detonations melted its entire crust; that's what gives it its high albedo." I liked Ruffian Jack; he could have been a good combat artist. I forgave him his constant habit of lying.

"Mr. Spinney," said Professor Angeluce in his penetrating, pedantic voice, "are you sure that that arthropod has been properly decontaminated? Might I ask its area of origin? Could it be the continental area known colloquially as the Mass?"

"I don't know, sir," said Spinney politely, patting his pet on the hard transparent case over one huge compound eye. "I found him washed up on the reef, half-drowned. I assure you that I have never probed his guts for protozoa, if that is your concern."

"What is your concern with the Mass, Professor?" asked Manies, his every syllable packed full of interest.

"My concern? My concern?" grated Angeluce. He gestured

irritably and one of his three cameras zoomed in for a close-up of his pale, pinched face. "I am a Scholar, sir. My doctorate is in the field of taxonomic microbiology, but I have a more than slight acquaintance with epidemiology. The Mass is this world's most fertile area for microorganisms, many of them potentially hostile to man. Insects often serve as vectors for such forms of life."

Annoyed and frightened, Spinney put one protective arm over his pet's narrow green shoulders. The mantis, its jaws ceaselessly working, twisted its sinewy neck to turn one jaundiced compound eye on Angeluce. Manies and Ruffian Jack laughed heartily; even Saint Anne Twiceborn allowed herself a smile. "No cause for worry, Professor," Ruffian Jack said. "My researches show that this particular species of mantis is native only to the eastern arm of Aeo. You notice the peculiar mottling on his inner forearms? We're quite safe."

"Indeed, sir," said Angeluce, visibly annoyed at their laughter. "You hold an Academic degree?"

Ruffian Jack scowled. "I'm an explorer," he said gruffly. "Even the Academy needs its legmen."

"Really, Professor," Manies said smoothly. "It's true that we are all laymen, but I think you underestimate us. My good friend Mr. Nimrod here has classified as many specimens as any Reverid alive, often at considerable risk to himself." All six of Manies' cameras flatteringly zoomed in on Ruffian Jack, and Jack immediately recovered his good humor. "Mr. Spinney is a noted historian as well as a distinguished poet. Even my very young friend the Artificial Kid has written several remarkable articles on chainlink weapons for the Reverid *Journal of Hoplology*, and is one of our planet's most accomplished camera programmers. It would be immodest of me to chronicle my own accomplishments, but I might mention in passing that I am the author of the Chemical Analogue Theory of the Body Politic. Saint Twiceborn is as yet a stranger to our shores, but I am sure she is as talented and intelligent as she is lovely. And here comes breakfast."

We left the railing of the balcony and moved to the oval wooden table. Manies' food programmer, Mr. Quizein, rolled through the door in his servochair, carrying the first course. Quizein was confined to his chair while he awaited the clone growth of a new pair of legs. He had recently lost both his legs to the attack of a ray while swimming on the reef. "Hello, Quizein," I said. "Haven't seen much of you lately."

Quizein pretended not to hear and served the first course, finger-sized breaded nerve clams with red sauce. I grabbed my chopsticks and dug in. They were delicious.

Saint Anne Twiceborn, her chopsticks idle, was staring at me, a bemused expression on her wide, freckled face. I had a camera follow her. Money Manies, whose alert, bulging eyes missed nothing, said: "My dear Saint Anne—do I detect the signs of homesickness on your lovely face? Even after two years in an oneill, the tug of one's homeland can be strong. Tell us, what brings you here? What force on Niwlind provoked your exile?"

Saint Anne reached up with an automatic gesture and smoothed a flat cluster of dark feathers pinned to her hair. She said softly, "I follow the path of righteousness wherever it leads. If to Reverie, so much the better. On Niwlind I was told that Reverie is a paradise—that no one has to work, and that the government is an invisible plutocracy. But I find that there is much work for me here. And it's true, Mr. Manies—I miss my poor flock. By now my government must have completed its policy of genocide, and my poor flock has been scattered and killed. I wish I would have done more for them. That's what makes me melancholy."

Said Manies, "You consider yourself, then, a force for good in our universe?" She nodded. Manies continued, "I have always found such doctrines very interesting. Tell us more about your work. It was with an alien species, am I right? The so-called moor moas—giant flightless birds, yes? And you consider them intelligent—you are convinced that they possess an intangible soul, essence, animus?"

Saint Anne touched the feathers in her hair again. "My heart tells me so," she said. "I freely admit that they are by no means as intelligent as humans, but they have their place in the cosmic scheme. That was why I organized demonstrations to protect their native moors from exploitation. Our government was callous and brutal, and many of my followers were driven to desperate, violent tactics. I was arrested and held to blame. The courts exiled me, so here I am."

Manies said, "Fascinating! I take it that the majority of your fellow Niwlindids did not concur with your estimation of the moas."

"Yes," said Saint Anne. "The moas have no language, they said. They have no hands, no tools, no history, no art. They devour their sick—they are given to mob stampedes—they attack and kill domestic animals as well as wild prey. They are irascible, warty-faced, ugly. Oh, they said many uncomplimentary things."

"All true, I take it," said Alruddin Spinney, pausing to tempt his mantis with a clam.

"Yes," said Saint Anne. "But they never lived with them on the moors. They never saw them dance."

"Can you tell me what inclined you to this friendship with the moas?" asked Manies. "Why did you do such an atypical thing?"

"All forms of life are sacred," said Saint Anne. "I felt the call, so I went."

"How did you prepare for this call? Was it prefaced by a long period of celibacy?" Again, she nodded. Manies' eyes lit up. "And I assume that you possess a fully functional reproductive system?" Another nod, this one rather hesitant.

"Such is my usual experience with such cases," said Manies with an airy gesture. "I suggest to you, dear Saint Anne, that your altruism and your repression of sexuality are intimately linked. I congratulate you on your adroit self-manipulation." He ate another clam.

"That's not so," Saint Anne said. "It's true that I have tried to purify myself with ascetic trials, but my innate goodness existed before that time."

"Really?" said Manies. "I suggest a trial. Let us determine how much of your goodness is natural, and how much cultural; how much you grow green and good from the heart, and how much you are twisted into predetermined shape like a human bonsai. Let us erase all traces of your sexual discipline. My Reverid pornostars are among the most accomplished sexualists in humanity. We could destroy your painful inhibitions with drugs, dear Saint Anne; and then you may fly with fiery wings into their embraces. I assure you that you would find your linkage entirely delightful. Many women would swear themselves into servitude for such an experience, but I offer it to you freely, in a spirit of liberating hedonism. Afterwards, we could see how many of your tenets you still held, and with what degree of firmness. Would you be willing to embark on such a voyage of self-discovery?"

Saint Anne hesitated. Finally she said, "I feel that you mean me no harm, Mr. Manies; so I control my disgust and repulsion. I must ask you not to make such an offer again."

Surprised, Manies said, "I meant no offense; my offer was quite sincere and grounded in a spirit of anthropological inquiry. Isn't that so, Jack?"

"Quite, quite," said Ruffian Jack, tugging playfully on the ends of his long drooping mustache. "The sexual attitudes of Niwlindids are endlessly fascinating. Take for instance the following case-history, which I can vouch for personally," and he told us a long and exceedingly improbable lie that lasted until Quizein came back in, took our plates, and left us with heaped bowls of saltgrass rice tastily fried with the savory meat of sandcrabs. From far away came the bright flash of a flying island detonating somewhere over the continent; we heard its hollow boom.

"It was our outrage at such decadence that gave our church its moral power," said Saint Anne. "I have always struggled against it; and I can see that this world, too, could use a thorough cleaning."

"You'll need a base for such an endeavor," said Manies hospitably. "Might I offer my home? I am willing to warn my many friends and guests about your predilections; I am sure they will make every effort not to offend you."

"No, thank you," said the saint. "I intend to see this planet's worst sink of depravity—the Decriminalized Zone. I saw tapes of the activities there while I was in decontamination. I think my efforts are most needed there."

"You're joking!" I said. "Why, you little ninny, you'll be beaten up and raped before you get twenty feet into the Zone. The Zone is the Zone—it's not a playground for crackbrained fanatics."

"Now I know where I've seen you before," she said. "I recognize your voice. You're that small spiky-headed fellow who beat up that great gross bellowing woman!"

"You saw my fight with Screamer?" I said. "Then you saw me win. My shin was fractured, but nowhere near as badly as her tapes showed. It's almost healed. Look at this cast." I swung my leg up onto the table and pulled up the loose leg of my fuzz-plastic formal pajamas. I was out of my fighting clothes, which may have accounted for her slowness to recognize me.

"And that weapon around your neck," she said. "It's just like the exercise device Secretary Tanglin used to carry. You even look like him!"

I was surprised at this reference to Tanglin. Put on my guard, I frowned. "I'm his son," I said slowly, telling my usual lie. "He came to Reverie thirty years ago."

"How horrible!" she said sadly. "To think of Rominuald Tanglin's blood and bone reduced to this! What a pity he's dead, and was unable to raise you, to give you some trace of his moral excellence!" She shook her head. "I pity you."

This made me angry. A small device on the back of my neck sensed this and sent a crackling rush of static electricity into my plasticized hair. It leapt up into bristling life. Money Manies, Spinney, and Ruffian Jack immediately pushed their chairs back from the table and got ready to retreat; my cameras took the cue and floated into combat formation around me. "What do you know about Rominuald Tanglin?" I said.

"Secretary Tanglin was my idol!" she said. "He was a great leader, a great man! At least, he was until his wife destroyed him and deliberately drove him mad. Why, he did more for the moas than any man alive!"

Suddenly Professor Angeluce, who had been placidly stuffing himself with rice, looked up angrily. "Rominuald Tanglin?" he demanded. "*The* Rominuald Tanglin? Tanglin, the demagogue, the enemy of science? The man who backed that neuter charlatan Crossbow in the Gestalt Dispute? Are you related to Rominuald Tanglin, young man?"

"Yes," I said. I put both hands on my nunchuck and pulled the chain down taut against the back of my neck. "Did I hear you call Professor Crossbow a 'neuter charlatan'? Surely my ears deceived me."

Angeluce went into a huff. "Are you attempting to threaten me, youngster?" (I heard Jack groan, "Oh, God, now he's done it.") "I am a Scholar, sir! I am here with the full backing of the Cabal and I warn you that they will severely punish aggression! My cameras are recording your every movement for a full report to the Academy as well as your own planetary government!"

I didn't say anything; I just stood up, whipped speed into my nunchuck, and cracked all three of his cameras. It took about two seconds. I sat down again. Angeluce was completely dumbstruck. I put my nunchuck back around my neck and released its handles. Spinney, Ruffian Jack, and Money Manies all got back into their chairs, from which they had leapt with alacrity as soon as I pulled my 'chuck.

"Thanks, Kid," Manies said in relief. "We all appreciate your restraint. Professor, tone down your rhetoric unless you want the Kid to split your head. Kid, I apologize for him; he's an offworlder and doesn't know Reverid etiquette. Forgive him, for my sake."

"All right, Mr. Manies," I said magnanimously. "For your sake, I'll deprive my fans of the entertaining sight of Professor Angeluce beaten to a bloody pulp." That remark about Professor Crossbow had roused my ire. I was familiar with the Tanglin-Crossbow alliance in the Gestalt Dispute, because Crossbow had told me about it.

On the other hand, I was now much better disposed toward Saint Anne. I had her pegged. She was one of the dozens, no, hundreds of women overwhelmed at a distance by Tanglin's charisma. I even liked her some. We shared a common distaste for sex.

Angeluce was puce with rage, but he wisely refrained from saying anything. Alruddin Spinney spontaneously decided that something had to be done to break the tension. He picked up his pet mantis with both hands and set it on the table facing him, where it bobbed and weaved alertly on its thick, spiny legs. Spinney stuck a shred of raw meat between his lips. "Kiss kiss," he said. "Kiss kiss!"

The mantis leaned forward daintily and bit out the meat and a small piece of Spinney's lower lip. "Yau!" cried Spinney in pain. "Death take it! He did it right fifty times in practice!"

We all had a good laugh at Spinney's expense. Then I gave him just a trace of smuff to kill the pain and dabbed on a little quikclot. After he had covered the tiny wound with a scrap of skinseal he was as good as new. While I was ministering to Spinney his mantis leapt off the table with a rattle of wings, hopped into my chair, tipped over my bowl with one spiny forearm and started to pick out the bits of crab.

Quizein came in with the third course, a thick, creamy, skate's-egg omelet with kelp salad. It was so incredibly delicious that Angeluce's appetite apparently overcame his anger.

"I assume you've already prepared for next week's Quincentennial, dear Manies," Spinney said, lisping a little. Next week would usher in the five hundredth anniversary of the first settlement on Reverie, Corporate Reverid Year 500. It was an occasion that meant a great deal to surface-dwelling Reverids.

"Yes, of course," said Manies. "I'll be quite busy; I've made so many commitments that I'll have to be everywhere at once. It should prove very lively. The social consensus seems to favor a harlequinade."

I had heard the harlequinade rumor, but now that it was confirmed by Money Manies, a prime social arbiter, the rumor had become fact. "Harlequinade, harlequinade," I said irritably. "I'm sick of these stuffy harlequinades. Why can't we have a satyricon, or even a splashfest? Death, I'd settle for anything."

"A splashfest would hardly be suitable for a state occasion,"

Spinney said with a smile. "Even a harlequinade would have seemed awfully wild and extravagant five hundred years ago."

Ruffian Jack chuckled coarsely. "Moses Moses would spin in his grave, if he had a grave that wasn't blown to atoms."

"Tut tut, do these aged ears detect a crude defamation of the memory of the Corporate Founder?" asked Money Manies rhetorically, chiding Ruffian Jack with two minimal shakes of one pudgy forefinger. "Alas, Jack, your simple patriotism has been painfully tainted. You raise a blush to the cheek of Reverid modesty."

Jack rolled his eyes, but for the moment he seemed to accept Manies' humorous rebuke.

"Moses Moses wouldn't merely spin in his grave," Spinney said darkly. "It was no ordinary grave. Moses Moses was entombed alive, in a cryocoffin. Unfortunately he was posthumously assassinated three centuries ago by the Fox Day blast. His announced intention was to thaw and return to life in Corporate Reverid Year 500. Politically speaking his reappearance would mean disaster; but speaking as an historian, I would have loved a chance to talk to the man. In many ways he remains an enigma."

"Who cares?" boomed Jack callously. "The past is dead, Moses is dead. He's been dead since Fox Day, anyway, and that's three hundred years!"

"But I remember Fox Day," Money Manies said in a remote voice. "I was amazingly young then. No more than your age, Kid. Death, I haven't thought about it in ages. Ages. It was quite a commotion, really. We really thought that the whole world was going to collapse. After all, the entire Reverid Board of Directors was wiped out—the Chairman's Building smashed to rubble—Moses Moses' cryocrypt blown up! Suddenly we had no government! It amazed everyone. Of course, the Board of Directors was never very vigorous after Moses Moses had himself frozen, but once they were gone we had nowhere to turn. Everyone feared terrorism—anarchy! But it never developed."

"No, it didn't," said Spinney. "I've studied the history tapes. That three-week period of no government was the most amazing episode in our history, if you ask me. All our cities, even the oneills, were hotbeds of rumor. Why had the Board met in secret session, after years of idleness? Who was responsible for the explosion? Then the Rump Board assembled itself—a Board even more lax and meaningless than the first—and suddenly the word was on everybody's lips. Cabal. Cabal. Reverie was ruled by a conspirator's council. Faceless men and women. Everyone agreed that they were all rich, all immensely wealthy, but that was the limit of agreement.

"We knew that they were wealthy, because the Corporate limit on personal wealth was the major schism of the period, and the only cause for a coup d'etat. The progressive faction favored a relaxation of the strictures; the old Board of Directors insisted on the primacy of the word of Moses Moses. Destroying Moses Moses was the quickest way to destroy his hold on Reverid society, to loosen the puritanical discipline of the Mining Years. That was the Cabal's motive. They had assassinated the entire Board of Directors, destroyed the Founder of the Reverid Corporation, and assumed control. Their immense wealth gave them spies and assassins everywhere, so it was useless to resist. No one could stop such ruthless efficiency. No one even knew the names or faces of the enemy!"

"Crap," said Ruffian Jack. "It's common knowledge that there are thirteen Cabalists. Seven are men and six are women. The men are called Red, Orange, Yellow, Blue, Green, Indigo, and Violet. The women are called North, South, East, West, Up, and Down. They live in their own oneills, disguised as ordinary orbiters, and they appoint the Rump Board through their agents. Any ten-year-old could tell you that."

"Any ten-year-old surface dweller," Spinney said. "Oddly enough, most orbiters believe quite the opposite. They're convinced that the Cabal dwells on the surface."

"Mr. Spinney is right," said Professor Angeluce suddenly. "The agent of the Cabal who met me in orbit assured me that the Cabalists dwell here in Telset, and in Sylvain, Eros, and Jucklet, the four largest cities." As always, I winced at the mention of "Jucklet." Jucklet! What a tin ear that Moses Moses had for names!

"You met an actual agent of the Cabal?" Manies said with interest. "That's a rare privilege, Professor."

"Not so rare," said Angeluce. "In the oneills your own name is mentioned quite prominently in connection with the Cabal, as you, sir, are no doubt aware. Some allege that the Cabal stifled your political ambitions. Others hint that you yourself may be a member."

"Me, a Cabalist? Law forbid!" said Manies. "I have enough trouble managing this menagerie, much less the planet. As for my political ambitions, perish the thought! I am a simple entertainer. And editor. And antiquarian. And social theorist. Oh, I wear many hats, but the thorny wreath of politics has never encumbered my brow, sir, I assure you."

"Excellent," said Angeluce. "Would that I could say the same for some of my misguided rivals."

The hypocrisy of this covert reference to Professor Crossbow disgusted me. Crossbow had chosen a political ally, Rominuald Tanglin, for Crossbow's interstellar war of words with the cobwebbed reactionaries of the Academy. I was a little unsure about the issues involved in the so-called "Gestalt Dispute"—it was before my time, after all—but I knew which side had my sympathies.

"And what do you call your own alliance with the Cabal, sir, if not 'political'?" I said. "Surely you've demonstrated that you need its bloody-handed help in the promulgation of your own senile meanderings."

"Bloody-handed, sir?" said Angeluce, squaring his shoulders. "I should think that adjective better applied to yourself and your fellow hoodlums, rather than to your planetary government. As for my alliance with the Cabal, you may call it what you like. I care as little for your language as you do for ordinary standards of human decency."

My hair rose, crackling. Manies, Jack, and Spinney quickly ducked under the table. I stood up. Angeluce stood up. I said, "I think your alliance might be best described, sir, as a double buggery of truth and justice. Your rhetoric is as low and hypocritical as your mind is narrow and mean. You, sir, and your treacherous Academic faction are an immense fishbone in the throat of human enlightenment!" Angeluce was turning white. "There is more information in one strand of Professor Crossbow's DNA than there is in the entire rattling, desiccated husk you call your brain!"

Angeluce folded his arms. "Feel free to resort to your usual dastardly violence, sir! As you can see, I am unarmed and unable to resist! Don't let the presence of a decent human being stop you!" He nodded at Saint Anne Twiceborn, who immediately leapt up from her seat to interpose her body between us. I was getting all this on camera and, unwilling to let her upstage us, I quickly sapped her so that she fell onto the table in a heap.

"Sir," I said, "I am sure you would prove as inept in physical combat as you are in a battle of wits! If your lack of weaponry bothers you, feel free to borrow mine!" I threw him my nunchuck. He caught it and, fumbling with it, he cried, "I would not soil my hands with such things!" Clumsily, he flung it over the railing and into the sea.

"You lout!" I cried. "My favorite 'chuck!" Ignoring my injured leg, I leapt over the table, grabbed him by throat and crotch, and hurled him over the railing to fall screaming into the sea. I had a pair of cameras follow him to record his impotent splashing and wallowing until the servants fished him out. Dusting off my hands, I returned to the table.

My host and his two friends crawled out from under it. "He had it coming," Manies said.

"I'll say," said Spinney. He picked up his mantis, which had found a perch on the blunt-cut brown hair of Saint Anne's head. It picked curiously at the flat cluster of feathers there.

"A great performance, Kid," said Ruffian Jack. "Really makes me wish I'd brought my own cameras."

"I'll send you a copy after I edit it," I said. I opened the sleeve of my pajama and injected two cc's of tranquilizer into the plastic drugduct in my left forearm. It soon calmed me down. Spinney and I set Saint Anne back in her chair. I slipped a little smuff into her mouth, checked the bump on her head—a small one—and splashed water in her face. She came to immediately.

"What happened?" she said.

"You fainted," I said. "The excitement overwhelmed you."

She frowned hesitantly. "I feel very strange. Sort of numb-tingly . . . all over." ·

"It'll pass," I said. "Why not relax and enjoy it?"

"Where's the Professor?" she asked vaguely.

"He left suddenly," Manies said. We all had a hearty laugh, and then Quizein brought in the fourth course.

At Manies' insistence, Dr. Kokokla, his personal physician, examined Saint Anne. He assured her that she was all right, gently pointed out that she had bumped her head, and offered her a sedative, which she refused. One of Manies' pornostars came onto the balcony, carrying my nunchuck, which she had carefully dried. I took it and thanked her; I felt uncomfortable without it.

"I've never fainted before in my life," said Saint Anne. "And I fail to see how I could have struck myself in the back of the head by falling face-forward. You can spare me your lying tact, sirs. I know that person struck me with that weapon!"

"Yes, so he did," admitted Manies. "Forgive me, dear Saint Anne; this spontaneous outbreak of violence was entirely my fault. I must own up to a miscalculation. I greatly enjoy the vigorous clash of disparate personalities, but I never thought that you would go so far as to fling yourself into the midst of a physical combat. Such grandiloquent gestures entail a certain risk!"

"Oh, stop groveling, Manies!" I said. "Yes, Anne, I slugged you. You upstaged me! As usual, our host is exquisitely considerate and polite; but don't expect the rest of us to conform to your bizarre notions! Now for heaven's sake, behave like a civilized person or I'll fling you over the balcony." A threat to severely pound Anne would only have roused her stubbornness, but the thought of being embarrassingly and disconcertingly thrown over a balcony made her reconsider. After looking at all of our faces, she took her social cue and sat down sulkily. After a moment she went back to her food. That's one thing about smuff—it seems to boost appetite and taste. It also completely kills pain, though it numbs, it disorients, it impairs coordination and sometimes hearing.

"Dear Saint Anne, thank you for being so reasonable," said Manies. "I give careful thought to picking the guests for these breakfasts, closely following the implied dictates of my Chemical Analogue Theory of the Body Politic—but sometimes I combine too sharp an acid, too bitter a base, and then I must deal with the following explosion! It's disconcerting, but often quite exhilarating! It keeps me young. I am a very old man, dear Saint; please allow me my quirks."

"I forgive you, Mr. Manies," said Saint Anne. "I believe that you have a good heart. And you have your own kind of wisdom, even if it be an ungodly one."

Manies beamed at this as if it were the most flattering compliment ever to touch his ears. Spinney and Ruffian Jack stifled smiles at her naïveté. "I am only fifty-two," Anne said. "You must have accumulated a lot of learning in such a long lifetime, even if you were never theologically trained. What is your Chemical Analogue Theory?"

Spinney and Jack rolled up their eyes, but the three of us were happy to hear it, as it gave us the chance to be silent and attack the main course, a tender roast tail of sea beaver that we ate with knives and forks.

"The Chemical Analogue Theory is, of course, an analogy," said Manies. He touched a stud on the heavy bracelet on his right wrist and in rushed his secretary Chalkwhistle, a neuter. Manies took pencil and slate from the neuter and began sketching as he talked. "As you are well aware, dear Saint Anne, the human body is an immensely complex system, in fact an ecosystem with its own flora and fauna. The same is true of the Body Politic, our human society. Their reactions, their structures are very similar. Now, the history of the human body is the history of its organic macromolecules, its linkages (pardon me) of separate atoms. Similarly, the history of the Body Politic is the history of many small groups and coteries, linked groups of friends. Of course, I would not go so far as to equate a single personality with a single atom. In most cases people would be better considered as small molecules; acids, bases, salts, et cetera. I often consider them atoms for simplicity's sake, however.

"Note that the effect of a single atom in the human body is almost negligible; but if that atom is included in the right molecule, its influence may be crucial! It does not matter which particular atom enters a molecule, you understand; the important thing is that it be the correct kind of atom, and attached in the correct molecular framework! It is the framework that counts, you see, just as the important thing is the relationships within groups of friends, rather than the friends themselves. Of course some atoms are comparatively rare, just as some personality types are comparatively rare, and they can exert a disproportionate influence; but it is the linkages that count.

"I regard myself as an enzyme, constantly endeavoring to link molecular groups into newer and more potent configurations. This breakfast is just such an attempt."

"In other words it's not who you are, it's who you know," Spinney said. Spinney, Jack, and I were shamelessly gorging ourselves; we had already heard Manies' ludicrous, disjointed theory several times. It was one of the most visible signs of his age. It was no stranger or crazier than other senile theories cooked up by people his age—Rominuald Tanglin, for instance.

"Correct! Such statements show an intuitive understanding of this principle," said Manies happily. "Let me offer a concrete example. Perhaps you recognize this molecule, delta-1 tetrahydrocannabinol." He held up his slate.

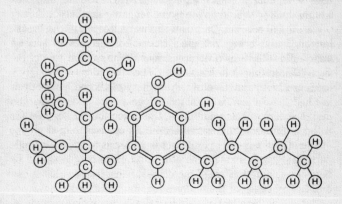

"This is a mild hallucinogen and euphoriant," said Manies. "As you can see, its structure is relatively simple; fifty-three atoms, all carbon, hydrogen, or oxygen, with no troublesome nitrogen or silicon as in so many drugs. I determined to deliberately replicate its structure as a Chemical Analogue, to determine its effect on the actions of the Body Politic. You may recall the occasion, dear Alruddin. It was the Mid-Year Satyricon, five years ago."

"Wau, do I!" said Spinney enthusiastically. "What a celebration! People were singing, shouting, laughing, crying, stripping off their costumes, linking right in the streets . . . howling at the Morning Star, diving off the Coral Towers . . . and at dawn there was a mass nude swim in Telset Bay! It was incredible, unbelievable!" He sobered. "You're not claiming you were responsible for that, Money Manies?"

"Responsible, my dear fellow?" said Manies with a cryptic smile. "You were one of the oxygens! It might have gone on indefinitely if one of my carbons had not eloped with someone else's hydrogen, breaking the structure down into a mere cannabinoid. . . . However, I consider the whole episode a strong point in favor of my theory. The experiment was well worth the effort of gathering together fifty-three hand-picked friends. Thank you, Chalkwhistle, that's all for now." Manies erased the slate with a touch of his thumb and handed it back to his secretary, who left. "Would anyone care for some sherbet?"

We all had sherbet, then had servants clear away the breakfast table and bring in lounge chairs. Manies passed around some mild after-breakfast drugs, and Spinney read us part of the new installment in his Telset Cycle. The eastern sky slowly reddened with dawn, and when the sun's vivid yellow rim touched the horizon we greeted it with shouts of acclaim. The placid waters of the great Gulf of Memory flamed up gold for an instant, then settled into the deep sapphire blue of daylight.

Breakfast was over; it was time to go home.

3

I now had one week to prepare for the Harlequinade, really an absolute minimum for a person in my status position. Most of the time I enjoyed status maneuvering—what Reverid doesn't?—but there were times when the endless minutiae and petty bickering made me sick, and this was one of them. I felt that it was aging me before my time.

The young can't begin to compete with the old in dominance games; the old have an overwhelming advantage in self-control, in experience, in knowledge of human motivation. But thanks to combat art and the Decriminalized Zone, the young now have their own social arena and their own rules of politesse. In fact, in many ways the combat art system has become a microcosm of the larger world outside. But it's our microcosm, where a young person at least has a chance at power—in the outside world you can only look forward to a hundred years of kindly, gentle, subtle slavery.

In this smaller world, I was a man to reckon with. Naturally I had my own client coterie, the Artificial Youth Faction. I restricted the membership to twelve, and the competition was intense, especially since I made it a point of honor never to beat up my clients unless they really deserved it.

The arrangements for the Harlequinade took time. First there was the problem of my costume. I made very little attempt to disguise myself, since the plasticized hair of myself and my twelve minions made disguise useless. Instead, I wore my usual fighting gear, barely camouflaged under a loose black-and-white smock and thin black flared pants vertically striped in scarlet. I also wore a simple black domino mask. Naturally I designed my own clothing.

Then there was the pressing matter of my palanquin. There was nothing wrong with the palanquin itself; Quade and I could easily unfold it, reassemble it, and redecorate it. The problem was choosing which six of my twelve clients would have the honor of bearing me about. The honored six would swagger intolerably, while the snubbed six would sulk. I had to arrange for everyone's rendezvous, and then go through the grapevine to establish a suitable location for my palanquin during the hologram display. I couldn't have cared less about the display, but socially speaking it was crucial that my palanquin be prominently placed.

I hated harlequinades.

Luckily, my good friend and fellow artist Chill Factor, co-head of the Cognitive Dissonants and chairman of C.D. Enterprises, was handling the details of the palanquin business. I got a call from him the day before the Harlequinade.

"Greetings, Arti, my little angel of violence!" said Chill. "How's the leg?"

"Cast comes off tomorrow," I told him. "What's on your mind, Chill?"

Chill looked harried; his sharp, narrow, glacially blue face had little puckers between his white, frost-brittle brows. There was a freezing beaded condensate on his cheeks and forehead and his icicle hair was half-an-inch thick in white rime. His status position was keeping him busy.

Behind him on the wall of his tape room was a map of the area in question, neatly marked off in a hexagonal grillwork. "I have you here," he said, rising from his console chair and pointing to the map. "You'll be next to Raphael of the Fourways and Todd Regewgaws of the Manglers. I'm just up the hillside a way, with Icy and a few of the Cogs—Twinkles, Hammer, Happy Daze—you know, the usual lot."

"I'll be there," I said. I was pleased at my position.

Chill looked relieved. He wiped his brow with the back of one ice-blue hand, cracking a thin layer of ice that had formed around his knuckles. Chill's refrigerated second skin was form fitted perfectly to his face, but there were a few small telltale bumps and wrinkles around his fingers. I still don't know how he supplied the necessary refrigerant power, but I suspect that it came from small engines hidden in his furry mukluks.

"You accept it, then?" he said. "Ah, that's my angel Arti. The status war this year has stricken me with grief, endless grief. Several areas are contested, including your own. I expect—well, not bloodshed, because fighting on holidays is gauche. But this will be the cause of many a bruise feud in the new year."

"I can hold my own territory," I said. "Call on me if you need help."

"Thoughtful, thoughtful," nodded Chill. "The Billy Club are the only ones on the Civic Detail, by the way."

I was disgusted. I despised police detail. The pay was great, but it was essentially a bribe from the Board of Directors to keep the combat gangs under control. Somehow the cunning old rascals had made the "Civic Detail" into a hotly contested honor. "Those bootlickers," I said. "What good are they? They couldn't punch their way out of a wet barrel. Crap, this could be serious."

"There was something else I meant to tell you," said Chill. He struck his forehead with the icy palm of his hand, then tore it loose with a shredding sound. "Ah yes. The mysterious gentleman in Red." He raised his voice. "Icy! Did I file that call under 'Grudges,' or under 'Threats'?"

"I think under grudges, darling," came Ice Lady's voice from off camera.

"Oh dear. I think the grudge file overflowed its capacity yesterday—you know these combat poseurs, Arti, taking a status demotion so, so personally—I must have lost the call. The man in question offered me five hundred fracs to beat you senseless."

"Was it anyone you knew?"

"He wore a red mask. He seemed old, though. Hard to tell, of course. Obviously he knew very little about the art, or he would have called one of your enemies, rather than me. In fact, I'm sure he has asked someone else already. He seemed quite determined."

'Five hundred fracs isn't bad pay."

"For you, my angel Arti, I would have demanded at least five thousand."

"You flatter me, Chill." I cut off.

On New Year's Day, the Artificial Youth Faction gathered together, to bear me in state through the Zone. The Decriminalized Zone was usually a lonely place. Most of the battered buildings were deserted.

Now, however, the Zone was clotted with people. As it always did, the sight of such a large crowd gave me a creepy sensation of awe. For the first twenty years of my life, I had been alone on the reef except for Professor Crossbow and my tapes, and the occasional rare visitor. Even after eight years in Telset, crowds disturbed me.

There were all the expected costumes of Harlequinade, with a decided historical bent this time: floater costumes, the somber garb of the Mining Engineers, the black and nebular yellow of Confederate officials, the decadent six-hundred-year-old finery of the Niwlindid Directorate, combined, mutated, exaggerated, adulterated with every atom of a playful and cynical Reverid ingenuity. There were others dressed as historical figures— members of the Board of Directors, favorite artists, composers, and scientists, or drowned swimmers from Aquaria, Reverie's ill-fated underwater city, or maddened plutocrats from the first rash days of expansionism; and then, crowding thick as swarming flies, the advocates of pure bizarrerie: people in fish costumes, dressed as insects, as birds, as crustaceans and coelenterates, people swathed in fur, or plated in skin-tight mirrors, people with no faces, or four arms, or eight legs; people in chains, in webs, in masses of bubbling froth; people dressed as the dead, the living, the not-yet-to-be, and the never-could-be. There were cameras everywhere.

It took a very special occasion to physically assemble Telset's scattered population, but this was it. The entire population was there: over three hundred thousand people. A crowd that large assumes an uncanny life of its own. Multicolored streams and filaments of people were pouring in and out of the crowd like the protoplasmic flow of an amoeba. Colored litters and palanquins were moving sluggishly above the heads of the crowd like food vacuoles. I rolled back the top of my palanquin and stood up as we neared the thickening edges of the crowd.

Cameras were drifting over the mass like hot droplets of grease over something frying. The crowd was making frying sounds; they were thousands of conversations, murmured propositions, shrieks of laughter, merging into an anonymous hiss and sputter like the sound from a blank tape, turned up far too high. Masked faces turned toward me; a murmur spread, because I had been recognized at once. Some people retreated from me, others advanced. I had a good view as the Artificial Youth Faction surged into the crowd.

I had delayed my arrival until midafternoon. The real fun would probably not begin until nightfall, anyway.

"You, sir! The gentleman in the black domino!" I looked down. I had been hailed by Emery Board, one of the minor members of the Billy Club. I recognized her despite her fish mask; she was wearing the rainbow armband of the Civic Detail. "This stranger has begged for an introduction." A huge lout in tasteless fringed leather clothing was standing at Emery's elbow. The stranger wore no mask. He was obviously not from Telset.

"You call yourself the Artificial Kid?" he bellowed, in a stupid breach of etiquette. He should have shown at least a token confusion over my disguise. I turned two cameras on him. "Why deny it?" I said easily.

"Why don't you hop out of that contraption and talk to me

man to man?" he demanded. "It makes my neck hurt to look up." Shocked titters arose from a rapidly growing group of spectators.

"My pleasure," I said. I leapt out of the palanquin and knocked him down with a kick in the chest.

He rolled with the kick and got up easily enough, dusting off his peculiar backwoods clothing with his rough, calloused hands.

"You're pretty clever with your feet," he said levelly. "In Jucklet we don't think much of feet fighters."

"In Jucklet you don't think much at all," I observed, winning a gratifying round of applause from the masked spectators. My cameras went into combat position. The six members of the Artificial Youth Faction set down the palanquin with sighs of relief and sat on it, grinning under their masks.

"I've seen you fight before, but I don't call that real fighting," the man said. "You don't feel pain. You use those chuka sticks. It's not man to man. It's opera stuff. It's faked! I'm more of a man than you, and I can prove it!"

The crowd was eating it up. Ribald suggestions flowed from their decadent lips. "Show us your manhood, then!" "Kiss 'im, Kid!" "Go on, Leather! Challenge him!"

I raised one hand for silence. From the corner of my eye I noticed that cameras were accumulating everywhere, which annoyed me; I hate bootleg tapes. "What do you propose?" I asked.

"Punch for punch," he said. "Man to man. No weapons. No dodging or defending. Last man to get back up loses. That's what I call an honest bout."

He knew as well as I did that those were impossible terms; it was my skill at dodging, defending, and blocking blows that made up for my lack of height and bulk. "Fine," I said. "You strike first." I dropped my candy-striped nunchuck and put my hands behind me.

As I expected, he swung for my chin. As the punch came in I leaned forward slightly and dropped my jaw. He punched me in the teeth. For anyone but myself it would have been a fatal gambit, but my teeth are a sturdy legacy from dear Old Dad.

They were all false, tooth-shaped white ceramic over a crystalline metal core, anchored solidly to one of the thin ceramic plates that armored my skull. He screamed and drew away his hand, dripping blood. I smiled evilly, skipped forward and hit him in the neck with the outside edge of the base of my hand. He fell down choking and soon lost consciousness. It was a nasty blow, but he was a nasty man.

I spoke quietly to Emery. "Get him to a doctor, Emery. You'd better hurry. I'll assume the charges." The man's neck already showed a dark stain; it was probably arterial hemorrhage.

I picked up my nunchuck and jumped back into the palanquin to a round of polite and somewhat intimidated applause from the spectators. If they had expected a long slugfest they were disappointed, but I wouldn't waste time being pounded for the sake of someone else's cameras. I pulled the cover of the palanquin up for privacy as the Artificial Youth Faction hoisted it with a grunt to their shoulders. I put salve on my lips to stop the swelling. My bravado in letting him strike first had cost me, but you don't win a reputation without taking risks.

Following the instructions that Chill had given me earlier, the Youth Faction made their way toward the area I had staked out for the hologram display. A nameless poseur had had the gall to park his palanquin in my place, and I had the Youth Faction dump him and stomp him soundly. We watched him crawl off as we broke his palanquin to pieces.

"Trouble, trouble, trouble, always trouble," observed a wry, vibrant voice. It was my best friend, the well-known combat artist, Armitrage. Armitrage had a lovely dark young woman on his left arm and a gentle, rather frightened-looking young man on his right. "These, sir, are my two new clients," he said, noticing my gaze. "For the time being you may address them as Jonquil and Coral." He struck a pose. "Have no fear, darling clients. I will protect you from this sinister ruffian." His two clients giggled shyly, cupping their hands over their mouths. I never learned which name fit which client.

Armitrage and I were so close that we merely played with the formalities of disguise. "Delighted to see both you and your complaisant lovelies, dear Stranger doll," I said. I invited him into my palanquin and offered him a flavored ice-stick. My housekeeper Quade, who had been faithfully tagging after me all this time, rushed up to offer sweetmeats to his two lovers.

"Where's your litter, 'Trage?" I asked.

He shrugged. "Left it behind," he said. "My aching death, these harlequinades bore the morals out of me." He sucked meditatively on his ice-stick. "It's as hot as the Morning Star out here. I can't remember when I've seen such a crowd, even on tape." I nodded. "I saw Money Manies a while ago," Armitrage said. "He had his Alien with him."

"Not again," I said.

"He never learns," Armitrage said sadly. "Even if he does learn, then he forgets."

"Yeah," I said. Even for an old man, Money Manies was unusually prone to peculiar lapses of memory. Most people thought that Manies was really forgetful, but I was convinced that it was one of his affectations. He was entirely too alert to be genuinely absent-minded.

"I understand the Clone Brothers are looking for you," Armitrage said. "I thought you'd settled with them."

"So did I," I said. "However, if they haven't learned, I'm always ready to administer another lesson."

"Want me to tag along today, in case there's trouble?"

"My gratitude, but no."

Armitrage shrugged again. "That's my proud Arti." He leaned gracefully back into the palanquin.

Most of the palanquins in the viewing area were down, and their tenants had left them to stroll about and socialize. The area just around us was crowded with combat artists and their young hangers-on. I spotted members of the Fourways, the Manglers, and the Perfect Stranglers.

Armitrage pried an artificial bubo from his neck and scratched under it. (I haven't mentioned as yet that Armitrage was disguised as an early Reverid settler suffering from a lymph infection.) "What are your plans now?" he asked. I shrugged. "Join me, then," he offered. "I'll keep you amused. You feel like some hot flashes? I've got some really nice Red Dust on me." Armitrage, besides being my best friend, also sold me my smuff. He was the drug supplier for many of the artists of the Zone—a very high-status occupation. "Maybe," I said. "I'd prefer something milder, though."

"Let's see what we can barter for, then." We dismissed our attendants and plunged into the crowd.

A man walked by us on stilts; Armitrage unobtrusively tripped him and sent him sprawling into a picnicking group of dancers from the third contingent of the Telset Ballet. Snickering, we ducked away behind the bearers of a litter. We detoured around a huge two-man pink palanquin belonging to a pair of lovers from the Perfect Stranglers, then almost stumbled over one of the Clone Brothers.

The Clone in question was squatting on the broken, weedgrown pavement with Jet Pink of the Stranglers, tossing polyhedral dice. He turned, saw me, and scrambled quickly to his feet. He was wearing a bright red bodysuit dotted with small metal studs. His mask was a stiff elongated band of white plastic that encircled his head; narrow red lenses hid his eyes. The plainness of this costume was strange for the tawdry Clones. It looked like livery, and its color could mean only one thing.

"Well," piped the Clone, recovering his composure. "It's the Mechanical Boy. How delightful to see you, Mechanical."

I looked him over, with contempt. "You shouldn't wear red, Clone doll," I told him. "It doesn't suit you."

"It hides the splatters of blood from those who offend their betters," said the Clone confidently. He stepped closer. I smelled the faint bitterness of cosmetic spices on his breath. He reached out slowly and laid his long, narrow palm across my cheek. "On behalf of my brothers and other selves, we challenge you, Artificial Kid. We challenge you! Bruise feud!" He slapped me.

I stepped back. "Tell your boss, the coward in red that hired you, that I will demolish him after I finish with his bootlicks."

The Clone pursed his lips. "Bootlick? Harsh words from the fawning pet of Money Manies."

My hair rose, crackling. Armitrage touched my wrist. "Don't hit him, Kid. He isn't armed."

"Right," I said. "I won't argue patronage with you, Clone.

Meet me in three days, midnight, at Rubble Plaza."

"Too late, too late," squeaked the Clone. "Haste is the essence of Red's request. No, we destroy you today, rash Kid."

"This is a holiday," Armitrage said indignantly. "Show some class, Clone!"

"See to your own health, officious and interfering Armitrage!" snapped the Clone. "The minor details of combat courtesy no longer concern us. Our new patron is powerful, and his commands predominate. Do not become his enemy!"

"If you attack the Kid today, you'll have to come through me first," Armitrage promised.

"Don't bother," I told Armitrage. "They can't force me to fight today. I'll pick my own ground and my own conditions."

"Think again, unwise Kid. You have ambushed and beaten us singly, but our corporate quartet will break you, tonight."

"All four of you intend to attack me, alone?"

"We have challenged you in accordance with the Code. Our techniques are our own business."

"In that case, I'll help the odds right now!" With a shriek of anger, I crushed the Clone's left instep with a heavy stamp kick and drove the handles of my nunchuck deep into his gut. He doubled over and I struck an overhand hammer-fist into the back of his neck. He fell in a heap.

As I administered smuff to the unconscious Clone, Jet Pink shook his head. "You attacked an unarmed man!" he said loudly, for the benefit of the crowd that had gathered during the argument. "Your arrogance calls for a heavy reprisal, Artificial Kid."

I gave him a deadly glare. "You know my communiqué line, Pink. For you, I'm ready any time." I pushed him aside and shoved my way through the crowd.

Armitrage caught up with me before I had left the palanquin grounds. By that time I had recovered my good humor. I clapped him on the back. "Come on, let's find old Oswald Pigment. I could use some White Light."

"Take it easy on the drugs today, Kid. That's my advice."

"Ha! I never thought I'd hear that from you, 'Trage!"

"You have a powerful enemy. You'll need your alertness."

"This is Harlequinade, dammit! No skinny little replica spoils my holiday. You saw how I disposed of him." I snapped my fingers. "Besides, no one fights today. How can they make me? I'll stay with friends."

Armitrage nodded slowly. "I'll see to that, anyway." Suddenly he grimaced. "Death, here comes my patron."

It was the lady Elspeth Milvain, Money Manies' closest rival, being borne in state in an immense flower-covered palanquin carried by a chain-gang of eight nude pornotapers.

"You there!" she crowed at Armitrage. "The ravishing gentleman with the disease! When can we tape that lovely body in action? We'll give you anything! Perhaps we'll even cure you!"

"Nothing can cure me but a healing kiss from the Queen of Beauty," cried Armitrage gallantly. He leapt athletically up onto her palanquin, sending the bearers staggering, grabbed Milvain by her feathered crown-mask and kissed her open mouth. Then he leapt back down and stripped the artificial bubos from the sides of his neck. "My recovery is complete!"

Elspeth Milvain laughed up into the higher reaches of hysteria and struck the side of her palanquin with her whip. Glaring blackly at Armitrage, her bearers shuffled off.

Armitrage watched them go. "The old bag," he muttered. "Here, Kid, see if you can help me tape these bubos back on."

Eventually we found our friend Oswald Pigment, surrounded by his aesthetic disciples, the Pigment Group of painters. He gave us some White Light, a drug which vastly intensifies visual imagery. From then on the day began to disintegrate.

To fully describe our drug-raddled wanderings would be tedious. There was one odd series of occurrences: we kept running into Money Manies, or people who looked like him. He was wearing a different costume every time we glimpsed him. I suspected that most of the multiple Moneys Manies were wandering holograms. Laughing, he admitted as much. "I told you I'd be everywhere at once, didn't I?" Somehow I got into a bizarre conversation with Money Manies' Alien, who was disguised as a human being. (There were those who claimed that Manies' Alien had actually once been a human being, but that was probably a slander.) The Alien was wearing a pair of infrared night-glasses that were fragmented into colored polygons like an insect's compound eyes. As usual, the Alien's face was hidden behind a thin white veil. Its false human skin looked rather dry and rubbery. "How good the crowd smells," the Alien observed. "I will never understand why people are not allowed to be eaten."

After night had fallen, Armitrage and I watched part of the hologram display from the beach, where members and hangers-on of the Cognitive Dissonants were roasting fresh-caught fish over a driftwood fire. I hadn't talked to any of the Cogs in weeks, and the occasion was pleasant. The food was good, the night was good, the drugs were fine. Even the hokey old holo-gram projections, stuffy, slow-paced stuff that only old people could enjoy, were fun to jeer at. From the beach, we could barely see the titanic, lumbering holos. Anyway, their color was off.

I hadn't planned on joining the Cogs on the shore, but Armi-trage had subtly steered me there—at some risk to himself, since he had a minor bruise feud going with Million Masks. It was all good will and camaraderie, however, until Armitrage began talking with Chains. I was close enough to listen in, since I had been staring in fascination at the links of Chains's light chain mail dress. Under the influence of White Light, her outfit was all splintered glittering.

"I talked to Brains today," Armitrage began, innocently enough.

Chains shrugged. "So what?"

"He was your man, Chains."

"Our breakup is no business of yours, friend." She hesitated, then said, "I couldn't live with him; he was analyzing us to death. He's too remote, too detached. He can't release himself. He's too smart for his own good—far too self-conscious. It drove me crazy."

"Words," said Armitrage. Slowly, he continued: "But love isn't words. Love is the other. It grows within you. It holds you. It warms you. It is its own being. It is a power, like fire. It cares nothing for the woman who thinks she owns it. It cares nothing for the man who thinks he can replace it. If you fight it, it will sour and poison you. If you suppress it, it will only sink deeper and destroy you."

"This tirade from you, Armitage?" Chains laughed mockingly. "I know your promiscuity. You'll link with anything that moves. I've seen your tapes."

"Did I say that was love? Brains still loves you. If he didn't, he wouldn't seek his own destruction so ardently. I'm asking you to save him. He's too proud to ask for himself." He sighed. "Pride is the great vice of us Reverids."

"You're beginning to bore me, Armitrage. Shut up, I'm warning you."

"You are too proud to admit that you need him."

Reflex took over. Chains suddenly screamed at him and went for his face with a tiger-claw grip. Armitrage blocked the blow and knocked her down, blacking one of her eyes. Chains challenged him and they agreed to meet in a week's time, Armitrage and his combat staff against Chains and her weighted manrikigusari. Armitrage then left.

I stayed. Sumo and I had a good laugh over Armitrage's sentimental posturings. We agreed with Chains that he had been insufferable. It was true, but I liked him all the more for it. I didn't understand him, but friends are all the better for a touch of mystery.

I stuffed myself with fish, then wandered about twenty paces down the beach to lie down and listen to the surf. I pillowed my head on my padded nunchuck. I had fitted the padding myself, because this nunchuck was a special legacy from Old Dad. It had been built for him on Niwlind, during one of his peaks of paranoia. The bottom of each club unscrewed with a quick twist of the hand, revealing the muzzle of a single-shot projectile weapon.

I had tried the guns before on lonely beaches; either gun would blow a hole bigger than my head in wet, packed sand. Guns, however, were forbidden in the Zone by the combat Code, just like blade weapons, stilettos, explosives, and other immediately lethal arms. Even my good friends the Cognitive Dissonants would have been honor-bound to beat me to a pulp for carrying such a thing, if they had known about it. If I had actually used it on someone, they would have reefed me; weighted my feet with chains and dropped me off the reef to be food for rays.

But this candy-striped nunchuck was one of my favorites. I liked having something special in reserve; I liked having a final card to play. That, too, was a legacy from Tanglin.

"Pssst!" The hiss barely reached me. Torpid as a poolful of carp, I hardly stirred. The hiss came again, and this time I looked around.

It was Brains. He was lying prone in a spiky growth of marsh-grass, about four strides away. He was peeking out through a gap in the thick blades of tall grass, his gaudy costume well hidden.

"Brains!" I said.

"Not so loud!" he said. "Come down the beach a ways. I don't want to be seen."

I lurched to my feet and met Brains again in a sheltered spot out of earshot of the rest of the Cogs, who were doing a ritual dance anyway and paying absolutely no attention. "Get down, get down," insisted Brains, crouching in the sand. "I mustn't be seen here. *She's* just over there."

"Who cares?" I said. "You're being ridiculous, Brains doll."

Brains clapped the heel of his hand to the transparent window set into his skull. "This is the thanks I get? I've got important news, Kid. I wouldn't come within a mile of that woman otherwise."

"Well, what is it?"

"It's your housekeeper. The tall woman, with arms like pencils. She's been taken. Kidnapped by the Clone Brothers."

I stared at him. "My client? My servant? But that's a blood insult. Clients are sacred! They're asking for blood feud!"

Brains shook his head. "I heard about the way they challenged you today. Now they're just trying to force you to fight."

I stood upright. "I'll rally the Cogs. This is going too far. This kind of transgression involves all of us. At least Chill and Icy—"

"No, no!" Brains said hastily. "Don't tell them!" He motioned me back down again. "Come on, Arti. You don't need a lot of

Cogs to hog your glory. This is a great scenario! Master to the rescue and all that. And I'll help you track them down."

"You?" I said.

"Sure, why not? We always worked well together in the Cogs. Didn't I bring you the news? Don't you owe me one? Give me a break, Arti. I've left the Cogs, you know. I'm trying to make it solo. A tape with the Kid would help a lot. Come on, please?"

I looked at him skeptically. "Are you in condition to fight?"

"I'm always in condition," Brains said, offended, flexing his arms. He was a fanatic for fitness. Maybe it was his lack of humor that had kept him from reaching top rank. "There are only three of them. You practically crippled the fourth one today, if what I hear is true. The two of us can handle them. I've fought the Clones before. And I brought my tonfa." He held up his rotating club.

"Well. . . ." I reached into my drugpak for my syringe and some stimulant. I injected a little into the plastic drugduct in my left forearm and breathed deeply as the rush cleared cobwebs from my head. Anger and confidence surged through me. "All right, Brains. You're on."

"Great! The Clones will never know what hit them."

"We have to find them first."

"Rubble Plaza, Kid. Their favorite turf. That's my guess." He was exultant. "Let's go, let's go! My new career is waiting in the wings. Come on, we'll redo the discovery scene." He shook himself. "Ready? One, two, three, four! 'Arti! Your servant! She's been stolen!' "

Once, Rubble Plaza had been the thriving center of Old Telset. Now it was the blasted, empty heart of the Decriminalized Zone. The transition had come in a single day, when the Fox Day bomb was smuggled into the Chairman's Building. Rumor said the bomb had been placed directly on the great black cryocoffin that was Moses Moses' resting place and living monument.

Now, at the center of the Plaza, stood the forty-foot bronze statue of Moses Moses, the Founder of the Corporation. White floodlights lit it from below tonight, and gave its immense metal face a sinister appearance. The titanic Founder seemed to be peering into the gutted five-story building that had once housed the Board of Distribution. The Fox Day blast had ripped the building's roof off and mashed its nearer wall into a shattered patchwork. The same for the Board of Records. The same for the Consular Library. I didn't know the names of the other broken buildings.

As for the Chairman's Building itself—once Telset's pride, stern and austere outside, but inside as rich and ornate as the Corporation's fantastic wealth could make it—it had been utterly leveled. Boulder-sized bits and pieces of it lay heaped everywhere, some with long jackstraw spars of metallic epoxy reinforcement jutting out. Chunks of the upper stories had been thrown as far as Telset Bay. Most of the building, however, had leapt out as a devastating wave of shrapnel that had knocked gaping holes even through the thick, solid, windowless walls of the surrounding structures.

It had never been restored. It would never be repaired. In itself, Rubble Plaza was a monument. For three hundred years it had been a place of silence. Now, part of the Zone, it was an artificial slum for the Zone's artificial thugs.

I liked Rubble Plaza. I felt at ease there. I had explored all the buildings, even the most hazardous, where the floors creaked ominously and the rotted ceilings were poised to mash you like a bug. Old people never went there. That was why I liked it.

Tonight, there were a few floating globes of light still left for the late stragglers or wanderers from the Harlequinade. Not many would come to this desolate place without a reason.

"They're not here," I said.

"They're probably lurking in one of the ruins hoping you'll show up," Brains said confidently. "Let's split up and flush them out."

I shook my head. "Better stay with me. You don't want to be caught alone."

Brains disagreed. "Nonsense. I can take care of myself." He whirled his tonfa efficiently. "Yell if you need help. I'll do the same if I have to. But I won't. Remember, they don't know I'm looking for them." He trotted off into the darkness.

"Hold on!" I said. When he replied, his voice was already eerily echoed from the tilted slab of a ruined wall. "Don't worry! I'll soon flush them out!"

This rashness was so unlike Brains that for the first time that night I stopped and soberly considered my situation. "This smells," I said, speaking aloud for the cameras. "This smells of a set-up." But it couldn't be. Brains had helped me too many times; we had fought back to back; we had guest-edited each other's tapes when I was a neophyte and he was already a hardened veteran. . . . Could it be that Brains so envied my success that he would betray me? Surely not if it meant helping the repellent Clone Brothers.

I would have plunged into the ruins myself in search of the Clones, but I had forgotten my infrared glasses. Stupidly, I had left them in my palanquin. I could see well enough to pick my way through the rubble, but fighting in the darkness was out of the question. If I met the Clones tonight, it would have to be by the statue of Moses Moses, in the glow from the floodlights.

I picked my way through the weeds and hip-high chunks of shattered masonry, looking for an area with good footing that was relatively clear. A floating orange light drifted over toward me, following its rudimentary programming, and my cameras switched lenses. About twenty feet from the statue's base, I found a clear area, about four strides square. The rubble there seemed to have been cleared deliberately. All the broken detritus had somehow been shoved off to one side, away from the statue, leaving scrape-marks in the gritty dust. No weeds grew there. The ruined scraps of heat-seared tile underfoot showed that this had once been the ornate floor of the Chairman's Building.

The Clone Brothers might have cleared this area themselves, knowing I would come here. It seemed suspicious. I checked the surrounding rubble for traps or hideyholes where the Clones might strike from ambush. I found nothing. The footing was solid and well-lit. Satisfied, I began pacing, stretching, clearing my lungs, doing my kata.

I heard a sound in the darkness. I leapt into a defensive position. A luminous white figure came toward me from the dimness, almost seeming to drift. My hair crackled and stood on end.

"Mr. Kid? It *is* you, isn't it?" I recognized the voice at once. It was Saint Anne Twiceborn. As she came into the light I saw that she was wearing her usual baggy white saint's garb, a shapeless sack that fastened tight around wrists, neck, and ankles.

I pulled off my flimsy Harlequinade domino mask. "Yes, it's me. What are you doing here? The Zone gets nasty again after Harlequinade. You're not even armed."

"We were hiding," said the Saint. "We saw a monstrous creature stalk by here, not long ago. It had great spiny jowls and a flattened pig's nose, and huge cruel arms with taloned fingers. It was naked, and it had no feet. It had hooves instead. Its legs bent backwards. It smelled awful. I've seen some horrible costumes today, but this was no costume, Mr. Kid. It was real!"

I laughed. "You make him sound terrifying! Why, that was just little Goaty, the gargoyle of the Zone. He's slow! He's stupid! Being heavily altered surgically—well, it slows you down. I could step on his neck as easy as crushing a bug." I considered. "Easier. I like bugs."

"He terrified us."

"What's this 'we' business?" I said impatiently. "Is there someone else with you, or do you have tapeworms?"

"I suppose you enjoy abusing those who have done you no harm," Saint Anne said tartly. "I've known people of that stripe before. Terrible things happen to them." She turned and called over her shoulder into the darkness. "Come on out, Mr. Whitcomb. It's safe now. I know this man."

A stranger walked gracefully out of the darkness. He was short, about my height, but broader in build, with a handsome, well-trimmed auburn beard. He was wearing an historical costume, a soberly cut black formal suit with white pinstripes, woven out of threads, in the antique style. He had no Harlequinade mask.

Whitcomb sat on a chunk of rubble at the edge of the small

cleared area. "Good evening, sir," he said politely. "I seem to have, ah, lost my way. This rubbled area here—" he waved one arm eloquently—"isn't this where the Chairman's Building once stood?"

"Yes, that's right," I said. For some reason, I took an instant liking to the old bearded man. I spoke to him kindly. "Listen, sir, you seem to be rather confused. Perhaps you're under the influence of some drug. That's all very well when the City's at play and the Zone is in truce. But the Harlequinade is over now. You shouldn't be in the Decriminalized Zone unarmed."

"Sir, I thank you for that warning," he said. For a long moment, he looked me over. Whitcomb's round, amber-colored eyes seemed to miss nothing. He said, "I feel that I should recognize you. Your face and that very tasteful hair seem familiar to me. You must pardon me for my apparent negligence. My memory has been affected—I suspect a breakdown in my computerized memory system. Perhaps I've seen you on tape before?"

"Very likely," I said. "Strangely, you look rather familiar to me, too, Mr. Whitcomb." I looked at him critically. "Maybe it's your costume. It looks like the sort of thing the old, pioneer Board of Directors used to wear." I stepped up close to him and touched the peculiar material of his sleeve. "A bit stern perhaps . . . stodgy . . . on you it looks good, however." I stepped back. "I tell you what, Mr. Whitcomb. You seem to be a man of substance, well worth bothering with. I'm sure you want to avoid the embarrassment of having your condition revealed publicly."

Whitcomb nodded quickly. "Yes. With all respect to Madame Twiceborn's suggestions, I'd like to avoid police involvement or any, ah, formal proceedings."

I nodded sympathetically. The old man's status was at stake. "These things can happen to anyone your age," I said airily. "What you need is competent, discreet treatment. My good friend Mr. Money Manies—you've heard of him of course— can help you recover your memory and restore you to yourself. There will be no charge. Mr. Manies is generosity itself."

"That's very kind of you, sir."

"People call me the Artificial Kid."

"Well, I'm very glad to make your acquaintance," he said. "My name is Amphine Whitcomb." He extended his hand. It took me a while to catch on, but I shook it. It's a custom you don't see much nowadays. He must have been very old.

"I'd like to take you home now, but other matters press," I said. "I could give you directions there, but my computer guards my house against intruders. Saint Anne, could I trust you with the password to the house? It's a bit complex—you never know when a spy camera might be watching or listening...." I broke off as I saw Brains returning from the ruins, adroitly dodging through the rubble. "They're coming," he gasped, then drew up short. "Who are these people?"

"Friends," I said. "But not combatants. Call them clients for the time being. Yes, I declare them my clients."

"Well ... Kid ..." said Brains hesitantly, "I hate to imply that your ability to shelter clients is in question, but for the time being I'd suggest that they withdraw."

"Let them watch," I said. "I'm ready if you are. Did you see Quade?"

"She should be released soon. That's my understanding," said Brains. One by one, he began shutting off his cameras. The Clone Brothers had arrived.

"A lovely night to you, poisoned and foredoomed Kid," said one of the Clones, mincing up out of the shadows. A long chain dangled from his hand, clinking delicately on the ground. "A night you will long remember ... a night that will make you wince henceforth at the mention of our name."

"He was supposed to be alone," another of the Clones told Brains accusingly.

Brains shrugged. "These are noncombatants. None of my doing. Our agreement still holds?"

"You will receive the rest of your recompense, helpful Brains. Our patron's resources are vast."

"Yes, so I've learned." Brains picked up his four dead cameras with a mournful look. He had already stepped carefully out of range of a surprise attack. "I can't bear to record this," he said. "Kid, I offer my regrets, but the reward was just too great.

My new lover's tastes are expensive. Call me when you get out of intensive care, and put the medical expenses on my tab. Believe me, I can afford it." He left.

"That's great, Brains," I shouted at his retreating back. "I hope to return the favor some time." I turned to Saint Anne and Whitcomb. "As you can see, I've been betrayed. I suggest that you run as fast and as far as you can." They exchanged glances, then began to back up rapidly, stumbling over rubble. Then they turned and fled into the darkness.

The Clones unlimbered their chains and drew nearer. They were all wearing infrared glasses, which gave them another advantage over me; otherwise I would have considered running and trying to out-dodge them in the rubble.

A peculiar hesitation gripped all four Clones. "Our tactics regarding your spindly client might seem provocative of blood feud, oh ignoble and much-outnumbered Kid," said the fourth Clone.

"And, indeed, we would enjoy your murder," said the first one, bravely.

"However, the loss of our best-known opponent would hurt our audience even if it helped our reputations. Therefore, you will be spared." This came from the Clone who was limping, badly.

"Your client is in the hands of Red, our puissant patron. She will be released when we deliver to him the tapes of your destruction. This occasion is imminent. Therefore, prepare to reap the whirlwind of our multiple wrath!"

I didn't wait. With a cry, I attacked the nearest Clone. I kicked him in the midriff with my steel-toed slipper, knocking him down in a tangle, and numbed another's arm with my chuck, but there were too many of them. A heavy iron chain hit my kneecap with crippling impact and I went down, squalling, kicking and gouging.

It was lucky for me that Old Dad had bequeathed me a tough, surgically altered body. My skull was sheathed with thin plates of ceramic reinforcement, and my teeth, all false, were white ceramic over a crystalline metal core. The leather body armor under my costume protected heart and kidneys, and my ribcage was reinforced. I needed it, because they gave me a terrible beating. My plastic hair helped a little with the blows to my head, but I felt the kiss of chains on legs and arms and chest and back and buttocks and padded groin. They turned me into a human drum that they beat in 4/4 time, chattering excitedly amongst themselves in the peculiar abbreviated vocabulary that they used with one another: "Pretty!" "Happy!" "Beat!" "Kick!"

As I lay there, battered and semiconscious, they slipped smuff into my mouth. True, they did it surreptitiously, but even the loathsome Clones were not devoid of this last shred of combat etiquette. Then they climbed with spiderlike agility up the great limestone pedestal of Moses Moses' statue. Hoisting me up by the arms and legs, they scuttled to the edge of the statue's base. "Kiddy off the statue, Kiddy off the statue!" they chanted happily, seizing me by the wrists and ankles. They swung me back and forth, gathering momentum: "One!" "Two!" "Threeee!" and they pitched me headfirst into space. I fell ten feet to land with a wet crunch on my back and shoulders. Magnanimously, they tossed down my nunchuck. I blacked out.

4

When I returned to consciousness my body was aflame with pain. With swollen fingers, I dug into the sealed pocket of my combat jacket and pulled out my smuff. Before I opened my eyes I swallowed it. The pain went far away and I sat up slowly.

I was not in my home, which surprised me. Usually, Quade came and got me if I had been severely beaten up. But of course, Quade had been taken. I saw that I was in an abandoned building with Saint Anne Twiceborn.

"Don't move!" Saint Anne cautioned. "Lie back down! You've been horribly beaten, Mr. Kid."

I snorted. "That should be obvious." I pulled off the thin, bloodied rags of my Harlequinade costume and looked myself over. It was ugly. "Feels like I broke my collarbone." I dug into the numbed flesh with my fingertips. "No, it's all right. What are you doing here, anyway? What am I doing here? I'm supposed to be at home being tenderly nursed in delicious luxury.

Why am I still out here in the ruins?" I looked at her suspiciously. "Did you drag me in here?"

"We found you unconscious and bleeding," she said indignantly. "What were we supposed to do?"

"How long have I been out?" I walked to the leaning, corroded door and looked outside. I checked the position of the stars. "Just past midnight. Where's my housekeeper? She should be released by now, unless the Clones have compounded their treachery." I checked the inner pockets of my combat jacket. "My locator is still on. She should have been able to find me by now if she's returned to my house." I turned my locator off and looked to see if I still had all six of my cameras. I still did. I turned to Saint Anne. "Have you seen my servant? Quade Altman?"

"I'm afraid not," Saint Anne said. "I've been hiding you in here for hours now. Please stop walking around so, Mr. Kid. You're a horribly sick man. Your pores are full of little black worms! They kept creeping into your wounds! If I hadn't found these tweezers in your pocket I could never have picked them out!"

"Little black worms?" I said, puzzled. Suddenly I realized what she had done. "Those were my follicle mites! You stupid fanatic! Those things *live* in wounds! They eat dead cells, they eat bacteria! Now it'll take forever to heal!" I clutched my head. "That was the worst thing you could have possibly done! I ought to pound you black and blue!" I snatched up my candy-striped nunchuck, but stopped when I saw her reaction of injured innocence. I looped the 'chuck into its usual position around my neck. I stared at her. "You're a very strange woman, Saint Anne. And you don't understand all this—this world of mine. Are you aware of the harm you've done?"

"I meant to help, Mr. Kid. We could have run away, but we stopped when we saw you suffering. I'm sorry, but how was I to know?"

"Did I ask for your interference?" I said rhetorically, but without much heat. She had deflated me again. "And stop calling me Mr. Kid, dammit. Call me Kid or Arti." I reached into my sealed jacket pocket for my drugpak and treated myself to a stimulant. The rush hit me harder than I had expected. I put my head between my knees and breathed shallowly until my head cleared. "There. That's better. Now let's have a look at me." I dug into a wound on my forearm and pulled back a flap of doubled-under skin. "At least you had the good sense to smear quikclot on some of these things."

"I saw you use it on Mr. Spinney a week ago."

"Pardon me while I strip." I pulled off my combat clothes and treated the wounds she hadn't touched. She averted her eyes. I laughed scornfully. "Some nurse you are! My death, with you around I'm lucky to be alive!"

I gestured her to her feet. "Here, make yourself useful for once. Help me smear on some of this skin oil." I brought out my spare packet of oil. "Come on, my skin won't burn your hands. This oil will feed the survivors among those poor mites you killed. You just smear it on my back. I'll do the threatening parts." I laughed, a little hysterically. The stimulant was getting to me.

"You need hardly regard me as a sexual threat, Saint doll. You could see that for yourself, without me telling you. I share your contempt for that silly, gross coupling." I smeared the oil all over myself. Luckily the mites multiplied rapidly in the right conditions and would soon be able to resume their healthful work. I put mite-permeable skinseal over the remaining open wounds. There was dried blood all over me, even inside my nostrils; I had lost a lot of it. My plastic hair was all clotted together; scalp wounds always bleed a lot. I felt dizzy, but it was probably just the smuff, and the stimulant would take care of that. I put my clothes back on.

"Let's go home," I said. "Where's your pinstriped friend?"

"Out in the Plaza," Anne said. "He's been wandering back and forth through the ruins for hours now. It seems to fascinate him. I warned him that it was dangerous, but he paid no heed."

"He's a strange one," I said. "I don't buy this amnesia story of his, either. It's no computer breakdown. He's too dazed for that. It's either drugs or suicide trauma."

Anne nodded slowly. "Something terrible has happened to him. He still needs my help."

"How did you run into him, anyway?"

"I met him for the first time early this morning. I was watching the Telset Ballet perform. I've always enjoyed watching dances. It's very wicked of me, of course, but if Telset's to be my home I'll have to accustom myself to seeing such things."

"How broad-minded of you."

"I wasn't wearing a mask, and had some difficulties because of it. I was standing quietly at the edge of the crowd. A man— Mr. Whitcomb—appeared at my elbow. I noticed that he wasn't wearing a mask either, so I smiled at him, and he said, 'I wonder if you can tell me, young lady—are most of the people in this crowd human?' Those were his exact words. I thought he was making a joke, but he was quite serious. He pointed out an eight-legged man nearby and swore the man was an alien. He said the man had tried to pull his face off."

"But mechanized legs show up at every Harlequinade," I objected. "In fact, they're kind of passé right now. And the man probably thought that Whitcomb was wearing some kind of incredibly detailed beard mask."

"We exchanged names, and then he asked me if I had anything to drink. He said he was afraid to ask the masqueraders for food or water. I gave him some juice. He seemed terribly thirsty. Then he began to ask me all kinds of strange questions—was I a corporate shareholder, was the Board of Directors still settled in Telset at the moment. He seemed bewildered. But he was very polite. Even charming."

"He's in a bad way," I said. "We'd better get him to my place in a hurry before he recovers. Money Manies loves little mysteries like this. Nothing pleases him more."

We crept out quietly into Rubble Plaza. Anne's hideaway bordered on it. We soon found Whitcomb sitting quietly under a tilted slab of shattered wall, staring at the titanic statue.

"Well, young citizen," Whitcomb said when he saw me. "Up again, I see. You certainly are of resilient fiber. I wonder if you could tell me—this is, of course, the famous statue of—?"

"Moses Moses," I said.

"Yes, I thought so," he said. He smiled and got to his feet. "I am at your service."

The buildings in the Decriminalized Zone, my own home included, are the oldest on Reverie. Most of them were abandoned painlessly; their peculiar starkness makes them repugnant to modern Reverid tastes. Modern Reverids prefer open, lavish, baroque homes, handcrafted out of native materials—Many Mansions, for instance. The buildings of the Zone were all constructed from orbit by drones, using the same techniques that had proven successful during the century-long Mining of the Morning Star.

First the island of Telset was fried with orbital lasers until sterile. Then orbital pods landed, laden with drones and raw materials. They were directed by the same tough-minded mining technicians who had enriched the Reverid Corporation with their manipulative skills. Their objective was to build a city capable of housing fifty thousand Reverids, about the population of one oneill.

The result was so uninspiring that most Reverids, who had already lived through one century in orbit and had made their big cylindrical oneills amazingly lavish and comfortable, simply decided to stay there. They could see all they wanted of the surface through their drones, which were often provided with a direct cerebral hookup and had reached a peak of development during the long and horribly complicated mining years.

We Reverids have no equals in our mastery of drones—"drone" meaning any one of several types of self-propelled mechanisms, piloted from a distance. We learned our mastery the hard way, mining the hostile, airless Morning Star by remote control. And when we settled Reverie, we put our knowledge to a thousand good uses—such as the floating cameras that make my lifestyle possible, and the computer-run armies of robots whose orbiting farms and factories make us continually richer.

The pioneer surface Reverids were much concerned with biocontamination; understandably, too, because Reverid protozoans are amazingly advanced. Most typical bacteria elsewhere, for instance, come in three shapes: spheres, rods, and spirals. There are plenty of those on Reverie, but there are also

55

rings, spiral rings, T-shapes, snowflakes, and crosses. I know. I've seen them through Professor Crossbow's microscopes.

The old buildings of the Zone were built by those expecting plague. They have thick doors, carefully insulated ventilating systems, and a lack of frills and furbelows where dust and trash can build up. The walls are thick masonry, lavishly reinforced with metal (which the pioneers had in plenty, thanks to their mining operations). Joints and walls are sealed incredibly tight with metallic epoxy; in the destruction of a building the epoxy is always the last to go.

All this proved grossly unnecessary when computer simulation revealed that eighty-two different species of Reverid bacteria, carefully introduced into the body, would provide all the necessary vitamin-producing and digestive functions, while killing other bacterial intruders. Getting the bacterial ecosystem set up is a long and arduous process, but after that it works fine, provided that you don't foul it up with the wrong drugs. Freed of their fear of disease, Reverids gradually abandoned the old drone-built structures. When the Fox Day blast destroyed the Chairman's Building and damaged many others, it was the end. Old Telset echoed, empty, while open, breezy, hedonistic structures bloomed up all around like limestone flowers.

But I'm a combat artist. I loved those old drone-builts. They're built like forts. My home, for instance, was my literal castle. It had three stories, one of which was below ground. It looked completely anonymous from the outside, which pleased me. High ramparts surrounding the roof hid my terraria, Quade's little garden, and the pergola, where we sunbathed. The house had only one door, but I had cut a few holes in the walls to get decent-sized windows, paned with tough crystal quartz and protected with heavy shutters and eye-traps. I had my own generator, my own well, my own recycler. I even had the building's old ventilation system repaired, and could make the old place tight against even a gas attack.

I had the place completely wired and my computer handled the alarms. I felt secure against attack and had taken, I thought, all the necessary precautions; even a few unnecessary ones, in homage to Old Dad's paranoid spirit.

But they had never been put into practice, until today.

I smelled the tear-gas from the door-trap canisters a full block away from the house. I broke into a run, despite the smuff-muted whispers from my legs that should have been shouts of agonizing pain.

Most of the gas had been dispersed by the night breeze, but my eyes still ran freely when I reached the door. It had been tampered with. There were scratches around the jamb and the door's edge.

I shut the cunningly hinged flaps that had hidden the blunt copper muzzles of the gas canisters. I put three fingers on the door's pressure spots, muttered the password, and pushed my way in.

Armitrage was already inside. He leapt up from the couch, but lowered his quarterstaff when he saw me. "You're alive!" he said. "My death, you're pulped! But you're alive!"

Whitcomb and Saint Anne came in; Armitrage raised his staff. "They're with me, Armitrage," I said.

Armitrage pushed the door shut with the weighted end of his quarterstaff, then flung his arms wide, showing his embroidered shirt front and handsome green sleeves. "Arti, I swear I'd hug you to this bosom if you weren't drenched in your own gore. From the way you've been savaged today, I was sure it meant blood feud. I've been sitting here, convinced that your precious self was in a ray's belly."

"Hardly," I said. "What's going on here? Where's Quade? And who tried to break into my house?"

"One at a time." Armitrage held up one hand and began counting off points on his fingers.

"First, a group of men in colored bodysuits showed up in the Zone tonight and set your palanquin on fire. They soaked it in some kind of fluid first. It burned to the ground. That's what the witnesses said. Second, your housekeeper was stolen by the Clone Brothers in the middle of a crowd of witnesses. They yelled challenges addressed to you while they dragged her off. And they caught up with you, didn't they? I recognize the impact marks of their chains."

I held up my hand. "You warned me. I admit it. You warned me."

"Third, someone tried to break into your house, and your

house alarms called me and woke me out of a sound sleep. That was the latest development. I got here as soon as I could, of course, but I didn't see the assailants. In fact, I couldn't see anything for your damned tear gas."

"Sorry, 'Trage."

"That's all right," he said winningly. "I lied about the sound sleep, anyway. I was worried."

"How long have you been here?"

"Maybe an hour and a half. It's been bizarre. Your Old Dad has been in, raving, on and off."

"Yes, he always does that when the computer alarms are triggered," I said. "Even during drills. Damn, I'd hoped to find Quade here. Instead, I find I've been attacked on all fronts! This is a crisis!" I hesitated. "Obviously I'll want to look my best. The three of you must chat while I get out of these bloody rags and into a hot bath. Armitrage, meet my friends, Saint Anne and Mr. Whitcomb. You know where everything is . . . drinks, drugs, snacks, tapes . . . ." I hesitated in the doorway, then stepped aside as my Old Dad paced alertly into the room, looking to either side with glittering, rapacious eyes. "A time of attack is no time for half measures!" he thundered.

"Right," I said facetiously. "Saint Anne, Mr. Whitcomb: my father, Rominuald Tanglin. Dad, keep them amused a while, won't you?" I snickered mischievously when I saw Saint Anne turn white and grab the edge of the couch for support.

I left the room and went downstairs to bathe, emptying the tub and running in new water until it no longer turned crusty red at the touch of my body. I cleaned my hair, put on new skinseal, examined the wourds and found them all squirming with mites. I put a few temporary stitches in the larger wounds. Then I put on a second set of my full combat garb and slipped on a thin overrobe. I returned to my friends.

Armitrage was talking intently to Saint Anne, who kept looking sidelong at Tanglin's hologram. Whitcomb was standing in the corner listening to Tanglin's lecture and sipping a glass of water. It struck me suddenly that Whitcomb didn't realize that Tanglin was on tape.

"Now I'm prepared to take action," I said briskly. Anne

looked puzzled. "Style is a weapon," I explained. "I could never allow my enemies to blunt my style. I'd be two-thirds defeated already. That's what my Old Dad always told me. Isn't that so, Old Dad?" I walked up to the holo and put my hand through his torso. He vanished. Whitcomb raised his eyebrows.

"Anne has told me how you were betrayed by Brains," Armitrage said. "Let's go into your tape room for a minute and discuss some private strategy."

"All right," I said. We left Anne and Whitcomb and went into the soundproofed tape room. Armitrage shut the door unobtrusively.

"Who are those two spooks?" he said.

"You mean Anne and Whitcomb? They're harmless." I laughed. "They're both sort of borderline crazies. Anne's a Niwlindid, and Whitcomb is ... hmm ... come to think of it, I don't know what Whitcomb is. I like him, though. Don't you?"

"I like the woman," Armitrage said. "What does she have to do with your Old Dad?"

"She knew him on Niwlind. He was her patron, or whatever they call them there. Do you really think she's attractive, 'Trage?"

"Anyone who can wear clothes that ugly and look that good has to be more than just attractive," he said. "She's a real heartbreaker. A blind man couldn't miss the way she looked at Tanglin, though. As for this Whitcomb character ... you know, I have a suspicion that he may be behind all your troubles."

"Him? You think he is Red? Well, what grudge could he have? I've never even seen him before."

"Are you sure, Kid? He looks awfully familiar, somehow. I could swear I've seen him on tape."

"Well ... at least we have him where we can watch him. This has gone far enough. I look better now—haggard enough to be dramatic, but not absolutely demolished. I'm going to call Money Manies and Chill Factor. I'll try to hire some of the Cogs as my agents in a bruise feud against Red. Manies can provide the financial backing, so I can meet Red on his own terms."

"Let me in on this," Armitrage said. "I see this as the first major art event of the year. And you'll need my help."

"Do you work cheap?"

"No, but you can trust me."

"Good point." We went back into the living room and opened up my communiqué line. I tried to put a call through to Manies. There was a blur of static, and an image appeared on the screen.

It was a circular rainbow, surrounding a cluster of six directional arrows.

"What in death's name is that?" said Armitrage. "Looks like a test pattern."

I touched my selector. "It's on every channel," I said, amazed. "Someone's been at my wiring! What an insult! Great sweating death, I wouldn't have believed there'd be a Reverid alive who'd stoop so low!" I looked sidelong at Whitcomb, but he looked as surprised as the rest of us.

"Well, that tears it," I said. "Now I'll have to walk over to Many Mansions and have a long heart-to-heart with my patron." My hair was up; I glared fiercely at my companions.

"I'll go with you," Armitrage said. "The noncombatants will be safe enough here." He opened the door.

There were four men and a woman across the street in an alleyway. The men were all wearing simple skintight masks and bodytights. One was in red, one in yellow, one in orange, and one in blue. The woman was Quade Altman. She was gagged. Two of the men were holding her arms.

"Those must be the people who burned the palanquin," said Armitrage calmly. He shut the door.

"And they have my housekeeper hostage," I said. "Armitrage, do you remember where I keep my rifle? You were always better with it than I was."

"I can't just gun them down," Armitrage protested. "It just isn't done!"

"Never mind that! Just go up on the roof and keep an eye on them while I see what they want!"

Armitrage left. "Let me talk to them," Anne said. "I'll be your mediator; they won't hurt me."

I glared at her. "If you try to upstage me one more time, I'll rip your lungs out! Go sit on that couch and shut up!"

I pushed the door half open and let two of my cameras out. "How did you like a taste of my tear gas, you kidnapping miscreants?"

The figure in red put a small, compact bullhorn to his lips. "Do not seek to irritate us further," he said, in a conversational tone that rang through the empty night streets like the voice of a god. "Resistance is useless. We have the power of the entire planet marshaled behind us!"

I drew back from the door while the others looked out. "What is he talking about?" I said. "Am I dealing with a megalomaniac?"

"Why are they dressed like that?" Whitcomb asked. "Red, orange, yellow, and blue? Isn't that awfully conspicuous, such bright colors?"

Saint Anne said, "Mr. Nimrod told us that the members of the Cabal were named after colors. Do you remember, Kid?"

"I remember," I said. "But what would the Cabal want with me? I'm not political. I'm not even rich, not by plutocrat standards."

Saint Anne said, "They can't like you very much. After all, you did call them a pack of bloody-handed murderers. You said that they were a fishbone in the throat of human enlightenment."

"I said nothing of the kind," I said. "That was the Academy I was insulting, not the Cabal. Wait! The Academy!" I grabbed my head and felt a dull throb of pain; it was time for another dose of smuff.

I leaned out the door again. "You there! The impotent old geezer in red! I offer you two choices! Release my client at once and go your way; or tell me your name so that I can declare formal blood feud!"

"You are in no position to name terms," said the calm, magnified voice. "However, since your impudence has been properly punished, we are prepared to be lenient. We will exchange your client for the man you hold, the old man in black!"

"I thought it might come to this," Whitcomb said quietly.

"I don't trust you!" I shouted. "Release my client first."

"Not likely!" said Red. "Send us the old man, or we will destroy your house at once with explosives!"

"You're bluffing!" I yelled. "An explosion would bring every artist in the Zone! They'd rip you to shreds!"

"You stubborn child! You force this action on us!" Red hopped up into the air and ripped the gag out of Quade's mouth. At once, a thin, hideous wailing poured out of her. It was wordless, and mindless, like the cry of an animal. I had never heard such frantic pain from a human throat. Shocked fury galvanized me. I jumped through the door and ran toward them, snarling.

Suddenly, from nowhere, the man in blue produced a pistol. I didn't even see it. It was blind luck that made my swollen knee give way; I fell, and a bullet thwacked into the door behind me, jolting it farther open.

My enemies then unwisely decided to rush the house. Armitrage shot the man in blue, who was holding onto Quade Altman with his left arm; he fell down with a scream and the others scattered as he crawled for cover. I scrambled back to my feet, grabbed Quade's arm as she stood there dazed and howling, and hustled her into the house. There was the crack of another shot from the rooftop and a second scream.

Once inside the house, Quade suddenly lost her voice in a fit of convulsive choking. The tormented look in her yellowed eyes filled me with insane fury. I burst through the door, whipped my nunchuck around and prepared to kill one of the wounded men, but they had already been dragged away into the maze of the Zone. I went inside, slammed the door, and stood wheezing and snarling with rage.

Armitrage clattered down the stairs, half-dancing with exultation. "Was that shooting, or was that shooting?" He threw the rifle aside and embraced Quade. "You're rescued, my elegant, elongated friend! Why no smiles, no tears of joy...." His voice trailed off vacantly and he suddenly released her as if he had been embracing a corpse. "My God, look at her head! Look at her arms and legs!"

With an effort, we got Quade to sit woodenly on the couch.

There were half-a-dozen ugly gouges in her scalp, and puckered red sear-marks on her thin arms and legs. "Those are burn marks," I said stupidly. "My God, she's been tortured." I shook her gently. "Who could have done this to you? You, my harmless innocent?"

Something in my tone seemed to reach her. Her eyes opened wide, showing eye-whites stained with yellow film, and she screamed again. Then she started thrashing, without co-ordination. Armitrage and I held her down and slipped smuff into her mouth. Soon her cries declined to whimpering and silence.

"She must be in shock," I said.

Armitrage shook his head. "I'm afraid not, Arti. Look at those eyes of hers. Are they often like that?"

"Yellow, you mean? Sometimes. I don't know why."

"Well, I do. She's a syncophine addict, and she's in withdrawal. I wonder where she keeps her stores. Syncophine's not on the market any more. She may have her own supply somewhere, but she'll have to go cold turkey now."

"Why? Why can't we ask her where she keeps her drug, and give her some?"

"Look. Look at those gouge-marks in her scalp. She's been memory-wiped. You've been talking to a new personality."

"But that's murder!" I hugged the unresisting, unresponsive Quade to me; she was like wood. Tears scalded my eyes. "I promised to protect her. I gave her shelter. She was *mine!* How dare they rob me of her life? This is it! Blood feud! I declare blood feud! Professor Angeluce, you are a dead man!"

Anne looked up, startled, from where she was pillowing Quade's head. "Professor Angeluce?"

"Yes," I said bitterly. "I'm certain that was him in the red costume. I recognized his voice and the way he moved. Now I'm going to kill him. Armitrage, will you help me?"

"Sure. Who is he?" After we had explained, Armitrage said, "Unless he's with the Cabal, then where did he get those hired bullies? Men like that don't work for a smile and a thank-you. But the Cabal has plenty of money. They must be backing him at least; otherwise, he wouldn't dare wear their livery. I don't like this, Kid. I'd be happy to spill the Professor's brains, whoever he is. But the planetary government . . . they're a little beyond the sticks and chains stage. They blew up the Chairman's Building. They killed the Board of Directors. They killed Moses Moses."

Whitcomb said, "The Cabal is the planetary government?" Amazed at his ignorance, we nodded. "They killed Moses Moses?" We nodded again. "This is all news to me," Whitcomb said. "I am Moses Moses."

Moses Moses took advantage of our dumbstruck silence to explain himself. His ornamental cryocrypt in the Chairman's Building had contained a dummy; the canny Moses had hidden his true cryocrypt beneath the building in a secret, heavily armored and completely automatic sanctum sanctorum. At precisely the stated date, he had been warmed up, stretched the stiffness out of his muscles, dressed himself, and come up through the rubble. That explained the cleared patch in the rubble at the base of the statue. "It's a good thing they didn't build the statue twenty feet further over," he said.

"You're Moses Moses?" I said at last. "Somehow I had always imagined you to be . . . well . . . *larger*. More mythic, somehow."

"Sorry, I'm flesh and blood," said Moses with a wry smile. "I expected a different world when I awoke, but I assure you I never expected *this*. I thought there would at least be someone to greet me. I never suspected that the center of my city would become a wasteland." He sighed. "It was a shock. I didn't know where to turn. And now it seems I've been recognized. I was recorded on the cameras of the men who beat you up, Artificial Kid. Their master must have recognized me and panicked. He tried to track you down to find me, even tortured your housekeeper to get her to help them break into your home. But she must have kept faith. Otherwise we would all be dead, I'm sure. They are obviously ruthless men. No doubt they wanted to wait here to ambush us."

"Yeah," I said. "The Cabal could hardly allow you to live. You must be the worst threat they could possibly face. You're a hero, you're the Founder of the Corporation. Holy Death, on Reverie you're the closest thing to God."

"I thought you looked familiar," Armitrage said wonderingly. "Excuse me, but . . . well . . . could I shake your hand? You've always been an idol of mine." Solemnly, they shook hands. Armitrage looked at the palm of his hand as if he expected it to glow with a sacred aura. "Wau," he said. "This is truly an unexpected privilege."

Except for poor Quade, we all shook his hand. Somehow the old ritual made us feel better.

"We'd better leave here," Armitrage said. "They're sure to return, and if they find us we'll be killed or brainwiped. Those portable brainwipers are terrible. You saw what it did to Quade. The Cabal protects its secrets."

"Yes, we've got to care for Quade somehow," I said. I looked at Armitrage. "You're the only one of us they haven't seen yet. . You take Quade to the Cognitive Dissonants. Chill Factor can take care of her. Besides, he's the only one I can trust."

"How much should I tell him?" Armitrage said.

I shrugged. "I'll leave that to you. I'll take these two to Money Manies. He's the only person I can think of who could fight the Cabal on their own terms." I glanced at Saint Anne. "It's our only hope. Now that we've seen Moses Moses, our lives are forfeit, no matter what we do."

"But Professor Angeluce said that Mr. Manies was a Cabalist himself," Saint Anne objected. "Why don't we simply go to the streets and announce that Chairman Moses has Come Again? We'll soon have a crowd of loyal supporters around us, and we can get them to do what's best. Besides, we have the right on our side. The Cabal are usurpers. We shouldn't skulk around in the dark, like them. We should declare ourselves."

"Maybe so, but not in the middle of the Decriminalized Zone," I said. "They're armed, and they may have explosives. Besides, we should announce it to the whole world, not just a small group. Otherwise, they could kill us all, and then claim that the Second Coming was just a rumor. We need an announcement on tape, a released speech that six million Reverids can see at once. That way there'd be no way to stop us. Besides, if everyone knew, then the Cabal would have no reason to single us out—unless we got in the way while they were trying to kill Moses Moses, of course. And Money Manies can help us. He has access to more channels than any Reverid on Telset Isle. We have to have his help, or we can't survive. Armitrage, run upstairs to the storeroom and get us all some infrareds while I see to Quade. Get all my smuff, too. You know where I keep it."

I would have liked to take the rifle with us, but it would have attracted unwelcome attention outside my home. In any case, I still had my shotgun nunchuck. My arms and legs were stiffening up; they were blue and purple and swarming with mites. They felt hot to the touch. I didn't hurt, but the body has its own wisdom, and it wanted to be flat on its back. But there wasn't time to indulge it.

By the time I had finished ministering to Quade, Saint Anne and Armitrage were telling Moses Moses about the events of the past four hundred and twenty-five years, a process that was obviously going to take a very long time. They gestured excitedly and slapped their foreheads and backtracked and interrupted one another loudly. They all had infrareds on. Anne and Moses Moses had put on pairs of my night-party glasses, frivolous ornamented numbers that fit them very badly and looked completely ludicrous on them. Armitrage had Quade by the arm; he was tall and the top of his head came almost half-way up her forearm. I put on my infrareds and everything went black and white and shiny. "Ready?" I said. We left.

5

Armitrage and Quade left us at the door; Armitrage agreed to rejoin us at Many Mansions as soon as possible. Saint Anne, Moses Moses, and I walked quickly east. We reached the beach without meeting anyone of consequence, then headed south to the docks where I kept my little boat, the *Sea Whip*. I had half-expected it to be guarded, but the Cabal apparently hadn't had time to take that precaution. They must have been scrambling for some way to meet this unexpected emergency, and the long habit of sloth slowed them down. It's impossible to be both quick and secret.

I hadn't taken the *Sea Whip* out in two months, and there was a dense growth of weed on her hull. We got on board and cast off. She was sluggish; the night breeze off the reef was only mild. I took her down the channel and about half-a-mile off-shore, where we wouldn't run the risk of holing the hull on coral.

By this time I was beginning to hurt quite badly. I took more smuff and heard the first telltale buzzing in my ears. I got off the little gunwale and stretched out on the deck so I wouldn't fall overboard; my equilibrium was shot. I was hungry, too, and the only food on board was four stale bars of oneill synthetic chocolate. I gobbled them down.

Saint Anne was giving Moses Moses her grossly biased view of Reverid history. Moses kept nodding and saying, "Really? Amazing, fantastic!" Moses Moses was at least three hundred subjective years old, probably closer to three-fifty, but he hadn't lost his zest for life. For him, his reawakening must have been a lot like a rebirth. He assured me that he could pilot the *Sea Whip*, and of course he knew where Prospect Point was, though in his day no one had lived there. I stretched out and went to sleep.

We reached Many Mansions about two hours past midnight. A Harlequinade party was still going on far down the western slope of Prospect Point, in one of the Mansions' beach outbuildings. At the top of the slope I saw a glow through one of the heavy one-way windows in Money Manies' private chambers, where no one was allowed to set foot but himself and his wife Annabella. Even his faithful secretary Chalkwhistle was excluded; Manies treasured that small three-roomed core of privacy. I was glad Manies was awake and separated from his usual horde of sycophants and hangers-on.

We tied up at Manies' dock, next to the *Albatross*. I glanced at Moses Moses and laughed. "No one could possibly recognize you behind those glasses," I said. "At least we're safe on that point." We left the *Sea Whip* and climbed up the slope to one of Many Mansions' numerous doors. I tried it; it was locked. I rang the bell and waited. Eventually Chalkwhistle answered it. "Hello, Kid," it said. "What happened to you?"

"Open up, Chalkwhistle," I told it brusquely. "I've got to talk to Manies."

Chalkwhistle looked apologetic. "Sorry," it said. "I've been told to admit no one. Why not go down the beach and join the party? Mr. Manies will be there some time before dawn."

"Sorry, Chalkwhistle," I said. "Emergency." I popped Chalkwhistle on the head with my 'chuck and it went down, its arms flailing. I stepped inside. We dragged Chalkwhistle aside onto a comfortable section of carpet, shut the door behind us, and locked it. We made our way through panelled corridors rich with mobiles and objets d'art to the door of Manies' private chamber. Manies must have been watching us through a house alarm system because he opened the massive, well-oiled door before we reached it.

"Kid!" he said. "What a peasant surplice." With an unsteady swing of his arm he gestured us into a richly decorated sitting room across the hall. Behind him, his wife Annabella came out, shut the door behind her, and ostentatiously locked it with a thumbprint. We heard heavy bolts and magnetic seals slide into place. Annabella was a slim, dark woman with enormous green eyes who had once been Manies' top pornostar, although she had never had a speaking role. She never spoke. She had the litheness of age but that was all I knew about her. Manies collapsed into a tapestry armchair. Annabella sat on the floor before him and wrapped her arms around one of his legs. Silently, she stared at us.

Manies' face was flushed and he kept nodding his head and tapping his fingers in rhythm. Saint Anne, Moses Moses, and I were too anxious to sit down. "Take off your glasses," I told Moses Moses. "Mr. Manies, do you recognize this man?"

Manies moved his head in Moses' direction, but his goggling eyes skimmed blankly over him. "My dear Kid," he said laboriously, "if it weren't for that lovely lovely hair I wouldn't even recognize you. And is this Saint Anne, your wife? Have you both discovered the happy happy joys of linking, at long last? I congratulate you. I felicitate you."

I sighed in heartfelt desperation. It was pitifully obvious that Money Manies had picked this night of all nights to take a powerful hallucinogen. He was completely wrecked. I addressed myself to his wife. "Annabella doll," I said, "I know you never speak, and I certainly wouldn't expect you to do it now, even though the political future of the planet is at stake. But this man is Moses Moses, the Father of the Corporation. He isn't dead, but the Cabal wants him that way, and they're sure to kill all three of us. We desperately need your husband's help." She stared at us stonily. "Can't you even nod, or anything?" She gave us all the lively response of a dead dugong.

Now Saint Anne tried. "Mr. Manies," she said. "We're your friends. Our lives are in terrible danger. Can't you help us?"

Manies blinked. He fidgeted uncomfortably and rubbed his nose. "My dear Saint Anne, how can I help you when you keep changing shape? Go to my pornostars. They understand your problem. I insist you enjoy yourself!"

Moses Moses said, "This man has taken a powerful drug. Look at his eye dilation."

I nodded. "I'm sorry, Mr. Chairman. I had no way of knowing. Neither did he. It's just an unhappy accident. He's a good man, and he would have helped us if he could, I'm sure of it."

"He's beyond helping us now," Moses said. "We'd better think of a new plan of action."

Manies nodded once and kept nodding, apparently unable to stop himself. "So you've guessed my little secret! My apologizing apologies. I didn't expect your visit."

"That's all right, Mr. Manies," I told him, forcing a smile. "I'll write you a note, and you can read it later when you're not having so much fun." I stepped to his desk, opened it, and took out a sheet of his creamy deluxe stationery. Like many of the older generations, Manies sometimes wrote letters, rather than bluntly stating things face to face over a communiqué line. I wrote Manies a quick note, explaining all the important details on a single sheet of paper. I folded it and handed it to Manies, and on the third try he managed to stuff it into the breast pocket of his red quilted drugging jacket.

"So you are the famous Moses Moses," said Manies hospitably. "You know, you died when I was only twenty-three, and that was a long long long time ago. Do you still read Riley?"

"Yes, Mr. Manies," Moses Moses said soothingly. I had to give him credit for presence of mind. He knew better than to press old Manies; had Manies fully grasped our situation it would very likely have sent him into a terrible panic fit. "He was my favorite author."

"Yes, I know," Manies said, going into his nodding routine again. "I have all his surviving works in my library—a complete edition of your first reissue. You saved him from oblivion."

"Yes," Moses Moses said. "I was very lucky to find that old microtape."

Manies smiled. "Like myself you are an antiquarian! Of course his *Flying Islands of the Night* is the longest surviving piece. Do you remember the verses that go:

> "O Prince divine! O Prince divine!
> Tempt thou me not with that sweet voice
> of thine!
> Though my proud brow bear the blaze of a
> crown,
> Lo, at thy feet must its glory bow down,
> That from the dust thou mayest lift me to
> shine,
> Heaven'd in thy heart's rapture, O Prince
> Divine!"

"How could I forget them?" asked Moses Moses with a sigh. "That's the confrontation scene between Queen Crestillomeem and her son Jucklet in Act One."

"Crestillomeem?" I said. "Jucklet?"

"Yes," Moses Moses said happily. "Wonderful names, aren't they? So evocative." Saint Anne and I traded amazed glances. The expression on Anne's face suggested that she had a mouthful of thick mush and was looking for some place to spit it out. Moses continued, "And what about those majestic verses in the beginning of Act One?

> "Lo, launched from the offended sight
> Of Aeo!—anguish infinite
> Is ours, O Sisterhood of Sin!
> Yet is thy service mine by right,
> And, sweet as I may rule it, thus
> Shall sin's myrrh-savor taste to us—
> Sin's Empress—let my reign begin!"

"It's marvelous," Manies said. "Crestillomeem, the prime creation of Lord Aeo, revolts from pride in her own beauty and is banished from heaven! What imagination! What a thundering cosmic scheme! I don't believe there's another work like it in the whole of literature."

"Did you say 'Aeo'?" I said. "I often wondered why anyone would give a name like that to a helpless, inoffensive continent."

Moses Moses frowned. "What do you mean? It's a perfect name. It rolls with superhuman majesty. Say it to yourself a few times. Aeo, Aeo, Aeo. It's perfect!"

I shrugged. "If I were a mass of land that big I think I would demand the dignity of at least one consonant."

"How it all comes back to me," Manies mused. "I haven't read Riley in a hundred years. Isn't it something how memories seize you in a state like this? As Riley says, 'All havoc hath been wrangled with the drugs!'"

"I must admit that I myself have neglected Riley," said Moses Moses with an introspective knitting of the brow. "I haven't read his work in twenty years, subjectively speaking. To think how his work inspired me in my youth, when the Corporation was myself and three men in a beer hall! I must say I'm glad to have met you, Mr. Manies, despite the circumstances. You have recalled me to myself."

"Think nothing of it," said Manies magnanimously, fidgeting in his chair. "Might I offer you an invitation to breakfast here next week? My guests would find you fascinating; they don't often meet the dead."

The usual slow ease of Reverid repartee was out of place in our predicament. "Listen," I said. "Let's give some thought to escape. It's only a matter of time before the Cabal thinks to look here for us."

"Where could we go?" said Saint Anne. "Besides, we promised to wait here for your friend Armitrage."

There was a pinging sound from the heavy bracelet on Money Manies' wrist. "Oho!" he said in annoyance, puffing out his cheeks. "Chalkwhistle should be taking my calls. I dislike disturbance!"

"Wait," I said. "It may be important. Answer it, I'll take the call." Manies fumbled with his bracelet and a holo of Chill Factor appeared in the room.

House cameras floated in to cover Manies. Irritated, he waved them to me. Chill looked haggard, but he brightened a little when he saw me. "Kid!"

"Has Armitrage reached you yet?"

"That's what I called about. He was here with your house-keeper. He gave us a really strange story, do you confirm it?"

"Yes, Chill, it's true."

Chill clutched his forehead. "Kid, you amaze me! Things like this can only happen to you! My little angel of intrigue, your news has stunned me like the blow of a hammer!"

"Spare us the histrionics, Chill; you can act them out and splice them in later. Quade all right?"

He nodded. "I got a strange call, Kid. From Instant Death himself. He's declared blood feud on all enemies of the Cabal in Telset. You in particular."

"That was quick," I said.

"They have some guns, Kid. They've transgressed the Code. The Cogs are completely outclassed. Instant Death has enough firepower to slaughter every artist in the Zone. He gave us a choice, Kid; stay with you and get shot, or throw in with them and take a cut from the Cabal. He's talking more fracs than any of us could earn in ten years."

I nodded. "I understand, Chill. Did he mention why I'm the Cabal's enemy all of a sudden?"

Chill looked guilty. He lowered his voice. "No, Kid. They didn't mention him. The Chairman."

"I've seen him, Chill. He's alive. Look." I waved one camera to Moses Moses, who looked into it and nodded once. "I know about him now; that's why they have to kill me. The Cabal will try to hush up the Second Coming for as long as they can; even if they can't, it won't matter much if they manage to kill the Chairman. Don't try to challenge them. Play along. Can you hide Quade?"

Chill started at the question; his eyes were fixed on Moses Moses in awe and amazement. "Hide her?" he said. "Sure. We'll take care of her, make sure no one sees her. But you'd better leave Telset. We can't protect you from guns. No one can. Go to Jucklet or Eros if you want to stay alive."

"Better cut off before someone can tap the line," I suggested. Chill waved once. "I'll spread the word," he said, and vanished.

Manies looked sick; the realities of the situation were beginning to percolate through to him. "Perhaps you should leave, Kid. I believe I am about to peak. I won't be good company."

"Right," I said. "Sorry, Mr. Manies. Perhaps we can get away before you're implicated."

An explosion shook the house. "I retract that statement," I said. I started unscrewing the base of one nunchuck handle.

It didn't take them long to find us. Saint Anne and Moses Moses had ducked down quickly behind the desk and an ottoman. When they came in they found Money Manies and I sitting in two armchairs, quietly conversing. Annabella Manies was still silently holding on to her husband's leg; he must have been the one oasis of certainty in her twisted universe.

There were two of them: the Stag, and Slummer. The Stag had a red pennant flying from one handsome antler; Slummer had a rag of red cloth twisted around one shabby arm. They were two of Instant Death's best men. Slummer had a small pistol, probably one of the few firearms the Cabal could scrape up on short notice. The Stag carried a heavy mace, his usual weapon. Slummer pointed the gun at me. "You're both under arrest in the name of the Cabal."

"Oh, I surrender, I surrender," said Manies cheerfully.

"Me too," I said. "We won't fight."

Stag and Slummer exchanged puzzled glances. "Well," said Stag. "I'm glad you're taking this so easily."

"Stag doll, what did you expect? I might fight the Instant Death, but the Cabal? Be reasonable. I don't buck the odds."

"But we've declared blood feud," Slummer said in his peculiar grating voice. Slummer had bent, rickety legs and always talked as if he were suffering from a lung disease. He dressed in filthy rags. "You've got to die, Kid."

"No," I said. "I'm betting the Cabal will change their minds when they see I've given myself up. I can probably get off with a partial brainwipe."

Stag looked around suspiciously, whacking one of his floating cameras with one antler. He was one of the rottenest camera programmers I've ever seen. "What exactly did you do, anyway? I can't figure out how a shrimp like you could do *anything* to bother the Cabal."

I gestured casually with my nunchuck. The base was unscrewed and ready to come off with a pull of my hand. "Why should I tell you?"

Slummer looked almost apologetic. "You might as well, Kid. This is blood feud. We've been ordered not to leave you alive. It's a dirty shame, too, if you ask me. I've got all of your tapes."

That saved his life for him. "Well," I said, "for one thing I've violated the gun code," and I blew off Slummer's left leg. He fell to the carpet, squalling. I jumped out of the armchair, evaded the hasty swing of Stag's mace, and whipped the chain of my nunchuck around one of his antlers. I yanked savagely and heard his neck crack. He fell, unconscious, but it didn't kill him.

Slummer had passed out. I ripped off some of his rags and put a tourniquet around his leg, just over the knee. I grimaced. His leg was still barely attached, and it was ugly.

"God," I said. "Guns really lack style." I picked up Slummer's little pistol and tucked it into my waistband. I screwed the nunchuck back together and dosed Stag and Slummer with their own smuff. Then I violated the artists' Code again; I stole some of their smuff. It deeply embarrassed me, but I needed it. I looked up at my cameras. "I'll have to cut this part later," I said.

Manies was staring transfixed at the thick pool of Slummer's blood on his carpet. "I'm sorry," he said. "I'm afraid I find this performance just too too strongly stated." He reached tremblingly into his drugging jacket and pulled out a small red bulb with a white jet nozzle. He squirted a puff of black dust or vapor into each nostril, inhaling sharply. He passed out not long afterward. Annabella Manies still said nothing, but she began to stroke her husband's knee with one hand, very slowly.

I gestured Moses Moses and Saint Anne to their feet. They got up, averting their eyes. "Come on," I said. "We'll all die if we stay in Telset. We'll take the *Albatross* out to sea. I hope Armitrage has enough sense to hide himself."

Chalkwhistle was still unconscious when we got to the outside door; it had been blown to splinters, but the bulk of a chair had protected the neuter. We all put on our infrareds as we stepped outside. We heard shouts and thumps from the beach-house; they weren't party noises. Probably the Instant Death had looked there for us first.

A bullet ricocheted screaming across the paving stones outside Manies' doorstep and threw stinging powder into my shins. I jumped backward, crowding Anne and Moses back into the house. The bullet had left a long scar in the hard travertine; it had come from further up the hillside, to the east. This particular wall of Many Mansions faced north to the sea. The direction of the scar in the rock showed that the sniper would take a while to reach a position where he could shoot through the shattered doorway. We started piling up furniture as a barricade. We heard the rapid thumping of his footsteps as the sniper came sidling along the wall, and we took cover. He never made it. We heard a solid impact and the unmistakeable sound of a body falling to earth. In a moment I peeked outside.

I saw Armitrage leaning over the sniper's body. "Look," he said. "It's Orange."

"Good," I said. "How did you manage?"

Armitrage grinned. "I was up on the roof," he said. "When he came running along the wall, I just leaned over and gave him a nice thump in the head." He shook his weighted quarterstaff.

We dragged Orange back inside the house and peeled off his skintight mask. He had an anonymous, handsome face, the product of cosmetic surgery. His rifle was so complicated that none of us could figure out how to operate it; we couldn't even find the trigger. He also had a long, nasty knife attached to his belt. He wasn't carrying a memory wiper, which was too bad for him. My hair crackled. "Don't look," I said. I opened his jaw, put the tip of the blade against the roof of his mouth, and hit the pommel with my hand. It went in deep, so easily that his skull might almost have been hollow and held together with a kind of black fiber. At the thought of this I trembled with a long, sickening thrill.

Armitrage licked his lips. "Let's reef him," he said.

"There's no time," I said. "Besides, we don't have the weights. Let's get out of here." My hands wouldn't stop trembling. He was the first man I had ever killed.

We ran downhill back toward the docks. Two of the Clone

Brothers were there; they had found the *Sea Whip* and were busy demolishing her with their chains. They were making a lot of noise, but they stopped their high-pitched cries of excitement when they saw us at the docks.

They tried to climb out of the *Whip* and onto the dock. It would have been better theater to beat them up, but there wasn't time. I started shooting at them. Either Slummer's little gun was horribly inaccurate, or else the smuff had destroyed my aim; they jumped into the water and swam to safety under the dock. I think I may have winged one of them.

Armitrage, Moses Moses, and Saint Anne jumped aboard the *Albatross*. I stood guard while Armitrage and Moses Moses raised the mainsail. They were both shaken and it took them a long time, long enough for the Clone Brothers to work up courage and begin taunting us from beneath the dock. One of them sent out a camera to watch us and I wasted a bullet on it, which missed.

"Blood feud, Kiddy!" they called out. "Blood feud!" You would have thought they were having the time of their quadruple lives. "Red wants your red blood! Blue wants your blue veins! The Colors will cut you up and the directions will scatter the pieces!"

I cast off, so smuffed that I fell into the water and almost lost the little gun. As I pulled myself aboard, the joints in my elbows made weird popping sounds, giving eloquent testimony to tissues strained to their limits of endurance. My arms were swollen to twice their normal size, and I could feel a few of the wounds seeping up with blood beneath the skinseal.

A brisk breeze blew up off the reef and we put out to sea. In the light of the open doors of the beachhouse we could see innocent hedonists hustled out at gunpoint. The Cabal had probably made a bad mistake in hiring the Instant Death, but perhaps they were the best henchmen they could get on short notice. I was glad that we hadn't met Instant Death himself. He was one of the very few people on the planet who inspired me with real physical fear.

The *Albatross*'s sails were blue plastic and were soon lost in the darkness. No doubt the Clone Brothers gave the alarm as soon as they could, but by that time we were out of rifle range.

6

We put up the jib. Moses Moses took the tiller. It was three hours past midnight; I could tell by the position of the stars. As Telset dwindled to a dark lump on the horizon the four of us gradually relaxed. For a long time we said nothing, sunk in our private thoughts. I took a wound kit out of one of my sealed pockets and got out needle and thread. I stripped, pulled the skinseal off one of the larger wounds, and started sewing it up. It was black with mites, which were doing a wonderful job and would soon have the swelling down. I felt a rubbery stretching sensation as I stitched up a loose flap of skin; it always feels very odd, even when it doesn't hurt. I used a special thread; the mites would eat it after it had done its work. Armitrage helped me sew the wounds on my back. Like many multisexuals, he had a very gentle touch.

Finally Saint Anne said, "What do you think will happen to poor Mr. Manies?"

I shrugged. ("Don't do that!" Armitrage said.) "I don't know," I said. "There's never been a crisis like this before. Money

Manies is a pretty popular figure. He practically owns six channels and has access to dozens more. If his programming is disrupted, it'll change the lives of hundreds of thousands of viewers, floaters and grounders alike. I don't think the Cabal would want to do anything that obvious; they've always stayed in the background since Fox Day. I'd guess that they'd try to make some kind of deal with Manies. But I don't know what kind of terms he would demand."

"But what if Mr. Manies decides to fight?" Saint Anne said.

"Fight what?" I said. "The Cabal knows all about Manies. Where he lives, how he lives—he's published enough lifetapes so that everybody knows his habits. But the Cabal's a phantom. Sure, he could attack the Instant Death and get a lot of people killed, but he wouldn't have touched the Cabal itself. How could he prevent a Fox Day in his own home? It would be easy enough to smuggle explosives into Many Mansions and blow the whole place to atoms. He'll be forced to compromise with them."

"I think they made an error by hiring the Instant Death," Armitrage said. "The Death have no class. They're louts and bullies. They're bound to rouse a lot of resentment. Besides, every time the Cabal gives an order there's a chance that someone will trace it back and discover their true identities. Then they'd be vulnerable. The temptation to strike back would be hard to resist. I know I would, if I could."

"Sure you would, now that they've attacked you personally," I said. "But I don't think the average Reverid would. After all, you could hardly call the Cabal an oppressive government. They've always been very careful to cover their tracks. They have the Rump Board to carry on the minutiae of government for them—distributing stock and the like. Besides, their real power is in their money. The Rump Board is just a sort of shell. The Cabal has always left well enough alone. They just want to be left in peace so that they can hoard millions of fracs. That's always been my understanding, anyway."

"Millions of fracs?" said Moses Moses, aghast. "How did they get into such a position? The Bill of Incorporation forbids any stockholder to hold more than three shares of stock. That was the very cornerstone of my social design! Why in death's name would anyone want so much money? One share of stock guarantees all the necessities of life, plus a nice discretionary income. Was pure greed so powerful?"

Armitrage had finished sewing up my back. He patted new skinseal into place, then turned to Moses Moses and spread his hands apologetically. "The Bill of Incorporation is a dead letter," he said. "Of course, your signature at the bottom makes it a sacred document, but it doesn't give it any more relevance. Besides, there was so much discretionary income! A thousand fracs a year, each, for millions of people! Naturally it started to accumulate in the hands of those who wanted it. Collecting money became a kind of game. And the Board of Directors was awfully lax. Their powers were so strictly limited that they had to depend on prestige, and when you left they lost a lot of it. They were trying to reassert their power when the Fox Day blast wiped them out. Then there was only the Rump."

"You could hardly call the Rump a government," I said. "They only handle routine matters, and most of that is done by computer anyway. I've seen tapes of the Rump in session. It's nothing but talk. Real mud-belching stuff. They only meet once a year."

Armitrage continued, "It's a ceremonial position. Some people say that the members of the Rump are directly appointed by the Cabal, but I don't think that's true any more. I think that the Board members retire when they get sick of it and sell the office to the highest bidder, or give it to a friend. There's not much turnover, though. They may be impotent, but they love to hear themselves talk."

"What about voting?" demanded Moses Moses. "The Board of Directors is supposed to be elected by shareholders! One share, one vote!"

"Oh, voting's outdated nowadays," Armitrage assured him. "Anyone with a complaint just calls up the central computer directly. It's programmed to respond to personal communiqués. Why get involved with the Rump Board?"

"But they're supposed to be your advocates! They're supposed to obey the will of the shareholders! Doesn't anyone ever complain about it?"

"Sure, you can complain to the computer if you want," I said. "But the computer's riddled with taps by now, and it keeps all its messages on permanent file. It'd be easy to find out who spoke up against the Cabal; then the Cabal could buy them off or arrange an 'accident,' if they thought it was necessary. But they're very tolerant. Except, of course, when their existence is directly threatened, like we threaten it."

"Doesn't it bother you at all to have lost your liberty?" Saint Anne said.

"Liberty?" I said. "Death, I don't know. The Cabal has ruled Reverie for three hundred years; that's longer than the Board of Directors ever did. I can tell you this much, though. I own four shares of stock. And if the old Board was still in power I wouldn't even have a profession. They would never have allowed combat art or a Decriminalized Zone. Or bet-slavery, or smuff, or personal servitude, or pornotapes, or the patronage system."

"Or multiple sexuality, or radical surgical alteration," Armitrage said. "Hell, we Reverids were used to the Cabal. They were like old shoes." Armitrage and I both sank into gloomy silence as we both realized how much we had lost, and how much more we stood to lose even if we survived. Moses Moses had returned and the Second Coming was bound to turn our world upside down.

We were trapped, too. Even if Armitrage and I clubbed Moses Moses and took him captive to the Cabal—a loathsome act of treason—we would still be killed, because we knew too much. Besides, a blood feud was on. I had sworn to kill Angeluce to avenge the murder of my servant Quade, and that meant war to the death with him and the Cabal. Any enemy of the Cabal would be a friend of ours, and their worst enemy—Moses Moses—would have to be our best ally. Armitrage and I both knew this.

We exchanged glances. Under his cheerful exterior, Armitrage was a moody, sensitive sort, and he seemed to be rapidly despairing. To cheer him up, I said, "Look at it this way, Armitrage. If the Cabal kills us, then that's it, zip. We're dead and it doesn't matter any more. Besides, everyone dies. But if we live, we'll be the heroes of the age. We'll be incredibly famous. It'll be the performance of our careers. This completely transcends anything we've ever done before, and just think, we're getting it all on tape." I gestured at his cameras; he had four of them, big clunky eyes with three lenses each and top-notch audio pick-ups.

"You're right," he said. "I have about two months' worth of tape left. Of course, I can always go back and erase what I've already recorded. It's mostly personal memory stuff—personal pornotapes and the like. There're a few good fights, too, but like you said, they pale compared to this. We're pretty lucky, really. We're in a privileged position. I just wish I'd been warned—I could have put everything in the computer and started off with clean, fresh, crisp tape." He looked up moodily at his cameras. Then he reached into the baggy sleeve of his fighting robe and pulled out his comb. He turned it on with a flick of his thumb-nail and started to comb his long luxuriant black hair with prac-ticed flicks of his wrist.

Armitrage was appallingly handsome, with his clear, sea-green eyes, his milk-white skin, his straight, surgically corrected nose (broken many times), his full lips and beardless face. But he was completely without vanity. What many others had mis-taken for vanity was only a dedicated combat artist's concern for image. If he had a weakness it was his forthright, careless passion for sex. Like most multisexuals his bloodstream was a seething tide of hormones and libido stimulants. He had spent a year as a pornostar but quit because his hundreds of tapes were flooding the market. He then turned to combat art so that he could continue to support his personal entourage: two women, two men, and another multisexual. He always had at least five people around to minister to his personal needs, but his person-nel were always changing because of his lecherous taste for novelty. Armitrage was a legend. He was only thirty.

"Say," he said suddenly, "I wonder what they're going to do about my new tapes. I had a great tape of a fight with Steam Engine that's supposed to premiere in four days. What about you, Kid?"

I shrugged. "The last thing I did was a tape critique for Cewaynie Wetlock. I was doing a gang tape but it fell through."

Armitrage smiled. "I saw that critique. Getting soft in your old age? You treated her a lot better than she deserved."

"Show some class," I told him. "Cewaynie Wetlock's great. You just don't understand Art with a Capital A." I was glad that Armitrage had cheered up enough to tease me. I let him do it because we both knew I could beat him up any time.

Armitrage leapt to his feet. "Hey, I bet Money Manies has some spare tapes here on board! Let's search the hold and see what we can find!"

The *Albatross* was a wooden catamaran, thirty-five feet long, fifteen across. Her two hulls were both sheathed in thin white ceramic to prevent the attack of teredos and boracles and to protect her against sharp coral. There was a wooden cabin on board that would sleep six, but I had already looked through it. It had Manies' old fishing equipment, which he no longer used, but kept for guests. It also had a dusty shelf full of vacuum-sealed provisions in glass jars, some with unhealthy-looking marbled streaks that suggested a choking death by poison for anyone unwise enough to eat them.

Money Manies was notorious for his reluctance to discard anything, which was unusual even among tidy, cycle-minded Reverids. It wasn't that Manies was methodically thrifty, far from it; he simply never threw anything away. He had seen so much of the past crumble and decay that it bothered him to see it happen to his own personal effects, to see entropy devouring his past even as he left it.

Though he seldom used her nowadays, the *Albatross* was still Manies' favorite boat. She was almost two hundred years old (though she had been repaired and refurbished so many times that hardly an atom remained of the original craft).

Armitrage opened the trap door to the port hull and climbed down the short stepladder into the darkness. "What do you see down there?" Saint Anne asked curiously.

"Junk," he said. "Wau, it smells down here. Looks like it hasn't been cleaned out in decades." We heard echoic clunking and scraping as he grabbed something below decks. Saint Anne went to the hatch to peer in and he handed her a collapsible, incredibly old-looking tapescreen. "There's a little generator to run it, too," he said. "But it looks broken. I'll have some trouble getting to it. Here, Anne, help me get some of these antiques out of the way." He began to hand her things through the hatch.

Moses Moses was still piloting; we were heading due north. He was a good pilot, relaxed yet alert and keeping an eye on the sonar. As usual, the Gulf was calm. Our course was north, not because we had a destination, but simply because it was the quickest way to put distance between ourselves and Telset.

Although Money Manies was one of my oldest friends, I had known him for only a fraction of his long, long lifetime. Succumbing to curiosity I began to pick through the heap of objects Anne and Armitrage were piling on the deck. There was a neatly folded bag full of spare sails and coils of spare line, a dusty case of handsome, spotless fishing knives, a plastic valise full of old navigation maps with a sextant and star guide. Their copyright date read C.R.Y. 380. Money Manies had been a mere two hundred and thirteen years old when they were published.

Armitrage handed Anne a square, black album. She opened it, looked inside for five seconds, then gasped and clapped it shut. She dropped it to the deck as if it had scalded her. I opened it. It was an album of porno stills, featuring an incredibly young-looking Money Manies. The nose and eyes were his, but the lips were thin and cruel and he was wearing a close-fitting tall red hat adorned with slick-looking swollen bulbs. He wore a pair of fetishistic thorny black bracelets around each ankle as well, but nothing else. I broke into helpless laughter at the next still, in which all three participants were fully clothed. It was like an essay on the history of Reverid fashions. Judging by the immense, jutting lapels, feathered sleeves, and elastic webwork of colored strings that crisscrossed their legs from waist to ankles, the picture was at least two centuries old. "Hey, Armitrage, come up and have a look at this," I said.

"Just a sec," he answered. Then he emerged from below decks, carrying a small generator crusted in old, dried-up grease. He dropped it to the deck with a crunch, and its starting handle snapped off with a pleasant metallic *sproingg* and fell into the Gulf.

"Crap," Armitrage said. "Oh well, it probably wouldn't have

worked anyway." He took the album, glanced at it briefly, then began to thumb through it avidly, with a critic's eye. "My word, look at that," he said, pointing at a picture of Money Manies and two friends suspended in harnesses above a parquet floor. "That's really hard to do. Takes a lot of technical skill, Kid."

"I wouldn't know," I said. "They look like idiots." I looked at him. "Did you ever try anything like that?"

"Well, of course. But never with anyone quite that large." He looked again and winced a little.

Anne had gone down into the hull. She emerged, smiling. "Look what I found!"

I looked at the peculiar object she had located, a squat, fluted cylinder of metal and glass with a thin wire handle. "What is it?"

"It's a lantern, of course! Haven't you ever seen one?"

I took it from her and looked it over. "I don't understand. Where's its lens? Where's its power source?"

"Here, silly, I'll show you." She took it back and shook it next to her ear. "It still has some oil in it. Now these little sticks here are called matches."

"Why?" said Armitrage. "What do they match to?"

She shook her head, shaking off his question with a peculiarly Niwlindid gesture. "I don't know. I haven't seen a lantern like this since I was a little girl. My great-great-grandfather, the Catechist, used to have one. He lent it to me sometimes. Now, you see, you pump this little rod like this to get pressure up— then you raise the chimney like this and light one of the matches." She rubbed the colored end of one of the sticks across the deck and with a pop and faint hiss it burst into flame. Surprised, Armitrage and I took a step back. The lantern lit with a whoosh and a dirty yellow light illuminated us. Anne replaced the chimney, and I heard four faint clicks as Armitrage's cameras switched lenses.

"It's a lighting device!" Armitrage said. "How bizarre! Look, Kid, it uses flame for light. How wasteful! Think of the waste heat." He clicked his tongue.

"Interesting lighting effect, though," I said. "Makes you look good, 'Trage."

"You think so?" he said, pleased. "Let's try the other hull and see what we can find there."

Happy now that action distracted us from our anxiety, Anne, Armitrage, and I immediately began to ransack the starboard hull. The first things we found were a dozen books, some spoiled by sea water. Armitrage tossed them aside incuriously, as he had never learned to read. He found a pocket autoharp, but unfortunately it was missing two strings. I fourd a hexagonal chessboard for three players, but Anne didn't know how to play.

Armitrage caressed the smooth top of a hip-high machine, cylindrical and studded with orifices and extrusible prongs. "Recognize this, Kid?"

"Sure, I've seen enough of them," I said. "Better make sure it's in working order if you want to use it. It's just about the oldest one I've ever seen. Sure is ugly."

"I think it looks sort of sweet," Armitrage said. "I might have known old Manies would have at least one of these on board. For those long solo voyages, you know." He bent over and briefly kissed its plastic top. Anne, who was carrying the lantern, looked at him curiously. She obviously didn't understand the machine's use at all.

"Can anyone tell me what these are?" she said. She showed us a metal cylinder with a connected ring-pull and a pair of lace-up plastic shoes with wheels attached to their soles.

"Good lord! Are those really shoes with wheels?" Armitrage said. With a wry expression he twirled their small metal wheels with the palm of his hand. The wheels whizzed along merrily on noisy ball bearings. The strangeness of the outré sight caused us all to break into loud, incredulous laughter that lasted almost five minutes.

Finally we threw the peculiar shoes aside. I tried pulling the ring-pull on the metal cylinder. An inflatable life raft, its fabric rotten and all its pressure gone, bloated its way flabbily out of the cylinder to lie in a blobby orange heap on the floor of the hold. We stared at it silently.

"Is that the only life raft on board?" Anne asked sepulchrally.

"I think I saw another one in the cabin," Armitrage said

doubtfully, but the carefree hilarity was gone from his voice. The sight of the musty-smelling orange raft, puffed and flabby like a gigantic slimemold, put a damper on our spirits. Petulantly, Armitrage kicked it with his pointed boot and it ripped loudly.

We continued to search the hold. We found other strange objects: a life-sized glass eyeball, a pair of crab gigs, a plastic tent, a glass bottle full of moldy white tablets, and a half-crushed wicker hamper containing two empty bottles, the fossilized crumbs of a meal, and a carefully folded, blood-stained handkerchief. There was also a square lacquered box full of small hook-shaped flanges of metal, of unknown function.

At last we found a heavy wooden trunk behind a dirty shroud. It proved to be full of clothes, musty, rustling antique clothes, many discolored with age, others actually woven out of threads of cloth fiber. We hauled the trunk up on deck.

At this point I offered to spell Moses Moses at the tiller, but he politely assured us that he was not tired. Armitrage and I stripped and started to try on the clothing. I saw Anne's eyes widen as she learned for the first time that Armitrage was a multisexual; even old Moses Moses seemed a little taken aback at Armitrage's surgically altered wealth of endowment.

All of the clothes were too large for me, which piqued me considerably. They fit Armitrage well, though. Particularly striking was an open-throated black one-piece, somber yet extravagant, adorned with dozens of soft, black, rubbery spines. Armitrage donned the accompanying wide-brimmed spined hat and studded, square-toed boots. It was impossible to resist his charm as he stretched and pirouetted, striking out briefly and precisely with his combat staff. Admiration and envy overcame me. "Armitrage, you amaze us all!" I cried. "Such antique majesty! Really, it touches me to the heart." I embraced him. Flattered and pleased, he hugged me close and kissed my forehead. "How marvelous to be praised, even by a captive audience," he said. "It is rather striking, isn't it? Anne, won't you try something on? You must be sick of that old white bag by now."

Anne stiffened. "This is the uniform of my order," she said.

'But you must've worn it for days now! Say, you'd look delightful in this." He pulled a sleek ankle-length gown thick with glimmering pink scales from the bottom of the trunk. "This would complement your eyes beautifully." He ran his hand across the smooth inner fabric. "Ah, its texture is delightful. Imagine this clinging deliciously to your skin. Here, just feel it." He handed it to her.

"It's regrettably thin," she said, holding it up with a frown. "Really, I have no need to flaunt my body in a garment of this kind. It promises actions I have no intention of fulfilling."

Armitrage smoothed the brim of his spiny hat. "Such rigorous self-discipline," he said mockingly. "Very well, I'll try it on myself." And he did. It looked marvelous on him.

Anne was visibly disturbed by Armitrage's graceful, ambivalent posturing. She turned her attention to the *Albatross*'s old charts. "Perhaps it's time we plotted out a course for ourselves," she said. "Where do you think we should go, Kid?"

I examined the maps in the lantern light and frowned. "It's a good thing we have the sonar," I said. "The reefs have grown miles since this thing was printed. Let me see. I suppose it would be best if we headed for Jucklet. It's the only large city on the continent. Sylvain is way the hell on the other side of the planet and Eros wanders, of course, so it's out. It'd be safer to stay on water rather than going overland, so here's our course. We could head north and leave the Gulf through these gaps in the atoll here, the Straits of Circumstance. Then we'll be on the outside of Aeo, and we can sail along the reef, here, west, and then southwest, and then south, you see, paralleling the circular shore of the continent. By the time we dock here we can disguise ourselves, and the hunt for us will have cooled off a little. There's a little settlement on the edge of this bay, though it doesn't show on this old map. I forget the name of the place."

"Let me see," Moses Moses said eagerly. "Jucklet was just a village when I entered cryosleep." I showed him the map. "My, how it's grown."

"But Jucklet is far into the mountains here," Anne said. "What are they called? The Crater Mountains? That's a peculiar name."

"They're peculiar mountains," Moses Moses said. "They're

artificial. They date back about three billion years. They're bomb craters."

I looked at the map. "They're big craters."

"They were big bombs."

"They made a magnificent landscape, though," Armitrage said. "All lakes and woods and ridges. I've been there. There's no combat art, though."

I shrugged. "Jucklet's a hick town. The population's pretty well thinned and scattered through the mountains. That's good for us, because we won't attract too much attention when we enter town. If we just get smelly and hairy enough, we can pass ourselves off as backswoodsmen. Of course, then we're still faced with the problem of fighting the Cabal. But at least in Jucklet we'll have resources to draw on. We're completely harmless to them on this boat."

"Let's not get ahead of ourselves," Moses Moses said. "The Cabal is aware of our predicament too; they can follow our logic. We can't expect to sail there unmolested."

Armitrage sat down gracefully on the wooden deck. "What do you advise, then, Mr. Chairman?"

"Oh, a little patience," Moses Moses said. "It's my experience that, if you wait long enough, Time will drag your enemies, dead, past your door. The Cabal will expect us to land and begin agitating for their removal. Instead, we could put in at one of these hundreds of small offshore islands, and hide the boat. If we simply lie low for a little while, it'll drive them crazy. They will think one of two things: that we are dead, or that someone is harboring us. If they think we're dead, they'll stop looking for us, and we can return to Telset in safety. If they think we're being hidden, they'll intensify their search in the major cities. But don't you think that would arouse resentment against them?"

"Sure," I said eagerly. "Not only that, but it'll spread the rumor that you're alive. All Telset has probably heard by now. My friend Chill Factor knows the truth, and Telset is wired. Rumor moves at the speed of light."

Moses Moses was pleased. "There, you see?" he said. "By attacking an enemy who ducks aside, the Cabal will upset itself.

One should never strike at an enemy when he expects the blow and where he is braced for it. One should confuse the enemy first, so that his reactions are slow and inappropriate. They expect us to challenge them; so, we will duck that challenge. They will strike at us with all their force; they will miss us, and look like fools. Their morale will be hurt. They will not know where we are, or when we intend to strike. We will have turned the table on them. We will be the New Cabal. We will be hidden in the shadows; they will be open and vulnerable. By trying to protect themselves from all possible modes of attack, they will spread themselves thin."

Armitrage laughed incredulously. "You mean we can do all that just by disappearing? Without striking a blow?"

"Yes," said Moses Moses. "I think it would be the most disconcerting scheme we could hatch against them."

"Ha!" said Armitrage gleefully. "That really cracks me up! It seems so simple once it's explained! That's genius, Mr. Chairman. Pure genius!"

Moses Moses shook his head modestly. "No. Just elementary strategy."

"How long would we have to remain in hiding?" I said.

"Not too long," said Moses Moses. "Three, maybe four years."

"Four years!" I said, aghast. "My death, that's half my career! I'll be forgotten, washed-up, a has-been! Things move fast in combat art!"

"Four years is a big chunk of my lifetime!" Armitrage objected.

Moses Moses smiled indulgently. "When you get to be my age, you'll see four years for what they really are. An eye blink. A moment. A small interlude. And we're operating on the Cabal's time scale. The Cabalists are old. Aren't they?"

Armitrage and I traded disgusted glances. It was self-evident that the Cabalists were old. Only old people could have kept up such a long and elaborate charade. Of course, the original Cabalists must be dead by now, but we could rest assured that their successors were old as well.

"Well, Armitrage," I said, "once again we're buggered by ancients."

Armitrage nodded gloomily. Suddenly an idea occurred to him and an expression of sly glee touched his face. With naïve duplicity he suppressed it. "Four years isn't that bad," he said, with a judicious air of compromise that fooled no one. "Time passes quickly in pleasant company like this. It beats being dead, anyway."

"You've got no argument there," I said. I yawned. "But what about my house, my friends, my mobiles." The words sounded flat and pettish, even to me. Here we were, playing with the destinies of millions, and I was insisting on the primacy of my narrow, personal world. Embarrassed, I pretended a deeper fatigue than I felt. "I haven't slept in hours," I said. "Let's postpone any decisions until I've had some sleep. Is that agreeable, Mr. Chairman?"

"Of course," Moses Moses said kindly. "I only offer suggestions; I don't intend to dictate. All our lives are equally at stake, so each of us should have an equal voice. As for myself, I believe I'll stay awake until dawn. I've had such a long sleep that I hesitate to return to it."

I walked into the cabin and pulled aside the fresh, scented sheets on one of the two lowest bunks. It was dark, but I could see well enough with my infrareds, so I didn't turn on the light. As I stripped I felt an intolerable weariness settle over me; my battered body was finally taking its due. I took a little smuff to sweeten my dreams, slipped into bed, and slept, lulled to sleep by the comforting hum of my cameras, and the slap of waves on the hulls.

"Kid! Mr. Chairman! Wake up!" I swung my feet out of bed, focused blurry eyes on Armitrage's face, and felt a hot flush of pain course through me. I found my combat jacket and took some smuff. I felt better. "What time is it?"

"Four hours past dawn," Armitrage said. He was in his combat robe and was holding Slummer's tiny pistol in one hand. "You've slept almost ten hours."

I started to dress. Moses Moses, who had been sleeping perhaps an hour, pried open gummy eyes with a pitiful look of confusion on his bearded face. Old people often suffer such disorientation immediately after waking; their brains are so crowded with dreams. "What's the matter?" he asked vaguely.

"It's a glider," Armitrage said. "Anne saw it. I was snoozing out on deck." I saw that Armitrage's skin was slick with the anti-tan lotion he wore in sunlight; it kept his skin milk-white. "I thought I'd wake you up. It might mean trouble."

"I'll check, Mr. Chairman," I told Moses Moses. "You'd better sleep. We'll need you to pilot at night, anyway."

"No," Moses Moses said. "No, I can't sleep now. I'll go with you." He began to pull on his pinstriped suit; I saw that he slept in a white one-piece underall. His arms and legs were remarkably hairy, with reddish-brown hair the color of his beard.

With a touch I restored my cameras to full function, then adjusted my jacket, slipped into my pants and shoes, and looped my nunchuck around my neck. I went out on deck with Armitrage, wincing at the bright yellow sunlight. I shaded my eyes with one hand; my fingers were no longer swollen. "Where is it?" I asked Anne. She was at the tiller.

Without a word, she pointed. I saw a black speck silhouetted against the looming, faraway bulk of a morning thunderhead. It was a black sailplane with extremely long, thin wings; as I watched, she climbed, lifting on a thermal with the bright precision of a razor.

Armitrage looked at me seriously. "Here, try these," he said, handing me a pair of red plastic binoculars.

"Where did you find these?" I said.

"Under my bunk. Go ahead and look. You won't like it, though."

I looked at him sharply and then used the binoculars. I caught the long-winged sailplane just as she banked and I saw the white skull motif stenciled on her black wings. "It's the *Kite*," I said, lowering the binoculars. "Instant Death's sailplane."

"Yes, I recognized her, too," Armitrage said simply. "He's a very good pilot, isn't he?"

"He's the best," I said. "The best on Telset." I handed the binoculars to Moses Moses, who had joined us, his beard still half-crushed from the pillow. Moses watched the plane briefly, then turned to focus on the pale, white gasbag of a flying island, shrunken with distance, trailing its rooted burden of mud. His composure calmed us all.

"What do you think?" Armitrage asked me.

"He's come to kill us," I said. "I'd guess a bomb. That would be instant enough for his taste, don't you think?"

Armitrage nodded. "Yeah. We're about forty miles out. If he sank the boat, we'd drown for sure."

"He'll have to make a bombing run," I said. I hefted my nunchuck. "Maybe he'll come within range of my scatter gun." I tried to color my voice with a hopeful vindictiveness, but I failed. The gun had a very short range.

"Let me try for him with the pistol," Armitrage said. "I might be lucky. The rest of you should stay in the cabin, in case he's using a rifle. Maybe he is. It would be much better theater that way. More elegant."

"I imagine that this tape is for a very exclusive audience," Moses Moses said drily. "I imagine that the Cabal favors efficiency over aesthetics."

"Let me fire at him, Armitrage," I said. "Why should you have the best role?"

"Ha," said Armitrage. "I've seen you fire this thing before. You couldn't hit a holothurian. Besides, I'm not smuffed."

"Well, I'm staying out here," I said. "If he swoops in low enough, I'll blast him."

Armitrage checked the gun. "Three bullets left. Not an overly generous allowance." He looked down at me, his eyes shining. "There are a lot of things I haven't expressed. Things I haven't accomplished. Projects I haven't tried." He looked up at the sailplane. "My brain teems with them."

With sincerity, almost with morbid gaiety, Saint Anne said, "The universe is kind to those who die in righteousness. I'm not afraid."

"Look," Armitrage said. Instant Death had gained all the height he wanted. Now he peeled away from the long spiral of his thermal climb and came toward us from the south. Briefly, he dipped his wings. "He's saluting us."

"A nice gesture," I said. Two of my cameras had already switched to telephoto, and they followed him in as he began his sleek and lethal dive.

"You should get into the cabin," Armitrage said. "Or better yet, into the holds. They've got that ceramic sheathing, you know. That would be some protection."

"No," said Saint Anne. "I want to see. It's rather pretty, really."

"Yes," said Moses Moses. "If this is death, let's savor it, as we savor all forms of experience." No one moved. The smell of the Gulf wind was sharp and briny and vital. It seemed to me that I had never really smelled it before. A small school of shiny fish skipped frantically across the ocean's surface, evading a predator. The sails flapped twice. No one said anything.

The *Kite* was beautiful. She had a wingspread of at least sixty feet. She was extremely lightweight, but perfectly rigid. It was almost a pleasure to be killed by a craft so elegantly engineered.

She came toward us, toward our stern, as if sliding down a chute. Armitrage braced his legs and lifted both arms, his left hand gripping his right wrist. I heard the pistol go pop . . . pop . . . pop. I threw myself overboard.

The explosion was jarring and I felt more than saw a chunk of wooden shrapnel tear into the water beside me, trailing sizzling bubbles. I held my breath. The weight of my metallic pants, my jacket, and nunchuck was slowly dragging me down. I heard pieces of the *Albatross* pancaking down into the sea all around me; then everything turned dark. For a moment I thought I was hit, but then I saw that the *Albatross*'s tattered mainsail had settled directly over me. I put my chuck around my neck and frogkicked my way out from under the sail. I came up for a welcome breath.

What was left of the *Albatross*'s deck was already awash. The explosion had dismasted her. Both hulls were shattered and shipping water. I saw a wicker hamper bob out of one hull, puffed out by a big rush of dirty bubbles. Quickly, I kicked off my metallic trousers, leaving myself in my padded combat groin-brace. After that I was able to tread water.

Wiping salt water from my eyes, I looked around and spotted Saint Anne. Her baggy white saint's garb was sealed by elastic at wrists and ankles; the air trapped inside was keeping her afloat. I swam over to her. "Are you all right?" She looked very strange with her blunt-cut hair plastered to her oval skull.

"Yes," she said. "But my legs. Something hit me across the backs of my knees. I can't feel much."

"Do you want some smuff?" I gasped out. A few yards away, Manies' shattered clothes chest sank, belching wet blobs of fabric.

"No," she said loudly. The explosion had apparently partly deafened her. "Where are the others?" She lifted her voice. "Mr. Chairman! Mr. Armitrage!"

There was no answer. I looked up. Instant Death had already caught another thermal and was gaining height for the long glide back to Telset and success. "Blood feud," I murmured to myself, but I felt disgust at my own dumb bravado. He had finished us.

I swam back to the wreckage of the *Albatross* and climbed onto the slippery top of the cabin, still a foot or two above sea level.

I was already numb with smuff, so I looked myself over quickly to make sure that I had no further injury. I was not worse off than I had already been.

Looking around, I saw the welcome sight of Moses Moses and Armitrage, both clinging to a splintery, ripped-up chunk of wooden deck. I signaled to Saint Anne and then dived off the cabin top to join them. Even as I left her, the *Albatross* blew air with a slurping, sucking sound, and began to glide easily, prow-first, to the bottom of the sea.

I swam to their chunk of wreckage. It barely kept them afloat, so I stayed away, treading water. They both looked severely shaken. Moses Moses started when I touched him. "I can't hear anything!" he shouted. "I think it deafened me!"

"Are you all right?" I shouted back. He read my lips and nodded. "It knocked the breath out of me! But I'm better now!"

I nodded and swam to Armitrage. I was alarmed when I saw the greenish, bloodless tint of his skin and his eyes, half-closed. I grabbed his cold, wet shoulder. "Armitrage!"

"I'm smuffed," he said. "I can barely hear, too. I took all the smuff I had. It was waterlogged."

"Where are you hurt?" I said. "Let me get skinseal over it."

He shook his head weakly, moving waterlogged black curls. "I didn't get him, did I?"

I glanced at the retreating sailplane. "No," I said. "But I think you scared him, 'Trage."

"I lost the gun," he said. "Couldn't hold on to it."

"It's all right," I said. I looked up. "Look, we still have all our cameras." It was true. Their tough casings had resisted the blast and they had come floating back to their masters, respecting their programming. For some reason it cheered me. I felt that I had not yet lost all my resources.

"I didn't want this to happen," Armitrage muttered. "There was supposed to be time. Time to win you to me." He looked at me, his green eyes stung with sea water and tears. "I have to tell you now. I love you, Kid. I always have. And you would have loved me back. I had plans. I would have been patient. It wouldn't have hurt you a bit, to love me back. It doesn't hurt to love. It just feels wonderful." A gout of blood filled his mouth and he spat it out, choking. In pity and horror I shouted, "No!" and tried to embrace him, to hold him up; and my right hand sank wrist-deep into the warm tangle of his guts. Bloody scum rose to the ocean's surface.

"You're dying," I said.

He said again, "It doesn't hurt. It just feels wonderful." He closed his eyes. His hands slipped from the broken deck and he started to sink; I caught his head in the crook of my elbow and held his face above the water. He said nothing. In a moment I heard his death rattle. Sobbing, I begged him not to die: "Armitrage, Armitrage, don't!"

Moses Moses swam up to help me. He looked into Armitrage's face and saw the blood on his mouth. "Is he dead?" he shouted.

I nodded, already raw-throated and racked with sobs. "I'm sorry," Moses yelled. "Let's get him onto the deck!"

We pushed the lax, unresisting body onto the splintered, floating boards. When I saw the way the explosion had ripped open his elegant body, I felt a tearing pain of revulsion and grief.

Anne approached, swimming clumsily toward us in her enveloping bag. It was easy to spot us now by the cloud of cameras. All four of Armitrage's cameras hovered around him, sucking up his gory image. Anne stopped at a distance, treading water. She seemed amazed to see me cry.

A minute passed. I ducked my over-heated face into the cool sea water, and stopped my tears. They I heard Anne shriek. "Something touched my legs!"

A broad black shadow rippled smoothly by us, just under the surface of the water. Moses Moses screamed, "Rays!" and we swam for our lives.

I had to turn to look. They were the big mid-ocean rays, dapplebacks, their broad leathery wings almost thirty feet across. There were at least three of them; I heard the explosive puff of air from their blowholes. The concussion and the scent of blood had brought them on us. I saw Armitrage's dead arms jerk upward as one of them snapped up his feet and dragged him beneath the surface. The water roiled, whipped to froth by their long, venomous tails. Another ray flopped up out of the water and crunched up two of his cameras with a single bite. After that I put my head down and swam after the others.

We were exhausted after two hundred yards. "My clothes," Moses gasped. "They're dragging me down!"

Anne helped him struggle out of his wet jacket; I pulled off his heavy, clinging trousers. I was about to let them sink when Anne panted, "Kid, wait!" While Moses floated on his back, exhausted, Anne took the trousers and knotted their cuffs. Then she put her head underwater and blew air into the waist. After several breaths, the legs puffed up taut, full of trapped air. By holding the waist underwater, Anne had turned the Chairman's trousers into a crude pair of water wings. Red-faced and wheezing, we all clung to them for support. The wet fabric held the air quite well, though we could see it slowly hissing out through the cloth in streams of tiny bubbles.

By floating on our backs and clinging to the air bags, we were able to float comfortably. Moses Moses had a coughing fit that cleared his lungs of sea water. "I can hear myself cough," he said loudly. "I'm not deaf then. Just stunned. Are you all right, Saint Anne?"

"Yes," she said. "I think a broken board hit me across the backs of my legs, but I'm all right. I'm just bruised, not bleeding."

"My ribs took a beating," Moses Moses said. "And I scratched my hands on that wreckage. It hurts, but I'm not bleeding either. How about you, Kid?"

"Not a linking scratch," I said bitterly. "If I'd stayed on board with him—"

Moses Moses laughed quietly. "Why feel guilt, Kid?" he asked gently. "He wouldn't have grudged us a few more hours of life. I don't care to spend my last moments in pain. Will you give me some of your drug?"

I was ashamed that I hadn't offered it sooner. "Of course," I said, pulling the watertight packet out of my combat jacket. "Don't spill any. Just a taste should be enough. You want some, Anne?"

Her face showed pain warring with taboo. "No," she said finally. "Not right now. But thank you, anyway."

I carefully resealed the packet and tucked it away. After a moment I said, "Do you think it's worth the effort to try to reach shore?"

Moses Moses shrugged. "I think I prefer the rays to exhaustion and drowning. But I'm open to suggestion."

"Perhaps we should try," said Anne. "It would be better morally to die fighting."

"The current is bearing us northward," Moses Moses pointed out. "Let's die comfortably instead. After all, who's to know?"

I looked up at my six faithful cameras, still hovering over us. "I wish I had some way to get my last tapes to an audience," I said. "But the cameras stay with me. What a shame. You know,

I almost regret that more than dying. After all, I've already died once."

"Really?" said Moses Moses. "A personality death?" I nodded. Moses smiled. "I thought so. I thought I recognized your age in the way you walked. It's hard to disguise."

"You're the first one to notice it," I said.

"Possibly," Moses Moses said. "Perhaps the others simply kept quiet about knowing. After all, it's your business, not theirs."

"Right," I said. Moses Moses took the hint. He stretched out his arms, his hairy fists loosely clenched. "Look at those clouds!" he said admiringly. "Their incredible height never ceases to astonish me. It's the depth of the atmosphere, and the length of the day here. So far, far superior to Niwlind. You children can hardly imagine it."

"I can," Saint Anne said. "I am a native Niwlindid. But you're right, Mr. Chairman, they're beautiful. So pure and white. The clouds on Niwlind are squat and gray. Over the moors, they are torn by the wind, knocked flat, scalloped. Like dark metal beaten flat with hammers. You can hear the wind all the time, the bleak wind. It's different here." She shivered and wiped wet bangs away from her forehead with one hand.

Moses said, "I haven't seen Niwlind in . . . let me see . . . it must be six hundred years now. Six hundred years. Two long lifetimes. Tell me, is it still ruled by the Directorate?"

"No," she said. "The Directorship still exists, but now it's a ceremonial office. Real political power has been taken over by the Director's First Secretary. The current Secretariat is held by a woman named Janet Decross, but she in turn is just the tool of another woman named Crestillomeem Tanglin."

Moses Moses nodded. "No surprises there. There's always been some power behind the throne, some damned courtier you have to buy off, sleep with, or blackmail. It's so rotten on Niwlind . . . rotten with age and inertia . . . I tried to start over, you know. Start over clean, with a new planet, a new society, a new world view, new morals and assumptions. I wanted to just sweep out all that choking garbage that was laying waste to people's lives, to give them a chance to find themselves, to express and explore themselves, beholden to no man...." His words sounded vaguely familiar. I recognized the strains of the Reverid Bill of Incorporation. "But it never works out like you hope. Just when you think you've pinned it down, it squirms away again. And people just don't understand! You point at the sun, and they'll spend years discussing your index finger! For years you build a monument, and when you lay the last brick the foundation shifts!" For a moment his face showed a titanic anger, but with a mercurial change of mood he laughed, mocking himself. "Listen to me talk! I had my chance. I gave it my best. I owned a planet, I led a people. How many men can say that much? I have no regrets. At least I die on my own world."

Impassively, he looked at us. He had an expression one often sees on the faces of the very old: as if they were looking at everything from a vast distance. Finally he said, "I've dragged you with me to death. I'm sorry, but frankly I'm glad I don't have to meet it alone. Since I have a captive audience, why shouldn't I tell you a story? After all, we may have hours left. We have to amuse ourselves somehow. If you like, I'll tell you the story of my life."

"I'd be honored to hear it," Saint Anne said simply. I nodded. "Why not?" I said. "It's just the three of us. We have no reason to hide anything from one another. If there's time, I'll tell my own story."

"So will I," said Anne.

"Good," said Moses. "Then I'll start."

7

"I was born . . . let me see . . . eight hundred and ten years ago,
on Niwlind. I was probably bottled, but it may have been a natural birth, I don't know. I know that I was raised in a government crèche, but my earliest memories date back to when I was
about nineteen or so." His heavy brows knotted painfully as he
sifted through the detritus of centuries of memory. "This would
be a lot easier if I had my computerized memory, but it's down
in the basement with my cryocoffin, of course. Ah, I have it.
Louise. Her name was Louise. My name wasn't Moses Moses
then, I had some other name, I forget what. I had a job at the
Bureau of Orbital Research and Assessment. We monitored the
resources satellites. It was a pretty good job, really, for a nine-
teen-year-old, but I hated it. I was a bright youngster. Louise
was my boss. She was about eighty years old. A child really, but
I thought she was the ultimate in sophistication. I knew she
slept around a lot, and that seemed very wicked and exciting.

"I don't know how I got her attention, I suppose I swaggered
around a bit, making up for my height In those days it bothered

me to be short, I forget why. I imagine she thought I was cute. One day she called me into her office, and she gave me a demonstration of her skill, which was considerable. I was shattered, completely stunned. Naturally, I lost my head. I swore eternal constancy, begged her to be mine alone, told her that I loved her desperately, that I'd sacrifice my life to her pleasures, her tiniest whim. I was completely enslaved. It must have amused her.

"She toyed with me for a little while—two years, maybe. Of course, back then, two years seemed like forever to me. The other bureau workers were sick of my being the office favorite by then; on Niwlind sex was a very political thing, especially when you held a government post. Finally she told me we had to break up for the sake of the bureau.

"I threw tantrums. I ranted and raved, I threatened suicide. I had a hot temper and a lot of determination. I told her that I was destined for great things and I wouldn't let such minor, cheap crap destroy my happiness. If the government got in my way I'd crush the government; if society got in my way I'd build my own society. She couldn't help laughing at that, and her laughter wounded me deeply. I insulted her, maybe I even tried violence. She finished our affair then and there and had me fired from the bureau.

"The years after that were very hard. Hundreds of doors were closed in my face. I was denied any post in the government. My savings ran out—I had very little, because I spent most of my salary on gifts for Louise. Suddenly I was poor. I lived with the poor, and for the first time I saw their miserable, barren, hampered, dehumanized lives. Sometimes they actually starved, and the damned mechanized police were everywhere. The Confederacy complained about it. Planetary governments aren't supposed to allow their populations to starve. But what did the Directorate care? They never saw the poor. They literally thought that starvation—*which was a fact*—was a vile rumor. Of course they never checked for themselves. They never had time, they were too busy holding their posts and plotting against rivals. Life was stratified. And in its way, the life of the very powerful was as narrow and rigid as the life of the very poor.

"Slowly it dawned on me that our whole society was suffocating. We had locked ourselves into a closet, and we could only escape by breaking down the door.

"By the time I was thirty I had become completely radicalized." He paused, meditating. "Thirty—that's a good age. Imagine growing up to be thirty. Then imagine doing it eleven more times. You see? Now you know what it's like to be my age. I'm three hundred and seventy years old." He smiled distantly and went back to his story.

"By that time I had gotten over my affair with Louise. She was only the catalyst, after all. But I hadn't forgotten what I told her.

"I had learned to control my temper and hide my feelings. I realized that I must rigorously discipline myself before I could have even a chance of success. I thought of entering the Academy, but I realized that they gave no courses in revolution. I worked at a succession of odd jobs while I tried to educate myself. I was drawn inexorably to the greatest source of information on the planet—the Consular Library at the Confederate Consulate, which at that time was in the city of Miclo. Do you know that city, Anne?"

"I've never been there," she said.

Moses shrugged. "Planets are big places. At Miclo I took a job in industrial design, designing clock faces and digital readouts. Now came my first act of really consummate cunning. I swallowed my obsession, and for five years I applied the full force of my intelligence to my job, which I passionately hated. I lived a life of ruthless discipline. I unhesitatingly trampled and betrayed my fellow workers. I lived in a spartan cell, I had no friends, and no recreations. In my spare time I read textbooks on design. I was promoted by leaps and bounds. Finally only one man stood between myself and control of the enterprise. When my chance came, I unhesitatingly compromised him and ruined his career. Then I bled the company dry by embezzlement and finally sold it for far more than it was worth to a woman I controlled by blackmail. I was then forty-five years old, rich, and insane.

"I was literally and clinically insane. I heard voices, I felt that my limbs were detached from my body, and I knew that my many enemies were trying to kill me.

"I invested my wealth, but I had become so intensely paranoid that I couldn't bear the sight or smell of human beings. I fled to a very remote area in the planet's polar icecap, the farthest place I could think of. You, Kid, have probably never seen an icecap. They are harsh and terrible places, but not without their own weird beauty. I paid well for a prefabricated, self-sufficient retreat, which I built myself, alone, with my two hands and two primitive construction drones.

"I lived there for two years and went through a traumatic personality change. I adopted another name, and I returned to the Consular Library with my sanity restored but my resolve undiminished!

"I was looking for ways to design a whole society from scratch. There were plenty of examples—mostly miserable failures. Part of the problem was that it was impossible to start with brand-new human beings. The converts to the new society always brought along a cultural hangover from their areas of origin.

"Most of the very worst failures were those based on religions and airy moral convictions. I decided that mine would be based firmly on self-interest. I looked for a sound structural basis and I decided on the corporation. Citizens would be shareholders, so that everyone would profit equally from the collective endeavor.

"Since work had driven me mad, I decided to abolish it. For that I needed a get-rich-quick scheme, a corporate investment that would supply the revenue to support an entire society. Of course, you know what I eventually found." He pointed upward. "It was the Reverid Morning Star."

He stopped momentarily while Anne and I ducked underwater to blow more air into the flotation bags, which had gone flat.

"By this time I was fifty, still a youngster. I had reached full maturity, however. By the time I was sixty I had ingratiated myself with the Confederate Consul General and had taken a position as his Chief Archivist. It was then that I discovered the works of Riley. I had them reprinted at my own expense, in translation of course, and they were a planet-wide sensation. I was wealthier than ever and now famous as well. The usual seductions of fame offered themselves, but I refused them. Instead, I adopted a carefully calculated demeanor of modesty and common sense. I knew that I would need such a reputation when I offered my harebrained scheme to the public.

"During the next forty years I slowly laid the groundwork for my plans, never hinting them to a soul. I was offered a lucrative position with the planetary government, and I refused. This really electrified my contemporaries. When they demanded my reasons, I let it be known that I objected on moral grounds. I never polemicized, I never raised my voice; in fact, I never made my moral grounds exactly clear. I mentioned the plight of the poor of course, but mostly I just fed them with witty platitudes I had scraped up during decades of reading. Frankly, I kept a little notebook full of platitudes on my person at all times. They proved invaluable." He paused. "Men will give their lives for an idea, if it's large enough and not exactly clear to them.

"The real reason for my refusal was the fact that I had already thrown in my lot with the Confederacy. I needed the Confederacy badly, because they were in legal control of the planet I wanted, this very planet in fact. The Academy was investigating the planet for possible colonization at the time, and I knew from my sources that they would clear it. I could get it, for a price.

"Luckily the Academy was moving very slowly, as it always does, and the planet demanded a lot of investigation. There was quite a bit of concern over the microbial life.

"At the age of one hundred I married for the first time, and at one hundred and twenty I married again. Both times I married for money. My wives and I were still friends when we separated, and I jumped from moderate wealth to an immense fortune. I started my charitable works: preserving wildlife, endowing libraries, feeding people, housing and clothing them. This was another tactic I had learned from the past. That way I preserved my moral stature and my money. Was it hypocrisy? Was it schizophrenia? I've never decided.' He shrugged again.

"I already knew that I would have to fight the Niwlindid Directorate tooth and nail. Naturally, they had grown to hate me, as they hated any power they couldn't corrupt or envelop. I knew that there were two sources of power I could turn against them: the Confederacy, and popular support." Suddenly a thought startled him. "The Confederacy still exists, doesn't it?"

"Of course," I said. "It's grown weaker since your time, though. Too much decentralization."

"Yes," Moses said. "I could see that coming. At any rate, it dawned on me that the time had come for popular agitation. I had to make myself such a nuisance to the government that they would be glad to see me go, no matter what the cost to their own resources. When I was one hundred and thirty, I changed my name to Moses Moses and started the Corporation.

"My plan was to mine the Morning Star. To strip a planet as it had never been stripped before. To blast it. To rip it. To turn it inside out and seize the metal of its core.

"I envisioned a cloud of oneills. Big, cylindrical orbital cities, the kinds the Confederates live in. I foresaw my people living in these cylinders, building drones, programming them to rip a planet. I knew there was a market for the metal, but the initial investment would be colossal. Ruinous. But Niwlind was ripe for ruin.

"I hired the best engineers I could find, and I paid to train others. I spent money like water. I was a man possessed. I got the necessary plans from the Confederacy, the documentation for oneills, and I paid them in the coin they liked best. Espionage. Yes, I committed treason—I confess it frankly. They joined me in plundering Niwlind, and many a Confederate official returned from my home planet rich. But I needed information only they could give me.

"The cost in human suffering was terrible, but it was blamed on the Confederacy and the Directorate, not me. Does that bother you, Kid, to know your life was based on the pain of the helpless?"

I shook my head. "That was six hundred years ago. They're all dead now, anyway."

Moses Moses smiled blandly. "It didn't bother me either. Their misery only drew them closer to me. I would have spared them their pain if I could, of course. I loved power, but I wasn't a sadist. Besides, I was offering them a chance to escape. They could never have had that chance without my genius. I could not afford to be hampered by useless guilt.

"Decades passed. I was battling the lethargy of the very old, and there's no lethargy like it. I started small. I endured twenty years of slander and ridicule, preaching, publishing, taping, testifying, pleading, arguing, begging, threatening, pimping, blackmailing. Then the young, the restless, the desperate began to flock around me. I picked good men and women for my apostles. You must have seen their names in your histories: Bowmarshay, Deeder, Quinn, Miniott, and all the others. The first members of the Reverid Board of Directors. They were all good people, the best I could find. They believed in me, and in return I gave them meaning for their lives.

"They had complete faith in the facade I had built for myself. And I had to stay within the facade, because I would have died rather than disappoint them. I had plenty of followers eager to do my dirty work, so I was able to retreat to a lofty moral eminence. Thanks to my long self-discipline, asceticism was very little effort for me, but it made an immense impression on people who were used to nothing but venality and greed. And this is the part you must believe . . . *my mask became my face. I became Moses Moses, the prophet, the leader.* I had started my people moving; now I was swept along by their tide. They had made me their lord and without hesitation I sacrificed everything for their happiness. . . .

"I had no private life, no selfishness, no will of my own, no *thoughts* of my own. In a very real, literal way I ceased to have an identity. I was the people's will made flesh. This seems bizarre and mystical, I know; it would have seemed so to me, if I had ever given myself time to think about it. But I never did. It absorbed me completely, like a dream, like a womb. I have memories of course: I gave speeches, I organized, I gave orders, I checked plans; I left the planet, I moved into the first oneills with the pioneers, I operated a mining drone like the rest, always like the rest. But it seems so vague to me now, as if I were entranced, as if I were someone else. It was a kind of madness, a kind of possession. I had built myself a role, and it swallowed me. I had burned away like the dross off molten tin; the only thing left of me was a shining tin god.

"I was like that for almost seventy years, until I was two hundred and twenty. We had already had the oneills operating for twenty-one years, and we had scraped up enough metal to begin to build our own oneills, to establish our independence from Niwlind. We had even begun to supply a trickle of money to the Confederacy; their lust for cash was incredible, and dammit, we were buying a planet, or at least the right to one. My plan was working. The long purgatory on the oneills was changing my Niwlindids into a people of their own, with their own customs, expressions, and ways of thought. Life on the oneills was grindingly hard at first; let no one tell you differently, I was there, and I *know*. Our supplies from Niwlind were grudging to say the least, and none of us were experts; we blundered time and again, and every time we blundered, people died. A life-support system is merciless; it knows nothing of pain, only the laws of mechanics. But we learned fast. We had to learn to stay alive. We went through the flame, and it tempered us. It made us what we were. It made you what *you* are.

"When I was two hundred and twenty-one, an accident occurred in my oneill, which was of course the center of government. It involved a newly constructed mining drone, which had not yet been dropped to the surface of the Morning Star. It was orbiting not far from the edge of the oneill when its laser malfunctioned briefly and sent a small pulse of pure light completely through the oneill outer wall; as it happened, right where I was speaking. This was not an assassination attempt as many people have claimed. It was only a deadly accident. My poor secretary, Madame Deeder, was killed immediately and the screams of the crowd were swallowed up by the roar of decompression. I looked and I saw naked space through the hole, which was no more than ten inches in diameter. Of course it would have taken weeks to empty all the air of the oneill through such a tiny hole, but my only thought was for the safety of my audience, who were trampling one another in panic. Naturally we kept the oneill spinning at Reverid gravity, since Reverie was to be our home; the zero-grav oneills came later. But I digress.

"To be brief, I saw them panicking; I heard the terrible roar, I saw it ripping up chairs, the podium itself, and I reacted quickly. I flung my body over the hole and blocked it with my chest. Of course I blacked out immediately under the crushing impact. I knew I was dead, because I knew I had given my life. But I wasn't dead.

"Things would have been different if I had died a martyr's death; they would have gone more to my plan. A dead man's hands can be crushingly strong. But I wasn't dead, because they healed me. It took them days to rebuild my body, but they succeeded, because they loved me. But when I opened my eyes again, I was no longer Moses Moses."

He sighed. We saw the lick of lightning against a distant thunderhead. Moses Moses' auburn hair had dried and was stiffened with brine. The skin of our hands had begun to wrinkle, as waterlogged as stewed fruit. It was almost noon and the glare off the sea was blinding.

"Oh, I kept the name," said Moses Moses. "I always kept the name. But I had lost that inspiration, that possessive zeitgeist. I knew my role, and I played it well, but now I was only the actor, not the man. Somehow they sensed it. I know this is the truth. No one ever spoke of it; maybe they never realized it consciously. Our lives went on, but they lacked luster, as if poisoned by anticlimax. That was it, the turning point. After that, the rot began to steal into my plans.

"I had lost it. Now that I think back on it, it amazes me to think how long I kept it. But now I was returned to myself, and the schemer had replaced the saint. It sickened me. When I tried to go on with the charade, it choked me; I felt that it was sucking out all of my life. I tried to delegate my authority to those I trusted, to go into retirement. It took me years. God, they were sickeningly coy. Oh, wonderful Moses Moses, they said, the heroic near-martyr, such statesmanlike modesty! As if we could go on without our very heart and soul! It cost me a tremendous effort to put power into the hands of the Board of Directors. When I picked them I had picked loyal followers, not statesmen. They were constantly deferring decisions to me. It lasted throughout the rest of the Mining Century, until I was three hundred miserable years old. God, what didn't I give for those people?

"One day I woke up and realized that we were rich. Fantastically rich! Our first concern had been to buy off the Confederacy; that came relatively quickly. Then, with their help and astronomical bribes, we were able to corrupt the Academic survey team and get the planet released to us before their study was complete. We were impatient; they'd already been studying it for two hundred years and they still weren't satisfied. We promised to take great care concerning the microbial life and I personally assured them that we would stay out of the Mass, which seemed to be the area they thought most dangerous. It's an ugly area anyway, all that mold and fungus, and who needs that when there are hundreds of thousands of beautiful, rich tropical islands? Then we turned our money back to Niwlind and paid off our investors; once that was done we declared our political independence. They didn't like it, of course. They called us traitors, but what could they do? The expenses of interstellar war are completely ruinous, and we had the support of the Confederacy who controlled the interstellar pilots. We were beyond their reach.

"And still the money kept pouring in, exponentially. We spent it on terraforming at first, building the big oneill gardens so that food would no longer be a problem. And I encouraged it, because we'd lived on green scum and yeast for years. Then we bought knowledge, trading metal for technology, so that we had the very best available food synthesis and vast orbital greenhouses tended by computer-run drones. Drone technology was our own, of course, we'd carried it as far as—or farther than—any other human people, so we placed the heaviest reliance on our own expertise. Drones were our slave labor force; we wanted a huge pyramid of drones to support a tiny apex of human aristocrats. So we built them in incredible numbers, until there were more drones than people, then twice as many, four times, six times, ten, twenty. And we built oneills to house them, for manufacturing, for energy, for food, communications, transportation. And as far as possible we kept them simple. We never allowed our computers to mock human sentience, because we'd learned from the lessons of the past.

"As money poured through our dwelling oneills, we were unable to resist making them beautiful. In my original plans they were only campgrounds, orbiting arks if you prefer. But after a century one feels differently; you learn to love the work of your own hands, to think of it as home. And oneills have their advantages; the lack of gravity at their cores for instance. That gave rise to hundreds of different pursuits from sports to sex, things that made us uniquely us, that people were loth to give up. Just as we started colonizing the planet, some oneills began canceling their centrifugal spin, going completely floater, like the Confederates themselves. They orbited Reverie, because it's such a beautiful planet, but they'd made their decision to stay in space and there was nothing I could do about it; it would have ripped the social fabric. I set an example by moving down to the planet, and I lived in those ugly drone-built fortresses that I'd helped to construct myself. They were uncomfortable and hideous, and every time a fresh wind blew in off the continent we would all come down with some minor ailment. We kept a close watch on our health, of course, and there weren't many fatalities, but we were constantly hampered by precautions. There were endless tests and inoculations and immunizations, and most of us were at a low level of illness much of the time—rotten little ailments like colds and diarrhea, stomach aches, low fevers, sticky eyes, peeling blisters on the hands and feet, bumps and itches—not dangerous things, not really challenging things, just trivial annoyances that sapped the will instead of strengthening it. After all, we were pioneers, and even with the full backing of a powerful technology, a pioneer faces difficulties. But the orbiters didn't see it that way. With a camera drone you can experience much of Reverie, sight and sound, without risking illness, from the lavish comfort of your oneill. You're not weighted down by gravity; you don't get sunburned, you don't get sand in your shoes. With a direct cerebral hookup you can even get good approximations of touch and scent. It was just too tempting to stay in orbit, to see the whole planet at a glance instead of a few acres through a tiny quartz window. They didn't want to struggle any more, and after the Mining Century, who could blame them? And oneills are close to self-sufficient, they have to be, since each is its own life-support system; an oneill naturally tends toward insularity, toward becoming a city-state. Our good communications prevented that, luckily, but nevertheless they were hard to control. . . .

"Things slowly got better as the decades passed, faster and faster, each one seeming to take less time than the last. The older settlers became immunized, we were able to see more, travel more, develop customs of our own, to take advantage of the incredible bounty of this planet. We grew to love it as a mother rather than fight it as an adversary. It's so beautiful, it's a gift. It had an intelligent race once. I often wonder what they were like. It was thoughtful of them to destroy themselves and leave their planet to us."

He grinned sardonically. "Death comes to us all, though not so quickly as it came to them. Death is rooted within me, it travels along every nerve. A man is lucky to live to three hundred. With a purpose in life, something to focus his will to survive, he may see three hundred and fifty. But the urge to die is as strong as the urge to live; it only manifests itself more subtly. After I passed three hundred, my death began to assert itself. Subtly at first, then more urgently. The degenerative process is peculiarly horrifying."

He looked at both of us, slowly, earnestly. "It started with the breakdown of memory. Distant memories had been blurred for a long time; I had depended on my computer to sort them out for me. But then I found myself prey to increasing absent-mindedness. I would forget the events of days or even mere hours past. I would forget if I had eaten a meal, forget errands and appointments, repeat myself in conversations. Then it became more intense. I suffered from the nightmarish feeling that I was living a single week over again; I began to suspect, insanely, that time had doubled back on itself, that I was trapped in an endless loop, like a tape.

"I felt that I was becoming thinner—stretched out into an intolerable, vulnerable state. I began to slip into the classic degenerative syndromes of extreme old age, the state we call Panan. Do you know what Panan is? Does it still exist?"

"Yes," I said. "I know what it is. It's pananesthesia—a sort of overall numbness."

"That's not half of it," Moses Moses said. "It involves physical numbness, of course. In its worst state, you can smash your fingers in a door and not even notice it until you see the dripping of blood. But it's a mental numbness too. Your strongest emotions, your deepest convictions run out of you like water from a broken jug. Apathy devours you. Black depression settles in, suddenly, without warning, and when you least expect it. You feel horribly distant from life, as if you were encased in glass, and other people seem like puppets. You can almost see the strings." He shuddered.

"God, it even hurts to talk about it! The pleasures that rooted you to life, that made it seem worth living, are leached away. Sex for example. I've been impotent for a long time now—decades. Aphrodisiacs would restore the function of my body, but it was as if it were happening to someone else. You feel out of phase with your body, as if you had drifted away from it. That's the very worst part of it. It's madness, a madness peculiar to the old. You begin to suspect that your body is useless, that it drags you down. You begin to hate your body, you begin to hate yourself. Your catch yourself inflicting small punishments on the body; you become accident prone. Most old people die by accidents, by indirect suicide. Only a few have the nerve to confront death directly and take their own lives.

"I didn't want to die. Consciously, I hated the idea of death. Unconsciously, I planned my own destruction. I convinced myself that a shock would restore my appetite for living; I took up mountain climbing, gliding, diving. I confronted these natural risks, and I manufactured more of my own. It didn't work, but it did show me the opposite side of the coin. It's called Hyperas. From hyperasthesia, of course.

"In many ways Hyperas is worse then Panan. Instead of being distanced, you feel suffocatingly close. Instead of feeling numb, you are hideously sensitive. Whispers sound like shouts and shouts like earthquakes. The softest clothing chafes you. The tastiest food is cloying, sickeningly rich. You notice everything, even the tiniest things that you never realized existed. Not merely people's faces, but the dirt in their clogged pores, the stubble in their follicles, the split ends in individual hairs. You notice the smallest, most fleeting expressions; people behave like slapstick clowns, mugging everything. You can tell what they say before they say it, what they'll do before they do it. Actually this is true for most old people; it's a matter of experience. But in Hyperas, your perceptions become so acute that it dehumanizes people. They seem like programmed drones. You rob them of their free will, and suddenly it seems that they never had any.

"You notice so many tiny details that you smother under the rush of information. It drives you frantic. It forces you to retreat from your usual haunts into a less cluttered environment; a bare room, for instance. I tried that, but I became painfully fascinated by the texture of the wall, by the weaving of the sheets on my cot, by the dust motes in the air, even by self-induced ringing in my ears. During my worst attack I retreated to a sensory deprivation tank; warm water, silence, darkness. It seemed to work; I calmed down. But when I finally came out, I was completely engulfed by Panan. From then on, the two states alternated, sometimes in a single day. When I realized that I was being driven to suicide, I decided to postpone my final confrontation with death by putting myself under ice. I started preparing my cryocoffin. When I had this task to distract me, my sanity was restored. I suppose the cryosleep was close enough to death to satisfy my destructive urge, so it granted me a respite from my self-torment. I picked what I thought would be a significant date for my reawakening; I thought that the marvels of the distant future would distract me long enough to provide a few more decades of life. If the Panan returned, I would kill myself, or go back under ice again. That way I could extend my life almost indefinitely.

"Also, there was an element of vanity. Naturally I wanted to see how long my social handiwork would last. Curiosity was a good enough reason to live. It aroused my interest, it broke the shell of apathy. So I did it. I never thought it would end in this, though I was prepared for disaster. I carefully hid my coffin, you remember. But I never anticipated this." He shook his head. "At least it relieves me from the moral effort of suicide. People tell me that suicide, deliberate, self-conscious self-destruction, is the only way to die with dignity. But I never believed that. The perfect death, for me, would have come quickly, without warning, as it did when the drone pierced my oneill. But death had his chance then, and he failed to get me. Since, then, I've resolved on life. When the rays come to get us, I suppose I'll fight them! That should be a sight to see."

He laughed lightly, mocking himself, but without bitterness. "I've said enough. Who'll be next to tell their story?"

Anne and I exchanged glances. Anne's freckled face was sunburned; it was noon and the burn would get much worse if we lived until sundown, nine hours away. "I'll go next," she said.

"All right," I said. I looked overhead. A flock of dark, long-winged birds were flying west in a V formation. Perhaps one of the towering, white-piled thunderclouds would drift over us and shade us. Perhaps it would even rain on us. Although we were neck-deep in water, I was getting thirsty. I tried not to think about it. The hunger was worse, anyway; as usual, the smuff stirred my appetite.

8

Anne said, "I believe in God, the catalyst of life, the core of the universe, the essence of good. I believe in good, and I believe in evil, and I have sworn to support the first and destroy the second. I believe in a soul, which is manifested in matter, but is different from matter and superior to it. God breathed life into matter, because God is pure soul, and the souls of all living things return to God when their stay in the realm of matter is dissolved by death. Evil comes when the pure and passionless soul is polluted by material lust and greed. The way of salvation is to purge the soul of evil and return to the good. All forms of life contain some good, because they all come from God; therefore all life is sacred and not to be wantonly destroyed. Such is the creed of my Church; such is my creed; such is my faith."

After this strange statement she fell silent for so long that I thought she had finished. I was annoyed and amused. "That's it, then?" I said mockingly. "That's your life story?"

"That is the core of it," she said. "The rest is only personal details."

"Well," said Moses Moses with an air of humorous restraint, "perhaps you should go ahead and tell us a few of them. Maybe you'll find it easier if you start with the history of your Church."

"The history of my Church is the history of my life," said Anne with a quiet womanly dignity quite amazing for one sunk to her neck in sea water. "I was born into the Church, because I am the great-granddaughter of the Mysteriarch. She is the leader of our Church, and her father is our greatest theologian, the wisest man alive. He is five hundred years old."

"Impossible," said Moses Moses and I, together.

She shook her head. "It's the truth."

"Then he's had a memory wipe, probably several," I said. "How do you know he's that old? What proof can he offer?"

"Church leaders never lie," Anne said indignantly. "Sometimes they prefer to meet questions with silence, but they never lie. Men and women are not born to destroy themselves; that idea is the lie. Those outside the faith die early, because they tear themselves apart with frustration and despair. Their lives are pointless; they have nowhere to turn; they have no goals in life nobler than the gratification of their own vanity. Their lives are empty! Hollow, echoing, empty! They have nothing to live for! They have nothing beyond themselves! Is it any wonder that they die? No. The wonder is that they manage to live so long. God put no limitation on life. Those who follow the path of righteousness can live indefinitely, because they dedicate their lives to God.

"Their lives are healthy, because they are dedicated to a noble purpose, the noblest there is: they do good. They do good, and they avoid the black paths of suicidal evil: Hate. Envy. Greed. Luxury. Sloth. The dissolutions of the flesh. They avoid all those things. They avoid all those things and they focus their eyes on the sublime." She looked piously upward. "That's why our creed has spread, slowly but surely. Now there are over a million men and women in our Church family. We are a force to be reckoned with on Niwlind."

I said, "What's Niwlind's current population? About six billion, right?"

"Six point two billion," she said. "But our million are the best

117

among them, and the rest will see the light in time."

Moses Moses was aghast. "Are there that many people now? How did it get so overcrowded? There were only three billion when I left."

"It was evasion of the population laws," Anne said calmly. "Everyone does it. People need children, you know; it's a very deep-seated need. I intend—well, I intended to have children someday. It's too late now, of course."

I was interested. "Really?" I said. "Do you favor artificial insemination, or were you going to give yourself to some man's sweaty fleshy embraces?"

Anne looked at me coldly. "Marriage is a sacrament. It is a meeting of souls. Marriage in the Church transcends carnal lusts." I nodded skeptically. She frowned. "I didn't expect you to understand that. Obviously it's completely beyond you."

I was annoyed. "I don't pretend to understand sex, but I know hypocrisy when I see it."

"That doesn't suprise me," she said cuttingly. "You claimed to be Tanglin's young son when you're really hundreds of years old. Obviously you're an old hand at hypocrisy."

"Why, you mudbrained idiot," I began, but Moses Moses interrupted. "Children, please," he said smoothly. "Let's avoid squabbling. These are my last hours. Let me live them in peace. You'll have your chance to explain yourself, Kid. Let Anne have hers."

My anger evaporated. "Yes, of course," I said. "Go ahead, Anne." I relished the thought that she would soon know the full truth about Tanglin, and our relationship.

Anne said, "The Uplands on Niwlind are one of the planet's oldest areas. They are a high plateau. The air is thin and it is cold and windy, especially in winter. It has never been heavily populated. Even now most of the development is in mining camps. But that is where the Mysteriarch founded our Church Sanctuary, and that is where I was born, fifty-two years ago.

"Only the initiates know the full extent of Sanctuary. Visitors only see the domes and churches that cling to the side of the rock. Sometimes rumors are heard about the tunnels in the valley cliff wall. They do not realize that there are miles of tunnels. And not all the tunnels were built by men.

"The Upland Plateau itself is grassy and arid. We chose to dwell in the canyons, great, deep river canyons that the water carved over millions of years. The rock is the continental shield itself—there is no sedimentation, no colorful layering in it. It is black and gray and sometimes, rarely, dark red. The canyons are thousands of feet deep and sometimes miles wide. The rivers are thin and sinuous and in some places they are blocked by falls of rubble. Then thin, deep little fjords appear, and there are rapids. The water is dark and very cold.

"Every morning and every evening, with sunrise and sunset, winds whip through the canyon, and they howl. If you listen carefully you can hear voices in the howling, but it is best not to listen to them. The wind tears at everything it touches—that's why the plants of the valley floor are almost all roots. They are small and gnarled and tough, but if their seeds land behind a windbreak then they grow tall and put out hard stiff colorful flowers whose petals can scratch glass.

"Even as a little girl I didn't like the valley floor—it is too dark, the walls are too high. I wanted to live on the moors instead. The moors are windy too, it blows all the time. But it blows steadily, not with the brief killing violence of the morning and evening valleywinds. And it is open. You can see the sun and the dark battered clouds and the knee-high grass and smell the little flowers and see the little denizens of the plains. There are beetles and grasshoppers and flutterbys, and little marmots and rabbits and goats, and of course moas. The moas are best." Anne reached up slowly and touched the sodden cluster of dark feathers pinned to her hair.

"I was a good girl and I understood the truth of the catechism almost from the first, and I was better even than they expected me to be. Until I was ten I stayed almost all the time in Sanctuary, because I was an illegal child and the old habits of caution die hard. But after a while I was given a forged identity and I went through my Borning and I took my adult name, Anne.

"Then I was allowed to go up the steep trail from the valley floor up to the moors, where I worked in the gardening domes with my uncle and cousins. During prayertime in the mornings and evenings, when the valleywinds blew, I was able to go out on the moors to meditate. I saw my first moa when I was twelve. It was an old moa—an old female with dirty feathers and big pendulous wattles on her neck. I was wandering, and so was she. I wasn't frightened, although mother had told me that in the first days of Sanctuary a child had been pecked to death by big rogue moas. The old moa wasn't frightened either. She just backed away slowly and then ran off over the grass on her great thick scaly legs.

"That night I dreamed that I was wandering over the moors and I came into a depression like a grassy bowl. And I dreamed that in the middle of the depression was a big circular track of beaten earth, like a big wheel, with eight dirt tracks like spokes. And in the dream something called me to step into the center of the wheel, but when I stepped over the boundary of the circle I woke up.

"In the morning I told my uncle about the dream. We of the Church know about dreams; they come from the depths of the soul, and therefore they are close to the Great Soul that is the author of consciousness and dreams alike. We put on our plains boots, and we took our hiking staves, and we went out into the moors to look for the wheel, and on the second day we found it. It was a dancing ground of the moas, such as few human beings had ever seen. We could see their big three-toed tracks in the beaten dirt, and we saw the strange flat mushrooms that grow in the dung of moas all around its rim.

" 'I knew we would find it,' my uncle told me. 'The Catechist, your great-great-grandfather, dreamed the site of Sanctuary long before we found it, and your grandmother, my mother, dreamed the site of the Iron Caves before the landslide exposed them. Look into your heart now, child, and tell me what we must do.'

"For a little while I knelt in the blowing grass and prayed, and the answer came to me. And I said, 'Uncle, you must leave me, and I must stay here. Something calls me to this spot and I must answer the call as best I hear it.' So my uncle left me."

"But moas are dangerous," Moses Moses objected. "They're carnivorous; I've seen them fed in zoos. Those big beaks could rip off a man's arm."

Anne nodded. "Yes. I've seen them tear moor goats to pieces in less time than it takes to breathe. But I wasn't afraid, although I trembled. I pulled my hood over my head and laced my gray cape around my shoulders and pulled on my gray gloves and leaned on my staff of gray stonewood. I stared for a long time at the wheel with the eight spokes.

"The sun began to set and it grew colder, and when the first pale star shone on the eastern horizon the moas began to appear. There were big blue-wattled males, and big red-wattled females, and little moa chicks no higher than my knee. They came in utter silence, because they are mute. I didn't move at all, and none of them seemed to notice me. Then they danced. They ran around the circle, and they danced across the spokes, dipping their heavy heads, and spreading their wings, and leaping in the air. They danced until it was dark and I could not see them moving but only heard the thump of their feet in the dirt. After a while even that sound faded, and I sat down in the grass and drew my knees to my chest and covered up in my cloak and slept and dreamed. I dreamed that I danced with the moas in the form of a moa. In the morning I walked back to the gardening domes, which took all day. In the evening my stomach began to cramp and hurt and I bled for the first time.

"I went to the dancing-ground many times after that, but I did not see any moas. When I was fifteen a mining expedition came to Sanctuary and the illegal population retreated into the tunnels. Everyone circumvented the population laws, and, until Rominuald Tanglin legitimized the illegal population, any of us could have been arrested and our parents heavily fined. And illegal people were denied the protection of the law as well—we could be robbed or beaten or raped and we wouldn't have dared go to the police. Of course there were no such criminal problems within Sanctuary. Our Church family was well disciplined—we all knew one another and did not tolerate crime. But the miners were terrible. They wouldn't have come to prospect if the Reverid Emigration hadn't taken so much of our metals, by the way—that was one of the legacies you left us. But I don't blame you for struggling to leave such corruption. The police had their agents among the miners. The Directorate didn't like the idea of a powerful religious group with their own city and they sent their census takers to harass us.

"But we were not helpless. We had the right on our side of

course. We appealed for the help of Rominuald Tanglin and put what power we had into his coalition. We had many Church brothers and sisters all over Niwlind, though Sanctuary was our holy city and our headquarters.

"Naturally I personally had very little to do with this—I was in my teens when the mining controversy first began. But I followed the controversy avidly, we all did. We hated the miners, who brought vice and brutality with them and tried to exploit Church members for sexual purposes. We tried to expel them, but the demand for the metal was great and we were overruled politically.

"I was still fascinated by the moas. When the Legitimation Act came through and I was granted my own identity, I was free to study them without harassment—thanks to Rominuald Tanglin, of course. Since we Church folk and the miners were the only people on the Upland Plateau, and since that was the moas' only habitat, I became one of the planet's top specialists on moas. I was very patient. I followed them on foot, I made no threatening gestures, and when I could I left them food. They grew used to my scent, to my presence. I often roamed with them for days. I had my own flock. I gave them names.

"But the mining went on at a redoubled pace, and foreign Niwlindids poured in from all over the planet in a rush. More than once I found moas shot dead or caught in cruel traps. The moas were not entirely innocent, of course, but it was their land. The intruders were ruthlessly developing their sacred places. Yes, sacred places, you needn't look so surprised—why should they dance so, if not to worship?

"The intruders were afraid of the moas, and with good reason. More than one wanderer on the moors was found with beak-marks on his bones. I can only say that my flock never killed a human—they lived near Sanctuary, where Church folk defended native life with their own bodies if need be. The miners were anxious to exterminate the moas, and they started the bureaucratic process that would have granted them that right—or that wrong, I should say. But thank God for Rominuald Tanglin! He got wind of this evil procedure. His upright soul was filled with righteous indignation.

"He visited Sanctuary in person. We gave him the finest reception we could—after all, by this time he was First Secretary, though his position was shaky. He seemed pleased by our acclaim, but it was hard to judge for sure, as he was in many ways a peculiar man. Those strange sticks linked with a chain—the weapon you use, Kid—he kept them with him at all times. He never let them get farther away than his fingers' ends. He, of course, never put them to the ignoble uses of violence, though. He used them only for healthful exercise, I can assure you.

"Secretary Tanglin spent several hours in close conference with our Mysteriarch. They got along famously, which very much pleased and surprised us, as the Mysteriarch usually had a short way with outsiders. She was over four hundred years old and did not tolerate sin easily, but apparently she found the Secretary to be morally sound. Or maybe it was the Secretary's famous ability to charm.

"You can imagine my shock and surprise when I, myself, Anne Twiceborn, was called to their conference chamber. Of course I had no right to be in such a place. I had not even been canonized yet—in fact I was only twenty years old.

"It was the most exciting thing that had ever happened to me. Never in my most cryptic dreams had I had a hint of such a thing—meeting the planet's First Secretary in person! And not merely a First Secretary, though they are rare enough, but Rominuald Tanglin! I was so excited that I actually cried. I must have committed fifty sins of vanity that day—it was shameful.

"I can remember every word the Secretary said. It was very strange. I had never moved in such exalted circles, so I didn't know what to expect; but it was very odd even so.

"The first thing I noticed was the strange way the Mysteriarch was behaving. She and Secretary Tanglin were both sitting in formal armchairs, and he was in his usual position, the one you always see in the tapes: with his right leg hooked over his left knee. And she was in the same position! It was so unusual for her that I gasped a little. And he said smoothly, in that famous voice that I had heard a thousand times, "This is her? Well, Alice! That's more like it! Oh, she should do famously!" Then he did something very peculiar. He held out his hands in front of him and made a little square with his thumbs and forefingers. Then he looked at me through the little square, moving his hands around so that he framed my face.

" 'She's marvelous,' he said to the Mysteriarch. 'You say she's your great-grandchild? Well, it's easy to see where she got her looks.' He grinned, and the Mysteriarch smiled and said, 'Thank you, Rominuald.'

"I was amazed. I couldn't have been more surprised if the sun had changed color. They were calling one another by their first names! Perhaps it wasn't so surprising in the Secretary—he was called the People's Friend, after all, and he was known for his informality. But the Mysteriarch! Crossing her legs under her black robe! Smiling! Answering to the name Alice! I hadn't even known her name *was* Alice. She'd always been just the Mysteriarch to us. I couldn't imagine what had made her do it.

"Then the Secretary spoke to me. 'I'm very pleased to meet you, child. I am Rominuald Tanglin. And your name is . . . ?'

"After an embarrassing pause I stuttered, 'Anne, Mr. Secretary. Anne Twiceborn.'

" 'Anne,' he said musingly. Suddenly he nodded. 'Anne. A fine name. Couldn't have thought of a better one myself. Marvelous, be sure you keep that name. How old are you, Anne?'

" 'Twenty, sir,' I said.

" 'Twenty!' he said. 'In many ways still our mental peak! Marvelous! Turn a little and show me your profile, dear. Have you ever been on tape before? Have you ever used tape?'

" 'A little,' I said. 'I've taped the moas in their native habitat.'

" 'Excellent. Then you'll be a new face. Your delightful ancestress here informs me that you know the moas very well indeed. How many years have you studied them so far?'

" 'Five, Mr. Secretary. Three years full-time.'

" 'That's all?' he said, frowning. 'Still, that's remarkable for one so young. I just wish they were better known before I. . . . You have a lovely skin considering the time you've spent outside, child. Those freckles would melt the heart of a man on ice. Do you like moas, child? What would you do to save them from their persecutors?'

" 'Anything,' I said.

"The Secretary turned to my great-grandmother. 'I like this child of yours,' he said. 'She gets to the point with alacrity. I think she'll do just fine. Are we still agreed, then?'

"The Mysteriarch nodded. 'Yes, Mr. Secretary.'

"'Excellent.' He lifted both hands and fluffed up the curls in his hair. He really was very handsome—it wasn't just the make-up.

"'Anne,' he said, 'will you come with me to the capital? I can't offer you anything but work and suffering—and this at your tender age, as well. But I need you and that means the planet needs you. I want you to speak for the moas, since they have no voices. You may be the only person on the planet who can save them. It will destroy your privacy and your peace of mind and change you forever. But your help is crucial to their cause and my cause and the cause of all of us. Will you do it?'

"I looked at the Mysteriarch and she nodded slightly, and I said, 'Yes, Mr. Secretary.'

"He said, 'Good. I knew you wouldn't fail me. I could tell it just by looking at your face. A lot of people will be looking at that face of yours in the months to come, Anne. And I know they'll see the simple honesty and goodness that I myself see in it. Ah, these Uplands are a stern land, but they breed fine, sturdy women. You'll carry quite a burden on those square little shoulders of yours, child—the kind I carry myself. Such burdens can be galling. Sometimes they'll make you weep. But they'll make you strong.' He turned his head to my great-grandmother. 'When can she leave for Peitho?'

"'As soon as you like, Rominuald,' she said." Anne broke off suddenly and said to Moses Moses, "Peitho is the planetary capital now. In your day it was Miclo."

Moses Moses nodded. "I've never heard of it. Built after my time, I suppose."

Anne nodded absently and drew in a deep breath. "Then the First Secretary got up from his armchair and stepped off the dais and to my side. He put both his hands on my shoulders and looked down into my eyes. He was tall—taller than you. Kid, by three or four inches."

"He must have been wearing block heels," I said.

"He said, 'This is sudden, Anne, I know. We'll be leaving tomorrow, and I'll be taking you from all you love best. You may not see this land again for months—maybe longer. You'll move into a new world—a complicated world, full of danger and ruthless sin. It will confuse you, and hurt you terribly if you are not careful. I'll have to guide your steps at first—you'll have to depend on my advice, and obey it, even if you don't understand all the reasons behind it. You see the sense in this, don't you?' And he looked into my eyes with his wise old eyes—like yours, Kid, but bigger and shinier, like black whirlpools.

"And I said, 'Yes, Mr. Secretary. I'll follow your advice. You will guide me.' And I looked away, because his stare was so intense. I couldn't meet his eyes.

"'Good,' he said. 'When we leave tomorrow we'll have a long talk together on the way to the capital. There will be cameras and lights and noise and more people than you've ever seen in your life. But Anne, you won't be afraid, because your cause is just and *I will support you*. Do you follow me?'

"'Yes, I follow you,' I said, but I only whispered because I was about to cry. He embraced me for a moment, and then he turned and bowed to the Mysteriarch, so low that the two sticks leaned down from his neck and touched the floor. Then he left the room without another word. When the door closed behind him I couldn't hold back my tears. I flung myself at great-grandmother's feet and cried into her lap.

"She said nothing but only waited patiently until I had recovered myself, and she dried my eyes with her black skirt. 'I'm glad you cried, my child,' she said, 'because those tears will have to last you for a long time. They must be your last tears, do you understand? You will have to be brave from now on.'

"'Oh, Madame, what shall I do?' I asked her.

"She was quiet for a few minutes as she tapped the deep waters of her holy intuition. 'Do as he says,' she said at last. 'Ah, I hate to trust you to him, a man with as many sins as he has hairs. But I must. I've spoken with him, dear, and without meaning to, he has opened his heart to me. He is mad. He is the only one who can help us, but he is mad. He has many enemies but he has built others from the ghosts of the past, the far, far past. His fears obsess him, and his end must be near because death has already set his seal in the lines of that man's face. And yet I must trust you to him.

"'It may be that he will try to corrupt you. He might find that an amusement for an idle hour, and he is a charmer, isn't he? Repulse him if you can, but do not anger him. Give in to him rather than risk his anger. The survival of our faith outweighs one young woman's personal modesty. Child, you cannot sin if your heart remains pure. Remember that.'

"'I will, Madame,' I said.

"'Then I have one last word of advice,' she told me. 'Beware of his wife! He trusts her absolutely, and that worries me. Stay away from her!'

"'Yes, I will,' I said, and that was all she said." Anne sighed wistfully. "That was the strangest day of my life. It meant more to me than any days that followed, even the last day of my trial, when I was sentenced to exile. I was famous for a while, you know—more famous than you, Kid, because six billion people knew my name. I won't bore you with the political side of my life—I hated it anyway, and I only did it out of duty. And it certainly wouldn't have meant much to you, Mr. Chairman—a man who could buy and sell a whole planet. I only wanted to save a small patch of land and a few of its birds from the great devouring mouths of the six billion. And in the long run I failed even in that.

"If the First Secretary had lived longer we might have won. I thought we had won at first, when Mr. Tanglin passed the Biome Preservation Act. But he declined rapidly as his wife undermined his sanity with subtle hints and horrible skill and probably drugs and poison too, I wouldn't doubt it. Too many of her enemies have died convenient deaths. She is a devil.

"He left for Reverie just two years after we met. He taught me everything I knew about taping and testifying and talking to crowds, huge crowds sometimes, hundreds of thousands. And after his madness seized him then his enemies tried to blacken his memory, claiming that he'd done all kinds of horrible things. It was typical of those cowards, slandering him when he was unable to fight back. Later we learned that he had killed himself. I cried for days. I loved him. Purely. And he never said an impure word to me, or made an unclean suggestion. He always treated me with pure affection and respect."

I smiled sadly at these last words. All the dignity and conviction in the world couldn't have masked that tiny undertone of regret. I looked at Moses Moses; his face was grave and impassive, but he must have caught it too.

"Thirty years have passed since I last saw Secretary Tanglin," Anne said. "A great deal happened, of course. For the first five years I agitated. Those were the days of my finest commitment, when I felt most exalted in the right. When I thought we had firmly defeated the opposition, I went back to Sanctuary. But I had changed, of course, as the Secretary warned me, and I found Sanctuary very constricting. I returned to the moas and followed them for ten years. I taped their dance, and I learned bits and pieces of their peculiar language. It is all gestures of course, movements of the head and wings and feet, and some other element—scent probably, but I'm not sure. They hurt me several times, but I had the scars removed when I returned to public life after the repeal of the Preservation Act.

"That was when the slaughter began. We preservationists joined together in a united front. The preservation issue attracted many followers other than Church members. In fact we Church folk were greatly outnumbered, but we led the others because of our firm moral stance and strict ideology. We were considered the movement's most radical elements until the violence began. It was about this time that I was canonized.

"I was arrested several times during nonviolent resistance sessions. I was jailed for almost two years. I saw people killed in riots and I threw my body between combatants sometimes and I was beaten with the rest. I saw injustice and violence and hatred. And it was real violence, with real pain." Anne looked at me with a frown.

"My trial lasted two years. I'm certain that Madame Tanglin had something to do with it, though that could never be proved, of course; she was much too clever. The movement put its whole force into the trial. We wanted to bring the persecutors to their knees. And we lost. The sentence was supposedly very light. As if they didn't know that the death of the moas would be the cruelest punishment they could inflict on me.

"They sent me here. The Confederacy has no love for Niwlind, so news is scarce. And I can never return, so I'm dead to Niwlind, and it to me."

She sighed. "I never thought I could love any place but the moors, but these islands, this beautiful sea. . . . I think I could have been happy here, if circumstance had let me. I'm not sorry to die, but I'm sorry not to have seen it all." She fell silent as a cloud drifted mercifully over us, plunging us into cool shadow. "I guess that's all I have to say."

Moses Moses and I said nothing; we were both touched by the simple sincerity of her story, but for different reasons. I felt sorry for Anne. I did not doubt for a moment that Crestillomeem Tanglin had destroyed her career and had her exiled. What chance did poor Anne, Tanglin's pawn, have against the malignant woman who had destroyed Old Dad himself? It would have been like a five-year-old child clenching her tiny fists to fight a combat artist.

A bathetic rush of mingled emotions washed through me like the synergetic effect of a dozen different drugs. Despair at our situation, grief at the death of my best friend Armitrage (I felt a sharp pain of loss—how he would have loved to hear what I had just heard), pity for Anne, the bitterness of irony and my own flinty self-possession, and above it all, a peculiar cosmic humor that was beyond all this and beyond all self. I smiled, turning by long habit so that the cameras could catch me at my best angle.

"Anne, you're getting sunburned," I said. "Let me give you my combat jacket. You can use it for shade." Treading water, I unlaced it and pulled it off. "Don't lose it," I said. "It has all my smuff and my camera controls."

I adjusted the jacket so that the stiff collar shaded her face while the back of the jacket was supported by her oblong head. "Thank you, Kid," she said. "I'll take good care of it." She seemed glad that I hadn't mocked her. Her gratitude embarrassed me. I reached unobtrusively inside the jacket and touchset the controls so that they would continue to follow me rather than the jacket. I needed the comforting presence of their attentive lenses as I told Anne and Moses my story.

9

"I'm sure it will be no surprise to you, Mr. Chairman, to realize that I am Rominuald Tanglin. Or rather, I was once Rominuald Tanglin. Our relationship is a peculiar one, rare enough so that there are very few terms for it. At any rate, Secretary Tanglin underwent terminal personality disruption and I now inhabit his body. You can call me his son, his clone, his successor, or anything you please.

"This happened twenty-eight years ago, so you might call that my age. That makes me the youngest of the three of us by far, and I have the tastes and appetites of the young—well, some of them, anyway. I have what old people call the vices of the young—impatience, impetuousness, carelessness, cruelty. No doubt you could name several more, Anne. I've had mine named often enough. Named to me by old people, of course, old people who slaver at the idea of a young man following his own pursuits instead of their fossilized scheming. Since they deprived the young of any chance of making a mark in the world, we chose our own ways; is that so bad? And if it is, can you stop me? I have power and vitality, you see that I have no patience with argument, because words are the nets of the old, and old people are stuck waist-deep in their own approaching deaths and they long to lure the young into the mire as well. . . ." My voice died away and I shook my head in frustration. Long oratory didn't suit me; I shared Rominuald Tanglin's contempt for long-winded formal apostrophes. My best efforts were in the exchange of stinging insults, followed by the cry of combat, the sizzling crunch of impact. I was no orator, no politician. I preferred to make my point with a blunt edge.

"You'll be old yourself one day. Or you would have been," Anne said.

"I've been old! I've seen what happens to me—to him, that is." I looked at them suspiciously. "He went insane. You probably think that I'm afraid that the same thing will happen to me, that I'm afraid of age because I know I share his weaknesses. Well, it's not so! I'm independent of him, completely independent, I assure you. I don't share his vices, his weakness, or his madness. I've never met him, of course, but he left me an extensive collection of tapes, so I've seen him at his worst, and I know him well. His last madness took the form of a persecution mania. He claimed that humanity was riddled with cunning aliens impersonating people, who preyed on human vitality. He claimed his own wife was one of them. Leeches, he called them. I won't bore you with the details.

"I was born an adult, you know. Into an adult body. I was born able to speak and with a knowledge of basic trained behavior, table manners, hygiene, how to walk, run, swim, operate a keyboard. I was never a child, not really. I suppose that's why I chose to live in an artificially childlike body. As you can see, it's nothing like Tanglin's body; it's my own, dammit, mine! But although I was born an adult physically, I shared certain traits with other children. Innocence. Sensitivity. I was very impressionable. So when I saw Tanglin's tapes I was terrified. I've always thought of him as my father. Strong, cold, remote. And I could tell that he was tormented by exhaustion and fear. Oh, I believed in Leeches, very strongly. There were days when I trembled in terror in my bed. Nights when I could swear I saw withered hungry faces at the window. The fear was worse because I was so isolated. I lived on the continent, you know, on the eastern edge of the Gulf, northeast of Telset. Not far from here, in fact; only thirty miles or so. I rarely saw people except in tapes and broadcasts. It was just me and my tutor, Professor Crossbow."

"Professor Crossbow!" Anne said.

"Yes. Do you know it?"

"Of course I do, it was world-famous. So it's true. You were telling the truth." Tears came to her eyes. "I'm sorry, Rominuald."

"Don't call me that!" I shouted. "I'm not your lover, you dumb cow! Do I look like him? Do I talk like him? No, no, no! I'm my own person, I've proved that!" A weighty silence fell. Anne turned her face from me and wept quietly. Moses Moses looked on with an expression of cool remoteness.

I shrugged helplessly. "All right, so it makes me anxious. Put yourself in my place. It's like living in a house whose builder died mad. It's like having a ghost at your elbow. I'm his heir. I have his legacy. His reflexes, his speed, his altered body, his cunning. But what else did he leave me? What guarantee do I have that he will stay dead? How do I know that he's not still in here—" I tapped my head—"hiding and biding his time? It would be just like him, you know. A masterstroke of horrible cunning. And it would make him a Leech. Disguising himself as me. I'm sure the thought occurred to him just as it occurred to me, because our thoughts run in the same channels, how could they help it? But I don't believe this. I've overcome those childhood fears. A man like Tanglin casts a long shadow, but I'm out of it now. I have my own friends, my own reputation, my own fame. I don't owe it to him. Oh, I used his fighting skills, but his were academic. Gymnasium fighting. The act of a paranoiac. I put the edge on it. I made it a marketable commodity. If I met Tanglin man to man I could break his back in ten seconds." I was quiet for a while. The weight of my nunchuck was dragging me down a little, despite the buoyancy of our makeshift airfloat. I had been treading water for hours now and a rubbery fatigue was invading my legs through the tingly numbness of smuff.

"I've never told this to anyone before," I said at last. "Professor Crossbow was the only one to know, and I haven't seen it in years. It may be dead. It was old, as old as Tanglin. And it was a hermit at heart. Its studies meant more to it than anything, even its friendship with Tanglin. I loved that old neuter. It was probably the only friend Tanglin had. It could have destroyed me so easily—turned me into another Tanglin. But it let me go my own way, at my own speed. It took away the burden of sex. Sex destroyed Tanglin. It made him his wife's dupe. I know better. I have no wife. I have no lovers...." I choked on my words as I remembered Armitrage's last declaration. There hadn't been time to think about it. Now the memory was like a kick in the stomach.

"He loved you," Moses Moses said. Anne looked puzzled. "You overheard?" I said.

"No," Moses said. "But I could tell by the way he looked at you. And that woman in your apartments—the tall, frail one, that the Cabal murdered...."

"Quade."

"Yes, Quade. She loved you too."

"No," I said. "She never told me so. She knew it was impossible. She was loyal, that's all. Loyal and stubborn."

Moses smiled ironically at my naïveté. "Do you think she stood the torture because she was stubborn, Kid? Do you really believe that? Or did you know all along that she loved you? Did you know how she longed to hold you, to touch you, to mend your wounds?" I jerked my face up to look at him and we locked eyes. His ancient yellow gaze pierced me with its insight; he seemed to suck up the thoughts from my head. "Ah, now you remember," he said softly. "You remember how she tended to you, worked for you, obeyed your least whims. And your response, Kid?" He nodded, sucking in his lower lip. "Yes. You knew she loved you. You knew she burned for your embrace and you lorded it over her. You threw her scraps of your affection, you flattered her, you led her on. You won her heart and you kept your own cool and shielded. Just as Tanglin did with this poor girl." He waved one finger-wrinkled hand at Saint Anne.

Anne cried indignantly, "No! You don't know that. You weren't there, so how can you say such a thing?"

Moses Moses turned his calm gaze on her and she withered instantly. She almost cowered and I shuddered at the way he had dropped his mask, at the way he spared us nothing. The old are powerful. They see too much. Maybe that is what drives them mad. "I can guess," he said gently. "It's not for nothing that we say the young are cruel. The old are cruel too sometimes, cruel in their madness and their desperation to live; but the young are cruel naturally, like trees that grow and crowd out their brothers. They cause pain because they don't understand, because they love themselves wholeheartedly. They have not yet developed the self-contempt that poisons all our enjoyment, the wisdom that comprehends our own weaknesses. And when you first begin to gain that wisdom, then you'll look back on your youth, and you'll see all the pain you have caused. But," and he smiled, "those who die young are spared that. So you are both fortunate."

After that there was little to say. Anne and I traded glances and we saw the wariness and fear that the old man had inspired in both of us. For the first time I realized that Anne was warm and human. I felt a surge of friendliness toward her. "Anne, I'm sorry," I said. "I'll be your friend from now to the end, I swear."

"I'm sorry, too," she said. "I had no right to judge you. I'm just a fool, I suppose. A dupe." She shook her head bitterly.

"Don't say that," said Moses Moses kindly. "It's no sin to be young. It happens to all of us once." He smiled at me. "Sometimes twice!"

We heard splashing and turned to see a large school of fish swimming toward us, leaping above the water. They were skipperjacks, foot-long, yellow-backed, elegant fish. As they drew nearer we saw that they were a whole shoal; dozens leapt above the water, but there were hundreds, perhaps thousands, swimming beneath the surface in gleaming phalanxes.

"Will they hurt us?" Anne said. "What shall we do?"

"No, they won't hurt us," I said. "They're only skipperjacks. I guess they're migrating."

"They look to me like they're running from something," Moses Moses said. They were coming from the north. The current was drawing us in that direction.

"Here they come!" I said. In moments they were all around us. One of them leapt by and rattled my hair as I ducked. I felt their fins and scaly sides brush slickly against my bare legs. Anne shrieked. They were making no special effort to avoid us, and their fishy intimacies made us laugh in embarrassed half-revulsion. In half a minute it was over; they were gone.

"I wonder what that was all about?" Anne said.

"I don't know, but they've provided lunch," said Moses equably. He held up a large skipperjack which he had somehow snagged with his bare hands. It was still struggling weakly.

"Ugh," said Anne. "Do you expect us to eat raw fish? Take my share. I'd rather go hungry."

"How will we gut it?" I said. "We've got no blades."

"And the blood may attract rays," Anne said practically. "Maybe you should let the poor thing go."

"Let it go?" said Moses indignantly. I could see that he had slipped back into his shell, and I was glad to see it; his frankness had deeply disturbed me. "After the trouble it took me to catch it! I'm thirsty, aren't you? This sea water is far too briny to drink, but the juice from this fish would be—"

"Holy death, look at that!" I shouted. Something was approaching us from the north. It was deep under the water, twenty or thirty feet down, at the limit of clarity. But it was huge. It was hard to tell its exact size because of the distance, but it was at least fifty feet across, I would swear to that. The cameras back me up on this. They show that it was an oblong, black oval, and there is a suggestion that it undulated slowly. We drew up our feet in silent terror. It seemed to take forever to pass under us. When it was gone we felt the chill of an icy upgush of deep water.

Half a minute passed before we dared to speak. "What *was* that?" Anne said. Moses and I shook our heads; it was impossible to tell, and the placid seas of Reverie hold many secrets. "I lost my fish," Moses said sadly.

The afternoon passed slowly. We grew bored. Moses Moses had not slept much, so we stuck the back of his head into the crotch of the air-float and let him sleep as we floated on our backs. I kicked off my shoes, but I still kept my nunchuck; I couldn't bear to part with it. Besides, its explosive charge offered a quick, clean death if the rays were tardy.

After Moses had slept, Anne slept; then it was my turn. It was not very restful. I never liked to sleep on my back and the gentle swell of the water was not soothing. I was forced to sneeze brine several times and when I finally gave up the attempt to sleep I was crotchety and miserable. My wounds were beginning to ache again, and it was not wise to take smuff on an empty stomach.

By the time the sun went down we were in terrible shape. All three of us were sunburned, especially on our faces. Anne's was worst. If she lived, she would lose all the skin on her face. Her eyes were swollen and her lips were chapped. We were all horribly thirsty. Anne and I had washed out our mouths with the bitter sea water, though we hadn't dared to drink it, following Moses' warning. Even so, it had made our thirst worse. Anne's hair was a mess; even the feather ornament in her hair looked drab and soaked. My plastic hair had crusted up considerably with brine.

After sundown I put my combat jacket back on and reset my cameras. I even reattached the electrical charge to my hair, but the sea water had shorted it out. Luckily the camera controls were rugged. They were designed to resist heavy impact and soaking with blood, so the water hadn't damaged them.

"I wish it were over with," Anne said at last, as the first stars showed after a magnificent sunset. "Why are we going on? Is there any chance of rescue at all? Ocean liners? Airplanes that might spot us?"

"No, of course not," I said. "I know this area well; I used to sail out here when I lived off the Tethys Reef with Professor Crossbow. This is wilderness. I suppose there's a chance in a million that someone's pleasure yacht might spot us, but certainly not at night. The only other things that come out here are camera drones. We might stumble over one of them, but they're pretty rare, and who would want to tape the middle of the ocean? There are aquatic drones, but they stay underwater. And their range is limited. They can only see as far as their lights can reach."

"Well, why haven't the rays gotten us?" Anne said fretfully.

"How should I know?" I said petulantly. "Maybe they're just not very fond of human flesh. It probably tastes funny. We're alien to this planet. You know. Biochemically."

"I can't understand why the first rays didn't get us," Moses said.

"Armitrage was full of smuff," I said bitterly. "Maybe it poisoned them. 'The Effect of Smuff on Rays.' That sounds like one of Professor Crossbow's experiments."

Hours passed. A flying island blew up over the continent. None of us talked; our mouths were too parched.

At midnight it was my turn to blow up the float again. When I put my head underwater, I heard the incredible: a dull, resonant boom from deep below.

I surfaced and said, "Listen. Did you hear that? Put your ears underwater."

We all heard it. Loud booming, like the taut skin of a drum. "What could it be?" Anne asked wearily. None of us knew. "Fish, maybe," croaked Moses. "Some kind of sonar."

It meant nothing to us, but the fish knew better. We heard flopping and splashing all around us as fish fled in panic. It was too dark to see them. The booming grew louder and more urgent; we could hear it faintly even with our ears above the water. Several times we felt backwash as big animals swam past us. "The water's getting warmer!" Anne said. She was too tired to resist her fright; we were all on edge.

"Look!" Moses said hoarsely. "Look down into the water; do you see it?"

We all saw it; a scattering of dim phosphorescence, deep beneath us; it was impossible to tell how far. It seemed to be murky nodes or lumps scattered across the back of some huge animal.

"Is that the ocean floor?" Anne asked. "Is the water that shallow here?"

"It's too big to be an animal," Moses said. "It looks like some kind of web. See how the glowing spots spread out. Are they moving?"

"No," I said. "We're moving." We heard another series of mellow booms. "They're coming from those spots of light," Anne said.

"I think I'll swim down for a closer look," I said.

Anne said, "No, Kid! What if it's dangerous?" Moses and I both laughed hollowly; it made no difference, of course.

"Here, Mr. Chairman; hold my weapon, if you please." I handed him my nunchuck and began to hyperventilate. I reset my cameras. When I had taken a dozen deep breaths I felt the peculiar effects of excess oxygen in dizziness and tingling fingers. I half-emptied my lungs, doubled over to dive down headfirst and began swimming strongly. My ears popped; I held my nose and blew to equalize the pressure. My ears shrieked. At twenty feet I lost my buoyancy as the pressure compressed my lungs; I began sinking slowly, then more rapidly. Quickly, I cupped both hands over my brows and blew out a little air, to form a shallow air pocket over my eyes. The phosphorescent spots leapt into sharp focus; they were below me, about a dozen feet. I could see now that the glowing green blobs were spots on a tense web or skein of some dim, filmy material. The structure, or whatever it was, was huge. Even the spots looked five or six feet across, and there were dozens of them. Bubbles escaped from my fingers and sea water stung my eyes. The water was strangely warm and my lungs felt crushed. I struck out for the surface. It was a lot farther away than I had thought, but I made it anyway. I had to call out for Anne and Moses and follow their voices in the darkness.

"Well, what was it? What did you see?" she asked eagerly.

I shook my head. "I don't know. It looks like some kind of titanic jellyfish. It was odd—as I got closer the water seemed to get a little warmer. I could feel currents moving over it. I only saw a piece of it. I got the impression that it covers whole acres. An incredible area."

"Is it some kind of undersea mountain, then? A guyot, or something?"

"No, it looked like skin," I said. There came another rush of booms, the loudest yet. A stream of immense dirty bubbles that smelled like muck burst through the dark water around us.

"God, is it breathing?" Anne shouted. "It smells awful!" The booms merged into a crescendo. We could hear bubbles geysering up all around us. We seemed to hear a sort of strumming and straining and rumbling, half-muffled by water. We looked into the sea. The phosphorescent spots were moving in unison, shifting back and forth in a sort of straining undulation, and of a sudden they seemed to break free and began to float up toward us with a slow, horrible purposefulness.

"Here it comes!" Moses shouted. "Swim for it!"

"Stop!" I said. "It's too big for us, it's all around us!" And it was true. The bulk of the thing was unbelievable. We grabbed one another's arms and waited for the end.

We drew up our feet in panic but it came to get us anyway. We all cried out at once when the hot fabric touched us; and then it was lifting us up. We sprawled out on the hot webby surface like beached whales, and our pitiful little float collapsed like a burst bladder. We heard the thing below us popping and snapping and making sounds like damp sails flapping full of wind as it carried us up, and up, and up into the dark Reverid night. By that time we had stopped screaming and were merely clinging to the taut pale seaweed membrane with hands and feet. We had risen at least a thousand feet above the sea when a breeze blew up. Slowly, the immense bulk beneath us began to drift to the west, with the wind. Then we realized what had happened.

We were beached on a flying island.

10

We could see our surroundings fairly well, because of the yellow-green glow from the round patches of phosphorescence on the island's skin. The island's titanic flotation bag was made of hundreds of cells of thin, taut skin, clustered tightly together like a compressed froth of bubbles or the pips of a mulberry. Each of the dozens of outer gas-cells had its own broad, glowing node.

The three of us had slid half-into the dimpled margin between two large gas cells. The seaweed membrane of the cells was very taut and still slick with sea water; it was difficult to hold. We were not quite at the apex of the great dredge-balloon, but we were in no danger of sliding off. In fact, for the moment we were in no danger at all. The relief was incredible.

"It's a flying island," I heard Moses mutter. "A flying island," and I heard him dig his blunt fingers into the skin with a wet squeak, as if he couldn't trust the evidence of his senses.

"Yes," I said hoarsely. "We're safe! We're up in the air and we're safe!" A great wash of release from tension swept through me. My spirits rose up like the island itself and I burst into hysterical laughter. My throat was so dry and sore, though, that I heard a weak, wretched cackling that alarmed me.

"Oh, it's real water!" I heard Anne say in a voice of rapture. "Look, water oozing out!"

Moses and I both immediately scrambled to the spot with pitiful haste. It was true. A wet, sappy-tasting, brownish moisture was oozing up from the juncture of the membranes of two gas-cells. All three of us stuck our faces into it and lapped and sucked it up with a complete lack of dignity. There wasn't much of it. We had to run our noses along the trough, slurping vigorously, for several feet to get enough to fill our mouths. But it was wonderful.

After a minute or so I had soothed my tortured throat with the vented sap and I stood up. My legs wouldn't support me. After several efforts I managed to stand, and I felt the taut, hot skin of the balloon dimpling under my feet. I took a few springy steps and reached one of the glowing, phosphorescent spots.

The glowing node in the center of the cell was about six feet across. The gas-cell itself was roughly hexagonal and about twenty or twenty-five feet across. I prodded the glowing spot with the handle of my nunchuck. It broke through a thin crust and came up glittering with yellow-green paste. There was a sharp chemical reek and a slight sensation of heat when I held it up to my face. I showed it to one of my cameras and then wiped it off on the pale white cell-skin.

Standing up, I could get a rough estimate of the island's size. I could see a horizon all around me, about three hundred yards away in every direction. There were hundreds upon hundreds of glowing disks, one in every cell. It reminded me strongly of some of the round, multicellular organisms I had seen in Professor Crossbow's microscopes—"volvoids," he had called them. They had floated as serenely in their drops of water as this dredge balloon did in its ocean of air.

Moses Moses and Saint Anne were still worming their way across the juncture of membranes with their heads down and their haunches up. It would be hard to conceive of a posture less fitting for the Founder of the Corporation, or for a saint. I made sure that I caught both of them with my cameras.

"We're safe," I said. "And I've got it all on tape." My knees grew weak and I collapsed with a springy rebound onto my back, then slid slowly down to the broad crevice between membranes. The hydrogen beneath me was deliciously warm. I spread out my arms in sybaritic ease, pillowed up by the thin skin over the hot, explosive gas. I pulled off my combat jacket and padded, sopping groin-brace. A warm breeze curled over my naked skin. I yawned, helplessly, looking at the stars. Instant Death had failed. Angeluce had failed. The Cabal had failed. My vengeance would be terrible. I slept the smug and peaceful sleep of hopeful, murderous ambition.

I awoke at dawn, after eight hours of chaotic dreaming. The air was cold and noticeably thinner, but the balloon was still warm. I sat up. I was thirsty and terribly hungry and my pounded muscles ached abominably. The incredible panorama of fleecy sea-clouds far below us distracted me, but only for a moment.

Moses Moses was sitting nearby. "I'm starving," I said. "What's for breakfast?"

He laughed hollowly and my growling stomach sank. "What do you think?" he said. "I tried a taste of the glowing paste in those phosphor dots. I should have known better. It burned my tongue. As for water, there's still a little sap left, but it's been drying out all night. The island is venting its ballast." He shrugged. "I explored a little last night. The balloon's about two thousand feet across. There's probably something edible down in the mud it's carrying. Starfish maybe. But how can we get to it? We can't cling to the membrane. We can't climb down. We'd slip, and it's a long way down to the sea. We're marooned on the top of this thing."

I shook my head impatiently. "What do we do, then? Sit here and starve to death?"

"Not so loud," he said. "Anne's asleep, poor girl. She's exhausted." He considered. "I've thought of one possibility. We could rupture some of the cells and try to break our way through the center of the balloon down to the bottom. However, if we don't blow up, we'll probably smother in the hydrogen, or get squashed between two expanding cells when we're in the balloon's center. It doesn't look good, Kid."

"What about the cell walls?" I said. "Have you tried eating them?"

"Too tough," he said. "It'd be like chewing cloth. I admit I haven't tried it yet. I'm afraid to rupture one of the cells for fear of a detonation."

"So what?" I said. "The thing's going to blow up eventually anyway; they're built to blow up so they can drop their mud on the continent. I'm willing to give it a try." I yawned and prodded experimentally at the cell-skin with the handle of my 'chuck. "Wish I had a knife."

Moses Moses looked speculatively at one of my cameras. "You might smash one of your cameras," he said. "We could probably batter some of the metal into a crude edge."

"Smash my cameras?" I yelled. "Forget it, doll! Over my smuffed-out body!"

Moses spread his hands apologetically. "Just a suggestion, Kid."

"Well, maybe if it was life and death." I looked up at my cameras with a protective frown. The very idea of breaking them unsettled me. I'd rather break an arm, any day.

"I'll give it a try with my nunchuck," I said. "Maybe you'd better stand well back."

"Wait!" Moses yelped. "Get those cameras out of the way first, for death's sake! They might ignite the gas!"

"No, they're airtight," I said. I stood up, grabbed both handles in a reverse grip, and fell to my knees, stabbing into the fabric with both swivel-heads. The skin dimpled. I pushed down with all my strength. Suddenly it ripped open and I fell through the opened slash. I dropped thirty feet to bound resiliently off an interior cell. Hot gas whooshed out. I coughed convulsively. "God, it stinks!" I said, my voice squeaking.

"It's not pure," I heard Moses shout. "Smells like something rotting! Are you all right, Kid?"

I had no time to answer. The walls of the other cells were bulging in toward me as the broken cell deflated. I dropped my 'chuck around my neck and with a scramble and lunge I managed to grab an edge of trailing skin. I pulled myself hand over hand toward the surface of the balloon again, pushing away at the encroaching walls with my bare feet.

After a few moments the other cells reached the limit of their expansion, and a pit ten feet deep was left where the first cell had burst. I heard shredding sounds as the sealed junctions between the surrounding membranes adjusted themselves. I pulled my legs up as the interior cell membranes rejoined stickily just beneath my feet. I was now at the bottom of the pit, but I could climb out easily enough once I gathered the strength. The hunger and thirst had badly weakened me.

Moses cautiously approached the edge of the pit. "So much for that idea," I said.

"Oh, it wasn't wasted," he said. "With this skin from the burst cell we can make a kind of shelter out of this pit. It'll keep us out of the sun, at least. Anne needs that badly. Come on out, Kid, and help me spread it out."

I climbed sluggishly out of the dimple and helped Moses stretch out a section of the ruptured skin to serve as a crude tent or cave. The lightweight stretched skin felt peculiarly damp and elastic in my fingers. "Nice place to starve," I said.

"Nonsense," said Moses. "If worse comes to worst, you can fire your gun into the bulk of the island. We'll die painlessly in a second or two. And we're not without hope. Birds may roost here. I'm very hungry. My word, do you realize how long it's been since I last had a meal?"

"The last things I ate were some moldy bars of chocolate," I said wistfully. My mouth watered uncontrollably at the thought.

"Let's go wake Anne," Moses said. "She'll sleep more comfortably in there. The sun is fierce at this height; less cloud, you know. If she doesn't get shade she'll blister."

We found Anne sprawled out at the dimpled junction of three cells. Her face was vivid red and her eyes were almost swollen shut.

Moses shook the scorched fingers of one of her outstretched hands. "Anne, wake up."

Anne forced her eyes open and frowned painfully. "I had the oddest dream,' she said. "I dreamed I heard something bouncing and thumping around beneath me. Inside the island."

"Oh?" Moses said. He looked down at the cell beneath his feet, but the white film was opaque.

"Kid! You're naked!" She averted her face.

"Get used to it," I said.

"He's right, Anne," Moses said. With an effort, he stripped off his one-piece underall and flung it aside. "The salt in our clothes will abrade our skins. You'd burn badly without your clothes, but the Kid and I have made a sort of shelter for you."

"I won't take off my clothes," she said with determination. "Not much water got inside, actually. I'm perfectly all right as I am." The dried brine in her saint's garb must have made it horribly scratchy and uncomfortable, but Anne's bizarre modesty had martyred her. Moses looked at her doubtfully, then said, "Well, at least have a look at our tent. The sun's already up. Doesn't it hurt your face?"

Still unwilling to look at our nudity, Anne hurried ahead of us, falling down once or twice but bounding back onto her white-slippered feet. She stopped at the pit.

"Oh! This is fine!" she said. "Look at all this extra film. Why, we can make clothes from it. Hoods. Umbrellas."

"Good trick without any tools," I said sourly. "Anyway, you won't get me to wear any of that stuff. I have a tan."

"Stop taunting her and let her go back to sleep," Moses said patiently. "Let's go to the top of the balloon, Kid. We'll get the best view there. I'd like to see it while it's still cool, and while I still have the strength to walk around." At this depressing note Moses and I struck out for the apex of the balloon. The phosphorescent spots on the flotation cells were still glowing, but the stronger sun had made them pale. It looked as if they would soon flicker out entirely and begin sucking up sunlight for another eighteen-hour night.

The view from the top was incredible. There was no breeze, for we were being borne along at the same speed as the tradewind. "We're at least a mile up," Moses said analytically.

"Look," I said. "You can see Telset through those clouds." I pointed and a twinge of pain ran up my battered arm.

We could see the Gulf far below us, faintly wrinkled with

waves, and a white, tenuous plateau of morning clouds over the water. Sunlight glittered off the sea to the east, blinding us. To the west, perhaps a hundred miles away, we could barely make out the dark smudge of the continental arm. "That's our destination," Moses said calmly. "I imagine we'll reach it in four days. Maybe five."

"Plenty of time left to die of thirst, then," I observed.

"It may rain on us," Moses said. "We're still rising, and we should go higher and higher as the sun heats the balloon. But we're still not as high as a thunderhead. They go all the way to the troposphere."

"I've heard of flying islands destroyed by storms before," I said.

"Maybe we can collect some dew on the extra fabric," he said.

We heard a peculiar popping sound from the cell beneath our feet and we hurriedly retreated from its surface. "We'd better not put all our weight on one spot," Moses said. "The balloon may be weaker in places."

"Look out, it's ripping open!" I shouted. Before our eyes, the very topmost cell broke open in a neat slash, five feet long. We lifted our arms to shield our faces and pinched our noses shut, but there was no outrush of smelly, unbreathable air. Instead, a shaggy blond head and a pair of narrow shoulders pushed their way out of the opened slash, and their owner climbed out onto the top of the cell, clumsily, like a beached dugong. I would have recognized that red, gill-clad neck and those sleek swimmer's muscles anywhere, even in a place as strange as this.

It was my oldest friend, my tutor, my mentor, my only parent. I called out in stunned amazement and incredulous delight. "Professor! Professor Crossbow!"

Crossbow started violently and scrambled back a couple of paces on its hands and knees. Its fingers were webbed. It squinted at us hesitantly and rubbed its bloodshot eyes with one long-fingered, webby fist. "How did you get here?" it said in a breathy, asthmatic voice. "How do you know my name?"

"Professor!" I chided it. "It's me, Arti! Don't you recognize me?"

"Arti?" it said. "My old ward, Arti? It *is* you, isn't it? But what have you done to your hair?"

I reached for my plasticized hair self-consciously but recovered at the last moment. Hearing the Professor's voice had stirred many long-buried memories. "For death's sake, Professor, never mind that now! What are you doing on this island? I can't believe I'm actually seeing you! How did you get here?"

Crossbow got to its feet uneasily, as if it had not done so for months or years. "*I've* been here all along," it said. "Why did you come to my island? How did you know where to find me? This place is miles from the house. I haven't even been to the house in ages!"

"Professor, I'm overjoyed to see you, but I wasn't looking for you, I swear! We were marooned here by accident! We were shipwrecked!"

Crossbow's almost hairless brows drew together and it looked at us querulously. "Arti, you wouldn't trick your old professor, would you?"

"It's true, Professor, really! Tell him, Mr. Chairman." I turned to Moses Moses, who had unobtrusively stepped behind me. He had half-pursed his bearded lips and I realized that his nudity embarrassed him. "Yes, it's quite true," Moses mumbled indistinctly. I understood his chagrin. He and I both looked like naked ragamuffins while Crossbow was quite spruce in an iridescent blue bodytight and slim, embroidered belt hung with pouches and waterproof metallic instruments. It looked well enough, but there were lines in its face that alarmed me. The neuter looked old and worn. Years had passed since its last age treatment. Some of its bushy blond hair was threaded with white and gray.

"Now, Arti," Crossbow said patiently. "You wouldn't persist in a practical joke, certainly? This means a great deal to me; it's my scientific work. You shouldn't have interfered unless it was absolutely necessary."

"Professor, please!" I said. "Can't you see that I'm stripped right down to my cameras? Can't you see our sunburns? Can't you hear our rumbling bellies? Good God, we're collapsing of hunger and thirst!"

"We're in desperate straits, sir," Moses said politely. "Your presence here is a godsend. We beg your assistance for ourselves and our companion. We had no intention of interfering, I assure you."

Crossbow looked flustered. "Well," it said. "I must take you to my study station, then. There's water there, a few medical supplies. . . . Of course I wasn't expecting visitors, the place is . . . well . . ."

"Oh, no need for apologies from you, sir," Moses said winningly. "We are entirely at fault. Let me fetch our companion and we'll go there at once; we're at your orders." He turned and raced away over the rounded, inflated landscape.

Crossbow folded its arms and ran its tongue along the inside of its left cheek. It was a typical gesture that brought back the eight-years-past as if it were yesterday. "Now Arti, we're alone now," it said with a martyr's patience. "You know I can always tell when you fib. Now what are you really doing here? And where are your clothes?"

I brushed its doubt away with an impatient gesture of my hand. "I told the truth, Professor."

It blinked once or twice. "Really? How can I believe that? What are you doing shipwrecked, anyway? And who are these people with you? Now confess, Arti. Are you sure this has nothing to do with the Academy? Nothing at all?" It looked at me keenly. "Perhaps not you, but your friends then. Have they never spoken of me? Never asked you to help them find me?"

"No, Professor, of course not. Believe me, I'm really astonished to find you here. We were sure that we were going to starve to death. And I haven't seen anything of you in eight years. Not a note. Not even a whisper." I looked up at it curiously. "Haven't you heard anything about me, Professor? Seen my pictures in the gossip tapes? Or my combat art? Or read my work in the journals?"

"I'm afraid I haven't had much leisure time for amusement tapes," Crossbow said.

"I'm pretty well known now, Professor. Famous even."

"That's fine, Arti. I'm glad for you."

"Maybe you've heard of me by the name 'Artificial Kid.' That mean anything to you?"

"I wish I could say it did," Crossbow said. "I haven't seen much of people lately, these last, well, six or seven years. I don't spend much time above the surface. Not much time at all. Just my reports to the Academy. My own tapes, you know . . . that's a nice set of cameras you have, by the way."

"Thanks, Professor. Luckily, I can afford the best."

"I'm afraid my new reports may have re-opened some old wounds. The Gestalt Dispute was never quite settled, you know. At least, not to my satisfaction. Or your father's."

"Really?" I said. "Well, I'm in a position to help you politically, again. I'm running in pretty exalted circles now. In fact, that naked man you saw is the . . ." I hesitated, not wanting to further strain my old tutor's credulity. "Well, I'll let him tell his own story. It's pretty incredible. But it's true." I looked at him earnestly. "It's no trick, Professor. I'm mature now. I'm beyond that sort of thing. I have my reputation to uphold."

"Then you no longer put crabs in people's beds? Or tie them down with seaweed while they sleep? Or make fake insects out of glue and thread and leftover wings and legs?"

I laughed with forced casualness. "No, Professor, I've changed a lot, seriously. I'm the Artificial Kid now. I have hundreds of fans. Thousands. I have my own house. I own four shares." I hesitated again. "Of course, the situation's changed a little recently. In fact it's changed a lot." I coughed drily. "Let me have a little water and I'll tell you all about it."

"Of course. But here come your friends. Introduce us, Arti, do."

"Of course, Professor. The lady in white is Saint Anne Twiceborn."

"The Anne Twiceborn?" Crossbow said. "Incredible! But it is! It is she!" He started to walk clumsily toward them, holding his arms out a little to balance himself in the unfamiliar medium of air. I was glad that he had spared me the trouble of introducing the Founder of the Corporation. It would have been too much.

I saw that Moses Moses had slipped painfully back into his one-piece.

"You're Anne Twiceborn," Crossbow said. "Do you remember me? We met once briefly many years ago. At a reception in Peitho."

Anne shook her head. "I'm sorry, I don't remember. But I've heard about you, Professor, of course. And I'm so glad you're here."

Crossbow smiled shyly. "This is the least expected pleasure in my long lifetime, I must say. And you, sir?"

"I'm travelling under the name of Amphine Whitcomb," Moses Moses said with bland caution. "I'm very glad to meet a person so well known in the field of learning. The pursuit of knowledge is the one truly preeminent human endeavor. As was once said, 'The pen is mightier than the sword.'"

All three of us looked at Moses, impressed. "The pen is mightier than the sword." It was the kind of blunt, pithy aphorism that had made his perception and wisdom famous on two planets.

Professor Crossbow looked pleased and flattered. "I thank you, sir. Let's waste no more time, but hurry to your rescue and sustenance. I can see that you are all fatigued." It looked at us kindly. The sight of Saint Anne seemed to have temporarily relieved its suspicions.

Anne was no longer wearing her saint's garb. Instead, using no other tools than her hands and teeth, she had ripped a kind of crude poncho out of the pale, striated balloon fabric. She had stuck her head through it and cinched it around the waist with a long, ragged belt. It should have looked ludicrous, but she wore it with a kind of brazen dignity that made me stifle my smiles. When she walked it unveiled her pale, unshaven legs almost to the knee.

"Come along this way and we'll slip through the airlock," Crossbow said, walking unsteadily to the very top of the balloon. "I believe that two of us can fit through at one time, if we squeeze. I'm trying to conserve air pressure. Mr. Whitcomb, will you accompany me?"

"A privilege," Moses said quickly. The two of them squirmed through the long slash in the top of the cell and into a small, fabric antechamber just beneath it. Crossbow reached out, accidentally jabbing Moses with his elbow, and pulled the long slash shut. It was zippered. He must have opened another zipper inside, for the flaccid fabric blew out tight with a snap. We heard thumping and bumping.

"So that's what it was," Anne said dreamily. "I heard that while I was asleep."

"I've got to get my camera controls," I said.

"Oh," she said. "Here they are, I brought them for you." She produced my combat jacket from beneath the voluminous folds of her poncho.

Surprised, I took it from her. "You needn't have done that for me. Thank you."

She smiled tentatively. "Why not? It's as easy for us to be friends as enemies, isn't it?"

"Of course it is," I agreed.

She persisted. "And it's as easy to please people as it is to hurt them."

"Now you're gilding the lily," I said. I turned off the cameras and they fell, bouncing off the pale stretched fabric and rolling and tumbling off for quite a distance. We chased them down and gathered all six of them up like ripe fruit. Then we unzipped the airlock and slithered into the little fabric cul-de-sac. I zipped it shut behind us.

Anne drew a deep breath. "It's rather nice in here," she said cheerfully. "Like a womb, almost."

"I wouldn't know, I've never been in one," I said. I unzipped the long slash in the tight fabric beneath us and air rushed in. It was quite breathable. I peeked out.

The industrious Crossbow had burst through all the central cells of the balloon, evacuated the hydrogen, and replaced it with fishy-smelling, slightly stale air. I had no idea how he had managed this while the balloon was growing underwater.

Crossbow and Moses were already thirty or forty yards down a long, swaying rope ladder. The top of the ladder was glued securely to a long section of fabric. Tightened ropes attached the ladder to connecting cells every thirty or forty feet, and kept the ladder from swaying too violently.

The ladder itself was slightly twisted, like a DNA chain. In several places down this long, long central chamber, there were safety membranes, also equipped with air locks, that blocked our descent temporarily. They were obviously there to prevent the whole chamber from evacuating at once in case of an accident. They also made good places to sprawl out, sweating, and rest.

I turned on my cameras as soon as Anne and I began our descent. Anne went first, as she insisted on it. After forty feet of descent the pain in my pounded muscles was simply too great and I took some smuff. Buzzing filled my head. After managing a few more rungs I lost my grip and fell with a scream, almost knocking Anne from the ladder and narrowly missing both Moses and Crossbow. I hit the first safety membrane, which bowed deeply under my impact and then snapped back, flinging me into the air again. After some smaller subsidiary bounces I got to my hands and knees and dry-retched. My cameras, floating along sedately, caught up with me about this time, and I hid my face in my arms so that I would appear to be merely stunned. I had fallen almost two hundred feet.

I reached into my drugpak and injected the last of my stimulant. Sea water had somehow seeped inside my combat jacket and ruined my tranquilizers and some really good, mild, social hallucinogens that I habitually carried. All I had left was my smuff, a little quikclot, a packet of skinseal, and some pellets of powdered nicotine that Chill Factor had given me over a year ago. The rest was a pasty mess. "Well, death sucks it dry," I said with bitter profanity.

By the time the others had climbed down to me, my teeth were chattering with stimulant. Nodding uncontrollably I assured them that I was all right and raced through the airlock and down the ladder ahead of them. I went through four more airlocks at a tremendous pace and through a final skein to the Professor's study chamber, where I collapsed on the fabric floor with my heart racing and pulsating black spots devouring my vision. I couldn't even sit up until the Professor arrived and gave me water. All three of us castaways drank with many a gasp for breath. We then took salt tablets and ate some leftover fish that the Professor had prepared in his little pressure cooker. The food took the sharp biting edge off the stimulant and I stopped trembling and was able to look around without seeing spots.

With truly Reverid ingenuity—for Crossbow had been cloned on Reverie—the Professor had adapted itself to its surroundings without damaging their peculiar charm.

The cells were smaller on the underside of the flying island and the little cell that held the Professor's living quarters was no more than fifteen feet across. It smelled strongly of fish and sea water. The walls were of triply-reinforced fabric, neatly sewn together, and the room was cooled by a small fan set in the floor with a conduit to the outside. It was much cooler in the room than it had been in the long passageway through the balloon.

The Professor had not been expecting visitors. Fish scales and bits of cast-aside edible kelp were everywhere. The walls were decorated with frightening photomicrographs blown up big as doors: the immense slavering jaws of sand fleas, the spiny threatening elbows of water beetles, the cruel, jagged feet of barnacles. Two of the Professor's favorite mobiles dangled from the fabric ceiling.

Another wall held a mounting board with a number of specimens preserved in little square blocks of transparent plastic. The rest of the small round room was crowded with the Professor's machines: a generator, a refrigerator, a pressure cooker, a compressor, a small sewage recycler, a distillery with a large water tank, a microscope, an old tape screen and its antique cameras. The machines sat on tough mats of woven seaweed that prevented them from ripping through the layers of fabric in the floor.

There were other miscellaneous items about. There were kitchen knives and a cutting block, the Professor's foot fins and speargun, a few books and journals, no more than a couple of dozen; his clothing, his hammock, and suspended from the ceiling, an incredibly intricate framework of hundreds of thousands of colored beads linked with wire, glistening in the mellow light from a number of small yellow bulbs. The bulbs looked like transparent fish bladders stuffed with phosphorescent plankton.

Moses Moses looked up at the torus-shaped wire sculpture, then looked around the disconnected tangles of beaded wire on the floor; some with hundreds of linked beads, others with as few as five or six.

"I've seen a structure like that once before," he said politely. "You'll pardon my asking, but is it an Elder Culture space sculpture, or perhaps a replica of one?"

"No, Mr. Whitcomb," said the Professor with an uneasy smile. "But it does resemble one, doesn't it? How perceptive of you to point that out. The similarity had occurred to me before. But I doubt if there was an influence."

"I thought perhaps you had tackled the old problem concerning their reason for existence," Moses said. Naturally, he had no way of knowing the Professor's involvement in this problem.

"What do you mean?" said Crossbow warily. "I thought that question had been explored long enough to sicken everyone."

"You're in luck, Professor," I said, hoping to cover Moses' slip. "You're in the presence of a man who has never heard of the Gestalt Dispute."

"Indeed," Crossbow said. It ran its tongue along the inside of its left cheek again. "I take it that you don't closely follow Academic controversies."

"Not recently, no."

Crossbow shrugged its muscular shoulders. "I won't burden you with it, then. I'm hardly a dispassionate witness, as has been pointed out many times."

"No need for modesty here, sir," said Moses alertly. "If you have a theory regarding those mysterious objects, I'd be delighted to hear it." He squeezed water into his mouth from the nozzle of a compressible bulb. We had all been drinking out of them. I think they were fish bladders.

Crossbow shrugged again with feigned indifference, but I could tell it was pleased.

"It's been generally accepted that these sculptures had a religious function," Professor Crossbow said. "Most Academic archaeologists declined to speculate any further, but I did, and I suffered for it." With a heavy sigh the old neuter seated itself on a square canvas pack on the bowed floor. With a start I realized that the pack was a parachute.

"My field of expertise is taxonomic microbiology, but I have a more than slight acquaintance with reductionist doctrine," Crossbow said. It slipped with ease into its lecturing attitude. "Reductionism has been the gospel of the Academy for many centuries. Essentially, this doctrine states that all mental and physical actions, no matter how grandiose or subtle, can be broken down into a set of simple chemical interactions. Thoughts, for instance, are electrochemical interchanges between groups of neurons, and nothing more. Life is a series of biological tropisms which can be reduced to the simple terms of physics. It is a very beautiful and elegant theory. It was the belief of our ancestors, so it is hallowed by custom; for centuries it was held by all men of learning. I believed it to be quite solidly established; as solid as, say, evolution, on which all thinking men agree. A doctrine which seems almost self-evident, even though our language still holds remnants from earlier beliefs."

Crossbow lodged its ankle on top of one knee and brushed adhering fish scales from the sole of its naked foot. "My researches here on Reverie, however, seemed to hint at a flaw in our theory. I found that flaw in the behavior of the Reverid ecosystem. It doesn't behave like other ecosystems elsewhere. For one thing, it is vastly older. Life has existed on this planet for almost eight billion years. Life has even outlasted the planet's era of geological activity. Continents here are artificially created—huge ring-shaped atolls. The sea long ago eroded away the original continents. All the dry land on Reverie is the work of organisms, like tower coral, mudcumbers, sea beavers, even flying islands, like this one." It thumped the fabric floor beneath it with one webby hand.

"I found it hard to account for this kind of behavior. Why didn't life simply adapt to oceanic conditions, and let the shallow sea cover all the land? Why this apparent altruism of marine organisms for those on land? What genetic purpose did it serve?

"I found these questions unanswerable, so I appealed to my superiors in the Academy for help in my research. I was called to one of the Academy's deep-space oneill clusters to testify. I presented my evidence and a research team was sent to verify my findings. They took their time, of course; there is no rushing true scientific research. In the meantime I began to search for possible alternatives to a strictly reductionist world-view and it was then that I discovered the doctrines of Gestalt.

"Gestalt means that there is a hidden force in wholeness. It means that the totality of the bits and pieces of a whole are greater than their mere sum. There is a mystic force in a whole system, there is something else lurking in that web of interactions, those chains of feedback. The greater the system's complexity, the greater its gestalt! Man is vastly complex, and that complexity makes itself known in the phenomenon we call consciousness. This element of self-awareness is something that has always troubled reductionists, but they have tried to sideslip its intuitive evidence. They have built artificial consciousnesses for machines, though we all know how that turned out." Anne shuddered delicately.

"They have even demonstrated that consciousness is tied to matter by altering the brain and showing that this causes altered mental states. This was done centuries ago, and that destroyed the old, old doctrine of mind-body dualism. But I never espoused that doctrine, and the idea of gestalt is entirely different! The idea of gestalt acknowledges the presence of matter in mind, the presence of those physical actions and interactions. The only supposition it makes is that we do not fully understand the nature of these apparently simple events. A reasonable supposition, one would think. A theory that at least deserved a good hearing. At least I thought so." It buried the tips of its webbed fingers in its unruly yellow hair.

There was a long silence. I got up, poured some water into a dead sponge, and began to sponge the crusted salt from my skin.

The Professor looked up suddenly. "Oh yes, you asked about

the bead sculptures. I saw my first sculpture there in the University, while I was giving my testimony. Its peculiar beauty entranced me; they had several of them, and data on a great many others. They are found occasionally, but only in deep space, always looking as perfect as they did the hour they were launched, so many millennia ago. That struck me immediately—their element of permanence. They were not meant to be on display. They were not meant to be found or seen. They were meant to be permanent, untouched by time. And they were obviously constructed with extreme care—the relationship of every bead to every bead was so sinuously perfect, the angles of the connecting wires were so incredibly exact. The entire sculpture was a system, and since it was a system it must contain gestalt. And since it was so carefully protected—meant to outlast even the Elder Culture itself—it must be something very precious.

"I arrived at the theory that it contained a soul. Probably the soul of the person who built it. I'm convinced that they still hold souls, the souls of members of the Elder Culture. I wouldn't claim that these sculptures are conscious, of course. They've been extensively monitored, even cut apart bit by bit, and there is no transfer of energy within the structure, at least none that our instruments can monitor. But they live. I could sense it somehow. I have no proof of this. It simply made sense to me. It was an elegant theory. It accounted for both the great amount of effort invested in the sculptures and the fact that they were abandoned in the quietest wastes of interstellar space. But I kept this theory to myself, having no firm evidence to back it. I only brought it out, as a theory, in the worst heat of the Gestalt Dispute, and only then because Rominuald Tanglin urged it strongly on me. He had his own theories concerning the Elder Culture and they meshed to a degree with mine. But only to a degree. I take no responsibility for his doctrines during his final delirium."

"I thought one of the criteria of a scientific theory involved its being tested empirically," Moses Moses said. "Did you try that, Professor?"

The Professor made a peculiar quick fiddling movement with

its fingers, a typical gesture that expressed its frustration. "How could I, when Gestalt could not be monitored or quantified? What is it, actually, that makes a system a system? Oh, I made tentative experiments, of course. There was my ten-year involvement with the Reverid slimemold. It is a creature that begins as a cluster or grouping of amoeboid protozoa and slowly develops into a crude salamander-like form with an interior skeleton and a circulatory system. Later the salamander develops a cancer-like fruiting body and bursts into millions of protozoa again. I attempted to find the lowest threshold of interconnections—to tabulate the relationships between the original amoeboid bits that triggered the rapid development of the salamander—the lowest possible number of webbed interactions that each contributed gestalt to the living system, you see?"

Anne and Moses looked at him blankly. Crossbow shook its head. "It's been such a long time since I tried to express it to laymen," it said. "My friend Tanglin was always much better at it. If he were here he could make you understand."

"I've seen the tapes he made during the Dispute," Anne said slowly, "but I must confess that they didn't mean very much to me. The worst of the Dispute was well before my time. I heard other Church members refer to it at times, not very flatteringly, I'm afraid."

Crossbow nodded. "Yes, churches of all kinds are usually opposed to the Academy on principle. They follow their own dogma too closely to concern themselves with the dispassionate search for truth."

Anne looked none too pleased at this and it was then that I first noted the peculiar rapport that had sprung up between Moses Moses and Professor Crossbow. Obviously Crossbow was in a wary, suspicious state, and its suspicion should have focused on Moses, the only one of the three of us whom Crossbow did not know. But this was not the case. I noticed that the two of them kept exchanging brief glances, little two-second moments of eye contact. It was as if they spoke some private code of the very old, some intense rapport beyond the youthful crudities of speech. I had never seen anything quite like it and it bothered me at once.

"I have some ointment for that sunburn of yours," Crossbow said to Anne. It got up from its seat on the parachute and popped open the lock on a small waterproof case made of wood and green plastic. There was a little compartmented case inside. Crossbow produced a transparent collapsible tube full of gooey white paste. "Shall I put it on for you?" asked the neuter politely. "It may burn a bit at first."

"Thank you, no," Anne said. She squeezed out a small blob of paste, sniffed it, and made a face. Then she began to spread it on her cheeks.

Crossbow, as usual, was generous to a fault. It provided Moses and me with new clothing, two pairs of blue bodytights. Anne refused to wear clothing that clung so tightly to the body, so Crossbow tolerantly gave her needle and thread so that she could stitch her own clothes out of balloon fabric. He then warmed up his pressure cooker and shared with us his hardy wilderness fare: steaks of deep-sea fish, plankton puree, minced kelp, and sweet seaweed gelatin.

The three of us ate ravenously, but Crossbow merely toyed with its chopsticks. Finally it spoke in a low voice, its words obviously directed to Moses Moses. "I would like to make an appeal to frankness."

"Do you think that's wise?" Moses said. Anne and I traded worried glances.

Crossbow lowered its head and mumbled almost incoherently, "Perils of personal dominance. The mask becomes the face. Sieges of panan. Too many steps back . . . do you follow me?"

"Yes, of course," Moses said with deep, tender sympathy. The words meant absolutely nothing to us and Anne and I were alarmed. It obviously meant something to the neuter, however, for it actually blushed. I had never seen it blush before and I had thought that it was impossible.

"It's been a long time," Crossbow said. "Very well, all masks off then. A pact between us. You agree? We'll seal hands then." Moses put down his platter and took the neuter's slim, webbed hands into his own.

They were silent, staring into one another's eyes. Anne put down her chopsticks and I stopped wolfing down the gelatin.

She shivered. I was frightened too. It seemed to have grown colder inside our snug little bubble. For a long moment we heard only the impersonal hum of the generator and the quiet breathing of the two old people. Their breathing seemed to be synchronized. They were going through something that we didn't understand, that we had never seen before. They were both so incredibly old. Anne and I couldn't help it. We were overcome by a sort of superstitious dread. I felt that there was some sort of tainted power at work; an old, cold, strong power that could eat us up like a viper eats young birds. Moses had dropped his facade again, just as he had when we were floating in the water, convinced that we would die. His face seemed to shine and there was a look in his round yellow eyes that terrified me. A glance at Anne showed that she felt the same way. I wanted to beg them to stop, but I was afraid to break their eerie concentration.

At last they released one another's hands and Anne and I both drew a sigh of relief. I was deeply glad that she had been with me to share that peculiar ordeal, and her look at me showed that she was also grateful. It had lasted only twenty seconds but it had drawn us much closer to one another. I wanted to embrace her and sit and breathe in the warmth of young, human contact, but I didn't, for Crossbow spoke.

"You are Moses Moses."

Moses nodded. "Yes, Crossbow. I slipped past death and ran for the light with destruction gnawing at my heels. And I lived. I have nothing beneath me but a shell, but I live. It rasps away inside me until I echo with hollowness, but it has never caught me."

Crossbow nodded. "Yes, we are members of the same brotherhood. You have seen how my old friend compromised with death." It nodded sharply at me. "I found an anchor. He thought he had found one too, but she destroyed him. And even now my enemies pull at me. They seek to tug me from the sea bottom just as this flying island tugged itself from its rooted moorings and floated up into the airy thinness of despair. But they won't succeed. You can help me."

Moses shook his head. "I haven't the strength. I haven't your conviction. Ask the young people. They have the vitality you need, not me. I haven't anything—I even envy you what you have. You've studied life. You understand it. You have meaning. I have nothing."

"There is a way, Moses."

"You're mad."

"No! Did you see madness within me? No. Think, Moses. It is awful, it is dreadful, as all things of great power contain an element of dread. But it can be ours. It is immortality. It may be tainted. Tainted with great age. But we are tainted. How could we live but with a tainted life?"

The terrible intensity of their rapport seemed to scorch us. Anne could not bear it any longer. "Stop! Please stop!" She folded her small hands over her sunburned ears, and shrank into a ball, drawing up her arms and legs.

Moses and Crossbow jerked up their heads, the thread of their rapport broken by her cry. In an instant their friendly, genial masks were back on; they seemed to drop over the two of them like flesh shrouds naked bone. They stopped leaning toward one another; they broke their eye contact. Moses reached down and picked up his platter. Crossbow stood up and smiled its old parental, protective smile at me. It seemed to drape it over me as if it were an old, warm blanket. It seemed intolerably artificial; I just stared.

"I still haven't told you what I'm doing on this island," said Crossbow brightly, leaping to a new subject with the agility of a mountain goat. "My presence here must have shocked you as much as yours shocked me!" It chuckled genially but without much conviction. Anne uncurled and moved closer to me; we sat together on the floor, touching hips and shoulders. I felt the warmth of her shoulder through the fabric we wore. Moses Moses was eating stoically and apparently ignoring the neuter, but I could sense him vibrating inside like the plucked strings of an autoharp. I slipped my fingers around Anne's naked wrist and the touch seemed to calm us both.

"I discovered this island in its bud stage three years ago," Crossbow said. "I found it on a tape while I was mapping the sea bottom near my house, with undersea drones. I had tracked the life cycle of the flying islands before, with drones and tracers, but I had always wanted to observe one personally and do a great deal of necessary detail work. I was able to estimate this island's eventual destination by calculating the trade winds and the paths of other islands; in fact, to be frank, I chose this island because of its destination."

"The Mass," Moses Moses said.

Crossbow nodded. "The Mass." It seemed pleased that Moses Moses had guessed correctly.

"But we can't go there," Anne said in alarm. "That's a horrible place."

"The Corporate terms of settlement are supposed to forbid human exploration," I said, trying to keep my voice neutral. I didn't disapprove; I merely wanted to point it out. "And the drone tapes I've seen of the Mass ... well ... they didn't look promising." In my mind's eye I saw the nightmare landscape of the Mass: sticky pools slimed with white muck, leafless trees furred inches deep in bright mold, crawling things bristling with damp ridges of shelf fungus, breathless stillness broken only by dripping ... a landscape not of death but of fervid, fetid life.

"I've been there before," Crossbow said. "I wasn't able to stay as long as I liked. But I had time to make a crucial discovery." It looked at Anne and me, then it shrugged and smiled shyly. "I might as well tell you; there's no call for false modesty, as my friend Tanglin used to say. It was this thing—this organism." It pointed with one slim webbed finger at the tangled wiring overhead. "This is a model of its molecular structure—a very limited one of course, though the torus shape seems to be well established. You'll notice the helical gaps within the structure; there are twenty-three of them, though why that number I can't say. Notice the peculiar arrangement here at these genomes; you can see that by faulting and folding this long double chain is moved shut almost like a trap door." The neuter stood up and began crimping and bending a section of wire with its thin but powerful fingers. Anne and I watched nonplussed as a long chain of linked beads moved up over a gap in the structure, like jaws closing. A section of fatigued wire popped with the strain and half-a-dozen beads of varying color spilled to the fabric floor and rolled off drunkenly under the generator, but Crossbow didn't seem to notice.

"See how it covers up that helical gap!" said Crossbow, filled with admiration. "It can trap an entire chain of genes in there—a whole half-helix. You probably wonder why it doesn't hold them there by chemical means—why it uses this mechanical arrangement instead. Well, it does use chemical linkage to a certain extent. Of course it has to have a chemical catalyst to trigger this crimping movement. But if it used a completely chemical linkage it would induce too many mutations. A half-chain of DNA is very volatile chemically, you know! There are all those open-ended linkages, just looking for adenine, thymosine, guanine, to complete itself and initiate a new being! It's like a little box, you see? A little torus-shaped box to hold life itself!" The neuter's face shone with a saintly radiance as it prodded eagerly at the tangled mess.

"I call it the Crossbow Body—that's the name the Academy gave it. I'm still uncertain whether or not it lives. It seems to be as much a construct as a being. I can't decide how it reproduces. I'm not sure that it does reproduce. It seems to be immortal, like an amoeba, barring accident of course, barring dissection.... And yet it can't be sterile—there must be some mode of reproduction, or perhaps reconstruction is a better word. And as for the problem of its origin—well, I'm convinced that it is natural. I'm convinced that it is the product of a Gestalt agency that is not intelligence—that is not consciousness—that is an attribute of a world-spanning gestalt that transcends intelligence as completely as intelligence itself transcends instinct. It is a teleology! It has a purpose that transcends determinism! It has slipped free of the iron chains of evolution! And it is evolution that demands death! It demands all death so that the old can give way to the new! But the Crossbow Body escapes death. The Crossbow Body destroys the motive for competition between species. It destroys competition between the old and the new."

Trembling with excitement, the old neuter sat down with a sigh on the single parachute. Then it looked at me with reproachful amusement. "Arti, you don't believe me! Don't worry. You'll see the truth soon enough."

I smiled falsely. Crossbow's speech had sounded very familiar, in form if not in content. It sounded very much like the senile ravings of my old patron, Mr. Money Manies. And a similar motivation had triggered it, I felt sure. Members of the Academy were no more immune from aging than were laymen. It sounded like poor Crossbow was cloaking its obsession with death in a thick blanket of pseudo-scientific patter. Its critical faculties had been distorted by the bright promise of personal immortality.

Obsessions with the molecular workings of life seemed to be in the air among the oldsters of Reverie. No doubt it was our peculiar zeitgeist.

"Have you already sent your findings to the Academy, Professor?" I asked.

Crossbow nodded eagerly. "Yes. Three years ago."

I nodded resignedly. "Well, that explains the presence of Professor Angeluce, then. It just struck me. Taxonomic microbiology—that was his specialty, too, wasn't it, Anne?"

"Yes, I remember," Anne said, nodding.

Crossbow shrieked and convulsively grabbed the sides of its head with both hands. "Angeluce! They didn't send him, certainly!"

"They certainly did," I said grimly. "And a most unpleasant little bugger he is, too. I've sworn to kill him. If I live through this, I will."

"Yes," Anne said musically. "He called you a 'neuter charlatan,' Professor. After that the Kid criminally assaulted him—didn't you, Kid?"

"How do you know?" I said testily. "You were unconscious at the time." It had struck me suddenly that Crossbow's mad meddlings had been the root cause of the disruption of my idyllic existence. If it hadn't stirred up the embers of the old Gestalt Dispute, Angeluce would never have come to Reverie. I would never have insulted him and thrown him off Money Manies' balcony. He would never have attacked me and poisoned the minds of the Cabal against me. Quade Altman would never have been mind-killed. The Instant Death would not have declared blood feud on me. Armitrage would not have died. Sulkily, I ate the rest of my gelatin, darting occasional black looks at my old tutor. I felt like beating it up, but it was my oldest friend, and my Old Dad's last and best friend. I restrained the impulse. As the last of the stimulant I had taken wore off, I somehow found it in my heart to forgive the old neuter. After all, it was our host, and it had meant no harm.

The news about Angeluce had devastated poor Crossbow. It sat with its head in its hands, groaning a little from time to time. Moses Moses helped himself to more fish. I had finished eating. I got out Crossbow's old tape screen.

"Here, Professor, I'd like to show you a few things," I said.

We spent the rest of the day examining my tapes and explaining our horrible difficulties. We cheered when Angeluce fell in the water; we sobbed unashamedly at Armitrage's death, which was his final tape appearance but undoubtedly the very best of his career. My spirits soared when I saw the quality of the recordings. They were the finest I had ever done.

It did me good to be working in tape again; it reaffirmed my self-image. Crossbow's equipment, however, was so old-fashioned that I hesitated to do any real editing. I had plenty of tape time left—six months' worth of thin metallic image ribbon, so I didn't erase anything. I spent several happy hours, however, cleaning and oiling my cameras.

We fell asleep at sunset after eighteen exhausting hours of wakefulness. I woke up at about two hours past midnight. I took some smuff, and when I got up for some water I noticed that Crossbow and Moses Moses were gone.

"Anne," I said. She threw off her thin fabric coverlet and sat up on the floor. She yawned. "What is it?"

"They're gone," I said, waving my hand at Crossbow's empty hammock. Crossbow had taken down some of its phosphorescent bulbs before we slept and there were peculiar multiple shadows in the little cell. My cameras resumed full activity as I touched the controls in my jacket. I put the jacket on and began to lace it up; I had already sponged the brine off of it.

"Yes," she said sleepily. "I saw them creeping out through a hole in the floor a while ago. They woke me up. Didn't you feel the wind?"

I shook my head. I always slept deeply when I was wounded; my body knew best. I was healing very rapidly, thanks to the actions of my follicle mites, which had struggled on manfully despite sunburn and prolonged soaking in sea water. The wounds that had required stitches were gummily sealed up and the big splotches of rainbow-colored bruises were turning paler.

I looked at the floor and noticed a thin zipper in the heavy fabric. It was another airlock, still damp inside with sea water. The new ventilation hole in the floor of the cell had been cut very recently, after the flying island had risen up from the Gulf; the old zippered airlock had been Crossbow's entryway into the balloon while it was still underwater. I opened up both sides of the lock and a heavy draft of wind swept through the cell. I turned off the ventilation fan, but not before a small cloud of dried fish scales, bits of seaweed, and fragments of beaded wire modelling had been swept out through the old airlock.

I slid onto my stomach and looked down through the hole in the loose flapping fabric of the airlock. It was dark outside. There was a short rope ladder, no more than twenty feet long, leading down into the darkness. Below it was an expanse of rich, black, smelly bottom mud, laced together with roots and cables—the island's payload. Seventeen thousand tons of it, the Professor had said. A forest of thick cables attached it in hundreds of places to the fabric of the balloon, distributing the strain of the immense burden. It was slowly drying out, at a rate that offset the loss of lift as hydrogen slowly seeped out of the balloon.

"Hey, look, it's the island itself!" I said. "Let's go down and see what the bag dragged up."

"Here, take one of the bulbs," Anne said, handing me one. "You go ahead, I'll come down in a moment." I attached the sticky side of the bulb to the fabric of my bodytight, at the sleeve. Then I went down the ladder, grinning secretly. Poor Anne, she was so embarrassed at her own natural functions that she couldn't bear to perform them with me in the room.

I climbed hand over hand down the ladder, carefully, for I

was a little dizzy with smuff. A crumbly, dried crust, interlaced with fibrous white roots, had formed in the sun-baked mud. It was thick enough to bear my weight, and I soon grew used to the pungent smell.

The Professor had told us that these seventeen thousand tons of rich black mud were grasped by roots into the shape of an inverted cone, roughly round and deepest in the center where it followed the island's tap root. The expanse of mud was about sixty feet across, and at its thickest it was eighteen or twenty feet deep. The entire mass had been wrenched up from the sea bottom, leaving a wide crater in the silent, black deeps now far behind us. Some of the island's volume was made up of the porous network of roots, but the rest was rich, prime mud, stolen by erosion and now returned, with interest.

I crouched down to examine the mud, digging into it gingerly with the end of my 'chuck. The white rootlets were incredibly tough. Trapped beneath their tendrils were tons of chipped shell, yellowed fish bone, and greasy mud half-turned to squashy slate. I dug up a long, ragged, broken ray's tooth and knocked the mud from it; it was as long as the width of my hand.

There were a few bottom animals scattered about, too weak, slow, or stupid to escape the island as it began its ascent: sea stars, thick, gut-colored bottom worms with armored heads, some tiny skates, some big-eyed flounders puffed up to bursting. I kicked one of the flounders over and a host of tiny crabs the color of roots ran out from under it, their minuscule pincers rich with rotting flesh. I wondered how the little scavengers expected to survive the detonation. Perhaps they would simply leap off the island once they had eaten their fill.

A few paces later I stepped into the mouth of something's burrow and almost tripped. I don't know what made the burrow but it hissed in annoyance as I skipped away.

It was Reverie herself at work. Even in this temporary ecosystem, life was stuffing itself into every available niche.

I saw Anne come rapidly down the ladder, her white garments floating out around her like a nimbus as she descended. She had given up wearing her saint's garb because we couldn't spare the water to wash its coarse fabric. She stepped daintily off the end of the ladder, her feet scarcely denting the crusted mud. She had a phosphorescent bulb attached to each shoulder.

"Oh, it's like a fairyland," she said, looking around wide-eyed.

"This filthy wasteland?" I almost said, but I bit back the words. Looking around, I made a conscious effort to see it through her eyes. I became aware of its peculiar beauty. It was the light that had done it; the pale yellow light of our bulbs, the wan greenish lights from the phosphorescent spots dotting the cells of the balloon, the weak bluish glow from clustered stars around the horizon. The jackstraw verticals of the hundreds of supporting cables gave the scene an eerie unreality, and if it weren't for the smell of the mud, you would swear that it was a mosaic—it was a broken jigsaw of shrunken plates of crumbly mud, linked by roots, touched with phosphorescent green amid the shadowed black of its interstices.

"It's pretty," I said. "I wonder where the Professor and Moses are."

Anne looked at me anxiously. "Kid, do you really want to see them? I'd rather be alone. With you."

I was touched. "Really? I thought you hated me."

She shook her head. "No, Kid, of course not. But Moses and Professor Crossbow are acting so strangely, and we're stuck here alone with them."

I smiled cynically. "You want me to protect you, then, is that it? How could I? If they wanted to kill us all, all they'd have to do is touch one little flame to that hydrogen up there and we'd all be tumbling lumps of charcoal." I enjoyed the look of horror that appeared on her face after this sadistic bit of teasing. "We'd be helpless. How could I possibly stop them?" Anne looked so unhappy that I repented.

"Oh, Anne, don't be so soft-headed. Crossbow's a gentle soul. When that precious hero of yours, Tanglin, was betrayed by all around him and sunk neck-deep in madness, Crossbow was the last friend he had. Crossbow was the person he chose to trust right up to death and through to the other side. Crossbow was the person he chose to raise him, to tutor him, to be his parent. No need to be afraid of it or of Moses either. They're old people. You have to allow them their quirks. They allow us ours."

"Kid, Tanglin was a great man. You should respect him. After all, you were him once."

"No. Never."

"You say that, but I see it differently. Now that I know, I can see the resemblance. You don't talk like him, but the way you walk, the way you . . . well . . . move your eyebrows, move your hands. I can tell. It's very strange. I think you're the strangest man I've ever met."

I shook my head. "Anne, you're so innocent! You're so full of silly delusions! When will you give up this dumb fixation about Tanglin? Do you think you were the only woman in his life? For death's sake, he had hundreds of followers like you. He charmed them. He made a science of it. It wasn't respect that made him treat you the way he did. When he first saw you he summed you up in fifteen seconds. Then he did whatever was necessary to make you obey him."

"That's cruel, Kid. And it's not true."

"Isn't it, though? You weren't even a warm body to him. You were a tool, a statistic. He couldn't even find the time to seduce you. You should thank your God that Crestillomeem Tanglin kept him busy, or your precious chastity would be just a memory now."

At last she was angry. "I didn't expect a lecture on sex from you! What makes you the expert? Do you think I know nothing about it, just because I restrain myself? I've been approached by experts in seduction—by wealthy, powerful, handsome men, and women, who would have offered me anything to sin. You forget that I was famous—that my seduction would have made any man's reputation. I've seen the temptations and I've turned away from them, which is a great deal more than you can say."

The justice in her retort annoyed me. "I've seen the gamut too—don't forget I'm a Reverid, and Money Manies' friend! I stay cool and detached, like Crossbow, because it's easier that way—and because sex ruined me once. It destroyed Tanglin.

He trusted his lover, and she ripped his insides out. I've learned by his mistake. It's just a complication. It's a lure I'd rather avoid."

"We're in agreement there, then," Anne said. She looked at me speculatively. "I like you for your frankness, Kid. I'd much rather hear that than the guile of some seducer, some deceiver. I've never had any patience with such people. They are uncaring. They cause pain and humiliation and exult in it. The best any such person can offer is a few moments of sterile pleasure that only detract from discipline and good works."

She looked at me again to see how I was taking it. I nodded a little, thoughtfully. She soon warmed to her topic.

"Our Church has a very common-sensical attitude, I think. They accept the role of sex in marriage, and the role of marriage in life. We marry only once. That is why we insist on a long betrothal period—ten years at least. If my cause had been successful . . ." Reflexively, she touched the feathers in her hair, lightly, as if she were touching a bruise. ". . . I might be betrothed now. I've always meant to marry and have children, so that I could continue the lineage of the Catechist. Now that duty falls to my cousins. I had other duties . . . too many other duties. Now that I live on Reverie, marriage is out of the question."

"You're still alive," I said.

"Yes, but I could never bring up a child in Telset. The moral atmosphere is too corrupt. A child is a sacred responsibility. It's no light decision, to create a life. And I am severed from the chain of descent. My child would be born outside the Church." She paused. "If I had this planet all to myself, just myself and the child's father, then things would be different." The fancy seemed to please her; she smiled. "I believe in life. I want life to go on, the life that came to me through my mother and her mother and her mother in a long chain back to the beginning of Life itself. But I'm not alone on this planet. I'm only isolated. And Church members marry only once. What Reverid would spend his life with me? Better to forget such things and devote my life and strength to my moral duties. You're a Reverid, so I doubt if you understand. But what do you think of that, Kid?" She looked at me. "I'm surprised you're not laughing."

"No, of course I'm not, but it sounds very odd," I said. "But knowing you as I do now I think it's about what I expected." Her little speech had roused an odd feeling in me—a sort of fascination mixed with distaste. It sounded so earthy, so prime-val—especially that remark about the chain of descent to the beginning of time. I had a sudden quick-flash vision of Anne, apelike, filthy, covered in skins, suckling a naked brat at one discolored breast. I shook it off with a rattle of plastic hair.

Anne looked at me curiously. "So now I've told you," she said. "But what about you, Kid? What about your ideas for the future, your ambitions?"

I shrugged. "Hadn't thought of it. Besides, all plans are off now. Now I just want to survive long enough to bash the brains out of Angeluce and Instant Death."

"But didn't you have plans before all of this started? What were they? Tell me, I'm interested, really."

I considered. "Well," I said slowly, "I'm still young, and still top dog in my profession. I thought I'd fight a few years more, accumulate a few more shares of stock, and then get out of ac-tive combat art while I was still at my peak. I wouldn't wait for brain damage or spine damage to put me out of it. And I'd stay in trim so I'd never have to refuse an honest challenge. And I'd probably run with the Cogs every once in a while, for old times' sake." I looked at Anne. She seemed to be drinking in every word, so I went on with a little more enthusiasm.

"Then I'd like to have my own channel," I said. "I'd edit ev-erything that went on it, personally, so that it was really top-drawer stuff. Then I'd become a patron, and get myself a talent-ed group of proteges to do all the hard work—you know, like Money Manies does. I'd just do the fun stuff—a little light edit-ing here and there, a few art tapes. I've always wanted to work with video mandalas, for instance. Then I'd get a few more channels, build myself an industry. The sort of thing you can run on an income of twenty-five or thirty shares. That's as rich as I'd ever like to be, really; anything more would be ridiculous.

Oh, and I'd move out of the Decriminalized Zone, and build myself a fine villa on the shoreline somewhere, half-buried in the reef, like Crossbow's old house where I grew up. With a dock, and an airlock, and a big stand of Tower Coral. Then I'd get a nice household going, with lots of parties and celebrations, and lots of interesting people to call me their patron, and lots of good art going on—the kind of art that'll make a name for you. And everyone would toe the line, because they knew if they didn't their patron would beat them black and blue. And I wouldn't grow old, either; if I felt myself going batty I'd just kill myself at once and put an end to it. Clean. Efficient. Straight-from-the-shoulder. That's the kind of life I'd like to lead."

Anne looked at me doubtfully. "It sounds rather sterile."

"Yes. Right," I said enthusiastically. "Sterile."

Anne slowly nodded, then looked away absently as if she had lost all interest. "Let's explore the island and see if we can find the others."

"Fine," I said cheerfully. "Let's. I could use some breakfast." I walked along lightly at Anne's shoulder, content to let her lead while I looked for interesting bits and pieces of stuff from the sea bottom. I had picked up a few shells and was crumbling the mud from them when Anne stopped suddenly and I bumped into her. "Hey," I said, and then fell silent at the tableau before us.

Crossbow and Moses were sitting on a spread-out section of balloon fabric, in a small clearing where the long support cables were especially numerous. They were sitting in the dark. I didn't see any of the glowing bulbs they had taken with them. Crossbow probably knew the whole area by heart, anyway. They sat cross-legged, silent; their eyes were closed. Their hands were palm to palm—Crossbow's webby ones to Moses' hairy ones. It was dark and it was hard to tell, but there was a hypnotic rigidity to their arms and a certain compression about the interfaces of their hands that suggested that the flesh was blurring—that their hands were stickily adhering—that their palms had blobbed together somehow like two bacteria exchanging genes.

Anne backed up quickly, nearly trampling me, then turned and ran. I stayed a little longer, curious, making sure that my cameras got it all. The two of them didn't move, they hardly seemed to breathe. It was eerie. As I stood and watched, a feeling of sickly nausea welled up in me from some place deep in my being, like a cold upwash of murky water from the ocean's bottom. I left too.

The rope ladder was still swaying when I reached it; I found Anne back up in Crossbow's dwelling quarters. She was pale, but seemed to have reasserted her self-control.

"Look at these shells," I said.

She didn't spare them a glance. "Never mind the bravado," she said. "What were they doing?"

I shrugged. "Ask them. I never saw anything like it. You want something to eat? I'm going to fix something." I opened the refrigerator.

"Are you going to eat at a time like this? Aren't you worried?"

"Yes, I'm worried, but smuff gives me an appetite," I said patiently. "How about some of these prawns? They look really good."

I was bolting down hot prawns in tangy white sauce when Moses Moses and Professor Crossbow came up through the airlock.

"It's a lovely night," Crossbow offered.

I looked at Anne; she was tight-lipped. I decided I'd better talk for the both of us. "Yes, I noticed," I said. "Have you eaten? I cooked some prawns."

"You look worried, Anne," Moses said perceptively. I decided to take the plunge. "Yes," I said. "There's something unspoken between the four of us."

"Oh," said Crossbow. "You noticed the problem with the parachute." There was an uncomfortable silence.

"The parachute?" Anne said in a small voice.

"Yes, of course," Crossbow said bluffly. "Moses and I had a chance to talk it over this morning, and there is no cause for alarm. It's true that we have only one parachute. And it's true that we haven't the slightest idea how to make another one—

not one that would work, anyway. But if we begin work today, with luck, we can cut one of the flotation cells free and use it to float down to earth well ahead of the detonation."

"Yes," Moses chimed in. "The island will lose some lift, but probably not enough to make it explode prematurely. On the other hand, if we wait until the last moment, when the island has dried out and is primed to explode, then our meddling will almost certainly blow us all sky-high—or perhaps I should say ground-low." He smiled charmingly. Both of them looked quite hearty. Their palms were brick-red, but it could have been the effort of climbing the rope ladder that had done it. Not likely, though.

"Luckily I have some hunting harpoons, some knives, and some spare glue," Crossbow said. "Under my direction, we should be able to do the work with a minimum of risk. However, we'll have to start work at sunrise. We can sleep through the hottest part of the day and start work again in the evening."

"There's not much time to lose," Moses said. "As the balloon fabric dries out and ages in the sun, it becomes brittle and volatile. And the balloon will be over the Mass in four days, according to the Professor's calculations."

"Right," said Crossbow. "And we ought to have the flotation cell cut loose from the island before the phoenixes come to attack it. Hopefully the phoenixes will ignore a target as small as a single cell, and I suppose it's possible that there might not even be phoenixes around the Mass. But I would imagine that there are."

"What are phoenixes?" Anne said.

"They're just small birds, about the size of a sandpiper—very pretty birds too, all orange and vermilion. Not much is known about them; I'd meant to capture a few specimens on this trip. Each bird carries a number of tiny eggs within its body, and the eggs become fully fertile only when the parent bird's body is charred by intense heat. The eggs incubate in mud. These phoenixes fly very swiftly, and they have sharp beaks. They dive at the island, fold down their wings, and punch right through the balloon fabric. That alone might generate an explosion, but I suspect that they have some other method of produc-

174

ing flame—perhaps by striking sparks off certain rough scales on their legs. We should see a great many other birds in the next few days, too. I believe I've already seen a few nightkites circling the island—I glimpsed their silhouettes against the stars. And by morning there will be seabirds in to search for crabs and carrion and insects. Many of them will carry the seeds of certain symbiotic plants, which they will bury in the mud. Oh, it's all very complex, and should be completely fascinating."

And that was that. For some reason, Anne and I couldn't bring ourselves to challenge them over their odd behavior, perhaps from fear of provoking something worse. Dawn found us on the top of the balloon, bristling with knives and harpoons, shivering in the cold predawn air of the altitudes.

Crossbow was tramping around one particularly large cell. "Here, this one looks good," it said. "I won't guarantee that it will be an easy landing, but it should slow down the three of us considerably."

"The three of us?" Anne said. She hugged her elbows and shivered. Her pleasant, broad-cheeked, freckled face was peeling horribly, skin shredding off in thin, dirty, tenuous sheets.

"Yes," Crossbow said. "I think the Chairman should take the parachute, don't you?" Anne nodded at once, self-sacrificing to the point of masochism, and I was willing to go along.

"Let's start by scraping off this luminescent gel," Crossbow suggested. "It seems to generate heat as well as light, and it probably has something to do with the detonation."

Anne, Crossbow, and I went to our hands and knees and began to scrape the yellow-greenish crust away with the blunt backs of our kitchen knives. We wrinkled our noses at the sharp chemical reek of the glowing paste. Moses collected it in a broad scrap of fabric, then walked to our balloon horizon to fling it over the edge and down to the mist-shrouded sea a mile below.

We soaked down the fabric with a little of the precious fresh water from a fish-bladder squeeze-bulb. "I hope this helps," Crossbow said. "All right, now let's attach the tethers."

The tethers were long reins of knotted balloon fabric, braided for extra strength by our dexterous saint. We glued them to the fabric of the cell we had chosen, using the glue sparingly, as there wasn't much left. The free ends of the tethers were attached to nearby cells.

"We'll open small slashes in the neighboring cells," Crossbow said. "We'll let them deflate slowly, to minimize the risk, Then one of us will have to crawl down through a deflated cell and cut through the attachments to the interior cells. With luck, some of the fabric may peel away spontaneously when the other cells expand to take up the deflated space. If we pull on the tethers, we may be able to peel it loose without having to break all of the connecting cells. We'll have to break at least six, and that represents a lot of lift. If we begin to sink too drastically we may have to go down to the island's payload and try to lighten it by cutting cables and dumping off mud."

"That won't be easy," I objected. "Those connective roots have it all webbed together into one big lump."

"We'll just have to make the effort," the neuter said. It stroked its red, feathery gills, which hung limp and moist at its neck. "Let's put it this way, Arti. If I hit the water, I won't drown. But I can't vouch for the rest of you."

"Do you have any spare gills?" Anne asked hopefully.

"Yes, but I can't do the necessary surgery," said Crossbow with a smile. We all laughed. Poor Anne knew very little about amphibious life.

Shading his eyes, Moses pointed into the sunrise. "Look, kittiwakes." We all turned to look, squinting. A flock of kittiwakes were coming in; we could faintly hear their grating, high-pitched cries.

They circled the top of the balloon once, screeching. Their blade-like black wings and long, elegant scissor tails flashed in the yellow morning sunlight. "They've come to search the mud for carrion," Moses said.

I looked at him, surprised. He seemed to have adopted the Professor's detached, Academic tone. Crossbow, on the other hand, paid little attention to the birds but stood with its chin in its hand, vigorously contemplating the problem before it, quite the resolved person of action. It took one of the instruments from its embroidered belt, knelt, and punctured the skin of a neighboring cell. We smelled the escaping gas at once.

"We'll see how this one goes before we attempt the others," it said authoritatively. Moses, nodding, stepped tentatively off to one side.

The first deflation went well and Crossbow quickly punctured the skins of the other five surrounding cells. The cells were naturally spherical; it was only their close packing that had forced them to assume a hexagonal shape.

The central cell expanded with the loss of external pressure and slowly rose upward, tugging at the slackened skins of the flabby adjoining cells. We heard a long, muffled shredding sound as the force of its lift began to peel it free from the sticky, clinging skins of the other cells.

"Excellent!" Crossbow cried. "I believe it will rip free of the cells beneath it without our having to cut. Quickly, Arti, help me slash it free of these others."

Crossbow and I leapt onto the collapsing fabric of the other cells and began slashing for all we were worth. My section of the fabric ripped completely and once again I tumbled downward into the balloon. I bounced off the resilient interior cells, keeping the presence of mind not to puncture one accidentally with my knife. It smelled terrible. I held my breath and cut away wherever I detected a strain on the fabric.

Two of my cameras were caught under the shroud, and my foot was trapped momentarily between the bulging edges of two expanding cells. I wrenched myself free, though, and had the satisfaction of seeing our savior cell rise up slowly from the body of the balloon, held only by shreds of white skin and our four tether lines.

I retrieved my cameras and, dancing adroitly so as not to get trapped again, I managed to scramble out of the deep, deflated pit. We heard muffled popping and peeling sounds all around us as the cells rearranged themselves beneath our feet. Anne and Moses were both knocked down.

Crossbow cut its way through a thin, flabby shroud and clambered out of the pit to join us. "There," it said. "That's fine. We'll leave what's left of the skin on it for now. When we cut the rest of the skin the cell will turn upside down, because we've attached the tethers to the top. Also. the remaining skin will help distribute the strain. I don't want to put too much of a strain on our glue bonds. I don't think it will rip free, but the tension might make the cell lose too much hydrogen."

"I thought I saw something slithering around in the bottom of the pit," Anne said.

Moses nodded. "Ah, yes. That would be the cell slugs. They live in the lining between cells. They eat sap. Isn't that so, Professor?"

Crossbow nodded briefly.

"I wish we could have caught a specimen," Moses said. I looked at Moses sharply. This was too much. The intonation was Crossbow's, syllable for syllable. Crossbow must have been aware of the mimicry, but it said nothing about it.

"Well, that's that," Crossbow said cheerily. "It went much more smoothly than I expected."

My ears popped. "Hey, we're descending," I said.

"Let's go back to our study," Crossbow said. "We'll go down to the island's payload. We can judge our rate of descent from there, and if necessary we'll cut a few cables and hope for the best."

Once again, we made the tiresome descent through the center of the balloon. The hundreds of rungs were a trial; they blistered Anne's hands, and I almost fell again.

We grouped together down on the crunchy, crusted mud. The morning sunbeams slanted in, cool under the balloon's immense bulk. Kittiwakes and shrikes were everywhere, perching on the cables, squabbling over the bodies of parched, bursting fish and filling the air with their cries. A few of them darted curiously over our heads, but most of them ignored us. Probably they had never before seen a human being.

Drifting with the tradewind, the balloon sank within fifteen hundred feet of the sea, low enough for us to see gentle swells chasing one another across its gilded surface. Then the heat of the sun inflated the balloon and it rose a little, up to perhaps two thousand feet. We drifted into a thin cloudbank, and dew began to collect on the island's support cables.

Moses Moses dropped to his knees and stared intently at the cracked mud. "Look at this mold growing," he said. Furry, greenish patches of some kind of mold were growing in the wet valleys between the cracked plates of mud. "Look," he said wonderingly. "This is life itself. This mold has seized the chance to live, if only for four days. Look how it accepts life, so completely, so gratefully. It has a great deal to teach us, if we will only deign to listen." He sighed. "When I look at this I feel that I have foolishly wasted my life. I've squandered so many years in pointless, useless strife, and all along, all these centuries, the secret has been here." He looked at us with tears in his eyes. "I want a chance to live again."

I looked at Crossbow. "Crossbow, this is your doing."

Crossbow shrugged. It had caught Moses' characteristic shrug perfectly; it was uncanny. "I need someone to complete my work," it said. "He needs someone to complete his. What could be more natural? By exchanging lives, we can revitalize one another."

"So that's what you intend to do?" asked Anne. "Trade lives?"

"We must," Moses said. "I can't go on the way I was, with madness nibbling at me day by day. And Crossbow's work is vital. I can lose myself in it."

"And I've given it the best years of my life," the neuter said bitterly. "But I've seen the truth I dedicated my life to, mocked by charlatans. I trusted the Academy. I trusted in the disinterested search for truth. I sincerely thought that they would want the truth revealed. I thought that they would rejoice in my discovery, just as I did. But I've been cheated by political maneuverings. The arrival of Angeluce has opened my eyes to their true motivations. I can't let him ruin my hopes as he did fifty years ago. And since he has the Cabal on his side, he has made them my enemy as well as Moses's. Death take him! I'll fight them all to my last drop of blood!" It clenched its thin, webby fists.

"Wait a minute, wait!" I shouted. "This is ridiculous! Listen to what you're saying! Moses, you can't do Crossbow's work. You've never been scientifically trained." I was furious. I shook my head, but my hair wouldn't stand up. For some quirky reason, that annoyed me even more than did their calmly stated madness. "You don't know a microscope from a micrometer. You don't know gram-positive from gram-negative!

"And as for you, Crossbow—my death, I never heard such idiocy! You? Politics?" My voice rose to a squeak. "What do you think you can do? What do you think will happen when we reach Telset? Do you think that the citizens are going to rush out, saying, 'Hurray, it's not Moses Moses, but it's the next best thing!'?" I grabbed his muscular arm. "Professor, you're a complete political nonentity! You haven't even been seen in seven years, and the Gestalt Dispute is completely forgotten! Do you think a wire model is going to topple the Cabal? We don't have a chance without the prestige of Moses Moses! He's the only rallying point we could possibly have! Good God, I don't know much about politics, but any child could tell you that much! You shouldn't need me to tell you this!" I lowered my voice. "Now, Professor, talk sense. Don't joke with us. It's easy to belittle Anne and me because we're young, but our lives are at stake. We're worried. Don't say such things, even in jest."

"I knew it was something suspicious even from the beginning," Anne said shrewishly, looking at the two of them through narrowed, puffy eyes. "Be serious. You can't just abdicate your responsibilities like this. None of us ever can. Mr. Chairman, this is your society whose future is at stake. You can squirm all you like, but it's your moral responsibility, and that's a fact. You can't just hide and get this—this person to rush out and lead all three of us to our deaths. You saw the kind of hoodlums that were pursuing us. What chance would we have against them, without you to help us? Are we supposed to live under the tyranny of the Cabal forever, as hunted fugitives? You know they'll kill us, just because we once saw you!"

"They might even turn it around," I said. "They might say we kidnapped you, took you from the island, and killed you ourselves. Without you there to prove otherwise, we haven't a chance. Now, be sensible. You can study biology anytime. The Professor can give you lessons. And Professor, you can study politics. You could help us by defaming Angeluce, and giving us a chance to kill him legally—if I can wait that long, which I doubt. Doesn't that make sense? Isn't that what you planned?"

"Frankly, no," said Moses. "My work here is too important to be interrupted by a political squabble. Politics is ephemeral. I'm dealing with eternal truths." He got up and brushed mud from the knees of his bodytight.

"And you underestimate me," Crossbow said loftily. "Even fifty years ago I gave them the fight of their lives, and I know better now. With the intuition of Moses Moses to help me, I'll turn the lot of them inside out. I'll make them wish they'd never been born. Besides, they'll be looking for Moses Moses. They won't expect me. When we get back to Telset, I'll burrow from within like a deadly parasite. I'll find Angeluce and destroy him. He couldn't escape me if he hid at the bottom of the ocean."

"That's the spirit," Moses said, but with the detached coolness of a spectator rather than the fervid warmth of a participant. "I'll drop the three of you off at the shoreline. You can make your way south along the coast until you are west of Telset, then float across the Gulf by boat. You're both accomplished sailors. You could manage the Gulf even in a homemade craft. I can lend you the tools. They'll be abandoned when the island detonates, anyway."

"And what will you do then?" I demanded angrily. "You'll parachute alone into the wilderness, right?"

"Right. But with Crossbow's insight to guide me, I'll be able to survive quite handily. After all, that's what it intended to do in the first place, right, Professor?"

"Yes, certainly."

"How do you expect to have Crossbow's insight when Crossbow is miles away, with us?" Anne demanded scornfully. Her answer was identical smiles from the two of them, smiles that chilled us both.

"When the transference is complete," said Crossbow bleakly, "I intend to adopt the name of Crossbow Moses. The Chairman will rejoice in the name of Moses Crossbow. Thus our internal exchange will be perfectly mirrored externally, as is only right."

"But you can't do this," insisted Anne, close to tears. "It'll ruin everything."

Moses shrugged. "As you may have guessed," he said, "it's already too late."

11

The next four days were hell for Anne and me. Moses and Crossbow gave up all pretense of normal behavior. They spent every spare moment in their strange communion. They ignored us completely whenever possible; when we forced them to confront us, they faced us as blankly as men in a trance. They refused to answer our most earnest pleas, our begging, our frenzied denunciations.

I regarded their insane behavior as a betrayal of all our hopes. Anne and I pointed out their folly in terms that a three-year-old could understand, but no; they were rapt in one another. I was ready to beat them both up, and, if that failed, to tie them up and threaten to drop them off the island. But Anne dissuaded me, and it would have looked rather mean and paltry on tape. After all, the two of them were obviously in no condition to fight. They ate almost nothing. They slept little. They looked pasty-faced and anaemic and both of them were given to fits of inexplicable trembling. We heard the two of them mumbling in their sleep at times: bits and pieces of garbled stuff, recited most horribly in one another's voices.

We took to sleeping on different shifts. Anne and I stayed up far into the day after Moses and Crossbow announced their decision, holding long fruitless discussions on how to get them to reverse the process. I blamed Crossbow for it; I was sure that the actual transferral mechanism was Crossbow's invention. Its knowledge of the chemical basis of mental processes was vast. For instance, it had programmed Tanglin's memory eraser. I was sure that this mind-exchange was something much deeper than mutual hypnosis, or mutual suggestion. It had something to do with the mysterious Crossbow Body, I was certain. If the Body could capture chains of DNA, as Crossbow said, then why not RNA, which was the basis of memory? Crossbow must have found some way to activate the Body, to make it behave as Crossbow wished. And who was better qualified to do this than its discoverer?

It was a risky and unprecedented venture. Only the looming specters of their own deaths could have driven them to it. Moses and Crossbow were old and exhausted. They faced the worst challenges of their lives without the confidence and energy to meet them. But they were too proud, cunning, and stubborn to die. There was one chance left to regain their lost vigor, and that was in an amalgamation of personalities. Their new composite selves would see the world with fresher eyes, defeating the weary staleness of extreme old age.

It would mean a descent into madness, with no guarantee of success. But Crossbow and Moses insisted on taking that risk, not caring if they gambled away our futures as well.

Without speaking to them, without making any formal arrangement, the four of us separated. Crossbow and Moses took over the study room, except for the brief moments when Anne and I heated our meals, and that usually occurred while they slept. Anne and I moved down to the island's payload, where we could escape the intolerable burden of their presence.

In two days, life had swept over the island like wildfire. It was a brief, ephemeral life, frantic and delicate. Perhaps most remarkable were the mosses and molds. Most of them must have been carried by airborne spores, but at least a few of them were borne in on the feet of birds; Anne and I found the muddy tracks of three-toed shrikes filled up within hours by bright orange fur. By the evening of the second day, a carpet of green mold covered the mud, giving the illusion of grass without its substance. It burst into powder under our feet. Curly red mosses appeared in clumps on the thickest support cables, and tiny bluish-white mushrooms sprouted in profusion, spreading out day by day into wider and wider fairy rings, like atolls. They too were tenuous; they crumbled at a touch.

Insects arrived in profusion, starting with a plague of tiny, lace-winged midges. For a few hours on the third day they were everywhere, "like snow," Anne said; by sunset they had vanished without a trace. There were a number of larger flies as well, and a large population of small, round, iridescent beetles, no larger than the nails of my little fingers. There were a few dragonflies, too, of the large, ocean-going size, big as forearms; and once I saw a small mantis, though how it reached that dizzy height on its filmy little wings I'll never know.

On the evening of the third day Anne discovered a series of damp footmarks in the dried mud. It was some large, four-footed animal; the marks of its blunt flippers were spread as wide as my hand. The tracks led to the edge of the island. They did not return.

Just before dawn on the fourth day, Crossbow Moses, as it was now calling itself, came to wake us. It did so by the simple expedient of shaking the cables on which Anne and I had strung our hammocks. I sat up and turned on my cameras. I looked at it bleakly. "So," I said sourly. "Back in the land of the living, are we?"

"No need for pointless recriminations, Kid," said the neuter tolerantly, its voice a distorted echo of Moses Moses's. It had never called me Kid before. It was then, bleary-eyed with sleep, feeling faintly sick, that I realized that my old tutor was dead. "What's done is done," it said. It had slipped past death, but at a price. Its old self had been destroyed; the old, muscular body was now animated by a strange, conglomerate personality. It looked weak, but whole, as if it had recovered from a long illness.

"Listen," it said. "Do you hear the roar of the breakers?"

I listened. I heard the murmur, far beneath us, carrying me back in memory to the beach at Telset. "Yes," I said. I hopped out of my hammock. Anne sat up, rubbing her eyes.

"Are we going to do the jump?" I said. "Is everything ready?"

"It's ready, but a new contingency has come up," said Crossbow Moses. "There's a heavy cloud layer lying low over the shoreline. We can't jump blind. We might land in coral. The surf would catch us and dash us to ribbons against it."

"Then what happens now?" Anne asked.

"We'll be borne inland," Crossbow said. "We might as well go up to the top of the balloon. If we see a momentary break in the cloud cover, we should go for it. Moses Crossbow did a star sighting an hour ago—we'll soon be over the eastern fringe of the Mass."

"Maybe the morning sun will burn off the clouds," Anne said hopefully.

"Maybe," Crossbow said.

Following the neuter, we climbed up the rope ladder into the study chamber. Moses Crossbow was there, twiddling bits of beaded wire in his blunt fingers and studying the convoluted, glistening web of the Body before him. The little room had been carefully swept and put into meticulous order. It was as if a demon of energy and neatness had invaded the room. Even Moses Crossbow himself looked unusually polished and trimmed. He was wearing an embroidered belt hung with instruments, his bodytight had been brushed until it shone, and he had trimmed his beard. Even his round yellow eyes had an unnatural twinkle; they were filled with a sprightly, ingenuous alertness that made me feel rather sick. One of Crossbow's books lay half-open near at hand; its spine showed a forty- or fifty-letter title that was all hexa-dexa-chloro-silico's. Moses had been reading it.

"Look at this, my dear fellow," said Moses Crossbow. Twisting a small chain of a dozen beads, he slipped it adroitly into a small space in the web of the Crossbow Body. "There, you see?" he said. "It was inverted, levo rather than dextro! Now it fits perfectly. The data is confirmed!"

"Why, how marvelous," said Crossbow Moses, but its voice had a polite congratulatory tone rather than a genuine interest. "Be sure to fit that into the micronotes—you know where to find them. The three of us will make ready for the descent; with any luck, we'll be gone indefinitely."

"Well, I wish you luck," said Moses Crossbow, leaping with nervous grace to his feet. "I'd come along to see you off, but you well understand that time presses. I haven't had much time during the transfer for note-taking, and my ecological records are in a frightful state. I must see to the Petri dishes; there are a number of molds that will expire at any time; specimens must be taken. And I've neglected my taping sessions. I'll be very busy; delightfully busy, every moment."

"This is farewell, then," said Anne. "We'll see you no more. You'll be alone."

"Oh, not alone, my dear," said Moses Crossbow distractedly, picking a bit of lint from one sleeve. "I'll be surrounded by life, you see. The whole planet hums with life. I will contribute my own small note to that vast orchestra." Suddenly he embraced her and gave her a light social kiss on her peeling forehead.

"Goodbye." He shook my hand, then embraced me as well; I could feel a light, tense trembling in his thick arms. He seemed to be keyed up to fever pitch. "Goodbye, my dear Kid," he said. "No doubt I will see the two of you again; you are destined for fame, and if you deign to visit a humble professor, I will be very happy to see you. Goodbye, Mr. Chairman."

"I won't fail you, Professor," the neuter said, an iron resolution stiffening its beardless jaw.

Moses Crossbow nodded. He folded his arms and ran his tongue along the inside of his left cheek. "Be so good as to put on these packs I've made," he said. "I've doublestitched the seams, but if they fail to hold I've put extra needle and thread in your own pack, Mr. Chairman."

"Thank you, Professor, you are thoughtful as always," said Crossbow Moses. It shrugged a heavy pack made of thick green plastic onto its muscular swimmer's shoulders. Anne and I struggled into smaller packs made of white island fabric. They were heavy. "What's in this thing?" I asked peevishly.

"Provisions. Supplies." said the neuter. "I've packed everything."

"Then I guess there's nothing left for us, but to leave," I said. I looked at the person who had once been Moses Moses. "Mr. Chairman," I began.

"Professor, please," said Moses with a polite smile.

I shrugged irritably. "Professor, then. I'm not sure why you did this, but I do have a parting word of advice, if you're willing to listen. Don't let anyone find you. Don't use the name Moses or the name Crossbow. Both will be your death warrant, if I know the Cabal. Change your name. Change your face. Hide for as long as you can."

"Oh, my intentions exactly," said Moses Crossbow, nodding blandly. "Don't think I've forgotten the rules of strategy. I'm not so rash as to confront our enemy directly, you can be sure of that. I'll disguise myself. And mind you follow your own advice, Arti, for your own transformation will soon be upon you."

With this last cryptic announcement, the ex-Founder of the Corporation turned away, dismissing us from his attention. Crossbow Moses leapt vigorously for the bottom of the rope ladder and we began the long, exhausting climb up through the bulk of the balloon. Anne used the sleeves of her fabric poncho to protect her blistered hands. My arms ached horribly, but I waited until we reached the top of the island before I took any smuff.

As we collapsed, panting, on the bulging cells, it dawned. The rim of Reverie's butter-yellow sun appeared on the horizon and we heard, faintly, screams of delight from the hundreds of birds resting amid the mud and cables of the payload below.

Crossbow Moses was the first to sit up. "We must have a look at the cloud cover below us," it said energetically. "I'll have to peek over the edge of the balloon. The two of you will have to serve as my anchor, once I have this rope tied around me." It slipped off its pack and pulled out a length of braided ceramic fiber. It tied the rope tightly but comfortably around its waist and we set off for the edge of the balloon.

When the curvature grew steep Anne and I braced ourselves in the crevice between two cells and began to pay out line to the neuter, who continued descending. I sent a camera after it.

"We're definitely inland!" we heard it cry out faintly. "At least two miles!" This surprised me. Since we moved with the wind, it was hard to estimate our speed without seeing the ground. There was no sensation of movement at all.

"How are the clouds?" I yelled at the top of my voice. Anne, sitting next to me, winced. "Terrible!" it answered. "We can't possibly go through this. Perhaps they'll get thinner overland." There was a long silence. Anne and I wondered aloud how fast we were moving. We made ourselves comfortable and paid out more line. An hour passed. Finally we called out again.

There was no answer. "Pull me up!" we heard it call at last. We did so; it came scrambling toward us as soon as it could get to its feet.

"Hurry!" it shouted. "Phoenixes!"

Anne and I leapt to our feet. "What shall we do?" she said. "The Chairman. . . ."

"There's no time for that," the neuter snapped. It was quite the brusque, hard-headed commander; my gentle old tutor was truly dead. "We've got to get to the mooring cables and cut free our descent cell. The whole island could detonate at any time!"

"But we can't just abandon him to die!" Anne insisted.

"Don't be a fool," snapped Crossbow Moses. "It'll take twenty minutes to get down the ladder; we'll all burn. He should be out on the payload by now; he can recognize a phoenix if he sees one. We've got to jump now, despite the clouds. We've gone miles inland, anyway."

Anne hesitated, then made up her mind. "You go," she said firmly. "I'll go to warn him." She set off at a run for the top of the balloon.

Crossbow Moses and I ran after her. When we reached the moored descent cell, it gestured unmistakeably with one hand. "Kid!"

I ran Anne down and hit her in the back of the head. Then I dragged her unconscious body to the mooring cables. "Good work, Kid," it said. "Make her fast to the cable with the hooks you'll find in the straps of the pack." Following its example as it attached itself, I did so. "Now take this knife and cut her free."

I did that, too. The single-cell balloon rose a little, Anne dangling free and swaying like a pendulum.

"Now attach yourself. Hurry! When I give the word, we'll sever our lines together!" With our frantic haste, it was the work of a minute.

"Go!" said Crossbow Moses. We slashed through the last mooring lines. For a moment we rose into the air, then, with agonizing slowness, we dropped down again to the surface of the balloon. Crossbow, who weighed most, was the first to touch down. It scrambled along daintily on the ends of its slippered toes, frantically trying to get us over the edge of the balloon. Wriggling desperately, I was just able to help.

"Hurry, hurry," gasped Crossbow. The cell's lift deprived us of the traction we needed to get up speed. We went through all kinds of panicked antics, which my cameras caught to embarrassing perfection. At least ten minutes passed before we reached the edge of the balloon. Anne began to come to just before we reached the steep, circular edge, but it took her a few minutes to gather her wits.

"You hit me again," she accused me groggily.

"It's too late to sacrifice yourself, so shut up and help us," I wheezed. Crossbow and I kicked away at the edge of the balloon for all we were worth, trying to push ourselves away from it. The curvature was such that we would kick away, descend a little ways, kick again, descend some more, and gain perhaps ten feet each time. It seemed to take forever, and all this time we were being borne relentlessly inland. At last we drifted down past the balloon's equator, and from then on we were free of it. However, we were still close enough to be engulfed in the fireball if the island went up.

"Look!" Crossbow screeched. Anne and I both flinched in terror as a bullet-like flash of red zipped past us, banking just at the edge of the island and careening off at astonishing speed. Flocks of seabirds burst up like fireworks from the island, diving toward the clouds below in noisy panic flight.

We also screamed a warning to the ex-Founder as we drifted past the bottom of the island, but we didn't see him anywhere. For the first time we saw the bottom of the payload, a titanic mud-black mass of tangled roots and dripping slime. Immense toadstools as big as beds had sprouted on its undersurface.

We continued to descend in a leisurely way, drifting farther from the island as we descended into a slightly slower wind. There was still no explosion. Minutes passed. Still nothing. We fell into a bank of clouds that shrouded us in white tenuous dampness. It was then that the explosion came, a flash that lit the cottony dimness followed by a deafening roar and a hot shock wave that half-flattened our little balloon and jerked us like puppets on strings. Our jaws dropped open as our whole bodies shuddered with the blast. We were too deaf to hear the squashy impact as the mud splattered to earth far below.

My ears rang as if I was stuffed with smuff. The two others were dim forms in the fog; I yelled at them, but could barely hear my own voice. My cameras, brushed aside by the rush of hot wind, floated back to me. I thought of swinging over to Anne, but decided against it. The tension might rip my tether line.

We continued to descend. It was impossible to judge our speed inside the cloud; we barely seemed to move, though I had to swallow several times to depressurize my ringing ears.

Suddenly we began to fall faster. The balloon may have cooled, or a tiny rip may have opened it. After a few moments we dropped through the bottom of the cloud layer.

A dizzying spread of land was beneath our feet, white and brown and green to my painfully contracted eyes. The sunlight was bright with morning and the sea was nowhere in sight. We couldn't even see the splashdown point of the flying island.

We were moving quite rapidly with a brisk wind, I could see that now. The tops of jungle trees were moving in the warm breeze, sweeping past under our feet. They were two hundred feet below us, and they looked tall.

I heard an indistinct mumble; I turned to see Crossbow Moses shouting and pointing at the trees below us. It made grabbing and hugging motions with its slender, webbed hands. It wanted us to seize the branches of the trees when we were swept into the forest canopy. I nodded violently to show I understood.

There were no signs of clearings or landmarks beneath us. This was part of the Mass; I could tell by the peculiar white blotchiness on some of the trees. The usual continental forests were every shade of green, but never white. As far as I could tell from our dizzy descent, the trees were otherwise normal.

Crossbow Moses dangled down farthest among the three of us; its feet rattled through the thinnest top branches of a tree as we were swept over it. It grabbed at a branch but the leaves stripped off in its hand. We crashed solidly into the next one and grabbed branches. The balloon tugged mightily at us and ripped Anne free, but she caught another branch further down. Crossbow and I gripped our branches like demons. I still had Crossbow's knife; I could have cut myself free, but that would only have increased the strain on the others.

Suddenly a gust of warm wind drove the balloon down into the tree and we heard the fabric rip. The balloon went flaccid almost at once, but it did not explode, and we were grateful for that. The strain abated at once. Crossbow and I cut ourselves loose.

The immense tree whose branches we gripped seemed perfectly normal; the whiteness of the Mass did not show on it anywhere. Its bark was smooth and gray; its waxy green leaves were as broad as two hands set side by side. The leaves were tri-lobed and smelled faintly of cinnamon. Smelly pale sap showed where our impact had broken and twisted some of the smaller branches.

"Ants!" Crossbow yelled suddenly. I could barely hear him. "Ants! Climb down, climb down! They're all over me!"

Suddenly I too felt a tickling on my feet and exposed neck. Tiny black ants were pouring out of large wooden galls attached to some of the twigs. I saw them doubled up, biting my feet vigorously, but the pain was very slight. It felt a little like a stiff hairbrush laid lightly on the skin. The ferocity of their painless attack alarmed me, however, and I descended as rapidly as I could, burdened as I was with the heavy pack. I crushed some of the ants on my way down, but that was a mistake, for they smelled horrible.

I could see as I descended that the jungle was divided into

three distinct vertical layers; a sunny canopy, where we had landed, a denser middle layer, crowded with the green crowns of the shorter trees, and, far below, a dappled jungle floor.

With my agility I easily outdistanced Anne and Crossbow and dropped the last ten feet to the ground. Satisfied that I would no longer annoy their beloved tree, the ants flowed off me in dense black streams.

My hearing improved with every passing minute and I became aware of the Reverid jungle cacaphony. The entire aural spectrum was as crowded with sounds as the jungle was crowded with life. I had heard these sounds before in drone tapings, but it was different to stand there, to feel the faint cool breeze, smell the odors, feel the leaf-crowded black humus under my feet. Prominent among the sounds was a piercing, rather oily-sounding double creak, endlessly repeated; insects without a doubt. It was interrupted occasionally by a mellow booming like an iron drum half-filled with water, and by low, almost subsonic, rumbles, like slowly moving doors with rusty hinges. In the upper register I heard the whine of passing bugs, the querulous, lean-throated cries of treetop animals, the warble and cackle of birds. There were other sounds, too; rustling, dripping, scraping. And these were only the usual ones; sounds you heard so often that they immediately faded into the background. The unusual sounds: roars, cries of alarm, territorial signals perhaps—were remarkable for their elaborateness. Where another animal would have settled for a simple bellow, a sonic-conscious Reverid beast had to introduce some arpeggio, some arresting variation.

Anne and Crossbow joined me on the ground; Crossbow was sucking a small scratch on one of its webs. "Those ants are so strange!" Anne said. "Why didn't they sting?"

"Oh, they stung, all right," Crossbow said. "But their venom has no effect on our metabolism. If you look carefully you can see the bites, but they're not at all inflamed."

Anne brushed leaves from her loose, balloon-cloth garment. "It's delightfully cool down here," she said. "I thought jungles were supposed to be steamy and sticky."

"That may be true on other planets, but Reverie is always a

special case," Crossbow said. "This jungle is the product of advanced evolution, not tropical circumstances. Reverid photosynthesis is very efficient. Because it traps more of the sun's energy, plants here can support a much larger population than plants on other worlds. And a jungle is more stable ecologically than other environments, because there is room in it for a vast variety of species. The stability of an ecosystem depends on its diversity; that is an elementary law. This jungle is billions of years old."

Anne laughed gaily. "I had thought this would be a horrible place. But it's beautiful, like a park! Look at those majestic trees! Why, it's marvelous down here. I like this much better than the balloon."

"Don't depend on a snap judgment," Crossbow said. "We still have the Mass to deal with before we can reach the shore again."

"I'm starving," I said. "Let's have something to eat before we start our hike. Smuff gives me an appetite."

Crossbow Moses looked at me reproachfully. "Are you still taking that drug? Why, you're almost healed. Your bruises are practically gone."

"Those are just the ones that show," I said. "Anyway, I hate pain."

"Very well," Crossbow said. It shrugged off its pack. "But we'll have to make our provisions last. Otherwise we'll have to live off the land, and in the middle of the Mass that entails some risks. The venom of the ants didn't affect us, but there are things harmless to Reverid organisms that will kill us as dead as sea shells. At one time I knew most of these things, but now my memory.... And in the Mass it's often hard to tell, as you'll soon see."

It dug into its pack and drew out three tasty seaweed cakes, part of the stock of travelling food it had saved for itself. "We'll have to eat sparingly, so you get only one," it said, passing them out. "The island was provisioned for one, not four." We bit eagerly into the dense green cakes. We had hardly downed the first swallow when we were assaulted by a horde of bright yellow butterflies. "Holy Death, what are these things?" I demanded, for I had never seen a butterfly before. I swatted at them ineffectually. The smell of the food seemed to drive the insects wild; they kept alighting on my cake. Crossbow mumbled something that I didn't catch, for it had wisely stuffed the entire cake into its mouth. I did the same, but I had to spit out bitter butterfly bodies and lost a good chunk of my cake, which fell to the jungle floor followed by a swarm of insects. Crossbow guarded its mouth with both hands as it chewed and swallowed. Our heads and shoulders were covered with them.

More and more of them poured in from the depths of the jungle. We couldn't even see one another, especially as they insisted on settling on our eyelids, even on my cameras. I went into a wild capering dance, but they clung to me as if I were a tree trunk. Finally I danced my way out of the enveloping cloud of insects and swallowed what was left of my cake. Then I pried a wetly adhering butterfly wing from the roof of my mouth. Bugs followed the scent on my breath, so I breathed through my nose.

Once we had swallowed the cakes, we were able to escape most of them. But a large number stayed with us tenaciously, clustering on our heads and around the flaps of our packs, which held more of the cakes.

"These are butterflies. Harmless," said Crossbow through gritted teeth, brushing them away as they sought to cling to his lips. "You won't see them on Telset, but they're common here. Come on, let's run."

We eventually outdistanced most of the butterflies, though at least a dozen of them clung to the strands of my plasticized hair. We sat down to rest on the lumpy knees of a huge tree with thin, light-red bark.

"It's the scent of the sea that does it, I suppose," Crossbow said mournfully. "Normally, when they follow that scent, it leads them to the site of an island splashdown. From now on we can eat inside the tent, if need be. By the way, the tent is in your pack, Kid, so don't lose it."

A number of the small yellow butterflies were climbing doggedly about in Crossbow Moses' bushy blond hair. Others sat sedately like little jewels on Anne's smooth, blunt-cut brown hair and her feather barette. I laughed at the sight they made; Anne looked at me and laughed back.

"Your hair looks different now, Kid," she said. "It lies down flat now instead of standing up all prickly."

I brushed my hair self-consciously, dislodging a number of flutterers. "It's growing," I said. "It's not plastic down to the roots any more, and it's bending on a hinge of normal hair. I have to re-do it every week, when I take my hormone treatment." I paused. "*Uh-oh.*"

There was a weighty silence. Crossbow said, "You didn't take any treatment with you, Kid?"

"How could I?" I said. "I didn't plan this trip. I left with an escort of bullets."

There was a second weighty silence as each of us considered the implications of this peculiar predicament.

"Well," said Crossbow at last, "there's no help for it, then. You'll have to go through a forced adolescence. You're in for a strange experience, I'm afraid."

"But I've been on suppressants for almost thirty years now," I said. "Who knows what the effect on my body will be?"

"The effects will be serious, no doubt about that," Crossbow said. "But almost all young males go through the process, and without the calmness of maturity to help them endure it. You'll just have to manage with the inconvenience until we get back to civilization. I'm sure you can deal with it."

"I don't suppose I have any choice," I said morosely. I snatched a butterfly out of midair, reacting absently as it fluttered too close.

"Don't kill it!" Anne said. Surprised, I shrugged and let the butterfly go. She looked embarrassed. "Look at the bright side," she suggested tentatively. "Your voice will change. You'll probably grow a beard. And when you cut off that plastic coating from your hair, you'll be unrecognizable. Already your skin color has changed—you're darker, and it doesn't have the greenish tint it used to have from that oil you used. The cosmetics are gone from around your eyes. If it weren't for your chain weapon and your cameras, no one would possibly guess that you were the Artificial Kid."

"Holy death, a beard!" I said, clutching at my face. Was there already a trace of stubble under my panicked fingers? "Good God, my image will be ruined!" My voice climbed into its higher registers. "I'll be finished! Washed up! The Cabal has probably already revoked my shares, burned down my house—how will I get the money for new treatments? Death, that stuff's expensive, it costs as much as smuff! And—oh no, what's even worse—I'll look just like Tanglin!" Clutching my head, I reeled back, looking straight into one of my cameras and making sure that another got a good side shot. "Just like Old Dad! My best friends won't know me! Poor Quade will scream and run when she sees me! What a catastrophe! Is this the end of the Artificial Kid?" I hadn't thought of poor Quade in a long time—a tear trickled down my cheek.

Anne looked at me, upset. "Don't take it so hard, poor Arti! Your career's not so important, is it? After all, when we reach Telset, we'll still have to stay in hiding. You'll have to give up fighting anyway, give up your fame. You should be thankful that you have such a good disguise!"

She had upstaged me again. Amazed at her gall, I dropped my hands and looked at her nonplussed. She looked back at me innocently, surprised at my sudden change of mood. "Right, right," I muttered in disgust. "Belittle my difficulties. Never mind, I'll probably have to edit all this anyway—it would never do to be seen with these linking butterflies in my hair." I stood up, washing my hands of the whole business. "Come on, let's get a move on."

Crossbow Moses got to its feet. "We're faced with a choice now," it said. "We can try to detour around the Mass, or we can plunge directly through it. If we detour it will take us much longer—weeks, perhaps. Our provisions will soon be exhausted. We could try to live off the land, but we risk death by poison. If we were at the shore, I could feed the three of us indefinitely, but the forest is not my area of expertise."

"Let's get to the shore as soon as possible, then," I said.

Crossbow nodded. "Water would be our worst problem if we took the forest route. But the Mass has plenty of water. It is riddled with stagnant karst pools, of course, and I wouldn't advise drinking from those, but it has a number of streams and a major river. If we can reach the river our difficulties are over; we can reach the sea easily, just by walking down the riverbank."

"What about the molds and bacteria?" Anne said. "The chances of illness?"

"It's true that the Mass is especially rich in microfauna, but if we keep up a good pace our exposure will be brief," Crossbow said. "We'll have to depend on our bacterial ecosystems to protect us. Besides, the forest itself is rich in bacteria. Our chances of infection would actually be worse if we were weakened by short rations and a long trek."

I looked at it through narrowed eyes. "You're hiding something, Professor. Chairman, I mean. You want us to go through the Mass. Why?"

Crossbow looked innocent. "I know the Mass better than the forest. That's all. Besides, I'd like you to see the Crossbow Body at work. You patently doubt my theories. What better proof can I offer?"

I shook my head. "If the Mass is so harmless, why has it been off-limits all these years? Why is its reputation so foul? They call it 'a thousand square miles of disease.' "

"Academy propaganda," Crossbow said confidently. "The Mass has only one disease, and that's the Crossbow Body. And that's no disease, that's a benefit. Trust me, Arti. Have I ever deceived you?"

"No," I admitted. I turned to Anne. "What do you think?"

Anne tore her eyes away from a small yellow butterfly sitting, tamed, on her forefinger. "We haven't any other guide or expert," she said. "We'd better accept its advice." And so we did.

12

We adjusted our packs. The heavy clouds that had been above
us all day were descending through the upper reaches of the
forest canopy. A silvery mist began slowly drizzling around us,
not so much falling as drifting. We felt dazed and lost as we
meandered among the shadowy columns of immense trees. The
underbrush was not heavy, mostly shade-tolerant herbs and
ferns, heavy with dew, with occasional lacework bushes dotted
with flowers. Fallen tree trunks were our largest obstacles. The
process of rotting was fast and riotous, and the fallen trunks
were slippery with orange shelf-fungus, fat-bodied slug-like
slimemolds with wet skins as varicolored as oil slicks, heavy
green carpet mosses, ferns with entangling stems as tough as ceramic fiber, and blood-colored puffballs that ruptured at a
touch to fill the air with stinking, choking spores.

We detoured when we could to avoid the fallen forest giants,
but it was difficult. The hole left in the forest canopy spurred
the growth of lush bamboos that crawled with fat, furry sapsuckers and chitinous marmosets. Immense dragonflies flitted

past us, snapping up mosquitoes that Crossbow would not let us swat. "They don't give diseases," he said. "They inject vaccines. After all, it's in their best interest to keep us healthy, so that we'll have plenty of blood." Their bites left no welts.

Sometimes we left the ground to clamber over rough-barked lianas that webbed whole groves together, their saprophytic roots sunk deep into the wood. Twice I had to fight off hives of hairy spiders that had caught my cameras in their tough, dense nets.

At noon we slept, slinging our light, balloon-cloth hammocks from low branches. After three hours Anne and I were awakened by a loud rip and a crash as Crossbow fell to the forest floor.

Mildew was devouring our packs and hammocks, and Anne's dress. Crossbow gave her a bodytight that was much too large. We repacked what we could into the tough synthetic fabric of our tent and slept, cramped and miserable, in the crotches of trees.

When we awoke, we slung the tent from a long wooden pole that Anne and I carried over our shoulders.

We marched until sunset. The terrain, which had been gently sloping, grew more difficult. We began to find immense lumps of primordial limestone, like gigantic toadstools, thrusting their rounded heads up through the thick forest humus. They were thickly crusted with fossilized shells and bones, and were densely festooned with creepers, ferns, tough bushes, and small trees whose naked brown roots gripped the rock like stiff snakes.

When night fell the forest grew incredibly raucous. From above our tiny campsite under the shelter of a weathered, crumbling knoll came rich howls of glee and showers of dead twigs and excrement. Booms and metallic screeches that seemed to come from everywhere and nowhere added a stirring counterpoint. We choked down wads of seaweed cake that already had the first lingering aftertaste of rancidness. Phosphorescent globes as big as eyeballs meandered through the branches above us, glowing red and blue and green, sometimes casting reflected pinpoints of light from the eyes of treetop animals.

When something large came thudding and snuffling past us, I decided I had had enough. "Let's build a fire," I said. Anne nodded eagerly; Crossbow said nothing but handed me a small flashlight from its pack.

I advanced on a nearby bush. It retreated warily. With a shriek of terror I attacked the bush and it exploded into its component elements: long, brown, multi-limbed twigs fluttering, green-winged leaves, even feeble, tiny-legged flowers.

"Don't hurt them!" Crossbow called out. I retreated to the shelter of our limestone overhang, trembling a little. Crossbow was squatting on its haunches, a melancholy expression on its face; the long walk had been hard on its aquatic legs. "It might have unforeseen repercussions," it said. "Everything is connected to everything else."

I looked at the other bushes warily. "Are they all like that?"

Crossbow shrugged. "Some of them," it said. "Mimicry is very advanced here." With a sigh, it sat on a patch of moss and propped up its tired feet on a fallen limestone boulder. It began to rub its legs with its webbed hands. "Actually that particular adaptation was camouflage, not mimicry proper," it said.

After a more successful search, I returned to the fire with an armload of dry leaves, twigs, and branches that had been sheltered from the mist. Unfortunately we had no lighter—Crossbow hadn't had much use for one in its aquatic existence—but Anne explained to us the principle of the bow-drill. By chafing away at dry, rotten wood till our fingers blistered, Anne and I produced a few feeble sparks that we fanned to a flame. As the dry leaves ignited with a bright flaring we heard a startled snort from perhaps six feet away. A small, burly, bear-like animal got up on oddly-jointed legs and stalked off into the forest.

"And take your bug-trees with you!" I yelled after it, heaping branches onto the fire.

We took turns keeping watch, Anne first. Insects were attracted by the light from our fire, but did not fly into it; they were precision navigators. As night's darkness grew denser, we heard rustling in the branches, and small furry animals with the tired, wrinkled eyes of debauchees ambled up out of the darkness to look us over. Occasionally these animals, which Crossbow called "squirrels," would catch a moth and eat it, but with an abstracted, bored air that suggested that they were doing us a favor.

During my watch, the last one, the fire burned low again. To save effort I dragged in a large log and heaped it on the fire, and a horde of ants large as crickets poured out of the log. The warrior ants had long nozzles in their heads and they assaulted us with spurts of glue and formic acid, so that we were forced to retreat to the top of the limestone crag that sheltered us.

We dumped our provisions out of the tent and pegged it to the top of the crag. We slept uncomfortably, painfully gouged by hard limestone lumps under the tent floor. We awoke well before dawn and sat up in the darkness, stiff with boredom. When it finally dawned we found that most of our shiny objects, including our knives and hatchets, had been stolen during the night. We also found that our seaweed cakes were riddled with tiny weevils.

"Oh well, they add protein," said Crossbow nonchalantly, and he ate them. Anne and I forced ourselves to follow his example. They had a nutlike, slightly bitter flavor.

We marched on. As the terrain continued to descend, springs grew more frequent, but the going was much rougher. The chunks of limestone appeared more often; the trees declined in height, and we began to see increasing signs of the presence of the Mass. Green tree-leaves were splotched with faintly furred patches of white. Damp furred masses like thin white throw-rugs clung to the trunks of trees. The ground grew noticeably damper underfoot, and some of the trees showed heavy knees and buttresses for support in the wet soil.

We began to spot pools and sinkholes. With a sigh of relief, Crossbow flung itself into a wide pool, sank beneath the surface, and did not return for half an hour. Then it came back, its ribs convulsing as it choked out a lungful of water, exulting over the network of water-caves it had found beneath the surface. While I climbed a tree in search of dead branches for a fire, Crossbow paddled around the pond, catching aquatic game with its long, agile fingers. We built a fire in a natural depression in a limestone slab and had roast turtle and fish steamed in bladdered pondweed. It tasted marvelous in our famished mouths, and we napped for three hours in the afternoon while Crossbow snoozed comfortably at the pond's weedy margin. Mosquitoes bit us, and I swatted one whose hair-thin legs were suspiciously furred.

We had to force ourselves awake again, but we could not afford to waste the daylight hours. Violating our natural circadian rhythms, we staggered to our feet and plodded on as if dosed with depressants. I took a little smuff for the soreness in my legs. The wounds in my arms and torso were already almost healed, and the busy follicle mites were devouring the edible stitches still sunk in the pink new flesh.

The forest was giving way to swamp. The trees were shorter and broader in the base, with thicker bark, and we found larger and larger areas where the earth squelched messily under our tired feet. We had to skirt more sinkholes and broad marshes where the shimmering water was half-hidden under the thick leaves of fleshy aquatic plants. Many of the plants were white, and there were areas where different species of plants were gummed together by a surface froth of sticky Mass material. The forest canopy overhead grew thinner and thinner and finally disappeared altogether in places, leaving the afternoon sun shining almost blindingly off glittering expanses of shallow marshwater.

Crossbow dealt easily with the water in our path; it simply plunged in and swam, leaving us to wade along as best we could, our feet wrinkling up in our shoes like stewed fruit. Sometimes we sank neck deep and paddled after the neuter, clinging to the airtight tent for support.

Finally we discovered that the wet ground beneath us had degenerated into the "trembling earth" of a true marsh. There was no honest dirt in it. Instead, we walked bent-kneed on wadded mats of decaying vegetation, some of them rooted in squashy mud but others floating free, buoyed up by pockets of trapped gas from decomposition. Luckily there were still many firm islands that had collected around the roots of groves of mighty aquatic trees. We dried off at the islands when we could, eating sparingly of berries from thorny marsh vines, weaving mats to sit on from the green waxy stalks of pliant rushes. Blobs of wet white moss dangled from the tree branches. We found several trees that were almost devoured with fur, but they seemed healthy; the cranes and egrets of the marsh nested in them without fear, and even thatched their nests with bits of fuzz.

When night fell we camped on the largest island we could find. While I looked for firewood I killed three snakes with my nunchuck. Crossbow had throttled an immense snapping turtle; he assured us that the turtles were safe to eat, while some of the most innocuous-looking fish were full of subtle poisons. We picked pink leeches from Crossbow's back while it cleaned the turtle with a tiny dissection scalpel, the only knife we had left.

Day in the marsh had been full of the cries of birds, but with night they slept and the night was alive with ghastly roars from furry mammalian crocodiles. Glowing blobs of swamp gas drifted over the waters. A few yards from our campsite we heard something huge emerge from the water, splashing and washing. We sat quietly until we heard it blunder off into the trees.

"The marsh drains into a major river a few miles from this spot," said Crossbow cheerfully. Its long immersion in the water had done wonders for its morale. "By late tomorrow we'll be strolling down the river to the sea."

We ate the turtle and fell into an exhausted stupor, trusting to our large bonfire to keep predators away. We slept almost twelve hours and awoke about six hours before dawn. We whiled away the time curing what was left of the turtle meat in the smoke. Anne cut my hair with the scalpel, leaving me with close-cropped stubs of rattling plastic.

Just after dawn I climbed to the top of the largest tree on the island, hoping to get an overview that would help us avoid the worst of the swamp. From above, the swamp was a shattered mosaic of green sawgrass, dark peaty water, and white splotches of Mass material, pitted and threaded by sinkholes and canals. As my eyes followed a morning flock of white egrets, I saw something that shocked me. It was the glint of sunlight off the metallic sides of a pair of huge camera drones. There was no mistaking their silhouettes; they were blunt cylinders studded with audio pickups and trailing jointed manipulative arms.

They were big ones; ten feet long at least. They were less than a mile away, cruising in a purposeful way over the swamp.

I drew my own cameras in close, fearful lest it should spot them with a telephoto. After a moment my surprise and dread faded into curiosity. The drones glided noiselessly off to the west, and I relaxed. I climbed down the tree and told Anne and Crossbow about the drones. Anne was interested. "Are they common here?"

"Hardly," I said. "But drones are the only legal way to view the Mass. I wish I'd known who their operator was. It could mean plenty of trouble for us. The drones themselves may be harmless, but they could track us and inform on us. We'd better try to hide if we spot them again." I hesitated. "Good God, what would happen if they caught me with my hair like this?"

"What about your own cameras?" said Crossbow.

"You don't understand, Professor. Chairman, I mean. I can edit my own tapes. I mean, here I am—covered with mud—cropped to the scalp—dirt under the fingernails—an unsympathetic editor could make me look like a buffoon! It could damage me professionally! It'll take an editor of genius to present this fiasco as the soul-stirring adventure I mean it to be." I looked around quickly and reflexively, making sure that all my lenses were clean.

We bolted down some chewy turtle meat and started slogging through the swamp again. While Crossbow wallowed unashamedly in the brackish water, Anne and I tried to pick our way through the firmest spots. Sawgrass cut us. Leeches nibbled our legs. Fetterbushes stuck their hooks in our skin and clothing. Broken milkworts drenched us with sweet greenish sap. Frogs clung to our heads. Algae plugged our nostrils. Silver darters tickled us and waterbirds flew at our heads, squawking, when we neared their nests. Our progress was maddeningly slow. Crossbow encouraged us, lolling on its back in the water, offering us the amused, confident advice that one gives to people without one's natural advantages.

Finally, when our legs trembled with exhaustion and our clothes and hair were caked with mud and pondweed, we discovered that the land was rising. The ponds grew shallower and were easily waded. Dry-earth trees, whitely blighted with Mass fur, appeared again. We found dirt that would support our weight.

"We must have made a mistake," Crossbow said, dragging itself out of the water with a reluctant frown. "The terrain should be falling, not rising. The swamp is supposed to drain here. Water can't run uphill."

"Spare us, Professor," I said, and Anne said, "It's so lovely to be on dry land again. This is the right direction, isn't it? It'll get us to the sea, won't it?"

"I suppose so," said Crossbow, "but it's peculiar all the same." We started walking overland, gaining our second wind now that the long frustration of the swamp was over. We had gone perhaps a mile through a small forest ("Intermediate growth," sniffed Crossbow, "not full climax. Couldn't be more than two hundred years old.") when we heard a wind blowing and noticed the movement of the treetops. The trees stopped in a broken chaos of white limestone rocks, and when we clambered over the rocks we realized that we had come to the edge of a long escarpment.

In the plain below us festered the center of the Mass. It was almost solid white, and resembled nothing else alive. We saw a nightmare landscape, twisted, contorted, visibly gummy and sticky, filled with lumpy spirals, convolutions, writhings of thick flabby fibers yards across. There were towers in it that might once have been trees, but they were draped with mangled, twisted strips and straps of sticky Mass fibers, as broad as highways. Parts of it seemed to seethe visibly even as we watched, like cells undergoing mitosis. Other areas were as wrinkled as the surface of a brain.

Half a mile to the east the swamp drained out through a gap in the escarpment in a low waterfall. Mist shrouded the bottom of the fall, but we could see where the stream from the swamp met the sluggish river, and, miles to the east, we saw the glint of the sea.

"This escarpment is a fault line," Crossbow said. "Fairly recent, too; a matter of two or three centuries. This explains the peculiar geology of the swamp." It leaned out precariously to examine the escarpment wall.

"Do you expect us to march through *that*?" I said.

Crossbow pretended not to hear me. "Look at those slicken-sides," it mused. "And look at that dark cluster of cave openings in the escarpment wall. I think I can state what happened here. It was the immense weight of the Mass. It caused the underlying network of caves to collapse. This whole continent is riddled with caves, you know. Limestone dissolves very easily."

"Listen, I'm not trekking through that mess unless there's absolutely no other possibility," I said. "Just look at it! It's ghastly! It's moldy! It looks like Death's cesspool! Isn't there some way we can skirt around it?"

Crossbow looked at me patiently. "Do you want to go back through the swamp? Look, we can descend by the falls, and then follow the river quite easily. It will be downhill all the way to the sea."

"How do we know it won't collapse on us? What if we get stuck in it, knee deep? What if we're eaten away by some kind of ravenous fungus? What if it eats our skin away and we sprout white fuzz all over our bodies. . . ."

"Look at that!" said Anne, pointing.

We looked and then leapt for the cover of a jumble of limestone boulders. It was a camera drone, almost certainly one of the two I had spotted above the swamp. It had the same tapered cylindrical body, the clusters of audio pickups, the pair of manipulative arms, cocked in a position of readiness like the arms of a preying mantis. It stalled momentarily in its patrol over the Mass, and then descended smoothly into one of the Mass's irregular corrugations. Cautiously, we crept out from behind our cover.

"I hope it didn't spot us," I said. "Those big drones have telephoto lenses and automatic tracking systems like you wouldn't believe. And that one's really big, it has room for all kinds of equipment. Infrareds, satellite hookups, odor analysis even."

"But could it possibly be looking for us?" said Anne.

"Professor Angeluce has an interest in the Mass," I said grimly. "And don't think that a drone is helpless. Those manipulative arms are computer-controlled. They move fast and they don't make mistakes. I wouldn't care to trade punches with a drone."

"Don't worry," said Crossbow Moses. "Once we are inside the Mass it'll be the merest good luck if it should find us."

"Hold on!" I said. "It's obvious that you want to hustle us into the Mass, but you might at least take the time to think up a good reason for it. Stop treating us like children. I told you that I'm not going into that poisonous dump unless there's no other choice."

Crossbow stuck its tongue into its cheek and crossed its arms. "Really, Arti, is this melodrama necessary? Your physical bravery should be beyond question. You've seen Mass material before. Did it bite you? Did it sting? What are you worried about? I've dealt with the Mass before. I give you my word as a microbiologist, and as an Academic, that you'll come to no harm." It hesitated at the look of open skepticism on my face. "Come now, Arti. The only reason for your fear is ignorance. It looks very impressive from this height, I know. Let me demystify it for you."

With a studied gesture it slipped into its lecturing attitude. "The Mass itself is made up of the Crossbow Body, its attendant micro-organisms, and elements of the Reverid gene pool. The micro-organisms are mostly advanced species of molds and yeasts, and they serve as a binder and an incredibly rich reserve of nutrients. The Crossbow Body traps genes, preserves them, and recombines them. It's like a gigantic Petri dish, that covers whole square miles. When the genes are recombined, they form a new organism, which is nurtured by the nutrients in molds and yeasts. And it spawns not just simple mold cultures, but species of all kinds: insects, mammals, birds. It's like a gene bank. And it's a permanent guarantee against extinction. It is the ultimate advance in the evolutionary battle against death."

"You're saying that birds grow in there?" I said incredulously. "Animals too? Without wombs to grow in? Without sperm cells or egg cells? And they grow to full maturity?"

"Well, rarely," admitted Crossbow. "Mostly they grow in little pockets of undifferentiated tissue, and then are broken down again by the Crossbow Body. But the number of captured genes is vastly increased every time that happens. When the concentration of genes of a single species reaches a certain critical point, then a full organism is sometimes produced. Of course its tissue is full of the Crossbow Body, and it serves as a vector for the distribution of the Body. And of course, if it dies, then the cells are broken down again and preserved in a new growth of the Body. It evades death, because its genetic constituents are preserved. The genes are the heart of life. The tissue is just an expression of the genes."

I looked out across the white, festering landscape. "I don't see many 'full-grown organisms' down there. There are a few things that look like trees, or things that might have been trees. . . ."

Crossbow shrugged. "Well, the growth of full organisms is a bit of an anachronism, anyway, isn't it? There is no need for adult organisms when reproduction is handled by the Mass. The only real purpose they serve is to spread the Mass by wandering. And once the Mass has taken over the planet, there'll be no need for that either."

"Taken over the planet!" said Anne and I in unison.

"An event in the distant future," Crossbow assured us. "The Mass is in no hurry. For one thing, it will have to produce an aquatic form before it can move into the seas."

"But that's horrible!" I said. "You call that living? Little bits of broken cells, trapped in white mush? No forests? No animals? No dance of predator and prey? No intricacy? No sensation? No intelligence?"

"I tell you that the Mass transcends intelligence! Do you think it has no intricacy, because your great gross eyes can't see it? On a molecular level, it is the most intricate creation in the known universe!"

"But it's just a mindless, devouring fungus!"

"Mindless? Remember that the basis of thought and memory is molecular. RNA is the sister of DNA. The transfer of genetic material from unit to unit of the Crossbow Body is incredibly complex. Think of the amount of gestalt implied in such an intricate system! Think of the powerful bulwark it presents against the forces of disorder! I'm not saying that its function is perfect as yet—there are accidents, admittedly there are accidents. But intelligence is a function of gestalt—a very weak function, from a very small system! But the complexity here has produced a gestalt function that surpasses intelligence like a bonfire surpasses a spark! Don't you realize—the Mass has defeated determinism! It has broken the rigid chains of evolution! It has become teleological! It is the quintessence of life—it is the enemy of entropy!" Crossbow looked searchingly into our faces. "How could words ever convince you?" it said. "I knew you could not be convinced until you had seen its power with your own eyes. That's why we must march through it."

"How do we know it won't grow on us and dissolve us?" I said.

"I am a vector of the Crossbow Body. So is Moses Crossbow. Did we dissolve?"

"You mean, if you die, you'll turn into a mess of white pudding, like that stuff?"

"The Body would dismantle my cells, yes. But that does not constitute death. My genetic content would be preserved. In all likelihood I would eventually be recreated. Whether I would be re-born in the full sense of the word depends on your definition of identity. I would be a clone. But all neuters are clones, of course."

"And if we're contaminated by the Crossbow Body while we're marching through the Mass, and we die, then we'll also be dissolved into white goo? That's what you're saying?"

"What's so terrible about that?" Crossbow demanded. "If you died in the forest, you'd be eaten by beetles and toadstools. If you died in Telset, you'd be cremated, or—what do they call it? Reefed? Eaten by sharks and rays? Is that any better?"

"Of course it isn't," Anne said vehemently. "What does it matter what happens to us if we have the misfortune to die? Our souls will be reabsorbed into the Infinite—these bodily shells will no longer be our concern. As long as it doesn't attack us while we're living, there's no danger. Isn't that so, Professor? Mr. Chairman, I mean?"

"Exactly," said Crossbow. "Come, we've wasted enough time in idle palaver. Let's find a way to descend the escarpment. No doubt the water draining from the marsh has carved a descendible channel. Let's try it." Crossbow got to its feet and began marching along the lip of the escarpment.

"I don't like this," I called after its retreating back, but it did not stop. After a moment Anne hurried after it. I had to choose between following Crossbow Moses, or plunging alone back into the swamp. That was no choice at all.

On our way to the waterfall it rained hard, soaking us through. Crossbow would not seek shelter; it merely fluffed out its dry gills in a self-satisfied way and trudged on.

The land sloped by the channel of the waterfall. The way was steep and slick. Mist from the last tumbling of the waterfall soaked us in an explosion of rainbows.

We stopped at the gushing, roaring pool at the foot of the fall. Long knotted white extensions of Mass fiber, like crippled stems of thick ivy, clung to the limestone base of the escarpment, white against white. "I can't go on," I said. "Let's pitch camp and catch a few hours' sleep before we plunge into the worst of it."

"Not here," Crossbow said. "Too scenic. It's a natural place for a camera drone. Let's seek shelter under that tree."

"Call that a tree?" I said, too tired even for derision. The object in question was tall, and it had a central column that might be considered a trunk, but its branches were long cable-like ribbon extensions that arced from the trunk to the ground. And the ground itself was bizarre. It had a certain granular quality—it was relatively dry—but it was not soil. It was milk-white crystals, loosely clumped, with puffs and domes of white fungus emerging from it. There were areas of round white lichen, like splashes of thick white paint.

We hid ourselves in a small, shadowy area under the tangle of branches. They would shelter us from prying eyes.

Anne and I pitched the tent. Crossbow dug its webbed fingers into one of the domes of white fungus. Crossbow tugged and twisted and the dome broke apart laterally like a splitting plate of mica. "Here, look," Crossbow said.

The dome was full of leaves. They looked like fossils, or more exactly, like plant specimens pressed flat between the pages of a book. Most of the leaves were ferns. They were perfectly formed, except for their whiteness and a touch of fuzziness.

Anne looked at the leaves and then looked at Crossbow. "Why, it's full of leaves, how marvelous," she said, but her intonation suggested that the sight had given her a turn.

I looked at the leaves. They gave me a crawly feeling. "What good does it do them to grow inside this pasty-looking lump?" I said. "They can't see the light. Look how pale they are."

"Oh, they don't need their chlorophyll, or any light," Crossbow said. "The nutrients in the fungus supply all their needs. Notice how perfect they are—without blemish or disease. They stay like this until they either emerge as full specimens or are genetically dismantled and reabsorbed into the Crossbow Body. And if we dig a little deeper—" The neuter shredded its way into the bulk of the dome. "Look. There's an insect."

A brown cricket, furred with white, crawled feebly out of a little pocket inside the white fungoid mass. It cleaned its feelers with its mandibles, then perked up and hopped off. "You'll find other insects, too. Mantises. Centipedes. Even predators, produced without the necessity of killing their prey. Killing is wasteful. The Mass produces life without the necessity of death."

"But what happens when they get loose?" I said. "There's nothing to eat here."

"Well, if they are born at the edge of the Mass, then they can sometimes enter the bordering ecosystem. Otherwise, they eat Mass material. They generally disintegrate then. If we're lucky, we'll find an animal in the process of disintegration. It's a fascinating thing to watch. Often the Crossbow Bodies within them carry the seeds of other forms of life. Even as the old host breaks down, another species spontaneously takes form within its tissues and breaks free. It's not painful. At least, it doesn't seem to be."

"I can't wait," I said sourly. We slept the sleep of total exhaustion and awoke about three hours before sunset.

We packed up and returned to the waterfall, then walked down the brook. The running water was full of green clumps of moss, small fish, and crustaceans, nibbling at the occasional blobs of Mass material washed in from the brook's stagnant bywaters. The running water seemed to protect them, but the stagnant pools at the brook's margin were scummed over with white. The bulging domes of fungus on the banks of the brook were full of Mass-grown pondweed and moss, as Crossbow proved by ripping one open. Others had been broken open from the inside by escaping animals.

We waded down the brook, preferring the algae-slick rocks to the clammy touch of Mass material. Crossbow swam as usual, leaving Anne and I to flounder along as best we could. Bridges of mold arched over the brook, casting shadows on the rippling water, and there were small gravel islands, no bigger than stepping-stones, where the Mass had established a beachhead and sent up clusters of fuzz.

When I could, I stopped to wash off the powder of spores. The touch of the Crossbow Body on my skin seemed to be driving my follicle mites wild with hunger. They were not native Reverid organisms—they were genetically altered, specially bred to protect my body from infection. They were devouring the Mass material wherever it touched me. They were fierce little creatures, and their digestive acids might be breaking down the Crossbow Body. I hoped so, anyway.

The texture of the Mass material was, surprisingly, rather pleasant. The tops of the life-containing fungus domes, for instance, were rather rough, dry, and pebbly, like reptile leather. Even the white fuzz that was so typical of the Mass showed a surprisingly intricate configuration when viewed from close range: the ghostly outlines of leaves and branches, the pointillistic silhouettes of animals. Still, I touched it only when absolutely necessary. Anne shared my caution, but Crossbow was recklessly indifferent.

Our quiet, wadeable stream ended at the white-mossed banks of a major river. It was sunset, so we decided to camp. We retreated to a dim nook in a lumpy, tortuous upheaval of Mass material; it was our only choice of shelter. Crossbow intended to sleep in the river, but changed its mind. Protruding from the brown water were the brow and bulging yellow eyes of some amphibious behemoth. The eyes were as wide across as the outstretched fingers of my hand. The body was hidden beneath the opaque peaty waters and its size was impossible to determine.

"Should we keep watch?" I said as we set up the tent on a furry flat space between two wrinkled white knolls. "There'll be no campfire tonight. There's nothing to burn."

"It's not likely that we'll meet anything on land large enough to menace us," Crossbow said. "The largest animals generally are disintegrated quickly. Besides, they don't learn the mechanics of predation because prey is scarce and they have no parents to teach them. If one comes blundering by, we'll hear it and wake up." So we went to sleep.

I woke up before midnight with a crawling sense of unease. I looked at Anne and Crossbow in the darkness inside the tent. Their breathing was quiet and even. I restored my cameras to full function and sat up. Anne stirred; it was crowded in the little tent, but I crept out without waking her. Crossbow always slept heavily, its old brain a riot of dreams.

I looked up at the stars and saw an immense shape blocking them. It was a drone.

It didn't move. It had been watching our tent, perhaps for hours.

The drone descended in absolute silence, its arms cocked in readiness. I readied my nunchuck to blast it, wondering whether I should cry out in alarm and reveal the presence of the others. With its infrared detectors it probably knew of them already.

Its arm moved with blinding speed and snatched up one of my cameras. I howled in rage and blasted it at point blank range.

A hole as big as my fist appeared in the thin metal of its underbelly. It sagged and listed to one side, but its arms were moving like lightning. It caught all my cameras with its jointed claws, one after another, as if it were plucking berries. I screamed piercingly and struck it as hard as I could on the elbow joint of one of its arms; the drone rocked slightly, and stuffed my last camera into a yawning storage aperture in its back.

"You linking thief! Give them back!" I screamed, and for the first time I heard my voice crack and shriek alarmingly in its upper registers. I leapt into the air and smashed one of its sound pickups; shattered plastic flew in every direction, but the drone did not try to fight back. Instead, it began to rise, tilting visibly and making, for the first time, a faint, strained humming. But it rose steadily and began to drift off toward the east.

"Leave me one, at least!" I begged, helpless now that it was out of my reach. I ran after it, hoping that its engines would fail, recklessly thrashing my way in the darkness through the knolls and walls and tendrils of the Mass. I could hear my cameras, faintly, complaining and buzzing as they tried to return to their master. A puffball burst under my hand and almost blinded me with spores; a few steps later, my feet caught in an ankle-high tangle of green vines and I went down on my face. In the half-second before I hit the ground I twisted and tried to roll, and the top of my head hit the ground and broke through a brittle white crust into a shallow pool of heavy, viscous fluid. A sharp, faintly pleasant chemical reek bit my nostrils. My scalp tingled where the fluid had touched it.

Anne and Crossbow caught up with me and helped me to my feet, out of the litter of green vines and broken fungus domes. They half-supported me as I sobbed uncontrollably. I looked around, half-blinded with tears, and for the first time in seven years the familiar, cheery presence of my cameras was gone. Gone. They were all gone. I made a motion to tear my hair; not only was it cut short, but the top of my head was crusted with thick white goo that was already dripping over my brow and ears. I screamed in rage, my voice cracking again, and looked around red-eyed for something to kill. I whipped my nunchuck around, but then slowed it and dropped it as I came to a stunning realization: why should I bother? The gesture would be lost forever. No one would see it but Anne and Crossbow, and they were not able to appreciate it; besides, they would forget. I was reduced to the ephemeral impermanence of the uncameraed. All my actions had been robbed of their true content, their true meaning. I slumped to the ground, sobbing apathetically.

I ignored Anne and Crossbow's querulous attempts to console

me; their words sounded like dry puppet voices. I said nothing. Crossbow went back to sleep, but Anne led me to the river, where she washed the crusted mush from my head. It stuck tenaciously. Some of it seemed to have soaked into the plastic coating on my hair. I washed my burning face in the murky water and stopped weeping. I could feel the muscles of my face growing rigid with bitterness. A fierce sulk came bubbling up like hot black oil from the cores of my bones. My face grew dark with congested blood. I trembled. "It'll be all right," Anne said. I turned on her, snarling, and she retreated to the tent.

I stayed awake until morning, while my furious anger declined into despondent worthlessness. Sniffing back tears, sunk in a slough of self-pity, I seriously considered flinging myself into the river to drown. Only the fact that the gesture would be wasted caused me to hesitate and abandon the idea.

By the time the first pale edge of morning lightened the sky, I had been awake ten hours straight, and I was exhausted and sick. My scalp tingled, and for the first time I felt the borderline nausea of hormone changeover. My suppressants had worn off, and a whole dancing, capering Harlequinade of male biochemicals were washing through my bloodstream, charging into hair follicles at lip and jaw and groin and armpit, triggering neotenic growth in my vocal cords, even badgering the pituitary into an atavistic state of alertness. I was too sick to notice the erotic effects, at least for the time being.

Anne and Crossbow had been awake for several hours. At dawn they came down to the river to get me. "We must be on our way," Crossbow said. "Now that the drone has located us, speed is of the essence."

"I'm sick," I said. "Go on without me."

"A ridiculous attitude," sniffed Crossbow. "Neither of us have cameras, but our zest for life is unimpaired. Consider how much worse things could be. The drone could have crushed us in our tent while we slept. Instead, it merely took your cameras. No doubt it was seeking news of the man it believes to be the Chairman. The drone's operator knew that your cameras must have news on Moses Moses. If its intentions had been hostile, it could have attacked us. I believe it was controlled by a friend.

One of your fellow tape craftsmen. Perhaps someone you know."

"You don't understand," I said. "My cameras are gone. It blinded me." My voice croaked horribly. I put my face in my hands.

"Arti, your forehead is blistered," Anne said. "You need medical attention. Besides, once we get to Telset you can get more cameras."

I shook my head. "You don't want to go with me, Anne. My suppressants have worn off. Hormones are turning me into an animal. I don't know what's happening to me. Besides, I'm worthless to you now. I've lost my cameras. I'm losing my identity, and that means I'll lose my following and my fame. No one will recognize me. I'm a liability. Not an asset."

Anne shook her head. "You should never be ashamed of something you can't help. Besides, there are just the three of us, now. We won't tell anyone."

Crossbow folded its arms. "Why give up now? We're on the riverbank! It's just an easy day's stroll to the seashore. Our difficulties are over. Stop sulking, Arti, it's beneath you. Just get on your feet and follow my lead."

Anne helped me up as Crossbow ambled downstream, its feet sending up thin puffs of spores from the thick Mass fuzz blanketing the riverbank. It had gone less than ten strides when a thick crust collapsed beneath its weight and it fell with a heavy splash into a corrosive pool of thick white liquid.

We rushed to the spot and started probing for Crossbow with the wooden pole we used to carry our tent and baggage. Minutes passed. We were about to despair when we felt a tug on the end of the pole. We pulled mightily and slowly dredged the neuter out of the thick, clinging fluid. Crossbow was clutching with both hands to the very end of the pole. It crawled out onto the pool's margin on its hands and knees, completely drenched in a thick coat of the reeking stuff. It retched fluid, forcing it out of its stomach and lungs and gills, then began crawling feebly toward the river, coughing. It half-fell into the murky water and disappeared beneath the surface. White scum floated up behind it.

The smell of the curdled white Mass fluid made my scalp start tingling again. There was already a network of tiny blisters across my brow and around my head, like a crown. Surprisingly, they didn't hurt, although the skin was red and swollen and swarming with follicle mites.

I sat on a shelf of Mass fiber to wait for the neuter to resurface. For several minutes Anne stood by herself, staring thoughtfully into the white pool where the neuter had sunk. Then she came to sit beside me, but said nothing. We ate the last of our stores, and my hormone nausea subsided a little. Half an hour passed. Finally there was a burst of murky bubbles near the shore and Crossbow came slogging out.

Its skin had bubbled up all over and detached itself in pockets from Crossbow's flesh. The poor neuter's skin was visibly waterlogged, and brown river water was seeping out of the blisters. Anne and I shrank back in horror. Crossbow coughed convulsively and spat out a thick white mouthful of mush. "I'm all right," it croaked. "It doesn't hurt."

"You're dying!" I yelled. "It looks like third-degree burns!"

"Just crust," it replied. "Look, it peels right off." It tugged at one of the blisters with webby, crusted hands and a wide strip of skin shredded off, revealing puffy white endodermis. "The only thing that hurts is these splinters in my hands. No, Anne, don't touch them. I'll be all right." It drew in a deep breath of air. The expression on its face might have been resignation. The blisters made it hard to tell. "Don't either of you touch me. I've ingested a great deal of the Crossbow Body. I don't know the effects. They may be serious."

"Is there anything we can do?" Anne said sadly.

"Of course. Follow me," Crossbow said, and kept walking.

Anne insisted that she lead the way, testing the firmness of the ground with our baggage pole, which she had washed clean. I carried our provisions on my shoulders while Anne probed the ground. Our progress was slow. Crossbow swam when it could, and the water seemed to help it. Most of the brown, blistered skin came off, but by noon the skin under the blisters was covered with little white bumpy colonies of Mass fur.

We pitched our tent and rested. Crossbow was delirious. It kept mumbling things, little evocative fragments that made me weep for my recorder. Things like: "She loves power, not you. And you must say the same for her," and, "Louise, you can't mean that," and, "But they're all dead. They've been dead for centuries," interspersed with bits and pieces of poetry and legal documents and scientific monographs. I was gray with exhaustion, nauseated with hormones and the sight of Crossbow's skin. I vomited twice. Anne kept us alive. She led Crossbow to the water; its eyelids were heavy with fuzz and it was almost blind. She bathed my blistered forehead and didn't flinch when a pocket of skin peeled away and revealed a tiny bud of green ivy, rooted in my skull.

We slept and then trudged on. Buds of ivy popped through my skin around my head in a dozen places. Crossbow's joints grew so stiff that it was hardly able to walk. Finally we attached ropes to it and towed it along in the water like a log.

By late afternoon the Mass was slowly being replaced by tough shrubs, then small trees, then riverside ferns and weeds and birds and, more and more often, mangroves. We could smell the sea. It was the heavy, dense-rooted mangrove so typical of the continental shore. When sunset began, we were wading around and through a network of thick round roots, scolded by aquatic birds and small, armored sapsuckers. We heard the roar of the surf, and it led us on. We were just in time to catch the last glimmer of the yellow sun on the blessed Gulf of Memory.

Anne explored for two days and found us a small patch of white beach amid the miles of tangled mangroves, where we camped to await Crossbow's death. There was a small freshet of water there, and the banks of the little creek were rich with deep black dirt. That was where Crossbow chose to stay. Its eyes and mouth were already webbed shut, and its joints were as stiff as wood. It had never removed the splinters from its palms, and that was where its transformation began.

It started slowly, as slowly as the growth of ivy around my head. It took whole months. The leaves grew in the damp spaces under the blisters on Crossbow's hands; when they were fully formed, they burst through the skin. We could do very little for Crossbow, but we heaped up dirt around the brown barky knobs that had been its ankles and made sure that it got plenty of water. Its fingers shrivelled into pliant twigs, bark crept up its calves, seaming its legs together, and its skull dissolved as strong, vigorous branches broke out through eyes and ears and mouth.

Anne and I lived on fish and crabs and clams and seaweed. We lived well. Even the ivy growing from my scalp seemed to thrive. Anne cut it for me when it dangled down into my eyes. My follicle mites prevented it from spreading any farther; it was confined to the areas where my head had been soaked in the thick Mass fluid. It didn't hurt, thought it bled red sap if Anne pruned it too close to the scalp.

I was growing, too. I grew three inches in a month, and it ruined three hundred years' worth of ingrained reflexes. I lost my smooth, fluid, self-aware grace, and it was replaced with adolescent gawkiness. For the first time in my life I found myself stumbling, stubbing my toes, dropping things. I even cut myself when I tried to shave with Crossbow's tiny scalpel. My career was ruined. It was useless to even think of resuming it.

We had no reason to return to Telset. Since my cameras were gone, we had no way to support our testimony. We had no political advisor, no leader who could rally resistance to the Cabal. We had no reason to risk our lives voyaging to Telset in a homemade boat. Even if we reached Telset, we had no guarantee that we would not be shot on sight.

Survival occupied our energies. When our tent wore out, we built a snug thatched shack out of mangrove wood and foliage, with my leather combat jacket for a door. We wove nets out of vines and bark and built fishtraps out of rocks and driftwood. We kept a hearthfire burning. We grew brown and lean and tough.

I had expected Anne to argue about our moral obligation to return to Telset. But Anne had changed, just as I had. One night in our third month, I looked at her curiously as we sat beside our driftwood fire. She had changed. It was not merely the long wisps and curls of tangled hair over her ears and the base of her neck. It wasn't the explosion of freckles under her sunburn, or her ragged bodytight, torn and stained. Something was missing. An element of tension in her face, a certain grimness around her mouth, was gone. She looked—not determined—only calm.

"You've looked different ever since you lost your feather brooch," I said. "The little ornament you wore in your hair. You never told me what happened to it."

"It was no ornament," Anne said. "It was a badge. I never wear ornaments."

"Did you lose it?"

"No. I gave it away." She hesitated for a long time, looking up at the night sky. Then, slowly, the words came to her. "Rominuald Tanglin gave me that brooch. He asked me to wear it for him, to wear it always. Especially on camera. It was supposed to identify me to the public. It was made of moa feathers, shed by the favorite birds in my flock. I wore it for thirty years." She looked at me intensely. "But its age doesn't matter. It was still made up of cells, the cells of the birds that grew the feathers, and cells have genes, and the genes are the heart of life. Some of the genes must have still been viable. I threw it away! I threw it into the pool that Crossbow fell in. It's been broken up and preserved in the Crossbow Body, forever. My birds can never die now. No matter what anyone does. I've saved them. I did it, no one else."

"That was clever," I said. I looked up at her with genuine admiration. The months with Anne had wrought a bizarre and drastic change in my way of expressing and feeling. She was the only audience I had left, so I played to her. At first, it had seemed a waste to feel *anything* without an audience to share it, but the deadly apathy wouldn't cling to me; there was too much else to do. There was the task of staying alive, there was the wind, there was the sun, there was the wet green ivy that circled my head and haunted my dreams....

I couldn't have hidden the effects of my puberty from Anne, even if I'd wanted to. Hair was appearing all over me, like the rank, coarse fur of an animal, long-buried in my flesh, but awake now and moving with irresistible, lazy power. It was the

Other, the Other Thing that Armitrage had spoke of; I was abandoned to it, and it grew inside me, wet and green and strong like ivy. I had dreams of flying, dreams of burning; even broken dreams of Tanglin's adult flesh, touched by ghost fingers of the women of the past. Anne was among the women.

Anne was the only woman. I saw her with new eyes, not the calm blackrimmed eyes of the Artificial Kid, but older, hotter eyes that showed slow heat shimmering just above the surface of her skin. I had never seen that the lines of a woman's body were curves; that they were not static, not just the outside layer of skin over muscle and tendon, but flowing and living. Before, I had seen proportion; now, I saw grace. When I had seen Anne's face before, I had seen her features; now, I saw a woman.

"I did it alone," Anne said. "No church could have helped me. I didn't need any church. I didn't even need Tanglin. It was Tanglin that put that badge on my head. It was only feathers, but Arti, it weighed so much! I fought so long to keep it there, even when the weight of it was crushing me. While my flock lived, I couldn't fail them; when I failed them, there was nothing left for me but shame.

"But how can I feel shame when there are only the two of us? We're marooned here. Reverie is a big world, but we only need a piece of it. This beach is our world, and we're the only people on it. You don't care what I did in the past. You don't care about me and the Church, or about me and Tanglin. That's what I've learned from you, Arti. I've learned not to care."

"I care, Anne. Without you here, I'd have died. You are the only person I've ever really known.... You are my audience, Anne, but you're more than audience.... Another person can be like a whole world, can't she? And we're all the world that's here."

"Yes, that's it!" Anne laughed then. It was a brittle, high-pitched laugh, with a cutting edge of hysteria in it; it sounded like chains breaking. She scrambled to her feet and ran down the beach. Sand scattered with each footstep. "There's no one to see us!" she shouted. "There's no one left to care! I'm dead to the old world, to the old things!" She spun around suddenly, looked at the sky, and stabbed her finger accusingly at one of the stars. "I'm dead to you, do you hear? I did everything you wanted, and now I've thrown you away! I'm my own world now. I'm my own people! I'm reborn! I declare myself reborn, right now! No one else can do it for me!" She sprinted suddenly for the foamy line of surf and threw herself into the sea. She poured briny sea water over her tousled head, three times, carefully, with cupped hands.

The shock of the cool water seemed to calm her. She came out of the water, dripping, and threw aside her wet clothing to stand naked, ankle deep in the foam.

"I am newborn," she said quietly. "Did you understand the ritual?"

"It's happened to me before," I said. "I wish it had been that clean and that easy."

"I suppose I'll keep the name Anne," she said musingly, digging into the sand with one naked toe. "I like the name Anne. Why shouldn't I keep it? From now on I'll do what I want."

"What do you want to do, then?" I said. Something awful was happening to me. My mouth was dry and my heart was pounding at my ribs like a madman at a prison door.

"I want to dance."

I got to my feet. "All right. I'll teach you."

"No," she said. "I'll teach you. First we draw the eight-spoked wheel in the sand, like this." She stooped over gracefully and began to scrape a wide circle in the damp sand. Trembling, I closed my eyes. I didn't want to see, for fear it would happen too soon. I pulled off the rags of my bodytight and dropped them in the sand. "The males go on this side, the females on the other. There seem to be only two of us, but there are really four: you and your older self, and me and mine. So, we begin."

The dance did not last long. Instead, we made love in the sand, like gods. "Rominuald," she said, and I shuddered in her embrace because the name sounded so right.

There came a day when we had been on the beach for five months. We had caught a huge ray with one of our heavy bone fishhooks and we were roasting it over a bonfire. They told us later that it was the dark pencil of smoke that had attracted them.

We heard the boat coming and we hid in the mangroves. They would never have found us if I hadn't recognized the boat as Ruffian Jack's exploring hydrofoil, the *Ruffian's Delight*.

Even then we were cautious. We didn't come out until we saw Ruffian Jack and Alruddin Spinney wade ashore, surrounded by clouds of cameras. When we came out of the brush we received a standing ovation and a round of cheers from Jack, Spinney, and their five-man crew.

Jack and Spinney ran toward us, grinning broadly. Jack embraced me. Spinney and his mantis embraced Anne. Even the crew jumped ship and slogged in toward shore, with more cameras, narrating the historic moment with off-satellite transmitters.

"A beard! I can't believe it," bellowed Jack, holding me at arm's length. "Is it really you, Kid? Or should I be calling you Mr. Tanglin now?" There were cameras all around us—a dozen of them at least. I looked into their lenses nonplussed. "What do you know about Tanglin?" I asked cautiously.

Jack laughed. "God's Death, boy, we've got all your tapes! Alruddin, look, he doesn't know! Kid—Arti my lad—they were beautiful! You're a hero! Anne's a heroine! A cult idol! And what about Crossbow, eh? What about its amazing discovery? Where is our sexless savant? I swear it's more of a man than any of us!"

I pointed to the tree. Jack looked. Cameras trained their lenses on it. "*Sylvaticum pinnatus*," said Jack absently. "Not native here. What's it doing this close to shore, eh? Lovely tree."

"It's Crossbow's grave," I said soberly. "We planted it there. It would have wanted it that way."

"You mean he's died?" said Spinney, letting go of Anne for the first time.

"It was an accident," Anne said, catching on fast. "In the Mass. A terrible illness. The long trek was too much for it."

"It was a martyr to the Cause," said Spinney sadly, tears coming to his eyes. It was the first line of what was to become Spinney's lyric masterpiece, "Martyr to the Cause."

224

"What's the situation like in Telset these days?" I said.

"Why, we've won! The Old Cabal has been annihilated! The New Cabal and the Reformed Board have everything under control. It was your tapes that did it, Kid. Tanglin, I mean. Angeluce is dead. Instant Death surrendered! Your tapes caused a planet-wide riot, a full-fledged Revolution! It's the greatest tape accomplishment in history!" Ruffian Jack waved his arms wildly. "Back on board, crew! It's back to Telset and a hero's welcome!"

Half-ushered, half-dragged by Jack's crew, Anne and I were heaved on board and surrounded by yelling, cheering sailors, who ripped bits of our tattered bodytights off for souvenirs and demanded autographs and statements for the planet-wide live broadcast. Jack gunned the engines wildly and the backwash from his craft's powerful engines nearly swamped the little hut Anne and I had built. We were in Telset in an hour and a half.

13

Our reception was half power-fantasy, half baroque nightmare.
The entire population of Telset met us on the docks. The shore
was black with people and packed so tight that citizens were
being forced chest-deep into the sea by the pressure of crowding. Every man, woman, and clone in the city was screaming
his, her, or its lungs out and setting off powerful, dangerously
haphazard fireworks that rained red-hot cinders on unprotected
necks and heads. They were chanting, too. "*Tang-lin, Tang-lin,
Tang-lin!*"

"Merciful God, I haven't seen anything like this since
Peitho," yelled Anne.

"Whose idea was this?" I screamed in Jack's ear.

"Money Manies', who else?" he said.

The screaming, billowing crowd was on the hair-trigger edge
of mass hysteria. Members of the Cognitive Dissonants and the
Fourways were trying to keep order. I noticed that they were
wearing new armbands, not the rainbow armbands of the Civic
Detail, but thick bracelets of linked beads.

"Go up to the bow and wave to them," Jack howled. "Go on, or they'll tear the city apart!"

Anne and I walked to the bow, joined hands, and waved. The crowd went absolutely out of their minds. In seconds we were in the middle of a maelstrom of cameras, bashing each other, cracking their lenses, spinning around in tight circles, going completely out of control as the drone wavelengths were overloaded with contradictory signals. When one of them knocked Anne down, I went berserk and started whacking them to rubble with my nunchuck. They were so thick that we couldn't see the crowd, could barely see each other.

Jack reacted quickly, gunning the engines and pulling us out of the dock, so rapidly that I was almost thrown overboard and Anne saved herself only by grabbing the brass railing on the bow.

Coral grated under the hydrofoils as Jack ran the *Delight* out to sea, ignoring the usual navigation channels. We zipped out of sight of the island, waiting for the cover of darkness while we monitored the riot on four channels, all of them Money Manies'. "My aching death, look at Hammer whacking the daylights out of that noncombatant!" I marveled. "Look, Ice Lady's whipping that man half to death! The Cognitive Dissonants are really beating the crap out of unarmed civilians! What in creation is happening here?"

"Oh, Chill Factor, your old friend, is part of the New Cabal now," Jack assured me. "He's in charge of keeping order, and he's doing it. Without guns, too. It hasn't been easy in Telset these last few months. Angeluce had a purge, you know. Eighty people were executed. Then there were the fatalities in the Decriminalized Zone—look, what's left of the Zone is coming up on screen four now."

"Good God, it's been leveled!" I cried.

"Yes. It was the scene of the first pitched battle between Old Cabal and revolutionary forces. It came just two weeks after you left—an abortive uprising in favor of Moses Moses. Word of the Second Coming got out almost immediately, of course. Angeluce lured them into the Decriminalized Zone and blew them sky-high. We learned later that he had been manufacturing explosives in an orbital oneill for almost two years."

"And my house?"

"Rubble. We saved a few of your tapes. Your computer's gone, though. I'm sorry."

"So am I. Poor Old Dad."

Jack smiled. "Oh, don't worry about *him*. His reputation's made. Imagine, all this time, and I never knew you were really Tanglin! Why, the news set all Telset on its ear. Look, that's where work is progressing on the new statue of Moses Moses. There's been no word on Crossbow Moses, by the way. Or Moses Crossbow, whatever you call him. You know, the one with the beard."

"Right," I said.

"At any rate, the true, original Moses is safely dead now, so we can deify him like a hero deserves." Jack guffawed. "I really liked the old gaffer. I'd like to shake his hand, or his successor's hand—whatever you call the guy who went down with the balloon. He was okay in my book. Shook the place up a little, through no fault of his own. Maybe it needed some shaking. Look, they're chasing the crowd back from the docks. Oooh, *that* was a shrewd blow. Looks like the worst is over now." He turned off the tapescreens from a central switch. "It'll be dark soon. I'll take you in to see old Manies. He's been anxious to have a good talk with the both of you. Congratulations. Celebrations. Parties all night. You know, the usual stuff."

"Right," I said again.

Money Manies did us the signal honor of meeting us at his private dock. "Darling Kid! You don't know how much this cheers an old man's heart!" he cried, embracing me and printing a wet social kiss on my forehead. "The days and nights I've spent, consumed with worry! But come in, come in! I'm just starting breakfast."

Manies touched his bracelet and the door of his mansion swung open. There were still a few raw bullet pock-marks on the wall that faced the sea. "Mementos," smiled Manies. He hurried us inside.

"You're looking well, Mr. Manies," I said.

"Thank you!" Manies said brightly, ushering us down the hall. "I've lost twenty pounds in weight, and I seem to have shed eighty years." He led us through a heavy, inlaid door into an interior dining room, lit by a glistening chandelier mobile. Wooden chairs thickly upholstered in dark red velvet rolled up to meet us, and then bore us to the table.

"Just a very small breakfast this time, with a few very close friends and allies," said Manies with a smile. "Let me have another look at the guest list." With a flourish, he pulled a roll of paper from a small pocket in one of his elaborate cream-colored lace cuffs.

"Let me see, let me see. . . . Are the place-cards out yet? I see they are. Well. We have my dear wife Annabella Manies, Mr. Richer Money Manies. . . ." He coughed self-consciously. "Arthur Tanglin—I understand that's the name you are going by now, Kid."

I shrugged. "I don't know how the rumor got started, but so be it. Obviously I'm not the Artificial Kid any more." I reached up to tug a lock of soft black hair and a leaf of ivy. Manies looked interested. "I've been meaning to mention that delightful headgear of yours. It's a far cry from the old spikes, but I find the change refreshing."

"Thanks," I said. "I've grown used to it by now, of course."

"My sagacious Arti. You certainly picked the right moment to change your image, I must say. You must let me supply you with some cameras before you leave. I'll have the house cameras record you at breakfast and give you the tapes."

"Thanks."

Manies looked back at his list. "Saint Anne Twiceborn — you haven't renounced your title, by any chance?"

"I am three times born, Mr. Manies." Anne and I were both suspicious. We traded glances of mutual reassurance.

"Professor Crossbow—I'm afraid we shall have to leave a seat empty, in its memory. A very great loss to science. How I regret never having met it. Ruffian Jack Nimrod. Alruddin Spinney, if he can tear himself away from his composing desk. He's working on a history of the Revolution, you know. Chill Factor and his Ice Lady. Your client Quade is fine, by the way;

they're still teaching her table manners, so she won't be here, but she survived the purge quite handily, thank goodness. Plus my very good friend Cewaynie Wetlock, down from orbit, and my Alien."

"Cewaynie Wetlock?" I said. "I remember her. I did a critique on one of her tapes just before I was chased out of Telset."

"Yes. She owned the big drone that discovered your cameras. She edited the tapes for publication, too. You'll love her. She's a very talented and sweet young lady, and very anxious to meet both of you."

Manies touched one of the studs on his heavy bracelet. "How long will it be, Quizein?"

"Another thirty minutes, sir. I'm having a bit of a time with the Alien's main dish."

"Oh." Manies chuckled. "That Alien of mine! Its biochemistry requires a special diet, you know."

"Who's your surprise guest?" said Anne.

"What, my dear?"

"You mentioned eleven guests. Even counting the empty seat for Crossbow, I see twelve chairs here."

Manies looked distressed. "You've spoiled it! Well, don't worry, he'll be here very soon. In the meanwhile, shall we beguile the time with a few tapes? I want you to see some of these, Mr. Tanglin. I want your comment on their technique."

Manies busied himself with his bracelet. A tapescreen appeared, sliding down out of the ceiling near the opposite wall. I leaned forward and rested my elbows on the table, which was round—one of Manies' affected bits of egalitarianism.

"I'm going to run this first one without the soundtrack, which was quite vile. This took place just after the massacre in the Decriminalized Zone after the first uprising." He ran the tape.

"It's Professor Angeluce!" I said.

"The late Professor Angeluce, yes."

"Who's the poor man tied up in the chair with the bag over his head?" said Anne.

"You'll see that very soon, as soon as he finishes his harangue—there!" Angeluce whipped the black bag from the head of his trussed-up victim. It was none other than Richer Money Manies.

Manies chuckled at our surprise. "Yes, it's me all right. Look at that expression of total fear on my face—maximum audience impact, eh? I had been arrested for 'collaboration,' just after you had made good your escape. My vocal cords were paralyzed, of course; otherwise, I would have protested quite violently, let me assure you. Now watch what he does with the gun."

Angeluce jammed the muzzle of a handgun into Manies' fat cheek and pulled the trigger. Manies' head burst apart, and wet chunks of it tumbled into the air.

"Very effective, eh?" said Manies grimly. "Those were raw terror tactics. A very sad and unsavory episode in our history, I'm afraid. Shall I run it over again?"

"God, no!" we said.

"Fine," said Manies. He touched his bracelet again. "You might as well come in now; I've run our brother's execution."

A few seconds passed. A second Money Manies ambled into the room.

"There were three of us," said the new Money Manies.

"Yes," said the first Money Manies, smiling at our manifest amazement. "There've been three of us for almost eighty years now. Luckily, the man who was caught and executed was my youngest clone. I suppose I can call that lucky, being the oldest clone. Though you would hardly agree, brother?"

"Don't we always agree?" said the new Money Manies with a smile.

The first Manies nodded. "Yes. The two of us were hidden in my privacy chambers when the Instant Death arrested our poor dead brother. We've spent most of our lives there, anyway, since we only appear in shifts. You must have known about my reputation for forgetfulness. Actually, my memory is excellent, but even with lifetapes it was hard to keep track of all three of me sometimes. Oh, we came out in force occasionally. At the last Harlequinade, for instance."

"We were everywhere at once," said the second Money Manies, chuckling genially. "I was the surprise guest of today's breakfast, by the way. It was a surprise for you and Anne. Everyone else knows by now. I had to reveal the truth when I staged my coup."

"My darling wife knew, of course," said the first Manies, "but she's a girl who knows how to keep her own counsel." He winked. "I married her because she had the skill to satisfy all three of us at once."

"Don't look so crestfallen, Arti," said the second Manies. "There was no way you could have guessed. We put all the talent we possessed into the deception."

"And it paid off, of course. I have another tape now. This is the tape of Angeluce being run down and torn to pieces by the Telset mob. It took place about two hours after I managed to release Cewaynie Wetlock's version of your tapes."

"Wait," I said. "I don't think either one of us wants to see it. We'll take your word for it."

Both of the Moneys Manies rubbed their chins with an identical gesture. "You've changed, Arti. There was a time when you'd be clamoring for a sight of such a splendid vengeance."

"Yes, I've changed," I said.

"Well, rest assured that the unpleasant Professor got everything he deserved. We found most of his body afterwards. The missing portions seem to have been taken for souvenirs by righteously outraged citizens. The death of two hundred of us left many with scores to settle." They sighed heavily. "It was the painful and bloody birth of a new age. I can't say how much I admire that ivy of yours, by the way—it looks so green and young and vigorous. You know, it would make a splendid symbol for the New Cabal. You wouldn't mind if we appropriated it?"

"Tell me what happened to the Old Cabal, first," I said. "That's the core of the matter. Angeluce was just their tool."

"Oh yes, the Old Cabal, the Old Cabal," said the elder Manies, nodding. "Well, the two of us have been working with Cewaynie Wetlock on that. A delightful girl, I can't tell you how much I admire her talent, especially in computer simulation. Could you believe she is only eighteen? She has genius, plus all the vigor and audacity of youth. I swear you'll love her, Kid."

"Tanglin."

"Yes, Tanglin, of course. Well, brother, let's run the first tape. Watch this closely, Arthur, I'll want your professional opinion on this."

The tape opened with an orbital shot of the glowing rim of Reverie. "Very effective, eh, Arti? She stole it from the beginnings of your combat tapes. She's your biggest fan. Yes, here it comes, just over the horizon—look at that! Can you believe it's simulated?"

"It's an oneill. One of the old-style models," I said.

"Yes, being an orbiter, Cewaynie knows them well. Now look at that rainbow insignia! It's the Cabal's oneill, where they're meeting in secret session! We'll put all this in the soundtrack, of course. We were hoping we could get you to narrate it."

"I see," I said.

"Of course, your voice has changed now. Oh, here comes the good part." A fat, glimmering yellow spacecraft lumbered onto the screen. It bore an insignia of linked beads. "These are the good guys—our side. Now watch them open up on that oneill. Bang! Wham!" The Moneys Manies gripped the arms of their chairs in excitement. "Look at the atmosphere gush out! Look at those pieces of debris! But it's not over yet! The oneill fights back! Lasers rake the vacuum! Wau, that was close, wasn't it? But now we fire again! The oneill splits open, it's a direct hit! They're abandoning ship. Count those little lifeboats, Arti— there are thirteen of them, no mistake there! But it's too late for the wicked Cabalists! The mighty hand of vengeance is upon them!"

The other Manies took up the narration. "These close-ups are marvelous, aren't they? Pow! There goes the first one. That was Red. You've noticed the crafts with the little directional arrows on them, I'm sure. Pow! Pow! Look at that one wobbling—we had to have a few misses for verisimilitude, you know—Pow! Pow! PowPowPow, two with one shot! Her technique is incredible, isn't it? I've never seen anything like it! Now watch her pursue them to the limits of the atmosphere. Look at those re-entry glows from atmospheric friction. That just slows them up, though—Zap! They're helpless! Well, that's the last of them. Wonderful, wasn't it?"

"Very exciting," I said stonily. "Good theater."

"Ah, I knew you'd say that. Cewaynie will be so pleased. That was just the surface-dwellers' version, though. We've done another one for consumption up in the oneills. As you recall, they believe that the Cabal had its headquarters on the planet's surface. All right, brother, run the tape.

"Now look at this. It's all done *underwater!* All with studio techniques, too, and by a woman who's never gone diving in her life—except with drones, of course. Notice the bead bracelets on the arms of these valiant frogmen. Those big guns they have are torpedo launchers. The design is authentic, too; I took it from the Confederate archives. Here we go, it's just past this rill in the ocean's bottom—look at that! The Cabal's secret headquarters, whole fathoms deep! No wonder we never found it, eh? It's wonderfully squat and evil-looking, isn't it? We were going to have some enemy frogmen come out of that airlock there, get in some exciting underwater hand-to-hand combat. But we thought that would be gilding the lily. You agree, of course."

"Right," I said.

"I knew you would. Now watch them firing their torpedoes. Boom! Blam! We'll put the sound effects in when we do the soundtrack, of course. Water carries sound quite well. I'm doing the soundtrack myself, since it's not Cewaynie's specialty. All right, here they come, puttering out in their little underwater lifeboats. You notice the insignia again. Too late for them, the hand of vengeance, et cetera et cetera. There goes the first one. Those rushes of bubbles are very dramatic, aren't they? Very visually exciting. Boom. Boom." Manies seemed to be losing interest. "Right, there goes the next one and the next one. Now, look at this, Orange pulls out of the way of the torpedo but it goes right on to hit Green. Bit of unconscious humor there, perhaps. Boom. Yes. Well, there goes the last of them."

"You're being very audacious," Anne said. "What happens when a floater and a surface dweller get together to compare notes on your stories?"

"Oh, each one will believe he's seen the truth, while the other has been suckered in by the official line. No? You don't believe so? Well, perhaps we'll release just one of them, then. It seems a shame. Which one do you think is better?"

"How about showing the truth instead?" I said bluntly.

"The truth? Oh. Well. The Corporation isn't quite ready for that as yet. The Gestalt Theory and everything. The Chemical Analogue Theory of the Body Politic. It's a very volatile situation politically. The Academy has disowned Angeluce of course—I saw to that. Even so, they were behind Angeluce all along. At least, they supplied his huge financial backing. They were determined to destroy Crossbow and all his evidence once and for all. But if the Reverid government embraced Crossbow's anti-Determinist theories, there would still be trouble. Reverie is just one planet after all, and the Academy is a very large enemy."

"That didn't stop Rominuald Tanglin," Anne said.

"Yes, and you see where it got him, begging your pardon, Arti."

"Well, privately then," I insisted. "Let's hear the real story, Manies. The truth."

"Well. Yes. The truth. Well, that's a bit of a ticklish situation, isn't it? A question of definition. Of perception. Of subjective interpretation." There was a double pinging from the bracelets on the wrists of the Moneys Manies. They looked up in some relief. "Ah, I see it's a topic that will have to wait till breakfast. Here come our guests."

Manies' wife appeared at the doorway and glided up silently to her husbands. She was wearing a remarkable dress of linked beads, but it was the wreath of fresh ivy in her black hair that caught my attention. A chair rolled up to her and she took it. It bore her to the table, between the two Manies.

Ruffian Jack came in, patently drunk. Spinney was behind him, carrying his mantis on his shoulder with a thin wire leash. Jack rumbled a greeting as they took their seats. They were both wearing wreaths in their hair.

Then Chill Factor and Ice Lady came in, smiling broadly, dressed very prosperously, almost to the point of bad taste. Chill had taken off his skin-tight, ice-blue mask, because there was a long, hastily stitched slash in his forehead. I saw that they both had new sets of cameras, big ones, almost small drones.

"Arti, our little angel, our star pupil, our salvation!" crowed Chill. "Let these arms embrace you, let this heart almost reach its melting point with gratified pride and joy!"

He embraced me cautiously, careful not to freeze my unprotected skin. Parts of the bodytight I had borrowed from Ruffian Jack stuck to his icy forearms.

"Anne, darling," said Ice Lady, swaying up to Anne and laying her whip gently and caressingly aginst Anne's cheek, "we've never met, but I'd like to thank you from the bottom of my heart for taking care of our little Arti, who's more than a son to us but our beautiful vicious brute and one freezing hell of a fine actor. You're welcome in our gang, anytime."

It was the highest compliment she could offer. Anne seemed to sense this. "Thank you, Ice Lady," she said.

"We've taken good care of your Quade," Ice Lady told me. "It was the least we could do for you, Kid. She's just fine, and dying to meet you. We've told her all about you. Is it true you've changed your name?"

"Yes, it's true," I said.

"Everything seems to be changing," sighed Chill Factor. "The Zone's rubble now. We meet on the beaches to fight, when we can. Mostly, we've got our hands full with the Civic Detail. Look at this rip in my forehead. Who would have thought a noncombatant could do that, eh? I tell you, the Revolution has got these people's blood up." He shook his head sadly. "The Instant Death's disbanded, too. Our best enemies."

Then Cewaynie Wetlock came in. She walked tentatively, with the hesitant, stiff-legged stride of an orbiter newly come to gravity. She was wearing a floater's blue overalls. She was painfully young, pale, and slender, with light blonde hair swept back from her forehead and caught in a beaded barette. Like everyone else, she was wearing an ivy wreath.

"You're the *Kid*," she said worshipfully, walking carefully up and seizing my arm for balance, with both hands. "I'm Cewaynie Wetlock. Gosh, can you ever forgive me for taking your cameras? I did it sort of on impulse—I was afraid Angeluce would find out I was exploring the Mass, and I was afraid I'd lose the chance. My telephoto picked you up almost at once.

If only my drone had had a voder unit! But I hadn t expected to find anyone in the Mass. Least of all you, Kid."

"Tanglin," Anne said.

The Alien came in, carrying a heavy tray with a hinged metal lid. Steam curled up around its edges. "Let's eat!' said the Alien from behind its filmy white veil.

The moving chairs predetermined our seating arrangement. Annabella Manies had her slim back to the tape screen. To her left sat the elder Manies, then Cewaynie Wetlock, Ruffian Jack, Alruddin Spinney, Crossbow's empty chair, the Alien, Ice Lady, Chill Factor, Anne, myself, and, finally, the younger Manies on Annabella's right.

Quizein, on his own two good legs this time, came in and deftly distributed plates, chopsticks, knives, and forks to all the humans present. To the Alien, he gave a round dish with steeply sloping edges and two pincerlike utensils that the Alien gripped with double-jointed fingers. The Alien had the covered dish to itself. Ignoring etiquette, it eagerly lifted the hinged cover a bit, snaked in a pincer, and nipped out a fatty-looking gobbet of some unidentifiable food. Heavy mandibular crunching came from behind its veil.

"This informal meeting of the New Cabal will come to order!" said the elder Manies with a smile, rapping the wooden table with the back of his fork. "Quizein. serve the first course, if you please."

Quizein brought in tiny cups of highly spiced soup, which we drank hot. Ruffian Jack coughed and reached into his brocaded coat for a plastic flask.

Manies belted down his soup. "Now," said the younger Manies, "I propose today's topic: The Truth!"

"Hear, hear!" said the company.

"I heard a true story once," said Jack with a hiccup.

"Quiet, Jack." The elder Manies looked around, beaming. "As you know, I've been preparing this presentation for some time. Now I know—and don't try to deny it—I know that some of you have an unhealthy skepticism concerning my Chemical Analogue Theory of the Body Politic."

"Aw, for Law's sake, Manies!" cried Jack. "Can't we postpone this till the second course, at least? If we gotta keep our mouths shut, we might as well have something in 'em."

"Really, Jack! These outbursts will cease or the New Cabal will have your shares declared forfeit." There was a derisive outburst of spirited hooting from the guests, especially the Alien, who caught on slowly but went on hooting long after all the other guests had stopped.

Both Manies waited tolerantly until the Alien grew tired and the second course had been served. "First," said Manies, "we must deal with the thorny problem of the existence of the Old Cabal. Put simply, our problem is this. How could one deal with an entity, or purported number of entities, who were universally acknowledged to exist, but could not be seen, touched, heard, smelled, or tasted?"

"There is only one such Entity," Anne said.

Manies smiled. "I think we can rule out theological implications for the time being. Here is our one solid piece of evidence: the destruction of the Chairman's Building, and the attempted assassination of Moses Moses. It is from this single piece of evidence—an occurrence three hundred years ago—that the vast mythology of the Cabal grew. Who was responsible for the Fox Day bomb? A long-neglected mystery. Many possibilities suggest themselves. A conspiracy is one. Perhaps it was a conspiracy, rather than, say, a suicide attempt by a deranged government official. But conspiracies are not long-lived. They dissolve once they have served their purpose. There may have been a Cabal once. Three hundred years ago. But does it still exist? It gives no evidence of persistence. I move that we dismiss the idea entirely!"

"But who rules Reverie, then? Who's been running things all this time?" I said.

"Ah, now we come to the crux of the matter," Manies said. He touched his bracelet. "Chalkwhistle, run the diagram, please."

An immense beaded network appeared on the tapescreen behind the two Moneys Manies and their wife. It was torus-shaped, and made of millions of varicolored beads.

"Thanks to your excellent camera work, Arthur, we were

able to reconstruct this and thus prevent a tragic loss to science," said the elder Manies sententiously. "This, of course, is the Crossbow Body, that marvelous, mystic construct that defies the laws of determinism. Naturally, due to the ticklish situation vis-a-vis the Academy, this information must not leave this room." Both Manies looked us over, jutting out their lower jaws with identical determined expressions. "Very well. Chalkwhistle, run the second diagram, if you would be so good. Ah yes, now we see it."

An identical diagram—I would swear it was the same one—flashed onto the screen. "Thanks to the splendid help of the Reformed Board and the help of certain very cooperative computer technicians, We, Richer Money Manies, have constructed this Chemical Analogue of the *entire population of Reverie!* It includes social, economic, and personal dominance factors. A remarkable resemblance, wouldn't you say? And the implications are unescapable! Reverie has been running herself! Reverie has been plotting her own historical evolution, just as the Crossbow Body fulfills the evolution of life on this planet! I should have reached this conclusion long ago, but my assumption that a Cabal existed had completely warped my calculations! Here, Chalkwhistle, run that pitiful tissue of errors that was my first reconstruction—mind you, friends, you must promise not to laugh. Ah, there it is. A wretched thing, isn't it? A mere circular tangle of beads! But remove the assumption of the Cabal, thusly . . . and you see that our social structure now has *twenty-three* specific gaps, corresponding exactly to the twenty-three storage gaps in the Crossbow Body! Friends, this is more than coincidence. I rest my case."

"You expect us to believe that?" I demanded.

"Arti, you are welcome to check the figures yourself. I warn you, however, that it will take you at least one hundred and eighty years to learn the mathematics. It took me two hundred, and I had the help of skilled tutors."

"Then where did Professor Angeluce fit in?"

"Angeluce," said Manies, "was merely a shrewd and unscrupulous manipulator. He had guessed the truth about the Cabal, and used our own mythos against us. His long-range goal was to annihilate the Mass and all traces of the Crossbow Body, thus liquidating the anti-Determinist evidence. I assume that he meant to use orbital lasers to fry the Mass. He meant to turn the greatest triumph of Reverid technology against us. He knew we Reverids would never freely agree to such a massive assault on our planetary ecosystem, so he concluded that he would have to force us by taking over our government. When Moses Moses reappeared, he realized that he would soon have a very serious rival, and took steps to eliminate him—steps that soon got completely out of hand."

"That's very interesting," I said. "I have an alternate theory, though."

Manies stared. "Wonderful," he said at last. "Let's hear it, by all means."

"Very well," I said. "Imagine a very old, very powerful, and very intelligent man, a member of an organization, not a Cabal exactly, but a loose alliance of the very old whose age and experience give them a piercing insight into human affairs. Imagine this man in a position of power, not crushing, overwhelming power, but behind-the-scenes control. It is not a lust for power and fame that motivates him. He is far beyond that. He is merely bored enough, and skilled enough, to enjoy playing the ultimate dominance game. Suddenly, two rivals present themselves. He uses the first rival to neutralize the second, then gives the first enough rope to hang himself. He operates with incredible, even self-destructive subtlety. When the fracas is over, he returns to his old position, and his old power, merely changing names and symbols to protect himself."

Both Manies looked shocked, then deeply pained. "Kid," said the older one pleadingly. "These suspicions are truly beneath you. Why, they're like Rominuald Tanglin's last days. Ah, I know what bothers you—stalwart freedom fighter that you are—how tactless of me not to mention this first of all. This is the deepest, most vital secret of them all—the existence of the New Cabal. I can tell that you dislike the sound of that title. Well, these people are the members of the Cabal. All of them. Your best friends. Oh, that's certainly not what we've told the public. They believe that we, Money Manies, are only the front man for a new group of conspirators, who have overthrown the old group and instituted a similar despotic rule. *It is vital that they believe that.* You remember those helical gaps in the structure? They would be filled if a true Cabal existed. *We must not be allowed to plot our own destiny.* The Crossbow Body does that for us. We are guided by the deepest forces inherent in life itself. A great new age beckons to us Reverids—salvation by a mighty force that transcends intelligence. If people began making plans to govern themselves—to resist the will of the Body—there might be another social upheaval like the one caused by Professor Angeluce. No one wants that. That's our secret power, we members of the Cabal—*we do nothing.* We will allow every man and woman and neuter to go their own ways in peace, to express themselves freely, beholden to no man."

I got up from my chair. "Crap, Manies. These are young people. They can't see through your subtleties. I'm not sure how you'll do it, but you'll arrange things to suit yourselves. You Cabalists always have."

Manies sat up and said with dignity, "My friends are young. Money Manies is the friend of all young people. Is there something wrong with that?"

"Don't get me wrong, old patron mine. I'm not your enemy. Rule Reverie if you want to. Play your games. Keep your last toe hold on life. If I were as old and wretched and desperate as you, I might do the same thing. Your pursuits don't concern me, as long as you don't cross me. There's only one thing I want you to tell me—an old score I have to settle. Where is Instant Death?"

Manies looked gravely concerned. Even Chill Factor and Ice Lady made sour faces. "He's left Telset," Manies said. "His gang has been dissolved. I know about the customs of blood feud, Tanglin, but you'll have to content yourself with that. Instant Death could have fought us to the bitter end, but he deserted Angeluce as soon as your tapes were shown and he learned the truth. We've granted him amnesty. We can't allow you to murder him. By his own lights, he was doing his duty to his government."

I pulled my nunchuck. It felt oddly slick in my hands; my

palms were sweating. "Don't make me angry, Manies," I said. "You disposed of Angeluce easily enough, but I saw that welcoming crowd on the docks. I'm not without power of my own, and I learned enough from Old Dad to know how to use it if I have to. Make things easy for yourselves, and tell me where he is. Don't force me to take drastic steps."

Manies blew out his cheeks. "I hardly expected this. Arthur, no doubt your analogous chemical make-up has changed. I see that we are reduced to a vulgar contest of will." He touched his bracelets. "Chalkwhistle, would you step in for a moment? Bring the weapon."

A few seconds passed. Anne got up and stood beside me, ignoring the plaintive attempts of her chair to persuade her to sit. Chalkwhistle came in, bearing a high-powered, oiled, and polished pistol on a small red pillow. Chalkwhistle gave me a black look. I had forgotten that I had knocked it down without warning, all those months ago.

Both the Manies pointed at the pistol. "There, you see, a deadly weapon, obviously in operating condition. We have ammunition for it, too, somewhere or other."

"In the desk drawer," the younger Manies said.

"Right, the desk drawer," nodded his twin. "There, that should convince you. Obviously, we possess overwhelming might. Needless to say, through the Reformed Board, all good friends of mine, we control all the ammunition stocks in Telset. If it comes to a showdown, we possess the power. You are helpless."

"Don't underestimate me," I said. "I have my own ways. I needn't resort to violence." I threw the nunchuck on the table with a clatter. "I can fight a social battle. Your charisma versus mine, Manies dolls."

"Would you really go that far for the sake of empty vengeance?" said Manies with a painful smile. "Kid, I love you like a son, but if you resist the will of the Body Politic, a thunderbolt will strike you. I'll have you assassinated."

"You wouldn't dare," I said.

"You think I lack the will and the ruthlessness." He sighed. "I regret that I have to make this demonstration." The older

Manies stood up. "Guests, friends, I apologize for this piece of rudeness, an unpleasantness which I would prefer that you not witness. I must ask you, as a personal favor, to turn your chairs and close your eyes. I assure you that no harm will come to Arti."

This was the true measure of Manies' control over them. They all did it. They did it without question or hesitation. All of them turned around, leaving only the two Manies, Annabella Manies, Anne, myself, and the Alien facing the table.

Manies gestured to the Alien. "And now, if you would."

The Alien turned its tray around and pulled it wide open. Despite the fact that it had been cleaned, steamed, and partially eaten, I recognized the object at once. It was Professor Angeluce's head.

The Alien closed the tray again, still chewing.

"I think you understand the depth of my conviction now," Manies said evenly. "Friends, you may return to the table. Again, I apologize."

"I'm leaving," Anne said. She walked quickly from the room.

"So am I," I said. "But I have one question for you, Alien. If I broke your head open, would it be hollow and held together with thick black fiber?"

The Alien only winked, and kept chewing.

I left the room. "Chalkwhistle will give you new cameras, and fresh tape," Manies called out. "Send me anything you do! It's always welcome!"

I slammed the door behind me and rejoined Anne in the hall. "It was horrible," she said, shuddering. "But Arti—I don't believe you should fight him. Not for vengeance. I've never believed in vengeance."

"I'm swearing off blood feud," I muttered. "I can't live that life any more. I can't compete with that. Oh bloody death—he had me so rattled that I walked off and left my nunchuck behind for the first time in thirty years."

As if they were listening in, Cewaynie Wetlock appeared at the door with my nunchuck in hand. "You left this," she said shyly. "Kid—Mr. Tanglin—I'm very sorry you argued with Mr. Manies, and I think he treated you *cruelly*. I know about your love for Armitrage—I edited it, remember? It's a legend already! I don't want to stay at some stuffy banquet. Listen. I want to show you all your tapes—what I did with them, how I handled it. I've seen every single tape you've ever done, I swear I have. I did it just like you would have. Won't you come to my house? I have a beautiful place, it used to belong to a member of the Rump Board, before Angeluce purged her. Oh, it's wonderful, and . . . well . . . you're not a child any more are you? Neither am I. I want to show you all the tapes. Then we'll make some of our own. I have a whole library of tapes. Armitrage's too. Even the weirdest ones. If you'll only say yes, then we could do all of the wonderful things on those tapes. Whatever you like. Or if you don't want to, then you don't have to. But come with me. Please?"

"I'm sorry," I said. "I'm leaving Telset immediately."

"Oh, but that would be tragic! Can't you spare even a few hours? It's night already!"

"Madame Wetlock," said Anne with strained patience, "don't you think you're assuming a lot?"

"Oh Anne," said Cewaynie Wetlock, putting her hands on her hips, "I love you like a sister, and you're a real heroine that everyone in Telset is crazy about, but there's a lot you don't know about men, and especially not Reverid men, and superspecially not about the *Kid*. Remember, I've gone through all of your hours together, and I know, well, everything about the two of you. Except what happened on the beach, of course. But I know you, and I know your weird moral code. After fifty-two years of celibacy, six short months on a beach can't have meant that much." She looked into Anne's face. "Nothing happened!"

"I see you have great confidence in your own appeal," Anne said stiffly.

"Anne, you're wonderful, and I admire you in a crazy sort of way, but you had your chance at Tanglin and you blew it! He's a man now! He's not a life-sized doll! I can give Arti things that you couldn't dream of giving—"

Then Cewaynie Wetlock sagged to the floor, wheezing. The incredible had happened. Anne had struck Cewaynie Wetlock in the solar plexus with the full power of a clenched combat fist.

I looked at her, amazed. "Don't say it," she said hoarsely, tears coming to her eyes. "I've struck her. I had no right to. What do you and I really know of each other? Our little world's been shattered now—"

"Anne," I said, "I'm leaving Telset and I'm going back to Crossbow's old house on the continent. I'm going to change my whole life, and I swear, if you don't help me do it, if you don't come with me, I'll kill myself."

"I'll come with you," she said. "I want to more than anything in this world."

We broke out of Manies' huge and suffocating mansion. Then we borrowed Ruffian Jack's hydrofoil. We picked up Quade and left Telset for good.

Crossbow's house was a shambles, but the three of us made it beautiful again. Quade is our daughter now, and she and Anne have taught me more about love and caring than most Reverids ever bother to learn. We'll have another daughter soon, if Anne's delivery is normal, and the doctors assure us it will be, even as they shake their heads at the eccentricity of a natural birth.

I'm happy here. It doesn't matter if my hair is long and curled, if I wear Tanglin's brocades and heels instead of leather. I do what makes Anne happy. And Quade is much happier, on suppressants. It's the only way to be a child. Just a few days ago she was playing on the beach, and when I joined her I found that she had made a little mosaic of seashells in the wet sand. "It's pretty, isn't it, Daddy?" she said, looking at me eye to eye from where she knelt, and as tears came to my eyes I said, "Yes, darling, it's beautiful," and I made a tape out of it that was a smash hit and took Telset, Jucklet, Sylvain, and Eros by storm. My new tapes, of my new life, have a vast appeal. I number my fans in the millions.

It's peaceful here. Money Manies is vastly supportive, and money pours to us from his networks. My position is perfect for him and his Cabal, since, like Moses Moses, I am a national hero safely retired to a pedestal.

Moses Crossbow's body has never been found. Perhaps he is waiting, like I am.

Just wait till the Kid grows up.

ABOUT THE AUTHOR:

Bruce Sterling, author, journalist, editor and critic, was born in 1954. He is the author of four science fiction novels: *Involution Ocean* (1977), *The Artificial Kid* (1980), *Schismatrix* (1985), forthcoming in ROC, and *Islands in the Net* (1988). His short stories have appeared in the collection *Crystal Express* (1990) and *Globalhead* (1992) and in the Japanese collection *Semi no Jo-o.* He edited the collection *Mirrorshades*, the definitive document of the cyberpunk movement, and co-authored the novel *The Difference Engine* (1990) with William Gibson. He writes a critical column for *Science Fiction Eye* and a popular-science column for *The Magazine of Fantasy and Science Fiction.*

His most recent book, *The Hacker Crackdown*, is nonfiction, describing the law enforcement and computer-crime activities that led to the start of the Electronic Frontier Foundation in 1990. He has appeared in ABC's *Nightline*, BBC's *The Late Show*, CBC's *Morningside* and on MTV, and in *Newsday*, *Omni*, *Whole Earth Review*, *Drugs Society & Behavior 1991*, *Mondo 2000* and other publications. He also does public speaking as a hobby, and has addressed academics, market experts, experimental media groups, phone regulators and state bureaucrats, among others. He lives in Austin, Texas, with his wife and daughter.

Exploring New Realms
in Science Fiction/Fantasy Adventure

Titles already published or in preparation:

The Day It Rained Forever by Ray Bradbury

Myth-maker extraordinaire, Ray Bradbury has created in his writing a world of uncanny beauty and fear. In this collection of twenty-three classic stories there are the gentle Martians of *Dark They Were and Golden-Eyed*, the killers of *The Town Where No One Got Off*, the sweet sounds of *The Day It Rained Forever* and much more. Glowing with luminous images of past and future, they resonate with the unforgettable mixture of nostalgia, fear and wonder that make him a science-fiction writer like no other.

Of Time and Stars by Arthur C. Clarke

A Tibetan monastery hires a giant computer to list the nine billion names of God – with terrifying results. A bored housewife encourages her laboratory-bred serving ape to take up painting – and astonishes the art world. A lunar exploration mission stumbles across a sentinel left by an ancient space-faring civilization. *Of Time and Stars* collects eighteen of Arthur C. Clarke's classic stories. Full of humanity, humour and solidly scientific speculation, this volume includes *The Sentinel*, the story that inspired *2001: A Space Odyssey*.

The Neverending Story by Michael Ende

Imagine an enchanted book, one so steeped in the magic and mystery of a distant land that you want it to go on for ever. Bastian, a lonely boy of ten, finds just such a book, *The Neverending Story*, and hides away to read it. There he learns about Fantastica, a remote kingdom ruled by a childlike Empress, now on the brink of death. Without the Empress, the whole future of Fantastica is in danger and all its creatures will follow her to the grave. Can Bastian set things right and save Fantastica from its fate? His quest, a bewitching blend of legend and adventure, will transport you to the magic place where dreams really can come true.

Exploring New Realms
in Science Fiction/Fantasy Adventure

Titles already published or in preparation:

Echoes of the Fourth Magic by R. A. Salvatore

When a U.S. submarine set out from Miami and was drawn off-course by the murderous magic of the Devil's Triangle, Officer Jeff DelGiudice survived the terrifying plunge through the realms. But his good fortune had a shocking consequence. He found himself stranded in a strange world awaiting its redeemer. Here four survivors ruled the corner of the once-great Earth with the ways of white magic ... until one of them tasted the ecstasy of evil. Thalasi, Warlock of Darkness, had amassed an army to let loose death and chaos, and only the hero promised in the guardians' legends can defeat such power. Now Jeff must face his destiny — in a dangerous, wondrous quest to lead humankind's children back to the realms of Light.

The Earthsea Trilogy by Ursula Le Guin
Wizard of Earthsea • The Tombs of Atuan
The Farthest Shore

As long ago as forever and as far away as Selidor, there lived the dragonlord and Archmage, Sparrowhawk, the greatest of the great wizards — he who, when still a youth, met with the evil shadow-beast; he who later brought back the Ring of Erreth-Akbe from the Tombs of Atuan; and he who, as an old man, rode the mighty dragon Kalessin back from the land of the dead. And then, the legends say, Sparrowhawk entered his boat, *Lookfar*, turned his back on land, and without wind or sail or oar moved westward over sea and out of sight.